ACCATTATACTCGGATCCCTTACTG
GAACTCTCCGATACCTCGATCGAGGC
GATCTCGAGAGGGTTCTTAGGATCTT
AGCTCGATCTCTATCTCGGCAATCGC
CTCT**DIRTY LITTLE LIES**TCAT
GATCTTTTCGATATCGATATCGAGGC
AGCTCGATCTCTATCTCGGCAATCGC
GCTCTCTATCTTCCGGGCAATTTTAA
GAACTCTCGATACCTCGATCGAGGC
GATCTTTTCGATATCGATATCGAGGC
CCAGCT**John Macken**AATCGAT
AGCTCGATCTCTATCTCGGCAATCGC
GATCTCGAGAGGGTTCTTAGGATCTT
ACCCATTATACTCGGATCCCTTACTG

BANTAM PRESS

LONDON · TORONTO · SYDNEY · AUCKLAND · JOHANNESBURG

TRANSWORLD PUBLISHERS
61–63 Uxbridge Road, London W5 5SA
a division of The Random House Group Ltd
www.booksattransworld.co.uk

First published in Great Britain
in 2007 by Bantam Press
a division of Transworld Publishers

A CIP catalogue record for this book
is available from the British Library.

ISBN 9780593056455 (cased)
ISBN 9780593056332 (tpb)

Addresses for Random House Group Ltd companies outside the UK
can be found at: www.randomhouse.co.uk
The Random House Group Ltd Reg. No. 954009

The Random House Group Ltd makes every effort to ensure that the
papers used in its books are made from trees that have been legally sourced
from well-managed and credibly certified forests. Our paper procurement
policy can be found at: www.randomhouse.co.uk/paper.htm

Typeset in 11/15pt Sabon by
Kestrel Data, Exeter, Devon

Printed in Great Britain by
Clays Ltd, St Ives plc

2 4 6 8 10 9 7 5 3 1

GCACGATAGCTTACGGG
AAATCTA**ONE**GTATTCC
GCTAATCGTCATAACAT

1

Dr Sandra Bantam watches as the knife enters her body again. There is a pause, a moment's respite, a chance to sense the burning wounds, to see the seeping red as the blade withdraws.

She lets out a scream, the pain coming out in bursts. She is numb and acute at the same time, dizzy, eyes opened and closed, shivering and sick. The blood which leaks out of her from a swarm of angry wounds seems to take her warmth with it. Dr Bantam has witnessed the handiwork of men like this many times before. Men who gouge and strangle and rape and kill. She has experienced the results and the aftermath on countless occasions. But never the event. The bitter, horrific, terrible event.

At first, almost a whole day ago, she thought there would be sex. Why else attack a lone woman in her home? Why else tie her up in the bedroom, naked and exposed? For an awful second she realizes she would rather have his flesh penetrate her than his steel. But that was never his aim. He wanted information. An onslaught of questions, sprayed out thick and fast. Where is he? Where is Reuben Maitland? What is he doing? Where is he working? What's his address?

Dr Sandra Bantam knows that capillaries are bursting in the whites of her eyes. She knows that she has lost a lot of blood. She knows that her core body temperature is dropping. As she fights for breath she wonders again why he wants Reuben so badly? What has he done? What does he need? And for a second, the only face she can see is Reuben's. In that instant she hates him with a pain which burrows as deep into her flesh as all the cuts and kicks and punches together.

And now there is no curiosity. Sandra considers the fact that the interrogation is drying up. What happens when torturers don't get what they need, she asks herself. The agony comes in a sickening wave and then subsides.

What then?

2

Sixteen Weeks Earlier

A hair. A dark hair. Kinked in the middle. The root still there, which is good news. He pulls the covers back further and brushes the sheet with his hand. A slight bobbling of the cotton; a warmth of friction against his palm. Another one. Two hairs, almost identical. He stands up and peers out of the corner of the window. The drive is empty. He is safe, for the moment. Suddenly detached, he walks into an adjacent room, telling himself, *This is a crime scene.* Reuben Maitland rubs some more amphetamine into his gums, pulls on a pair of unpowdered surgical gloves and takes a slim case back to the main bedroom. Using a pair of tweezers, he bends the hairs into a small clear tube and closes its lid.

He spends a further twenty minutes meticulously examining the bed, the pillows, the chair, the floor for any other evidence. The drug dilates his pupils and opens his eyes. His concentration is total and unblinking. The sound of a TV resonates up through the floor, his foot tapping involuntarily along. He finds a number of blond hairs, all of which he ignores. They have been very careful, he decides. The carpet has been hoovered, the pillowcases changed, the chair repositioned.

Through a partitioned wall comes the noise of a baby waking: tentative exploratory gurgles clutching for attention. Reuben Maitland realizes he has got to get out in a hurry. He leaves the bedroom and sheds his gloves, balling them into a pocket. Peering over the banister, he can just make out a childminder talking on the phone, watching TV, a magazine open on her lap. He notes a baby-monitor on one of the sofa arms. Outside the infant's room, he pauses, quickly weighing up his options. At eye level, animal letters spell out the name J-O-S-H-U-A on the door. He tries the handle and pushes it open.

Inside the nursery, a baby stares up, dummy out, mouth agape, oval in the way of six-month-olds. Reuben replaces the dummy and turns off the monitor. As he looks at the child, he is trying to forget twenty years of genetic training. The opaque blueness of its eyes, the wispy brownness of its hair, the blank features waiting to bud. Too young to tell, maybe. But there are other ways.

The infant starts to grizzle, so Reuben bends down and picks it up. He feels a flood of warmth seep into his speed-hardened muscles, the baby radiating unknowing love like a hot-water bottle. But leaking through are words and images and implications that Reuben is fighting to suppress. He tries to stop the ants' nest of suspicion in his brain forming itself into an army of logic.

'Tell me,' he whispers, reading the child's features. The shape of his ears, the width of his nose, the tinge of his eyebrows, the length of his chin all talk to him, but the words are muffled. 'Tell me,' Reuben urges.

Joshua gripes and complains.

'Not without your solicitor, eh?'

The baby stares over Reuben's shoulder and through the window. Reuben sees the change in the infant's expression and follows its line of sight. Outside, a car has pulled into the drive.

'Fuck,' he says. A dark-haired woman is sliding herself out of the driver's seat. She is pretty but looks hassled, carrying a stack of folders. Reuben has to escape, and fast. He scans the room, making sure he has left no contaminating evidence. He replaces the child in its cot and takes out his mobile, pressing an instant-dial button. The front door echoes to the sound of rattling keys. Reuben misses a breath. Then the rattling stops. He hangs up and glances over the banister. The childminder is busy ending her conversation and is rushing to turn off the TV. Reuben walks quickly down the stairs carrying his case. He dials another number as he does so, and the childminder changes direction and heads off to answer it. There are keys in the lock again. Reuben darts along the main corridor in the opposite direction, making for the back door. He hears the baby begin to cry. The woman enters, calls the childminder's name, and both of them ascend the stairs in mutual concern. He hears a brief conversation.

'How's he been?'

'Great.'

'Have you fed him yet?'

'He's just woken.'

Reuben changes his mind. He turns and creeps towards the front door, which he is able to open and close silently. Suspecting that he can be seen from the nursery, he edges to the side of the house, steps over the neighbouring fence and makes his way across the gardens of two more semis before reaching the road. His car is parked a couple of streets away. He places the case on the seat beside him and drives to the lab, focusing through the North London traffic, sweating from the close scrape, the air-conditioner struggling to cool his car. All around, vehicles suck in the city air and excrete it, slightly chilled, for the next one to consume. He knows what he has just done is illegal, and that there are other ways to find out. But when investigations have to be solved with one-hundred-per-cent certainty, forensics is almost always the answer.

The ants in his brain are starting to marshal themselves into columns, which march in defined directions. Questions and misgivings whiz around like the angry mopeds and taxis cutting in and out of his line of sight. He turns into the underground car park at GeneCrime. It is dark and forbidding, swallowing cars in the morning and spitting them out at night. Reuben's eyes dart in the rear-view mirror, noting the fairness of his hair, the shallow dimple in his chin, the tilt of his earlobes, the width of his forehead, the creases of his frown. There are other ways of finding out, he tells himself again. But still, Reuben leaves his car squatting in the dark, and swipes through a door marked 'Forensic Science Service'.

Inside, there is quiet. The nine-to-fivers have gone home. A few others remain, waiting for their supervisors to leave. Reuben is greeted almost suspiciously by the members of his staff he encounters. They mill around the extended corridors, chatting in laboratory doorways, unsure whether to call it a day. As he sits down in his office, Judith Meadows enters without knocking. She is petite and dark, and carries with her a look of gentle defiance. It is there in the straightness of her back and the serenity of her face. In the years that he has known her, Reuben has spent a lot of time wondering about his senior technician. He has the nagging impression that he will only ever scratch her surface.

'Judith,' he says, 'tell them to stop hanging about. I'm just catching up with a few things. And go home yourself.'

'Where've you been?' she asks.

Reuben swallows the bitter taste the powder has left at the back of his throat. 'Undercover sweep.'

'Anywhere exciting?'

'Residential address in NW10. Bit of a close one.'

'Any samples you need to hand over?'

He examines Judith for a couple of seconds while he decides. As he stares up at her, she looks like the caricature of a beautiful woman. Reuben has often found Judith attractive from certain angles but not others. At this moment, she appears almost

12

overpoweringly alluring. 'No. I'll sort it. Thanks.' He is hot; the room lacks ventilation. 'Any calls?'

'Eleven.'

'Eleven? Christ. What are they trying to do to me?'

Judith breaks into a sly smile. 'Do you want me to answer that?'

'Better not,' Reuben says, examining a small patch of wetness under his arm. 'Wouldn't want to drag you into all of this. Anyway, I'll see you tomorrow.'

Judith takes her cue, and her face regains its placid composure. She turns and walks back out. Reuben stares through the glass. Eleven calls. They are beginning to turn the screw.

Two adjacent laboratories, which are overlooked by his office, slowly begin to empty, research scientists glancing up at Reuben's window or making a show of tidying loose ends. He takes the clear bullet-shaped tube out of his case and squints at its contents. The kinked hairs are bent double, wrapped around each other like sunning snakes. So who are you? Reuben asks them. Who the hell are you? The only noise is the slamming of doors. Reuben realizes that the course of action he is about to take is inevitable. It is dangerous and immoral, and yet every atom in his body is screaming for him to do it. He feels almost like a passenger, being driven by curiosity and doubt, the amphetamine sweeping away misgivings and turning them into actions.

A sharp knock distracts him. Detective Chief Inspector Phil Kemp stands in the doorway, squat, short-legged, shirt tucked tight into his trousers, his pallid face asking the question before his lips get round to it. 'Are we ready to go?'

'Any day.'

'That's all I've heard for weeks. When, exactly?'

Reuben runs his fingers along the polished veneer of his desk. 'When I'm ready, Phil.'

'Look, how much further can you push this thing?'

'No further. Predictive Phenotyping is finished.'

13

'So what's the delay?' Phil Kemp demands, refusing to be fobbed off. 'This is the country's leading Forensics Unit. We don't sit around waiting for things to happen.'

'Come in and shut the door.'

The DCI obliges and takes a chair, leaning forwards, toes just about touching the carpet, eager and impatient. 'What is it?'

'You know what it is. Sarah's too hungry. And I think you're getting swept along for the ride.'

'Meaning?'

'I don't think Sarah Hirst understands the power of Predictive Phenotyping. She's itching to use it. I can see it in her eyes. There are rumours.'

'What rumours?'

'That someone's been delving about in the lab. That reagents have gone missing, or been used up out of hours. Look, Phil, we go way back, so this is between you and me. I'm sure it's not your CID boys – they wouldn't know a laboratory from a lavatory' – Phil makes a point of holding Reuben's eye – 'it's just I think Sarah's more interested in my invention than she should be.'

'But we all want it out there, Reuben. On the street. You can't blame her more than anyone else. The Area Commander is on to me on the hour. "When the fuck is Maitland going to stop pussying around with this thing?"' Reuben smiles at the impersonation. 'So I have to ask again. When is it ready?'

'And I'll answer you again, Phil. When *I'm* ready,' he says.

DCI Phil Kemp stands up and paces around. 'Rube, see this from my side. You know me and Sarah are being judged. At the moment, you manage the Forensics Section, I've got CID, and Sarah's responsible for everything else. But after the restructuring, one of us is going to be given overall jurisdiction.' Phil allows himself a short, bitter laugh. 'Since for some ill-conceived reason you said no to the job.'

'Administration's not exactly my thing.'

14

'The price you've got to pay when there's a lot up for grabs,' Phil mutters, staring down at his badly worn shoes. 'Overall commander of GeneCrime. It's what I want. And it's what Sarah wants. Badly. Which is what worries me. If she had your technique at her fingertips . . .'

'Trust me. I'm not taking sides. I just need a bit more time, and we can all benefit.'

'But time is the problem, Reuben.' DCI Phil Kemp pauses on his way out. 'And the longer you delay, the more you're going to get squeezed.' He shrugs briskly and leaves the room, his warning swirling in the agitated air which follows him.

Reuben turns away and stares out into the lab, where the last of his staff are hanging up their lab coats and slinking out of GeneCrime. When I'm ready, he whispers to himself. The plastic tube on his desk calls for him. He lifts it up and stares through it. When I'm ready. A number lights up on his mobile, which vibrates its way slowly across the desk, screaming for attention. Reuben picks the phone up and walks into the empty lab, placing it in the rotor of a large centrifuge. It stops ringing for a second, before starting again. Reuben turns the machine on, noting the Doppler effect as the phone begins to rotate, blurring into one long shrill note, the centrifuge picking up speed. Reuben holds his head in his hands. After a few seconds, the ringing is inaudible. He calculates that the phone is spinning at around three hundred revolutions per second. Pressing the Stop button, Reuben waits for it to ease to a halt. The mobile doesn't look too bad, except that the screen is inky black and the buttons have collapsed. He dumps it in a bin and walks over to a DNA sequencer. An involuntary muscle contraction clamps his jaws together. Maybe, the amphetamine tells him, the time is finally right.

The idea for Predictive Phenotyping had come to Reuben two years previously. Now, he almost wished it hadn't.

It was beautifully simple, the obvious extrapolation of what everybody knew already. As he walked around the lab assembling the materials he would need, Reuben tried to pinpoint the exact second within his thirty-eight years during which the notion had crystallized. He closed his eyes and allowed his mind to wander. He was in the back room of a dingy South London nightclub in early 2005, surrounded by police and forensic scientists. On the floor lay a man, face down, arms out, as if he were about to skydive through the sticky carpet. Reuben was dressed in a white hooded suit. He was examining blood samples and hairs distributed widely around the man. From what the Scenes-of-Crime Officers had divined, the man had been stabbed after a struggle. No one had seen the assailant. No one knew what he looked like or how dangerous he was. And there, collecting DNA specimens, the exact second of inspiration finally arrived. Of course Reuben knew who the killer was. He had left his entire identity in the very room with them.

Reuben realized that forty thousand genes, give or take, encode a human being, and that several hundred, directly or indirectly, affect our 'phenotype' – that is, who we are and what we look like. He knew that these included genes for height, weight, hair and eye colour, skin colour, nose length and width, ear shape, dental attributes, shoe size, lip form, chin cleft, body hair and everything else the retina could perceive. And that it also followed that several hundred more controlled our individual patterns of behaviour.

Conveniently, the attacker had just scattered all his characteristics around the scene of his crime. All Reuben had to do was to develop a system which analysed not just the sequence of a criminal's DNA, but also the levels of expression of their individual genes. And hey presto: forensics would become prospective rather than retrospective. You would know who you were hunting, what they looked like and how they were liable to act. Genetic profiling would no longer be a barcode. It would be a crystal ball.

Reuben pipetted a small amount of clear fluid into the tube and watched the hairs relax and loosen. The trouble with a crystal ball, he appreciated, is that it is only as good as the person who interprets it. And in the wrong hands, predicting the future can cause a lot of problems. However, there are times when the means are justified. Like when suspicions just won't go away. Like when people above and around you are taking liberties with your ideas. Like when an entire Forensics Unit needs to be shown just how dangerous technology can be. Reuben stared grimly at a plastic membrane. On it, barely visible, were almost two thousand individual spots. He turned his laptop on. The moment had come.

3

The loft was slowly cooling, the day's sun, which had been trapped between fibreglass insulation and clay roof tiles, gradually escaping into the night. Traffic noise from the street permeated the tiles, which seemed infested with gaps, and barely able to stop a shower. From within, the roof appeared inherently porous, and yet Reuben well knew that no rain ever made it through. He shrugged. Up close, what was safe didn't always seem so.

The rafters, as he made his way across, unnerved him. One misjudged step and his foot would be through the ceiling. It was like walking a wooden tightrope. He placed the sealed plastic bag he was carrying on a small boarded area, which resembled an island in a sea of timbered waves. Similar transparent bags, all packed with tightly wrapped case notes, Reuben's personal archive of investigations, sat slowly gathering dust and decaying. He ran his fingers over the stack, sensing the fine, gritty soot on the smooth glossy plastic. Within, so many ideas, so much work, such limitless concentration from his team. He felt suddenly humbled by their dedication and awed by their loyalty. Reuben was about to balance his way back to the loft opening when he spotted an old shoe box, with the single Biroed word 'Photos' staring forlornly out. He hesitated, the rumble of traffic in his ears. Then he stooped down and picked it up.

Inside were wallets and wallets of pictures. He chose one at random. Reuben and Lucy in the early days. They looked like different people. Without the weight of responsibility. With the potential for anything. Grinning insanely in front of a variety of backdrops. Reuben opened another set of photos; they were stuck slightly together, but still sharp and brilliant.

Mostly, they were holiday shots, each set of thirty-six exposures chronicling two weeks in the sun. But what they were also recording, Reuben noted sadly, were the short snatches of time between all the carnage, a flickerbook of one man's journey through the heart of atrocity. As he held each picture up to the unshielded light, names of cases came to him, like the gaps between the roof tiles. A holiday in Crete. The South Shields murders, 2001. Driving through the Rockies. The Tannahill brothers, 2004. Camping in Northern France. Bethany and Megan Gillick, 2002. Restless beach holiday in Spain. The Greening rapes, 2000. Reuben wondered whether he could see an extra wrinkle for every murderer he had put away.

Lucy called up through the hatch, bringing him round. 'You want to pass anything back down, darling?'

'No,' he said, glancing at a photo of his wife in her late twenties, temporarily blonde, looking magnificent. 'Just sorting a couple of things.'

'I'm going to have a bath. You'll be OK to climb down?'

One day, Reuben told himself, he was going to fit the loft ladder he had bought the previous year. He peered across the beams at it, still in its folded wrapping, sitting uselessly by the opening. Getting in and out was an act of scrabbling, climbing and jumping, and not for the faint-hearted. 'I'll be fine,' he answered.

He heard his wife pad along the landing, and a door open and shut beneath him. In the picture – Portugal, he guessed – they had

19

lazy summer arms around each other's waists, fresh quick tans with red outlines, a happy Mediterranean torpor about them. He wondered momentarily who had taken the picture, whether they had stopped someone and asked them to record for posterity that single moment of happiness, which would then sit in the breezy loft of their house. This was the opposite of *Dorian Gray*. While their faces were ageing and showing battle scars from the elements, there remained in the attic faultless pictures of their unlined visages.

The hot-water tank began to murmur and complain as Lucy drained it to run her bath. While Reuben opened the next wallet of prints, he pictured his Predictive Phenotyping grinding through the night. In the morning, with a little editing and manipulation, he would have his answer. Finally. He examined himself in a pair of swimming shorts, looking relaxed, tanned, lean as he always was. The eyes, hidden behind sunglasses, yet to see so much, a full decade of crime scenes, of mopping up other people's spills, of detecting the brutal misdemeanours of the few. Again, there was Lucy, before they were married, grinning obliviously, a glistening bathing suit, hair wet and shimmering, the photo saying, This is what happiness is; remember this moment.

And then there, at the back of the thirty-six exposures, out of place, slightly smaller, a different photo. A lonely desolate hill rising out of the surrounding flatland. The words Sedge Knoll came to him. Reuben leant his head slightly forwards and held the image against his closed eyes. He was still for a second, lost in its memories, until the amphetamine invaded, pushing snapshots of the day through his brain.

Reuben knew she had detected the speediness of his demeanour since he returned from work. Still holding the picture to his face, he resolved to cut down. But it wasn't that simple. Nothing was. At the moment, it was purely a matter of survival. And that was something he couldn't talk to Lucy about.

20

Reuben's phone rang, and he reached for it, his movements automatic and jerky. He listened to the recorded message, packing photos back in the shoe box as he did so. Then he edged towards the loft opening and lowered himself down, chemically strengthened muscles making it easy. He walked to the bathroom and stood outside, his forehead against the cold white surface of the door.

'Luce? I've got to go. Work. Something nasty.'

His wife's voice came back through the wood, dulled by the barrier, but her sigh still audible and clear. 'What, now?'

'Afraid so.'

'You've only just got home.'

Reuben glanced at his watch. It was nearly nine, when most normal people would be settling in for the evening. But Reuben knew that even if he didn't attend the scene, he wouldn't be able to relax. Questions and scenarios would eat away at him, chewing up his composure, making him unrecognizable to the version of himself languishing in the box in the loft. He ground his shoe into the carpet. That so many smiles could now make him feel so desolate. 'I know. It's a bugger, but until murderers learn to keep better hours . . .'

'Fine.'

Reuben loitered a second, the only sound the slosh of a full bath. He pushed his forehead hard into the veneer of the door. Lucy inside, lowering herself into the warm water. Lucy in photographs smiling for the camera. Lucy . . . Reuben stood upright again. Then he turned and walked downstairs, out into the night, into his car, back into the thick of whatever horror lay waiting for him.

4

Just two things distinguished the flat from any of the other residences squatting on shops facing Ealing Broadway. First, the carpet was saturated, so much so that the record store below had noticed wet plaster dropping from the ceiling in time to the beat. Second, and more unsettling, there was a man nailed to one of its walls.

Lost in an anti-contamination suit, Reuben examined a length of hose which led into the deceased's bloody mouth. It was plumbed on to the cold tap of the kitchen sink, which had still been running when the first officer arrived. The man's clothing was shredded, revealing a multitude of cuts, grazes and shallow stab wounds infecting his skin like a rash. Very little of him had escaped the assault, and that which had shone out as virgin areas of white dotted around his nipples and navel.

Reuben had been at the scene for an hour and a half since the call had dragged him from his loft. A small plastic rack sat beside him, holding variously coloured specimen tubes, many of which were already labelled and sealed. The afternoon's amphetamine, which had enhanced his concentration and dulled his unease, was ebbing and flowing in fits and starts. And while he worked, he couldn't stop picturing his laptop buzzing and grinding its way through the first ever Predictive Phenotyping assay.

Tracing a gloved finger along the line of the hose, he gently parted the victim's lips. Several teeth were shattered, the pipe pushed through a hole where upper and lower incisors used to meet. The molars had been superglued permanently together. On the carpet was a hammer. Reuben frowned, resisting the urge to scratch his forehead. He withdrew the hose, which trespassed almost half a metre down the dead man's oesophagus, and examined upper and lower jaws. Reuben was distracted, imagining the face his laptop would show him, so understanding was uncharacteristically slow. Superglue. Hammer. Hose. Water. He looked up suddenly from the notes he was making. The man had been drowned in his own front room without even getting his clothes wet.

Reuben studied a pair of shoes which entered his peripheral vision, walking over the sodden carpet to stand next to the body, and concluded that they belonged to DCI Sarah Hirst.

The footwear didn't lie. Reuben had always liked the way Sarah dressed, but he tried not to let it show. 'So let me make some presumptions,' he said.

'Go on.'

'Senior CID here at, what? Eleven p.m.? Dressed as if you're about to go out for the evening. So . . .'

'Yes?' Sarah Hirst asked.

'This isn't a routine murder.'

'Take a good look at the victim, Dr Maitland. Does that look like a routine murder to you?'

'The point I'm making, Sarah, is that there's an agenda here. I'm half expecting Phil Kemp to show up any minute.'

'He's on his way.' DCI Sarah Hirst sighed and ran a finger along the smooth line of an eyebrow. Her cheeks were pale, her eyes contrastingly brilliant. She was a year younger than Reuben, and it vexed him that her stellar rise through a blur of police titles had failed to tarnish her features. 'Heard you on the radio last week,' she said.

'And?'

'Thought you sounded tired.'

'Maybe I'm not getting enough sleep.'

'Why? What are you doing all night?'

Reuben checked himself. DCI Sarah Hirst had a way of opening the door to flirtation and allowing you to step in, for as long as it served her purpose. 'Working,' he answered.

'All work and no play makes Reuben a dull boy.'

'And what's so exciting about you?'

Sarah smiled. 'Great legs, good figure, exhilarating company.'

Reuben studied her for a second, lining her up against his wife. The thought of Lucy tugged at him momentarily before Sarah's voice brought him round. 'So, you got any good DNA?' she asked, her smile fading, the door closing.

'Difficult to say until we've excluded Mr Hose.' Reuben ran his tongue around the dry insides of his mouth. 'So who did it?'

'You're forensics. You tell me.'

'I refer you to my earlier point. If this is important enough to keep you and Phil from your gin and tonics, you already know something I don't.'

'This was Jonathan Machicaran, former informant and crack addict. Another sad case whose life was ruined by drugs.'

Reuben felt a pleasing rush of energy flex his muscles and stimulate his brain. 'That's terrible.'

'He'd recently given us enough on Mark Gelson to – Hi, Phil, you OK? – to start reeling him in.'

'Reuben. Sarah,' muttered DCI Phil Kemp.

'And does torturing and drowning a man in his own living room reek of Gelson?'

'Possibly. Mark Gelson runs a much-feared crack and smack operation which we've been infiltrating. But his whereabouts are unknown.'

'No witnesses. We don't have anything to put him here. And we don't have DNA for him,' Phil Kemp added.

'Aha. Here it comes. Now I see why you two are off your sofas.'

'Come on, Reuben,' Phil said encouragingly, 'we could be looking at his face in a few hours. We wouldn't need to have him in custody. We'd know if it was Gelson or not. And all of this if you'd only—'

'So where do you draw the line? Say Predictive Phenotyping suggests future psychotic behaviour in someone tested only for elimination. Then what? You'd just let him go?'

'Well, we'd . . .' Sarah Hirst stared down at her shoes, which were slowly getting wet.

'Look, I've been in the meetings, heard the rumours. As I told Phil earlier, I just don't think CID understands the implications of this.'

'Let me explain something to you,' Phil began, turning up the heat, as if this were an interrogation. 'Out there' – he pointed through the flat window, but because it was dark saw only himself pointing back – 'are eight million lives, banging and crashing into each other, running themselves into walls. It's hard enough if you're normal. But let's say you're not. Let's say you've been born with a predisposition to rape, to kill, to abuse. How difficult is it then? And when do we ever get involved with people like this?'

'Tell me.'

'When they've already raped, killed and abused. And usually not till they've done it again and again.'

'It's like medicine,' Sarah interjected. 'Prevention and cure. We need to be there at the beginning, before everything kicks off. We have to be *interventionist*.' Reuben pictured Sarah learning this word at a PR workshop. 'The days of waiting for criminals to do what we knew they would anyway must end.'

'It needs to be tested.'

'Then test it, for Christ's sake.'

'You don't understand. Proper trials take months – years,

even.' Reuben yawned. Holes were beginning to poke their way through the speed. 'And you want to use the thing now.'

'Then why not test it as we go along?'

'Do you really need me to answer that?' Reuben turned round to face the ill-fated man nailed to the wall, his skin hacked and slashed, drowned in his first-floor flat via a length of hose fed directly into his stomach. 'Let me ask you two something. You think Predictive Phenotyping could have prevented this?'

Phil and Sarah shrugged, almost as one, padded shoulders doing a Mexican wave.

'Look, it's good, possibly the most powerful thing we've ever come up with. But it needs to be handled carefully. I know what you think about me. I can sense your exasperation.' Reuben swivelled back to look straight at them. 'Give me a bit more time. I'll make it foolproof. We won't make mistakes.' He poured the victim's broken teeth into a plastic vial. They sounded like dice being shaken. 'Until then, there's no way I'm sanctioning it. Especially if it's rushed out to meet crime targets, or win the PR war, or further careers. Because in the wrong hands, this stuff is fucking lethal.'

Sarah Hirst turned and strode out of the room, high heels skewering the wet carpet, poking small square drainage holes through it. Phil remained, studying Reuben's features. His eyes were dull and opaque, his face jowled. A dark matt of stubble was trying to ooze out of his pallid skin. He was shorter than Reuben, and stared slightly up at him. Reuben sensed for the first time that their respective roles were pushing them apart; they were now closer to being colleagues than friends. 'I'm going to say this once, Reuben.'

'You have secret feelings for me?'

'Don't isolate yourself from CID. Play with us, not against us.'

'I suppose, just for the sake of convention, I should ask whether you're threatening me?'

Phil's expression softened. 'Jesus, no. We're all on the same side. Sarah's got her pressures, just like you've got yours and I've got mine.' He reached forwards to place a hand on Reuben's shoulder. 'Just try to compromise on this one. Look at it from our side. We use your technique, take a big step forward, we all look good.' Phil tapped him twice on the cheek. 'And then the Met promotes from within. Sarah or me, hopefully me, ends up Unit Commander, you get the budget and resources you need, and we'll all get back to being happy campers again.'

'One final thing,' Reuben said as Phil moved towards the exit. 'I just don't get the rush. GeneCrime is thriving. We've had several big breakthroughs in the last six months.'

'And?'

'There's something else going on here, isn't there?'

Phil held the door handle, which was wrapped in a clear plastic evidence bag. He hesitated. 'I've always admired your suspicious nature, Reuben. It's what has pushed you to the top of your field. But do me a favour, my friend. Turn it off from time to time. Or else who are you ever going to be able to trust? Me? Sarah? Your team?' Phil Kemp pulled the door open. Despite the hour, his phone beeped, receiving a document for his electronic signature. He stared at the screen and sighed. Then he raised his eyebrows at Reuben and left the room, whistling a tune without troubling any of the right notes.

5

A fat Chinese man walks as if he is wading through treacle, rolls of flesh rippling like waves. Two men following him separately begin to converge. One is tall, fair and lean. The other is shorter and darker, and is dressed as if he is just leaving a nightclub. It is late afternoon.

'Jehovah's Witnesses,' the taller man says as his new mobile rings. 'How might I direct your call?'

'Punishments, please,' his accomplice announces.

'Just putting you through. Praise the Lord.'

'Oh hello. My name is Jez. I'd like permission to carry out a shooting, please.'

'Busy street? Broad daylight? Obese Chinese man?'

'All of the above.'

'And, verily, thou shalt strike him down with a mighty vengeance.'

'Thank you.'

'Just don't miss him.' Reuben scans the busy pavement. 'Where are you, by the way?'

'Ahead of you, other side of the road, passing the pub with the flower baskets.'

'I see you. God, you look shit.'

'You don't look so good yourself.'

'I guess not, Jez,' Reuben acknowledges, swallowing a yawn.

'Late to bed?'

'Took a while to wrap up the drowned man.' Reuben had left the scene and returned to his lab, spending a sleepless night coming down from the amphetamine mania, methodically performing the world's first Predictive Phenotyping test. 'So, what about the target?'

'Red jumper, about to cross to your side of the road.'

'Got him,' Reuben says. 'I'm hanging up. Pass me the gun after you pull the trigger.'

'You're the boss.'

'Right, he's turning into the park. Let's do him out of sight. Catch up with you back at the lab. And Jez?'

'Yes?'

'Pray to Jehovah you get a clean shot.'

A gun appears and is passed from the fairer to the darker. The fat man wades into the park, kicking up litter. Behind him, two glances confirm the time is right. The weapon appears and its trigger is pulled in close proximity. The Chinese man cries out and clutches his neck. Blood appears through his fingers. The gun is exchanged. The men split up and walk away.

Ten minutes later, Reuben Maitland passes a small gun-like object to his senior technician Judith Meadows. Reuben notes that she appears happier than yesterday, her usually serene features pulled undeniably upwards. Judith takes the gun and asks, 'So how was it, boss?'

'Fair to middling.'

'And this is Run Zhang?'

'The very same.'

'And the gun itself?'

'Think we're going to have to modify it.' Reuben rubs his face, a greasy fatigue lurking in his skin. 'I'm not sure we need the retraction part. It seems to be hurting them too much.'

'Another squealer?'

'Like a pig. Mind you, I haven't spoken with him yet. Knowing Run he's probably checked himself into hospital.'

Judith positions the barrel of the implement in an Eppendorf tube. She swills the red fluid around before leaking a drop on to a microscope slide. 'So let's see what've we got,' she mutters, squinting through the eyepiece. 'Couple of million cells maybe.'

'Great.'

Judith turns and trains the full attention of her large dark eyes on him. 'You know what I heard this morning, Rube?'

'What?' he asks, momentarily caught in the depths of her irises.

'Someone's been fishing around in our freezers again. Any idea what's going on?'

Reuben holds his hand up. 'Relax,' he says. 'This time it was me.'

'Oh.' Judith is quiet, looking from the microscope to her boss and back, trying not to ask.

'You keep a secret?'

'Always.'

Reuben glances around. 'Predictive Phenotyping has just had its first outing.'

'You're joking! But what about all the—'

'Phil Kemp, Sarah Hirst and a lot of other people are going to discover exactly what happens when you open Pandora's box.'

'So who have you profiled? Mark Gelson?'

Reuben stares into the shiny lab floor and sees a distorted reflection of the laboratory and its upside-down personnel. 'No. And that's all I ought to say about it.'

Judith pauses for a second. 'At the risk of irritating my boss, could I at least see the actual Pheno-Fit?' She flutters her eyelashes. 'Pretty please?'

Reuben scans the lab. Run Zhang, theatrically clutching his neck, is making his way in through the heavy security doors. He stops to show off his wound to a couple of technicians. Reuben takes what looks like a colour photograph from his inside pocket and holds it up briefly for Judith to inspect. The Pheno-Fit depicts the 3D face of a handsome male with hazel eyes, wavy hair, a broad nasal bridge, and a sharp chin. In a textbox at the bottom right, the information '1.85–1.9 m tall, slim build, shoe size 10–11, athletic' is printed.

'Don't suppose you can predict his phone number?' Judith asks, absently flicking at her wedding ring through her vinyl glove.

''Fraid not. But what do you think about the actual picture?'

'Looks like you've finally cracked it. Can we have a go at it now?'

Reuben nods his head slowly. 'Any day,' he says, 'any day soon.'

'So what about the Psycho-Fit?'

'Medium intellect, a propensity for argument, poor ability to differentiate right from wrong.'

'Doesn't sound too dangerous.'

'That' – Reuben frowns – 'depends entirely on the context.'

'By the way, the new guy, Dr Paul Mackay, in due any minute to get his security clearance sorted.' Judith pulls her gloves off, removes her lab coat and smooths her skirt. 'OK if I go and bring him in?'

'Of course.'

'You going to do your trick?'

'I'm not feeling . . .'

'Come on.' Judith smiles. 'You know it freaks them out.'

As Judith leaves, Reuben brings the Pheno-Fit up to eye level and stares into its face. He experiences a dizzying mix of anger and apprehension. 'I don't know who the fuck you are, but I've got a feeling that we're going to meet pretty soon,' he whispers to it. 'And that it won't be good for either of us.' The Pheno-Fit stares back: expressionless and impassive. Reuben is both excited that his own technology works, and scared at the direction it is inevitably pushing him in. His furrowed concentration is broken by Run Zhang.

'Look, Dr Maitland,' Run points, shuffling over to reveal a small nick just above his collar.

'A graze,' Reuben answers, slotting the picture away.

Run is a forensics researcher, big and lazy, a mild hypochondriac who is disinclined to have anything shot at him in the name of field testing. He has only been in the UK for two years, and is still adapting to GeneCrime's predominant language of scientific Londonese. 'A graze? That fucking thing almost, ah, take my spinal column out. You told me it won't hurt.'

'It was only an exercise, my brave friend.' Reuben's phone announces that over the next few minutes he will receive fresh crime-scene footage. 'But we're getting there. Soon, we'll be able to do what we did today for real. Take an unambiguous DNA sample from a suspect in the street, with them feeling little more than a mosquito bite.'

'This fucking shark bite.'

'OK, OK. We'll redesign it. Grab a plaster from the first-aid box and I'll see if I can't stem the tidal wave of blood.'

Standing alone in the middle of the laboratory, Reuben watches a few members of his team huddled together in discussion. There is an awkwardness about them, a pronounced lack of coherency. He sees Mina Ali, dark, bony, her scowl lop-sided; Bernie Harrison, tall, bearded and serious; Simon Jankowski, centre parting, glasses, a loud shirt doing the talking for him; Birgit Kasper, mousy, stout, almost deliberately unremarkable in appearance and conversation. He flashes back to the Christmas party several months previously, observing a group of scientists out of the laboratory, drunk, having fun, racing round like a batch of lab rats released from their cage.

Reuben checks his watch, unfastening its metal strap and peering at the flattened hairs on his wrist. He feels like he has two different timepieces. The one he holds in his fingers now seems to count slowly and inevitably. The one he wore through the night was quick and erratic. He doesn't know which he prefers. Reuben stares intently at the back of the Dugena. Just visible are a series of scratches which surround its leverage point. He licks his dry lips, fighting a sudden urge.

'Nervous?' Simon Jankowski asks, pulling a blank lab coat over his Hawaiian shirt.

'What?'

'The interview. It's now, isn't it?' Simon tunes the lab radio and calls to his co-workers. 'Anyone want to hear the boss on . . . what station was it this time?'

'Radio Two.'

Several of Reuben's group desert what they are doing and amble over as Simon finds the station.

'. . . leading authority on forensic detection, and the scientist accredited with solving, amongst numerous others, the murder of the Harrow sisters Bethany and Megan Gillick, joins me now in the studio. So, Dr Maitland, thank you for joining us. What do *you* make of the government's newly proposed legislation to introduce genetic testing for everyone suspected – not just convicted, but *suspected* – of minor crimes or misdemeanours?'

Reuben half listens to his voice crackling out of the speaker, yesterday's words recorded and regurgitated. 'There are clearly two issues here. First, you mentioned the Gillick sisters. Now, we would never have made the link to the killer, Damian Soames, if his profile hadn't been on record from a pilot study we performed on Category B prisoners in the mid-nineties. So information in isolation often seems arbitrary or intrusive, but when you have the power to cross reference, as we do now, on a massive scale, it can suddenly assume a logic of its own. However, and this is the second point, the issue of civil liberty, particularly within a legal framework that almost exclusively predates the discovery of DNA, is paramount.'

'In what way? Surely the common good—'

'Look, when I buy a washing machine, my personal information – my address, telephone number, consumer habits, et cetera – go on record somewhere. They are passed around. I end up being called on the phone to see if I want to buy insurance or change my gas supplier. I get junk mail thrust through my letter box. Information at whatever level – be it shopping habits or be it DNA sequences – has to be handled carefully.'

'But there's an enormous difference between shopping and DNA-testing.'

'They simply reflect different scales of the same issue. Consumer profiling and genetic profiling . . .'

Reuben silently concentrates on his own words; his voice is calm, his answers are rehearsed, his arguments occasionally stretched and inflated for public consumption. This is one more in a long line of radio and newspaper interviews over the last year that have taught him what to say and how to say it. He wonders momentarily whether he has begun to sound too polished, question after question wearing his teeth down to the gums. Surrounding him, his group listen intently, smiling, occasionally looking from him to the radio and back again, almost wondering why his lips aren't moving. He takes in their loyalty and respect, and for a second enjoys the warmth. The interview continues, widening its scope, Reuben's position as an eminent authority on forensic detection pushing the debate.

'. . . and so we struggle to keep up. Always, laws are reactive, crimes are reactive, people are reactive, and yet technology is proactive. The potential is enormous. But potentially fantastic or potentially disastrous. That's what we have to decide.'

Reuben stares uncomfortably at the floor, glad that the cross-examination is beginning to draw to a close. He feels increasingly that while forensics nudges its way further into the public consciousness, maybe it should do so without him for a while. He can see battles ahead, and appreciates that he will soon need to cut out all distractions.

Finally, the interview ends and Simon switches the radio off. 'Show's over, folks,' he says.

'You should be on TV,' Birgit Kasper suggests, her face pale against her strikingly red glasses. 'Any offers?'

'One or two.'

Run Zhang grins. 'I don't know, boss.'

'Why not?'

'You got, ah, perfect face for radio.'

'OK, OK.' Reuben smiles. 'Any chance of anyone doing some work around here? The new guy will be here in a minute. Let's at least pretend to look busy . . .'

'You going to do your trick?' Mina asks.

'I wouldn't rule it out.' He winks. 'Now, people, let's catch some bad guys.'

Reuben watches his group melt away with gentle reluctance. Glancing up, he sees Judith reappearing from the far side of the lab with a tall man in tow. From the man's paper-thin air of confidence, Reuben senses that he is nervous about starting at GeneCrime. Reuben shrugs, replacing his timepiece. It is a building brimming with the bright and the sharp. He is right to be wary.

6

'Dr Maitland, do your trick,' Judith implores after Reuben has shaken hands with the new recruit.

'Judith . . .' he answers, a dizzying moment of fatigue draining his opposition.

'Oh, come on. I've told Dr Mackay all about it.'

Reuben finds Judith's demure persuasion hard to refuse. 'Dr Mackay?'

'I'm curious.'

'If we have to.' Reuben yawns and shakes his head. 'Right, Dr Mackay, here we go. We've only met once, when I interviewed you for the job. And during that time you told me nothing about your background, aside from your qualifications and vastly exaggerated work experience. So let me guess.' Reuben peers intently at the man before him, running his suddenly open eyes from left to right, from top to bottom, as if scanning his image on to a screen. He pauses, taking in a deep breath. Then he begins. His delivery is brisk and direct, serious but light, playing along with the game. 'You have an uncle on your mother's side with acute male-pattern baldness. Your father went prematurely grey. You are taller than your mother, but not your father. One of your parents has blue eyes, the other either blue or green. Your dimple comes from your father's side of the family. In temperament, you consider yourself to be more like your mother, but in actuality you are somewhere in the middle. Both parents are slim, tending towards the athletic. There is Nordic ancestry in your deep, dark past. You have relatively sparse body hair, and your stubble, when you haven't shaved it to make a good impression on your first day, grows with a tinge of copper. One of your parents – I'm not sure which – has slightly bucked teeth. You are highly intelligent and an above average sportsman. Judging from the relative length of your index and ring fingers, I would guess' – Reuben winks at Judith – 'that you are fairly well hung. How am I doing so far?'

Dr Paul Mackay shrugs. 'OK, I suppose.'

'Right. Let's step things up a bit. You enjoy, among other things, rowing and cycling. And you follow motor-racing and read American crime fiction, particularly Ellroy, Grisham and—'

'Where are you getting my hobbies from?' Dr Mackay asks, obviously unnerved.

'Your CV.'

'Picasso!' Judith exclaims. 'You cheat!'

'OK. Let's get serious again.' Reuben squints at Dr Mackay, his half-closed eyes blinking rapidly. 'So, here's the thing. Despite what's on your CV, you rebelled in your mid to late teens. Challenged authority, that sort of thing. Disappointed your parents. Did something serious. Went much further than the usual teenage mutiny. Maybe got yourself into some trouble?'

Dr Mackay shuffles uncomfortably. Reuben's phone tells him that the video footage is ready to view.

'Is he right?' Judith asks.

'About almost everything. But how—'

'Simple mix of genetics and observation. Key point: a previously pierced nose and earlobe, both well grown over. The other body and facial features speak for themselves, if you know how these things are inherited. It's really just Mendelian theory with a bit of guesswork and the odd generalization thrown in.'

'Scary, isn't it?' Judith adds.

'Why "Picasso", if you don't mind me asking?'

'He paints. Obsessively. Face after face after face. He's not bad, either.'

'Don't mind me.' Reuben grins, walking to the far side of the lab, opening drawers and taking out sample bags and sterile tubes.

'And has he ever painted you?' Dr Mackay enquires.

'I don't think he's ever looked close enough,' Judith answers quietly, when she is sure that Reuben can't hear. 'But there's something else you should know about him.'

'What?'

'He's different. Not like normal scientists or coppers.'

'How do you mean?'

'Do you remember the judge who killed his cleaner last year? The Jeffrey Beecher case? What you won't have heard is that when everyone else had given up, gone home, forgotten all about it, Reuben stayed at the scene. Worked through the night, just by himself. Even remained there till teatime the following day, refusing to quit. Phil Kemp and Sarah Hirst asked him to return to the lab, but he said no. We had nothing, no samples, no body, no nothing. The investigation was falling apart. And then, just as we were all going home on the second day, we got the call. Specks of blood in the hinge of a door, which must have been slightly open at the time of the attack. A fine mist of blood that had been missed by Judge Beecher when he scrubbed his apartment with the cleaner's own detergents. When we arrived there, Reuben had actually taken the front door off with a screwdriver. We got enough sample to tie Beecher to the murder. And despite no body ever being recovered, he was prosecuted and, as you may know, later confessed. All because Reuben wouldn't quit when everyone else had.'

38

'So you're saying he's thorough.'

'It's more than that,' Judith answers as Reuben re-enters the lab. 'He's damn well possessed.'

Reuben places a small collection of plastics into his case and closes it. 'My ears are on fire,' he says, but is interrupted by another insistent beep from his phone. He walks away, watching pictures of a murder victim taken from different angles on the screen. His mood darkens instantly, a cold grey depression leaking into his brain.

The dead man is in one of the most unusual positions Reuben has ever viewed a naked corpse. His legs are perfectly spread, at right-angles to his torso, like a gymnast doing the splits. Pelvic dislocation, Reuben mutters to himself, femurs ripped from their sockets, ligaments snapped, muscles torn. Reuben heads out of the lab and past a row of offices, viewing the video file as he walks. The victim's arms, in parallel to his legs, are crucifixion-straight, and his head is barely visible in most shots, hanging over the side of a bed. Reuben squints. The man looks like a giant letter H. But what really disturbs Reuben is what lies beneath. Spilling out, coiled and meandering, almost seeming to pulsate as if still digesting his lunch, are the man's small and large intestines. He has been pulled inside out, disembowelled, colon first. A large metal hook, slaughterhouse in origin, lies in front of the bed, dried blood on the carpet. From the colour of the intestines, the man has been dead for days.

As he crashes through a set of double doors, a close-up of the victim's face stares out of the screen. Reuben guesses Korean or Japanese. He looks away, momentarily troubled by what he sees in the expression. It is there in the flared nostrils, the open-locked jaw, the fixed pupils, features which smelt, tasted and focused upon an unimaginable evil. The address where the deceased drew his final breath flashes up on the display. Reuben plays the footage a second time, mental images of what caused the carnage lighting up his consciousness like slides in a lecture.

Reuben takes the lift to the ground floor, and enters the unisex toilets which squat near the security desk, locking the door behind him. Inside, he looks into the mirror. His eyes are bloodshot, red capillaries searching through the whites, coiled like lightbulb filaments. He sees the paleness of his face contrasted against the dingy walls of the toilet, and sighs that an elite unit should have such rudimentary standards of hygiene.

Reuben takes his watch off and lays it beside his mobile phone on the stained sink. He spends a few seconds removing its metal back. Sometimes, he tells himself, DNA is a real fucker. We are organic, driven by our selfish genes, sticks of rock with our letters running through, our characteristics and traits pushed to the surface for all to see. But those four little letters can cause more harm than an alphabet of treachery. He pulls a hidden plastic vial out of his watch, the size of its battery. Frozen on the screen of his phone, even through the grainy pixels, the horror in the victim's eyes is clearly visible. Reuben needs to be isolated and unshockable. He uncaps the tube and pours its contents into his palm, wetting his finger and dabbing the drug into his gums. By the time he reaches the scene, he will have stopped debating the broader issues. Reuben will be a forensics officer in the purest sense: attentive, alert and unthinking. But until then, the distresses of his existence are free to gnaw at him. He tidies up, flushes the toilet and leaves. As he walks past Security and out towards his car, he feels the Pheno-Fit in his shirt pocket rubbing against the left side of his chest. Beneath, his heart pounds out a frantic beat of uncertainty and premonition.

7

Davie was dimly aware of another presence. Bigger, wider and heavier. Walking shoulder to shoulder, pace for pace. Looking straight ahead. Davie tried to vary his tempo. As he slowed, the man slowed. As he speeded up then so did the man. He cleared his throat. Glanced at his watch. Another thirty-five minutes to go.

He had learnt a multitude of lessons in the last nine months. Never talk unless spoken to first. Never say anything that can be construed as direct or aggressive. Never catch someone's eye for more than half a second. Never ask questions. Never trust anyone who offers you something for free. In short, retreat into your shell, head just about poking out, staring up at the sky, willing time to pass.

The man brushed shoulders with Davie. Davie mumbled an apology. Now he was freaked out. It had been a deliberate contact. He walked on, hands in his pockets, hunched over, his jaw clenched.

'Tell me what're you in for,' the man muttered. The voice was gruff and educated, foreign consonants wrapped around English vowels.

Davie didn't look at him. 'B and E,' he said.

'Crack or smack?'

'Crack.'

'How long you got left?'

'Thirteen months.'

Again, the man brushed shoulders, harder this time. Davie edged away, but couldn't move far without leaving the treadmill of the path. 'I'll come and see you later. Block C, yes?'

Davie nodded silently.

'Floor B? Cell two hundred and twenty-eight?'

Again Davie nodded, scared now. The man knew his cell. This was it. The thing he had feared more than almost anything was about to happen. The man slowed his pace and dropped back. For the next half-hour, Davie was afraid to turn around. He had the unsettling feeling that the man was one step behind, watching, sizing him up.

After the exercise hour, Davie didn't break his stride. He just continued walking, heading through the quad gate and into the cool corridors of Block C, up the cracked concrete stairs, along the outside edge of Floor B and into Cell 228, and paced forwards and backwards, from wall to wall, from window to door, worrying the thin carpet of the floor. Fuck fuck fuck, he told himself. Occasionally he twitched slightly, maybe from long-term withdrawal, maybe from neurons which were drowning in cold adrenalin. One more lesson he had learnt in the nine months of his incarceration was that no matter who you knew, you were very much on your own. A figure appeared in the doorway, thickset, looming and intense. Davie stopped walking. 'Knock knock,' the man said. Davie kept quiet, trying to sum him up without staring. He was dark, and there was a brutality in the blackness of his eyes and the thickness of his eyebrows. His lips were full, his teeth, as he grinned, stained and worn. He took several paces into Davie's room and sat down on the bed. Davie's cellmate Griff sauntered in, took one look at the guest and left quickly, closing the door. From what passed between the two of them, Davie surmised that this had been pre-arranged.

'So,' the prisoner began, 'so, so, so. Davie Hethrington-Andrews. That's correct, isn't it?'

Davie nodded.

'Funny name, don't you think?'

Davie shrugged, as nervous as he had ever been in his life.

'Not many of you, are there? Hethrington-Andrewses, that is?'

'No.'

'How many in London, do you think?'

'I don't know.'

'Two. And guess what? They're both related to you.'

Davie's eyes widened. This was about his family. 'There's no money . . .'

'Quiet,' the man instructed. 'I'm not interested in money. I'm interested in your well-being.'

'How?'

'Let me just say that I have power over your future.' The man glowered up at him. 'Don't you think?'

'Yes.' Although he didn't know the man's name, Davie certainly knew his face. Everyone did. The man was unreadable, unpredictable and utterly sadistic. The prisoner all other prisoners feared. His anxiety jumped up a notch.

'And would you say that I'm a man who could influence your well-being?'

'Yes.'

'Now, don't worry. There's only one thing I want from you, and it won't hurt.' The man stood up to face Davie, and cut into him with his eyes. 'Unless of course you can't help me. In which case it will hurt so much that you will want to die.'

Davie didn't want to ask, but the question was left hanging, waiting to be plucked. 'What do you want?' Davie enquired quietly.

The man took a folded piece of paper from his trouser pocket. He flattened it out with his palm and passed it over. It was the front page of a scientific article. 'I want to meet your brother,' he said.

'My brother?'

'This is him, yes?'

The paper was entitled 'Towards Genomic Expression: RNA Evidence to Supersede DNA.' The third name amongst the authors was Jeremy Hethrington-Andrews. 'Yes.'

'You will ring Jeremy.'

'Jez. He hates being called Jeremy.'

'I want to see him when I leave here. I have a couple of things I need to ask him.' The psycho took a step forwards. Davie sensed his sheer power radiating forth, shrivelling all in its wake. He seemed to bristle with violence. There was a change in his features and his nostrils flared. 'Things that could influence your survival in here.' He struck a sudden blow towards Davie's face, which stopped millimetres short of breaking his nose open. Davie felt the air move over his opened eyes. The man moved his left arm equally rapidly and Davie flinched. However, the man allowed the punch to change direction, and instead wrapped his powerful arm around Davie's shoulder. 'You see' – he smiled – 'events could go in either direction. No one in here will touch you while you stay on my good side. Even when I'm released – in a few weeks – my people will look after you. So come on, get the ball rolling, sort things out, and you and I can be friends.'

The man let go of Davie and left the cell. Davie slumped down on the bed, relief washing through his veins, diluting his fear. As it dissipated, he began to shake, as if his terror had been the only thing holding him together. His cellmate entered and studied Davie's face.

'What the fuck did he want?' Griff asked.

'Not a lot.'

'Look, when someone like that comes to see you, it's never not a lot. Come on, what's he after?'

'He wants my help with something.'

'Like what?'

'Just a favour.'

From the moment Davie had been locked up, Griff had intimidated him. They shared a cell, but Griff had made it clear that it was his territory, and that Davie played by his rules. They had had one fight, which Griff had both initiated and won. Davie ran his tongue over his chipped front tooth.

'What favour?'

'Nothing.'

'Don't fuck with me, Davie-Wavie. Come on, let's have the news.'

Davie stood up and faced him. For the first time since he had arrived in the prison, he stared Griff straight in the eye, pushing his shoulders back. 'Don't ever ask me again,' he said.

'*You what?*' Griff screamed.

'I said, don't ask me again. And from now on, stay the fuck away from me.'

Griff's face hardened. His fists clenched and unclenched. Davie continued to stare at him. Griff reddened, conflict rippling through his muscular body. Davie held his nerve. Somewhere a bell rang. And then Griff turned away and walked back out of the room.

Davie breathed a long, cool sigh. The balance of power in Cell 228 had suddenly shifted.

8

Reuben remained at the crime scene until he was happy that all obvious samples had been collected. Between them, GeneCrime's SOCO team had fingerprints, hairs, saliva, blood and footprints. Whoever had enjoyed the protracted death and disembowelling of Kim Fu Sun hadn't been too fussy about leaving their calling card.

After dropping the various specimens into a lab freezer, he drove to the pub. The hands of the car's analogue clock hovered around 1 a.m. It was late, but a few of the stragglers would still be there. He knew he should go home, but that was something he couldn't do just yet.

Inside, only one person remained. Reuben was disappointed, but also secretly relieved that he wouldn't be on his own. Phil Kemp gave off the distinct impression of someone who had drunk themselves sober. He was sitting at a table surrounded by the empty drinks of others, bolt upright, staring into the middle distance. Reuben noted his half-empty pint of Guinness and carried another one over to him.

'I guess I've missed it all?' Reuben said.

Phil came alive instantly. 'Not so, big fella.' He grinned. 'I'm still here.'

'Great.'

'And Simon Jankowski's puking in the toilets.'

'Hell, I've been to worse parties.' Reuben sat down next to Phil and they clinked glasses. 'What was the turnout like?'

'Full house.'

'It was a long hard case.'

'Too right. And we nailed that fucker.' Phil raised his glass. 'To Philip Antony Godfrey and his three life sentences.'

Reuben joined the salutation, the ice cubes rattling in his neat vodka. He glanced around the dingy, enveloping interior of the pub. The barman looked eager to close up; only one other punter remained, a fat man hunched uncomfortably on a stool.

Phil was quiet for a second, lost in his thoughts. Then he asked, 'How's Lucy these days?'

'Good.'

'Copper's intuition, but you don't sound so sure.'

Reuben drank from his glass before answering. 'It's just . . .'

'What?'

'No, she's good.'

'It's been a long time.'

'I know, Phil. We'll get you round. Soon.'

'You certain everything's all right?'

Reuben closed his eyes and muttered, 'I love my wife, you know. I love my wife.'

'Maybe you should be telling her that.'

'Yeah. Maybe I should.'

'And the kid?'

'Fantastic.' Reuben glanced involuntarily at his watch. 'Though I missed another bedtime tonight.'

'Curse of the job, my friend. Like many things.'

Reuben felt the familiar burn of the vodka. He was coming down, bit by bit, but the drink would help. He glanced at Phil, who was burying himself deep in his Guinness. Was it all worth it? he asked himself. The personal and the professional ramming into each other, making things tricky, damaging friendships and relationships alike.

'I'd better go and check on Simon,' Phil said, standing unsteadily. He eased himself out from the table and swayed towards the Gents.

Reuben continued to ponder, shredding a beer mat, knowing that things were coming to a head. Lucy, Phil, Sarah Hirst and two unusually brutal and sadistic murders in as many days were gnawing at the remnants of the speed. Out of the corner of his eye he sensed a movement, and turned in the direction of the bar. The fat man was approaching his table. He smiled at Reuben and then sat down heavily in Phil's space.

'You Reuben Maitland?' the man asked brusquely.

'Who are you?'

'My name's Moray Carnock, Dr Maitland.'

'How do you know who I am?'

'It's my job.'

'And what might that be?'

'Finding people. Offering services. Protecting things.' Moray Carnock took a chocolate bar from his coat and offered Reuben a chunk.

'What do you want?' Reuben asked, shaking his head.

'I've got information.'

'So you're a grass?'

'Oh no, Dr Maitland. I'm no grass.' The man laughed heartily, and then pushed some chocolate into his open mouth. 'I've been called some things in my time, but grass, hell . . .'

'Well, what then?'

'Look, let me spell it out.' He glanced around the pub, sure that he couldn't be overheard. 'There was a *murder*.' His Scots accent rolled through the word, drawing it out. 'Let's say your people are investigating it. I have a lot of contacts, both nice and not so nice. I've been tracking someone as part of a commercial security suit. In the course of tracking this person, I have discovered something interesting about them that I doubt you boys know.'

'Which is?'

'So what I'm suggesting is quid pro quo. I scratch your back; you fill my pockets.'

'I don't work like that.'

'You're saying no?'

Reuben flared with anger. 'I'm saying leave me the hell alone, and don't approach me again.'

'Your final word?'

'My final word is goodbye,' Reuben answered curtly.

'OK, my friend,' Moray Carnock said, standing up. 'But remember this. Principles are a luxury in a murder investigation.' He flicked a business card on to the table, then walked back past the bar and out of the door. Before Reuben had time to think, Phil emerged from the toilets with a very pale Simon Jankowski in tow. Reuben stood up and felt for his car keys.

'Looks like we'd better get this boy home,' he said. 'Come on, DCI Kemp, play your cards right and I'll drop you back as well.'

Phil grinned, reached for the last remnants of his drink, and followed Reuben and Simon out of the bar. The grateful barman shouted goodnight and began to turn the lights off one by one. In his car, driving along the empty nocturnal streets of London, Reuben found himself wondering exactly what the Scotsman had been offering to sell.

9

Reuben opened his front door. He was restless and tired, a nervous feeling eating at his stomach. The house was still, the air cool, its occupants asleep. He walked through into his cramped study at the rear. It was a converted outbuilding with unfinished brick walls and a roughly tiled floor. A large desk in the corner supported the weight of a computer. Scattered around were multiple pots of water paint, a jar of slender brushes and a number of pens and pencils. Taped to the surface was a square of rough canvas. Reuben slumped in his chair and began the ritual. He started to sketch out the face of the corpse.

Reuben started with a soft pencil, before progressing to colours and tones. Drawing the victims brought them back to life. He gave them dignity, reconstructing them as they would have looked before the world chewed them up and spat them out. More importantly, this ritual brought him down from every crime scene. As his mind shook itself free from the final lurches of amphetamine, he would sit alone, restoring and re-establishing, touching and retouching, renovating and reanimating, letting the sickness bleed from his body. The drawers of his study were crammed with faces of the dead, two-dimensional representations of souls who had been stabbed, shot, strangled and scythed down in their prime. In this room, only good things happened. This was Reuben's sanctuary, painting his method of readjustment. Aside from Lucy, no one ever saw these pictures. They were purely for his own peace of mind.

Dipping his brush unsteadily into a coffee jar of water, Reuben appreciated that, unusually, he was struggling. He was stuck on the eyes of the corpse; all he could see were pupils frozen wide as they imprinted a final series of horrific images on the victim's brain while his guts were torn from his body. And as Reuben stared into the canvas, another face was tormenting him, poking through the surface. Its eyes were broader, its nose pinched, its hair lighter, its cheeks rosier. The visage of a baby. Smiling, innocent and untouched by iniquity. Suddenly Reuben stood up, crashing, too overloaded to paint away the horror.

He climbed the stairs and stopped outside his bedroom, before turning and padding back along the landing. Reuben read the letters J-O-S-H-U-A on the door of the nursery, and pushed it open. The smell seeped into his consciousness: urine, faeces, sour milk and nappy sacks. The odours were much more acute than they had been the previous day. Then, he had been on forensic autopilot, getting the job done, breaking into his own house. He lay on the floor and pulled a couple of blankets over him, wrapping them tight under his body, swaddling himself like a baby. Reuben listened to his son wriggling, kicking his legs, sniffling, tossing and turning, trying to be free of his own restraints. Focusing on a stationary mobile above the cot, Reuben once again felt the ants buzzing around his head, fighting their way into nooks and crannies, marching along neural highways.

In his pocket he still carried the Pheno-Fit. Two hairs in his bed predicted that a male whom he had never met had been spending time there. To his knowledge, no workmen had visited the house, no friends had dropped by, no . . . He quickly appreciated there were no other explanations. This was hypothesis-based research. He hypothesized that Lucy was having a long-term affair, and now he was in the process of proving it. Reuben reasoned that he should be scientific about the whole thing. If I'm scientific, he rationalized, I can't be hurt. Everything is just a question with an answer. But, screwing his eyes up, he realized that feelings and reasons are very different beasts. And no matter how logical he was, it hurt like hell.

But what to do? He took the picture out and squinted at it in the gloom. He ran over the crime scenes of the last forty-eight hours – the drowned man nailed to his living-room wall, the disembowelled corpse with the dislocated legs – his conversations with Sarah Hirst and Phil Kemp. He considered the fact that someone was rummaging around in his lab at night; the statistic that ten per cent of all babies don't share their supposed father's DNA; the possibilities; the impossibilities. Come-down paranoia began to join the dots between all the events of the last couple of days. Sarah Hirst was pulling the strings, masterminding events. The drowned man had been using his lab at night. Run Zhang was planning something with Judith. Lucy was having an affair with Phil Kemp. The fat man in the bar had poisoned Simon. Only Joshua knew the real truth . . . Reuben wrapped himself tighter. He recognized the signs of delusional behaviour.

To paper over the paranoia he ran through a mental slide show of images of Lucy. Almost hysterical two nights before their wedding. Hobbling around with a broken ankle. Camping in Northern France. Sitting unselfconsciously on the toilet while he bathed. Screaming at him during labour. Giving him head as they drove across Canada. Nursing him through a long bout of flu. Making love to him silently in the dark. Crying as he proposed to her on Sedge Knoll, a wet Somerset hill.

And then he cut to the present. The arguments when Joshua was in bed; the fractured trust; the terse atmosphere which had become the norm. A great marriage which was slowly, inexorably, going wrong, the love and respect diluting, the very things which had held them tight starting to unravel. He remembered the first time he had met her. It had been in a pub near her office, and Reuben had known instantly that he wanted to be with Lucy, that he would take more risks than with other lovers, that he would open himself up to her. Now, he felt shut, clamped tight and hidden away.

Reuben saw that some of this mess was actually his own fault. The long hours, the press interviews, the politics of GeneCrime: he was honest enough to acknowledge that none of these had helped his role as a husband. I know what I have done to you, my love, he sighed in the darkness. And now I'm going to find out what you have done to me.

Reuben reached through the bars of the cot and squeezed Joshua's hand. Eventually, he slipped into an uneasy unconsciousness.

At breakfast, Reuben studied Lucy's every action, images from the loft photos playing around with his mood. He was distracted and distant, a thousand notions washing through his brain as he spoke. In contrast, Lucy was tense, busy, rushed, a big day ahead of her.

'What are you looking for?' he asked.

'You got any cash?' she said, rooting through her handbag. 'The childminder needs paying.'

'Sure.' Reuben stood up and picked Joshua out of his high chair, wiping his face with a wet-wipe. 'Look, why don't I take Josh to nursery today?'

'Fine by me.'

'It would make a change, that's all.' He felt the warmth of his son, cheek to cheek, his solid little body clinging to the embrace, one hand tugging at Reuben's ear. When he held his son, there was no wrong in the world.

'I really don't mind. Now, where are my keys?'

'In the hall.'

She glanced at him and nodded quickly, her straight dark hair bobbing momentarily. 'Don't forget his bag. There're some spare bibs and a dummy.'

Reuben pictured the drive to the nursery. Sometimes when he dropped Joshua off, he arrived at work with a baby-sized hole in his stomach. Although the day quickly distracted him, it was still there, just perceptible, a space ready to be occupied again when he saw him at night. That was when crime scenes didn't drag him away.

Lucy managed a slender smile. 'Rough night?' she asked.

'Very,' Reuben replied, closing his eyes, his tired mind continuing to drift and explore, winding in and out of the conversation, and in and out of his problems. How did it come to this? he wondered. Functional, practical, mechanical. Where did all the fun go? The laughs, the games, the lunacy? Going out, getting drunk, flopping into bed in hysterics.

'And will you be putting in an appearance tonight?' she enquired.

Maybe this was just what relationships did. They lasted a number of years and fell apart. What had Lucy said to him in the early days? I have been unfaithful to nearly every partner so far. And Reuben would have been shocked, if the same hadn't also been true of him. They had promised each other that this was different, that this was a proper relationship, grown up and serious, years away from all that childish stuff with previous partners. They had got it all out of their systems, meeting in their early thirties. But had they really? Reuben looked at her. Did anyone really? 'Shouldn't be a problem,' he answered.

Lucy leant forwards and kissed him on the cheek. She smelt good – clean, fresh and natural – and he wondered again why she was betraying him. She wasn't inherently flirtatious, or needy, or exhibitionist. 'Good,' she said. 'You fancy a Chinese when Josh is in bed?'

Reuben nodded, still watching her closely. There had been no obvious behavioural signs. She was just different, colder, more withdrawn. For months, Reuben had fought the obvious. It was down to having Joshua, transferring love from husband to child. Her role in the family was changing. Certain freedoms had been sacrificed. He had tried to think it through in every conceivable way. Until the hairs in the bed. And then, almost instantaneously, he had stopped pretending. He had snapped from denial to resolution. 'Yeah, that would be good,' he answered quietly.

Lucy turned and strode out of the front door. Reuben walked Joshua into the living room and distracted him with a stuffed toy while he changed his nappy. Joshua kicked his legs and arms almost randomly, delighting in the mock screams his father gave each time he was hit in the face. Reuben blew a soft raspberry against Joshua's cheek, and a second and a third, his son's squealing laughter getting louder each time. Then Reuben picked him up. Reuben was silent for a moment. He stared into Joshua's smiling blue eyes, suddenly focused and serious, snapping to the point.

'Please forgive me for what I'm about to do,' he whispered.

He carried him into the hallway.

'But I need to know the truth.'

GCACGATAGCTTACGGG
TAATCTA**TWO**GTATTCG
GCTAATCGTCATAACAT

1

Reuben Maitland strode into a small cramped office on the first floor of GeneCrime and closed the door. Inside, Jez Hethrington-Andrews was playing a computer game and made a half-hearted effort to cover his tracks. Reuben looked sternly down at him. 'Relax, Tiger,' he said, breaking into a smile.

Jez grinned back. 'Fancy a go?' he asked.

'I'm hopeless.'

'Come on. I won't tell anyone.'

Reuben hesitated, appreciating that he would soon be asking Jez to take risks on his behalf. 'OK,' he said. 'Prepare to witness some wildly inaccurate shooting.' He sat down and began to fire more or less indiscriminately at a succession of digital zombies staggering towards him.

'You weren't joking.'

Reuben's eyes watered as he yawned. He had missed the best part of two nights' sleep. 'Listen,' he said, hammering the keyboard hard, 'there's something I want you to do for me . . .'

'Name it.'

Reuben took a disc out of his shirt pocket and passed it over, his eyes remaining glued to the screen. 'You have open access to all databases?'

'Aha.'

'Now, you don't have to do what I ask. Understand this – what I'm going to suggest doesn't follow protocol. Not by a long margin. You're going to need to keep this quiet.'

'I'm in.'

'Right. On the disc is the image of a suspect. I'm aware this hasn't come through the usual channels, but I want you to insert the suspect's face on the Serious and Sexual Crimes database. Flag it up as Priority One.'

'I'll do it now.'

'Is there a way of putting it on anonymously?'

'Nothing in the world of computers is anonymous.'

'OK, well, do what you've got to do.' Reuben was beginning to get inside the game, and to understand its mechanics. 'There's one more thing.'

'What?'

'Pattern-recognition software. Take it to the address written on the back of the disc. Use my authority and get it installed on the CCTV system. Drag Run along with you – test it out.'

'How?'

Reuben spent another few seconds maiming and destroying, before reluctantly handing the controls over to Jez. 'Get a digital photo of Run and place it in the search files of the CCTV system. Then ask him to walk back and forth in front of a nearby camera, and see if it picks him out.'

'By comparing its images with Run's stored photo?'

'Exactly.'

'You're sure? I mean, this all sounds a bit . . .'

'What?'

'Nothing. It'll make a change from shooting him in the park, I guess.'

'And, Jez . . .'

'Yes?'

'Not a word.'

As he paced back to his own office, along shiny corridors

humming with antiseptic, Reuben rang DCI Sarah Hirst's number. Things were finally moving. A new sense of calm settled his nerves, like a child falling asleep in a vehicle, happy just to be going somewhere. He had the opportunity to stall, to back out, to leave things alone, but was about to pass the point of no return.

'I was thinking about what you were saying the other night,' he began.

'And?' Sarah asked.

'Predictive Phenotyping has just had its first outing.'

'You're joking.'

'Seriously.'

'Mark Gelson? The Korean murder?'

'Not necessarily.'

'Who, then?'

Reuben entered his office and closed the door. 'Let's just say this is a double-blind trial.'

'Dr Maitland, try to be clearer.'

'The ultimate philosophy of science. In order to test something properly, you must have no notion of the expected outcome. By observing, we interfere.'

'Whatever you say. Fingers crossed.'

'Yeah,' Reuben answered unenthusiastically, pulling his wedding ring off, 'fingers crossed.' He noted the dent the ring had ground into the base of his digit. On the inside of the slim band he read the inscription. It simply said Sedge Knoll. He span it on its axis, watching it blur, glimmering, slowing, becoming unstable, falling over, vibrating on the desk, shuffling round in its death throes. 'You know, Sarah,' he said, putting it into a drawer, 'I'm going to need to call in a couple of favours if we're going to test this thing properly.'

The need in Sarah's voice was palpable. 'Name them.'

'Can you sanction a CCTV pattern-recognition trial? And clear it with Metropolitan CID?'

'Sounds possible. What for?'

'As I said. Double blind. This thing is going out into the field, and no one must know what to expect.'

'Come on, Reuben, give me a clue.'

'You'll see,' Reuben replied, sighing, 'but you may wish you hadn't.'

He hung up before Sarah had chance to ask him anything she might regret.

2

'OK, what have we got? Run, how about kicking off?' Reuben suppressed another in a long succession of yawns.

'We boring you, sir?'

Jez grinned. 'Maybe all those zombies have worn you out.'

'There're only two zombies wearing me out,' Reuben said. 'And they're both DCIs.' He glanced around the group of eight forensic scientists crammed into his office for their weekly meeting. These were the bright young things, recruited to GeneCrime from industry, academia and the Forensic Science Service. All of them, even the technicians, were as sharp as knives. Reuben liked it that way – it kept him on his toes. 'Sorry. Scratch that last comment. So what's going down, Run?'

'I think my neck's gone sceptic.'

'That's *septic*,' Jez corrected, sending a reasonable titter around the group.

'Ri'. Well, I'm extracting from Colon Man.'

'Let's have a little dignity, please.' Reuben rewound to the previous night. He smelt the obscenity of the death that had hung in the air. 'His name was Kim Fu Sun.'

'Think there's a link, boss?' Simon Jankowski asked. 'You know, with the hosepipe case?'

'I don't know. CID aren't pushing it. Mr Kim appears to have been executed, according to Pathology, a couple of weeks ago. Probable South-East Asian gang member. Mr Machicaran, on the other hand, known crack addict and associate of Mark Gelson, was tortured, presumably for information of some sort. Maybe no more linked than any other pair of unpleasant London deaths. But let's get our evidence straight and see what's what. Birgit?'

'I think we now have a pure sample from the Gelson/Machicaran case.'

'Think?' Mina Ali opened her fierce eyes behind her fierce glasses. 'What do you mean, *think*?'

'I'll know better in a couple of days.'

'Nothing less than certainty,' she lectured. Reuben imagined she was fighting the impulse to poke a bony finger as she said this.

Bernie Harrison, a gifted bio-statistician Reuben had lured from academia three years previously, took issue with Mina. 'Science is never a hundred per cent, forensic or otherwise.'

'What are you saying?' Mina demanded.

'We're all people, even you.' Bernie smiled. 'And—'

'Fuck you.'

'And people make mistakes. It's the way we're built. If you're so confident, let's have a look through your lab book, your sequencing, your profiling, everything you've done. You're telling me I won't find a single miscalculation anywhere?'

Mina let it drop. She was the group's scientific Rottweiler. Although she vexed Reuben considerably, she was nobody's fool. He liked to think of her as his internal control. If the evidence wasn't good enough for Mina, it wasn't good enough for court.

'Come on,' Bernie continued, 'even some of our own cases have been doubtful. You remember the GeneCrime evidence on the Edelstein rape? Inadequate, at best. Or the McNamara murder? Not to mention one or two recent convictions. The Brighton Rapist, the . . .' Bernie ran out of examples.

'Fine. Let's move on,' Reuben muttered. 'Science is flawed.

Forensics isn't always perfect. But Mina's right. We need to be one hundred per cent, and if we're not, we need to be open about what we do and don't know.' Usually, he welcomed the quarrel of sharp minds. Today, his own intellect was battling multiple diversions, an overwhelming range of unpleasant possibilities undermining his good humour. 'Judith. What's new with you?'

'Same old same old. People get murdered, samples come in, tubes get filled, people get arrested.'

'You having a bad day?'

'I'm just saying. And someone's still messing around with our stuff.'

Reuben scratched his knuckles against the stubble of his chin. He frowned and closed his eyes. When he opened them again he surveyed the eight faces in front of him intently. 'Who else has noticed anything odd?' Mostly, they met his gaze. Bernie stared resolutely into his A4 lab book, scouring a blue line into its faintly ruled pages. Mina, Simon and Run indicated that they were suspicious. 'So, Simon, tell me what you've observed.'

'It's nothing obvious. I don't know about the others' – Simon Jankowski glanced apprehensively around the group – 'but I might be imagining it. Twice in the morning I've come in and found equipment and reagents in slightly different positions than where I left them. That's all.'

'Mina?'

'Same.'

'Run.'

'I'm septical.'

'Nice one.'

'You know, I'm not sure,' Bernie said finally. 'Maybe we're just being paranoid. I mean, why would anybody want to play with our reagents?'

'I guess that's the point.' Reuben ran his eyes around his team, absorbing their frowns and their shrugs, their scratching and their fidgeting. 'So what do we feel about this?'

There was an uncomfortable silence. Birgit Kasper was the first to speak. As Reuben listened, he took in her plain features and logo-less clothes. Even scientists from Scandinavia dressed unlike any other section of society. 'I'm unnerved,' she said finally. 'This is freaking me out. There are issues here.'

'Like what?'

'Like irreplaceable evidence going missing, or being compromised. We handle the biggest cases here. I mean the implications, if someone *is* breaching lab security, are horrifying.'

'Everyone else?' There was a broad nod of agreement. Reuben flicked his lower incisors with the nail of his index finger while he thought. 'So how about this?' he suggested. 'We set a trap.'

'What sort of trap?'

'That's up to you,' Reuben replied. There was an expectant silence amongst the group. 'Come on, people, use your imaginations. It's what we pay you for. You're the whiz-kids with the fancy degrees, hotshots of the elite GeneCrime Unit. Some ideas?'

'Let's tag our stuff with isotope,' Mina proposed.

'And then what? Geiger the whole building?'

'There's something else we could try,' Simon interjected.

'Such as?'

'Wipe everything down tonight with ethanol. Then, tomorrow, let's take swabs.'

'So now we've got to DNA test GeneCrime?'

'Uh-ah,' Mina declared, shaking her head. 'Simon's got something. Internal Samples. Where DNA specimens are held for everyone in the building.'

'Hang on,' Jez said, 'I'm being slow here. We take swabs and compare them with the profiles all of us have on record for evidence exclusion. How the hell are we going to get access to that? You want someone just to walk in and ask for the whole lot?'

'Sounds like we've got a volunteer. I'll write you an authorization pass. So everyone swab the whole lot tonight before you leave. And keep this quiet. Accepting that it's not one of you, I don't want the culprit getting wind.' Reuben raised his eyebrows. 'Forensic officers chasing forensic officers. I like it. Right, people, are we all done?'

'My neck still . . .'

Reuben smiled at Run, ending his protests before they could even begin. 'OK. Same time next week. Let's get all those samples logged and mapped. Bernie? Let's catch up before lunch. And, Judith, can I see you for a second now?'

When the seven other scientists had traipsed out of the office, chattering excitedly about the trap, Reuben sat back in his chair. 'You know the question you asked the other day?'

'About the Pheno-Fit you showed me . . .'

Reuben pressed his forefinger to his lips and shhed her. 'Keep your head down. Big things are about to happen.'

3

Sinking into the soft, cushioned embrace of the sofa, Reuben let his eyes wander around the tatty lounge. He tried to see the room as a Scenes-of-Crime Officer would, walking in and searching for clues. There was a handful of cards on the mantelpiece, a couple of vases of flowers on the sideboard and an unopened box of Quality Street on the coffee table. The wallpaper, as he examined it, was at least twenty years old, and the heavy brown curtains of similar antiquity. The carpet was fussy and the furniture ornate. The overall impression was of time hanging in the still air, a room slowly and defiantly ageing, of a contented lack of progress.

Reuben watched his mother as she poured two cups of tea. For a woman on her sixty-fifth birthday, she was undeniably sprightly, almost at odds with the room and its air of unhurried decay. He wondered momentarily whether he would age as well as her, and concluded that at the rate he was going, he probably wouldn't.

'So how's work?' she asked, handing him a dainty cup and saucer.

'It's . . .' Reuben struggled to sum it all up. The heinous crimes; the stench of inhumanity. The enormous potential of technology; the even larger pitfalls. 'We're on the verge of something big. A breakthrough in the techniques we use. Something that could really make a difference.'

'That's nice.'

'It should be. I should be jumping up and down with joy, feeling proud of myself, dancing you around the room.'

'But?'

'But nothing's ever simple. You come to see that you solve one series of problems only to open another lot up. I don't know, Mum . . .'

'What?'

'It's complicated,' Reuben muttered. 'They even offered to promote me.'

'You turned it down?'

'Simple choice between more paperwork or less paperwork.'

'You do right. Stick to what interests you. You tell 'em this is the world-famous Reuben Maitland, and you won't shuffle papers for anyone.' She passed him a chocolate digestive and ruffled his hair. Reuben made a play of fending her off, like he was a boy again, and they both laughed. 'But you know,' Ina Maitland said, 'your dad would have been proud of you.'

'If he could have focused on me.'

'Oh, Reuben.'

Reuben bit into the biscuit. 'Come on. He was a drunk. He could barely see straight enough to recognize me.'

'Well, he did try. He really battled it. But it just had too strong a grip on him, that's what he used to say.' Ina Maitland glanced up at a photograph on the mantelpiece of a man in his fifties, slightly gaunt, smiling out at her. 'He could have been something, your dad. Something good. Instead of, you know . . .'

'Yeah, well.'

'Have you been up there recently?'

'Few days ago.'

Ina Maitland turned to her son and ran her blue eyes over him with a mother's acuity. 'You seem a little on edge, son. Not your usual self.'

'I'm fine.'

'I've noticed it the last couple of times you've been. You almost seem haunted by something.'

'Is that a question?'

'Just a mother's observation.' Ina Maitland took a slow thoughtful drink of her tea. 'Is everything OK at home? How're Lucy and Joshua?'

'They're fine,' Reuben answered, suddenly wanting to be honest with her, to blurt everything out, but unable to say the words. His own mother, who had always loved him, no matter what. But to say the words would be to accept that they were true. He was, he conceded, firmly in the grasp of last-chance denial.

'I thought you might have brought the little one . . .'

'I've just nipped out of work for an hour. Josh is at nursery, and Lucy's got a big case on the boil. You know how it is. But we'll drop by soon. Next week, maybe?'

'I'll look forward to it.'

Reuben stood up, making a show of inspecting his watch. 'I'm sorry, Mum, I'm going to have to dash. Lunch is over and I've got a busy afternoon. Just wanted to wish you happy birthday. When we come round, we'll take you out, have a proper birthday bash.' He grinned. 'Now that you're a proper pensioner.'

Ina smiled back. 'Always so busy,' she said, partly to herself.

Reuben had a last look around the living room. He kissed his mother on the cheek. A large part of him wanted to stay in the soft, enveloping atmosphere of comfort and stillness. But it was time to enter far harsher environments, places where time never stood still.

4

A fleshy guard drinks tea from a badly stained mug. His identity badge reads Tony Doherty, Assistant Security Officer. The handle of the cup is broken and the liquid is hot, so he is holding it delicately, alternating chubby fingers, blowing across it and taking small sips. Surrounding him like a huge psychedelic bay window is an expanse of CCTV monitors. People walk across one screen, jump on to another, blend on to a different VDU, only to reappear again in a new place, viewed from a different angle. Tony Doherty follows the multi-faceted progress of a thousand people, scanning and zooming, his avian eyes almost unblinking in their concentration.

The tea is cooling, and he begins to take larger and larger swigs, occasionally frowning and jotting notes on to a piece of paper. The street names of several of the roads are visible. They are in the Westminster area of London. A door opens and he drags his eyes away from the screens, reluctantly leaving myriad existences temporarily unobserved.

'Anything going on out there?' the man asks.

'The usual, Michael,' Tony replies.

'Nothing serious?'

'Not yet.'

'Police have asked us to watch Kimberly Street, especially

where it meets Mossfield Road. A gang of lads been causing trouble, hassling people, maybe selling drugs.'

'What time of day are—' Tony is interrupted by an insistent buzzing from his console. He looks at monitor 47, which has a small red LED flashing above it. He runs his fingers over the ball control and caresses the joystick. A man walking across the screen jumps to monitor 48, and a buzzer for this screen sounds. He is hurrying, glancing around, and appears slightly agitated.

'I'll be fucked.'

'What?'

'Pattern-recognition. The thing actually works.'

'Looks like it.'

'Right, Tony, I'll alert the station.'

Michael picks up a phone without dialling, and identifies himself. 'Supervisor Michael Chambers here at Drury Lane CCTV. We've got a target walking south down Newhall Street, just passing the junction with Old Road, left hand side, heading towards the pedestrian crossing by Boots. Wanted by the Euston branch. Special request.'

'He's crossing,' says Tony.

'Just crossing over. IC one, medium build, brown hair, carrying a case, dark suit, white or yellow shirt. Now he's stopping. Looking in a shop. Jeweller's maybe. Can't read the name. Checking his watch, glancing up and down the street.'

'Matissers,' Tony interjects.

'The jeweller's is Matissers. You on the way? Yes, we'll stay live. I can see the squad car.' On a monitor to the far left, a police car is beginning to speed across the screen, quickly jumping from VDU to VDU, leaping towards the man waiting outside the shop. 'He's moving again. Just a few yards. Stopped by what looks like a restaurant. Actually, I think he's meeting someone. An IC one female is approaching and waving. Dark hair, slim, trouser suit, also carrying a case.'

The two guards watch intently, leaning towards the vast bank of screens as the police car bounds on to the final VDU like a pouncing cat. The vehicle stops smartly and two officers rush out. One grabs the man; the other distracts the woman. There is the semblance of a struggle, and the woman begins to argue. The guards watch her mouth opening and closing, tension and disbelief carved across her face. The police push the man into the back seat of the car. The woman stands alone amongst several passers-by who have stopped to view the action. She watches the vehicle leave, before taking out her mobile phone and crossing the road. Two streets away, and just picked up by the cameras, Michael and Tony watch as the man is punched in the face in the back seat of the squad car.

'Gotcha,' Michael says.

Tony Doherty barely hears. He has returned his stare to the vast panorama in front of him, once again dredging the monitors with utter absorption.

5

Reuben stared silently at Lucy across the kitchen table. She was making a poor job of catching a button mushroom with a pair of disposable chopsticks. Neither had eaten much of their takeaway. For his own part, every time he levered a fresh piece of meat into his mouth, the coarse, dry wood of the chopsticks made him shiver. The single phrase 'trouble brewing' hung in the air, watching, waiting, ready to descend at any moment.

Although he was edgy, suspicious and unsettled, Lucy's behaviour since she had returned from work was even more erratic. She had made and returned a series of terse phone calls. She looked pale and fragile, and despite applying extra make-up to compensate, her unease still leaked through. Reuben longed to comfort her, to put an arm around her, to tell her things would be OK, as he had done a thousand times before. Instead he remained on his side of the table, chasing vegetables around the plate, his left hand gripping a glass so hard he thought he would break it.

'Tough day?' he asked.

Lucy stabbed a small cube of reddened pork and chewed it off her chopstick. 'Aha.'

Reuben was curious. Something was happening. 'So what's up?'

'Nothing.'

'There must be . . .'

'Nothing,' she repeated.

Reuben focused on his food. He had eaten all the good stuff. All that remained was rice, peas and water chestnuts. He stood up and slid the remnants into the bin, before slotting the plate in the dishwasher. 'I'm just saying you seem on edge. Is anything wrong?'

'There isn't anything to talk about. Now please drop it.'

Reuben walked away. The kitchen ceiling was low and felt as if it was pushing down on his head. Sitting alone on one of the two perpendicular living-room sofas, Reuben stared into the newspaper he had brought home from GeneCrime. Reuben rarely read newspapers. If he needed grisly details of serial inhumanity he could just peruse his work files. This copy of *The Times*, however, had been left in his pigeonhole, folded inside a large brown envelope, marked simply 'p 8'. From the kitchen, he could just make out the sound of Lucy crying. Reuben turned to page eight with feelings of misgiving. A quarter-page article in the bottom left had been highlighted with a blue pen. The heading was 'Crime Continues to Escape Police'. Reuben skimmed the text. Amongst the facts and phrases which entered his depressed consciousness were 'inner city serious crime is up 8% since last year' . . . 'drug-related murders, violent attacks, rapes' . . . 'police spokesperson Sarah Hirst' . . . 'frank and controversial admission' . . . 'a new approach needed' . . . 'cited the examples of two recent and brutal killings' . . . 'time for crime to feel the long arm of science . . .' Lucy walked in and sat down heavily on the adjacent leather sofa, dabbing her eyes. The article was bite-sized, designed to be consumed like chow mein, chunks of meat hidden amongst the rice. Reuben examined the envelope, idly wondering whether to send the flap to be DNA tested, or if a cartography expert could make a positive ID from the two-character inscription. Not that there was any need. It was clearly

Sarah's doing. Reuben's mobile rang and he put the paper down. 'Hello,' he said.

'Dr Maitland?'

'Yes.'

'This is Barton Street Police Station, Westminster. I'm sorry to call you after hours, but we've picked up a suspect, flagged by Euston, and we can't find his charge details. We were wondering if you could sort this one out.'

'I think you need to contact Euston direct.'

'We did, but they were none the wiser. Your name was attached to the arrest order.'

Lucy's mobile rang and she began to talk at the same time as Reuben. Their individual conversations remained confined to separate sofas.

'Hello? Lucy Maitland.'

'That's right,' Reuben said. 'I placed his details on the database.'

'But what's he been detained for?'

'The surveillance sweep was cleared by DCI Sarah Hirst. Or you might want to talk to DCI Phil Kemp.'

'Sex crimes? What the hell does that actually mean?'

'They're both gone? OK. What did you say his name was? And his occupation?'

'I see. But what evidence do they have?'

Reuben took a pen out of his pocket and scribbled 'Shaun Graves. Corporate lawyer' on the thin white margin of his newspaper. 'Right. And, just so I'm sure on this, tell me exactly what he looks like. No, I know that. Please, humour me.'

'I still can't believe Shaun would ever do anything like that.'

'OK. Got it. Medium height, slim build, IC one.'

Lucy turned slightly towards her husband. 'But it all seems so preposterous. I mean who the hell do they think they are, arresting him in front of me, in broad daylight, with no evidence?'

'And, just for my records, what colour are his eyes?'

'He's being moved?' . . . 'What, now?' . . . 'But where are they taking him?'

'Right. I'm on my way. Let me just check.' Reuben held his phone away and interrupted Lucy. 'Sorry. Work. Gotta go. You be all right?'

Lucy ended her call quietly. 'You can't get out of it?'

'I'm sorry. I have to go and see someone urgently. Everything OK with you?'

'Just one of my clients. Been arrested.'

Reuben stood up and reached for his coat. 'But you're not a criminal lawyer.'

'I know. He's asking me to go and get him.'

'What? Do you know him personally?'

'Not really . . .' Lucy tailed off.

'Don't know when I'll be back – a few hours at least.'

Reuben pecked Lucy on the forehead. He smelt her hair and for a second was unsteady on his feet. There was a finality in the kiss. It was all he could do not to scream. He left the house and rushed to the car. This was it. The moment had arrived.

6

Reuben drove the six convoluted London miles to GeneCrime. Cutting down side roads and funnelling through one-way systems, he had the notion that he was slowly circling his house, taking wider and wider concentric sweeps until he arrived. Even the SatNav appeared to struggle to direct him. When he reached the car park, Reuben pulled up outside the subterranean security office and signed a short form authorizing him to take a pool car. He climbed into a regulation blue Mondeo with subtle police markings and screeched around the sticky tarmac of the car park.

Some twenty minutes later, Reuben killed the engine outside a police station in the shabbier end of Westminster. The building was worn-out and greying, a tired witness to years of relentless crime. Seemingly, criminals leaked out like rats from a drain and officers returned them, over and over, neither side particularly gaining from the experience. The duty sergeant checked Reuben's ID and rang an internal number. Reuben examined the posters which lined the walls. They implored people to ring Crime-stoppers, or DrugAmnesty, or Vandal-Line. Please, they seemed to beg, do *something*.

The man who had called him, when he appeared, was thin and old, the word 'deskbound' cowering in the creases of his uniform. As his mouth opened to speak, thick threads of saliva appeared at the back of his tongue, as if moving his jaw was a rare event.

'I'll bring him up, then.'

'Good. But don't tell him who's collecting him or where's he being taken.'

'If you'll just sign the release forms.'

The man paced slowly back the way he had come and Reuben was suddenly nervous. The moment of truth. Two whole years of research and experimentation. Months of pressure from above. Eight years of relationship, three years of marriage. A six-month-old son. Seconds away from the intersection of every important timeline in his life. A horrible collision of all of his worlds. He hoped to God that he was less competent than he had imagined. Surely there was a good chance he had fucked everything up, and that he could go home to Lucy and Joshua, guilty of nothing more than suspicion and abuse of power. Please, he whispered to himself, please let the obvious logic be wrong. Please let there be another explanation for this situation. Please let recent events be a series of unhappy coincidences. Please let Lucy be faithful and loving. Please let the hairs in my bed have blown in on the wind. Please let my child be mine. Please let the detainee have no connection to Lucy. Please let the Pheno-Fit be inaccurate. Please let the CCTV recognition be wrong. Please let the restless ants in my brain stop. Please let everything return to the way it was. Please let me turn around without finding out. Please let me drive home in blissful ignorance. Please. A man being led forwards, scanning left and right, slightly stooped, smartly dressed but looking uncomfortable, an air of recent terror about him. The skinny PC behind, nodding to say here's your captive. The eyes, the skin tone, the chin, the nose, the height, the build, everything assessed and assimilated. The hair. Reuben sees two kinked hairs in a tube. The start of everything. He hears the phrase in his crashing mind: *Give me the hair and I will give you the man.*

Time goes into slo-mo.

'Shaun Graves,' the constable says, coughing and shuffling back the way he has come.

Reuben turns and walks out to the car. He opens the back door. Shaun Graves looks at him, his face haunted by physical shock. He is battered and broken. Here, standing bleeding before him, is the real power of the technology. Reuben suddenly feels sick and his legs weaken. He realizes that he is out of his depth, that he has pushed things too far. This stranger was never supposed to get hurt.

'Look,' Shaun spits, 'I don't know what the hell is going on but I demand—'

'Where to?' Reuben asks, numbness beginning to mix with his agitation.

'You mean I'm no longer in custody?'

'Where to? Get in and tell me an address.'

'Islington.'

Reuben pulls off, shaking, a multitude of unsettling notions flashing through his consciousness. He has the sudden need for drugs. He stares into the rear-view mirror, studying the features again, registering specifics – the width of the bridge, the kink in the chin, the darkness of the eyebrows. He notes the nascent bruises, the grazing on the right cheekbone, the cut above the left temple. Shaun Graves pulls out a mobile and dials a number. At a set of traffic lights, Reuben watches him, listening intently.

'It's me. Can you talk? Good. Look, it's been . . . a nightmare. The fuckers beat me up. For Christ's sake, I'm innocent. Jesus, this is going to be the biggest lawsuit these fuckers have ever seen. Are you alone? He's out? Good. I'm coming over. I don't care. There's doubt in your voice. I'm going to look you in the eye and convince you. The kid's in bed, yeah? I'm on my way.

Bye.' He pushes a button on his phone and leans forwards. 'I want to be taken somewhere different. Do you know Euston? The A40, yeah?'

'What's the address?'

'Melby Road. I'll direct.'

'No need,' Reuben answers. 'I know it well.'

He begins to join the dots of roundabouts and junctions back to his house. A film of sweat appears on the surface of his skin. It is so cold that it feels more like condensation than perspiration. Through the glare of headlights he sees the faces of Lucy, Joshua, Shaun Graves and himself. Reuben superimposes aspects and features, his mind racing as the car stutters between traffic lights. He asks himself the question which eats into the very heart of him. Is Joshua my son? He views the series of events underlying his suspicions. The police beating a man in their custody; the man having an affair with a married woman; the woman betraying her husband; the husband tracking the faults of others while ignoring his own. He links the sequence of failings of Lucy, Shaun Graves, CID, GeneCrime, of the whole of London. His visions are cut through with conflicts, memories of rights and wrongs, regret about initiating a course of events over which he has little control, thoughts of what is best for his son, of what is best for himself. He visualizes the scientific journey that has been taken, from DNA to protein to cell to hair to tube to RNA to picture to CCTV to arrest to sitting in the car with the suspect. He reviews the recent tweaks and improvements in Predictive Phenotyping which have successively brought the suspect into focus. He swallows the doubts, the errors, the potential limitations of the approach. He considers the dangers of the technique ending up in the wrong hands: the police attacking suspects with the blunt tool of technology.

In the mirror, Shaun Graves watches the outside world flash by, fighting his own demons, blood seeping into his expensive suit. They pass through a complex intersection, and Reuben sees the imminent collision of a number of existences. His thoughts concentrate themselves into a readiness for action. His unease distils into a restless hunger. In the last mile before home, he begins to breathe more quickly. Reuben is alert, ready, excited and scared.

The moment of many truths is fast approaching.

GCACGATAGCTTACGGG
AATCTA**THREE**GTATTC
GCTAATCGTCATAACAT

1

Waiting; waiting; an eternity of waiting; staring in the rear-view mirror; the eyes wild; the teeth clamping; waiting; giving them enough rope; waiting; counting; estimating; twitching; buzzing; the moment crystallizing; turning off the engine; jumping out of the car; marching down the drive; fists bunching tight; muscles swelling; breathing hard; swinging the front door open; down the hall; bouncing off walls; through the kitchen; striding into the living room; the two of them together; the arms wrapped tight; heads jerking back from the embrace; the fear in Lucy's eyes; the slow-dawning comprehension on Shaun Graves's face; the pointlessness of words; grabbing Shaun by the back of the collar; swinging a punch; the jarring connection of knuckle and nose; staring at Lucy; her inability to deny or explain; blood dripping on to the carpet; soaking in; making itself at home; an invading red permanency; running upstairs; pushing into Joshua's room; his stillness and innocence; kissing his hot forehead; leaving him; leaving him; packing a bag; throwing items in; clothes and toiletries; useless items of convenience; leaving him; looking at the bed; the tidied bed; the hoovered carpet; the carefulness; not careful enough; suppressing the notion that forensics fucks lives; hearing the commotion downstairs; descending; two stairs at a time; tears welling; mouth making funny shapes; trying to hold it together; trying so hard to hold it together; seeing Lucy comforting Shaun Graves; punching the wall; shouting; knuckles bleeding and swelling; hitting the wall again; anything to block the pain inside; the dents in the plaster; the flaking paint tumbling down; mouthing the word divorce; Lucy refusing to beg for forgiveness; Lucy refusing to walk away from Shaun; Lucy dabbing at the redness on Shaun's face; the last scan of the room; vision blurred by rage; picking up keys and bank cards and files; crashing through the kitchen; smashing wedding present plates and champagne flutes; throwing open the door; leaving it open; hopeful; desperately hopeful; heading out and away; into the road; into the warm air; into the cool car; engine firing; wheels spinning; looking back in the rear-view mirror; praying to see her running out; praying to see her in the street; praying to see her pleading for forgiveness; getting further and further away; swallowed by the London traffic; blurring through the disorder; fast and erratic; screeching round corners; wanting to drive headlong into walls; turning off the main road; being spat out near a hotel; a cheap hotel full of cheap people; checking in and drinking; drinking; drinking; vomiting; passing out; tossing and turning; drinking; too hot and too cold; sweating and shivering at the same time; endlessly repeating the word 'No'; the pitiless light pushing through the blinds; waking up alone; crying in the morning; the crushing, defeating hangover; the split-open knuckles; the sickening realizations; the gnawing truths; the utter desolation; the son, the wife, the house, the marriage, the job; the end of one life; the vacuum of another.

The new day brought a frantic series of phone calls. From Phil Kemp: 'We've got problems, Reuben. Serious problems.' From Sarah Hirst: 'What the fuck have you done?' From Judith Meadows, loyal Judith: 'Are the rumours true?' From Mina Ali: 'CID are baying for your blood.' Empty bottles lay on the bed, open wraps of powder were scattered across the flimsy brown table, and used-up clothes were heaped on the floor. And all the time, the redness continued to leak through bandaged knuckles, refusing to scab over and begin healing.

The next morning, the recriminations began in earnest. Lucy screamed abuse down the line, the news of Shaun Graves's intention to sue the Metropolitan Police Force emerged, and rumours of improper conduct within GeneCrime surfaced. There were more calls from Sarah Hirst and Phil Kemp, which insinuated a developing picture of misuse and impropriety. Reuben stayed in bed all day, drinking, vomiting and reaching out for the clawing comfort of institutionalism.

The third and fourth day melted into the fifth, powders blurring the distinction between night and day. Reuben ignored his phone, deleting messages without hearing them. He knew that senior CID were starting to take an interest, and decided to stay the fuck away from GeneCrime. And then came a visit from Judith Meadows. Reuben saw the shock in her eyes and tried to explain the whole mess to her in one extended amphetamine rush. The deceptions at home, the deceptions at work, the pressures from above, the hunger of CID for an untested technology, the relentless search for the truth, the not knowing, the need to find out, the pattern recognition, the hairs in the bed, the denials, the police beating Shaun Graves, the knuckle-jarring punch, the untenability of everything.

The sixth night, Judith stayed with him, pacing up and down and describing how his team had reacted to events. She told him that, mostly, he still had their loyalty, and that Run and Jez had been complicit in events and were keeping quiet. Judith said that many saw the pressures but didn't understand his actions. Eventually, Judith had fallen asleep on the other bed. Reuben lay awake and listened to her breathing, feeling humbled by her concern, weighing up ideas and notions and planning to get out of bed during the day. He decided to stop drinking to excess, and vowed to call Run, Jez and Mina, the ones he could trust. In the half-light of the morning he realized he was alone. Judith had gone, and only an indent of her remained on the bed. He quietly shaved and showered, before re-bandaging his broken knuckles. And then Judith returned with breakfast.

On the seventh night, Judith finally left. Reuben waited silently for the call to hunt him down. As he did so, he saw the weeks ahead. Night after night in a different room of the same hotel, sleeping and lounging on spongy beds, alone and isolated. And as he sat and wondered, picturing the bleakness of his immediate future, the single phone call he had dreaded all along pulled him back to the present. It had taken longer than he had imagined, which could only be a bad sign. They were being painstakingly thorough.

'Reuben,' Commander Robert Abner barked down the line, 'come and see me tomorrow.'

2

Despite the all-pervasive air-conditioning, Reuben was sweating inside his suit. As a general rule, Reuben wore suits only when absolutely necessary. Today there was no other option.

There was an element of going through the motions as he walked into the building and along its corridors. Reuben kept his head down, avoiding the stares of his colleagues. Even when he passed Judith, who was loitering by a coffee machine, Reuben focused resolutely on the thin carpet. He felt a sense of shame eating into him as the eyes of GeneCrime staff monitored him intensely, burning into him with accusations. Reuben appreciated that the rumours had probably gained a momentum of their own.

They were already seated in the Operations Room, waiting for him. Reuben pictured them arriving early, scheduling to meet half an hour beforehand, getting their stories straight, ironing out any differences of opinion. He ran his eyes from left to right: DCI Sarah Hirst, coolly professional in a tailored trouser suit and regulation white blouse; Area Commander Robert Abner, large and forbidding, jacket off, wide shoulders almost bursting out of his shirt; DCI Philip Kemp, slightly scruffy, but having made a noticeable effort to iron his collar and centralize his tie. By the care they'd taken with their outfits, Reuben knew his fate.

He pulled out the single chair which faced them across the

table and sat down. Phil refused to meet his eye. Sarah stared straight through him. Commander Abner grimaced briefly in welcome.

'So, Dr Maitland, I think we all know why we're here. Let's not have any illusions.' Robert Abner turned to his right. 'Sarah, why don't you kick off?'

'I'll be blunt, Dr Maitland. We've spent the last week investigating your recent actions here at GeneCrime and have discovered a series of inappropriate activities including . . .' Sarah glanced down at a sheet of typed, headed paper. '. . . misuse of FSS consumables and equipment; misuse of FSS staff time; misuse of FSS databases; misuse of FSS samples and specimens; misuse of CID time; arranging for false imprisonment; subsequent assault of a person under Metropolitan care . . . the list goes on.'

'Phil?'

'Right.' Phil Kemp stared into a similar piece of previously prepared evidence. 'Altogether there are seventeen accounts of inappropriate behaviour deemed to have brought GeneCrime into serious disrepute under Section Twelve of the Forensic Science Service Code of Conduct. Plus there are a number of unsubstantiated allegations that we have not had time to investigate fully.' He shuffled in his seat, deferring to the Commander.

Robert Abner turned his massive palms face up. 'Do you want to contest any of our allegations?'

'No,' Reuben answered.

'What the hell happened to you?' he said.

Reuben remained silent, gazing into the table.

There was a palpable disappointment in Commander Abner's face and voice. 'You turned it down, Reuben. Running this Division. You could have been great. Instead . . . look at you.'

Reuben stared back. Time seemed to get lost in the still air. 'So what now?'

'You know exactly what now.'

'That this will be quiet. Kept out of the papers. The truth glossed over for the good of the Division.'

'We may not have that luxury. It wouldn't be in anyone's interests to broadcast this. Not yours, not ours, not anybody's.'

'And how about the public interest?'

'The public need to believe in forensics, Reuben. You know that. And this is the flagship unit of the FSS, where we pioneer the advances which keep us ahead of the game.' Reuben briefly pictured Commander Abner addressing a conference of senior CID officers. 'The public don't want to hear that one of the country's leading scientists has been falsifying evidence.'

'I wasn't falsifying anything.'

'The point is you go out of here quietly and you don't say a fucking word.' Robert Abner scowled across the table. 'And remember, you still have a pension here. So I expect your cooperation.'

'Are you threatening me?'

'I am *telling* you, in your last few minutes under my command. We've got one, possibly two, maniacs on the loose, drowning and disembowelling as they go. Shaun Graves is going to sue the Met for wrongful arrest. We've had word that one of the broadsheets is about to run the story. We have to be seen to act decisively.'

Reuben cleared his throat, which felt tight and dry. 'There's something else here, isn't there?'

'What do you mean?'

'I've just made it easy for you to do what the Force has wanted to do for ages – to get rid of me.'

'Don't be ridiculous. We offered to promote you, for Christ's sake.'

'Out of harm's way.'

'Enough, Reuben. Sort yourself out, man. Mud-slinging is hardly going to help you at this stage.' Commander Robert Abner glanced sideways at Sarah and Phil. 'Is there anything more either of you two want to say?' His subordinate officers shook their heads slowly, almost sadly. 'OK. Dr Maitland, I have a written statement to read to you.'

Reuben avoided the Commander's eye. He knew what was coming, the words that had been catching him up for over a week. Once, a couple of years previously, he had sat where Sarah was now, part of a panel reading a grossly incompetent CID officer his marching orders. While Robert Abner went through the motions of dismissal, Reuben focused into the dark greyness of his suit, acknowledging that his time at GeneCrime was over, knowing that Sarah Hirst and Phil Kemp would soon be vying to take control of his section, appreciating that everything he had ever worked for was slipping away from him for ever.

Reuben didn't wait to hear the end of the announcement. He stood up and swung the door open. A CID officer escorted him out of the building in silence, past his laboratories, his office, the lockers . . . As he walked, the only positive thought amidst the pressing defeat was that Predictive Phenotyping existed solely on his personal laptop. In firing him, GeneCrime was losing the one technology it had been crying out for. The small dab of speed he had taken earlier began to run out of steam. They turned towards the exit. Reuben breathed deeply, taking a last drag of the building with him. He didn't stop until he rounded the street corner, letting the breath escape, the final remnant of GeneCrime seeping out of his body.

3

After the Formica blankness of his hotel room, Reuben found his mother's lounge even more cluttered and fussy than usual. He ran his fingers over his still-bandaged knuckles, feeling for the stitches that were slowly dissolving into his flesh. In the two weeks since his dismissal from the Forensic Science Service, he had rarely ventured further than a series of bars. The fortnight had lasted an age. Fragments of its truths stayed with him, playing themselves in endless loops of regret, anger and hurt. Through the sickness, the loneliness and the encroaching depression he had reached a momentous decision. But it had left him incredibly low, so much so that he had craved the comfort of maternal support.

Despite Reuben's silence, Ina Maitland continued to talk regardless, and he struggled to pick up the thread, distracted by the haunting image of an open wrap of speed. He tightened his aching fist. Reuben recognized that nothing in his life could truly get better until he got better. This was the first full week of cold turkey. He knew that amphetamines weren't excessively addictive, but all the same, they were clawing at him. Cold sweats, itchy skin, nausea, his teeth feeling raw, his heartbeat erratic . . . Reuben struggled for composure in the stifling front room, with its slow-ticking clock, which thudded through the still air.

'So you don't feel the need?'

'What?' Reuben asked, pulling himself back from the craving.

'To drink.'

'Not to excess.'

'A thing like that can ruin a life. Your father always said that. Even when they had him in and out of hospital.'

The dainty cup in Reuben's hand rattled against its saucer and he put it on the table. As ever, the picture of his father beamed down from the mantelpiece. It was a drunk's smile, an addict's smile, sad and desperate, the eyes focusing elsewhere. In his father's face, Reuben saw the root of his own self-destruction.

'Look, Mum, it's time I came clean. Lucy and I are splitting up.'

Ina Maitland held her son's eye. 'Go on,' she said.

The clock ticked lazily. 'She was having an affair. With a work colleague.'

'The bitch . . . Oh, God. What about Joshua? What's going to happen to the poor lamb?'

'Lucy's filing for custody. She says she's going to fight to keep me away from him. An exclusion order if she can.'

'But, surely, if she was the one having the affair . . .'

'It's more fucking complicated than that,' Reuben snapped. He hadn't meant to, but he was raw and trembling. He had an acute need for pain relief, for the bitter powder which would make him immune. 'Sorry,' he muttered.

'Oh, Reuben. I thought you were so happy.'

'So did I.'

'Poor Joshua. And what are you going to do about the house?'

'She's going to put it up for sale.' He could hardly bear to say her name.

'And all your things?'

'Storage. Till I get myself sorted.'

'You know you're always welcome to stay here.'

'It's a one-bedroom flat, Mum.'

94

'All the same . . .'

'I'll be fine.'

The clock beat out long slow seconds. Reuben's muscles twitched sporadically. It would be so easy not to think, not to feel, not to hurt. Get back to the hotel, ring a dealer, buy a few wraps, as uncut as possible, let a couple of days melt away, oblivious to the head-fuck of no wife, no kid, no job, no house. He picked up the cup and made himself drink its tepid tea, eyes closed, regaining control. Reuben stayed like that until his heart slowed and his muscles ceased spasming.

Misreading his discomfort, Ina Maitland decided to change the subject. 'Your brother seems to be doing well for himself,' she said. 'Came round again the other day.' Ina smiled, a youthful grin which enlivened her whole face.

Reuben looked down at his aching fist.

'He said you don't see much of each other these days.'

'Would have been good to see him.'

'You've got to keep in touch with your brother.'

'I would. Only Aaron . . .'

'What?'

'Nothing. I'll keep in touch.'

'Nice clothes and everything. Even offered to lend me some cash.'

'And did he?'

'I said no. But still . . .'

Reuben opened his eyes. At last his thoughts found something else to occupy themselves. He bit into an already well-worn thumbnail. Aaron with money could only mean one thing.

4

Aaron stood under a tree, smoking a cigarette. It was a thin roll-up with a hint of cannabis. A few drags and it was all over. He dropped it on the tarmac and dragged his trainer rapidly back and forth across it, shredding the paper and spilling the guts of its remaining tobacco. At his feet sat a baby's car-seat. Wrapped tightly inside a white blanket lay a doll with glassy blue eyes which stared up at Aaron, unnerving him slightly.

Aaron watched intently, waiting for his chance. A busy London nursery, with cars pulling in and out of the walled parking bay. Hassled parents extracting infants from seat restraints, persuading them in the direction of the door. Glancing at watches, tense encouragements, 'Come on, Fabian, Daddy's going to be late', tugging slightly at the wrist.

For the sake of camouflage, Aaron wore a smart suit jacket and a pair of clean jeans. City casual, he told himself. The kind of clothes that demanded no further inspection from nursery parents, an outfit that said, Let's talk business, but let's do it in a coffee shop. Aaron snorted at the sheer rigidity of middle-class impressions. The dogged adherence to the idiom Clothes Maketh Man. Still. In the twenty-first century. Lawyers in pinstripes, doctors in sports jackets, architects in collarless shirts, bankers in dark suits and black shoes. As if the last thirty years of labour changes had never happened. Uniforms for the uninformed. He nudged the car-seat forwards slightly, so that the doll's eyes lolled shut, unable to worry his consciousness with their dead, unblinking gaze.

A silver Mercedes stopped a few yards away, and Aaron leant back out of view, obscured by foliage. The mother within – pretty, busy, smart – lifted a one-year-old out and carried her towards the front door. Aaron craned his neck to get a better view of the car's interior and swore to himself. He took out another pre-rolled. It was raining, and the dampness seemed to invade the cigarette, making it hard to light. He persevered and checked the time. Eight-twenty-five. Peak kid-dumping time. Aaron clenched and unclenched his fists, readying himself.

A few drags later, an oversized Mitsubishi SUV entered the car park, and Aaron watched as a father of three attempted to round all his children up and encourage them forwards. This was no easy endeavour. Aaron wondered momentarily why anyone would put themselves through the lunacy of reproduction. The father was becoming flustered as various children wandered in opposite directions while he struggled with bags and nappies and bottles of milk. By his clothes, the man worked in finance. No normal person would look so solemn if he wasn't paid to do so. Finally, his flock were cajoled away from the spotless off-roader and into the building.

Aaron threw down his cigarette, picked up the car-seat and ambled over to the vehicle. He pulled a rear door open and slotted the baby-seat in. Then he climbed into the driver's seat. The keys were in the ignition. Aaron started the diesel engine and reversed slowly out of the space. If you needed distracted people, ones who would routinely leave valuables, briefcases and, occasionally, car keys in their vehicles, nurseries were the place to come. Easy pickings. And the more exclusive the nursery, he had learnt, the more distracted the parents and the better the cars. Aaron picked his way slowly across the car park, even stopping to let someone pull out ahead. He knew that dropping off children was never a quick event. Aaron also suspected that the nursery's CCTV system didn't record to tape. Either way, the trick was not to hurry or attract any attention. To blend in with the other parents. And in a nursery, there was no better way to ensure invisibility than by carrying an infant in a car-cot and driving slowly out, paranoid about running over someone else's brat.

On the main road, Aaron took a few moments to examine the interior of the Mitsubishi. A year or so old with less than ten thousand on the clock. A sought-after 4 x 4. He turned down a side street, slamming the heavy vehicle over a series of speed bumps, which did little to impede its momentum. In a matter of minutes, he was heading out of Chelsea, away into more familiar territory. Aaron pictured the father of three pacing around the car park, staring at the empty parking space in mild disbelief, shaking his head, making certain, charging back to the front door, ringing the bell insistently, striding in and demanding someone call the police, desperately trying to picture the fucker who had taken his pride and joy . . .

Aaron smiled. He would only own the car for a matter of hours, until he passed it on. But they would be sweet hours of victory. Before that, he would have to wipe the surfaces down for fingerprints, make sure he left no forensic evidence of his time behind the wheel. And then, enough cash for a fortnight of excess.

5

From the top deck, the bus took corners impossibly wide, seeming almost to hover over the pavements and roads below. As Judith Meadows talked, Reuben looked down on the heads of shoppers scurrying along, fighting for room, a clawing tangle of movement, pressing in conflicting directions. The bus swayed violently through a junction and Reuben gripped the metal bar in front of him. His attention switched to the knuckles of his right hand. Six weeks had seen the broken bones reconciled, the cuts stitch themselves closed, the swelling subside, and the lingering ache of contact with his living-room wall confine itself to memory. But it had been a slow process, an unrelenting pain which nagged at him, reminding him, healing with stubborn reluctance. He shook himself free from that night and the ensuing six weeks of a life which had been sucked inside out. While the bus staggered and tottered like a drunk, Reuben tried to lose himself in Judith's words.

'I told them I was cataloguing a few of our old cases, clearing freezer room, et cetera, and I noticed that several inventories were incomplete.' Judith was wearing a pale-blue blouse that Reuben had never noticed when he was at GeneCrime. The colour suited her. He pictured her picking her way through the crowds to buy it, flitting untouched between heavier, sturdier shoppers, nimble and quick. 'So Sarah asked which cases, and I said the Hitch-Hiker Killer, the Edelstein rape, a couple of others.'

'And this rang alarm bells?'

'You'd have thought so. She just said that they were closed, punters in jail, and a few tubes here and there wouldn't make a lot of odds.'

'What else?'

'Asked me to keep it to myself. Said she didn't want the rest of the team getting excited about the fact that a few tubes might have been mislaid.' Judith turned in her seat to face Reuben. 'I'm beginning to believe you're not quite as paranoid as I once thought.'

'Thanks.'

'Look, this is the leading forensics centre in the country. It's either unforgivably sloppy, or . . .'

'What?'

'You know what I'm saying. You've said it before yourself. Not in so many words, but when our reagents started getting used up, it was there in your eyes, in what you didn't quite spell out to us.'

'You trust the team, though?'

'Most of them. But GeneCrime's a big unit. A lot of people have access to the labs, the samples and the databases.' Judith toyed with her wedding ring, twisting it round her finger. 'It's not inconceivable, that's all.'

Reuben hesitated for what seemed to be long minutes, weighing up whether to involve Judith. In the weeks since he had lost everything he held precious, a new purpose had begun to form. From a budding, embryonic thought, it was starting to kick and thrash. Reuben's restless yearning for truth was gradually forcing him back to life. Day by day, he was piecing himself back together. Coping.

'You know, Jude, the more I think about it, the more I suspect I just gave them the excuse to do what they wanted to do anyway. Large factions of GeneCrime wanted rid of me, even before I went.'

'Why, though?'

'I don't know. But I intend to find out.'

Judith stared hard at him, a critical look which came from years of scientific rigour. 'But if you couldn't prove anything while you were there, what chance do you stand now?'

'I'll call you next week,' Reuben answered, making the decision. 'There's someone you should meet.'

6

The following week, on an overcast day in June, Reuben stepped reluctantly into a packed betting shop in Waterloo. The single word 'Loser' hung in the stale cigarette smoke swirling from the tips of a hundred roll-ups. All the men except one faced the same direction, searching the TV screens, quiet desperation in their bloodshot eyes, shallow excitement in their drawn faces. Near the counter stood a fat, untidy man, who seemed to have little interest in the horse races, football scores or greyhound results lighting up the screens. Reuben approached him, trying to gauge from his body language what his answer would be.

'Hey, Moray,' he said, shaking his hand. 'A betting shop?'

Moray Carnock glanced around himself as if noticing the place for the first time. 'Believe me, there's a good reason.'

'So you've had a few days to decide.'

'I guess so.'

'Well, what do you think?'

Moray narrowed his eyes, peering at Reuben from behind dark, bushy eyebrows. 'Poor background. Good education. Sometimes unsure of yourself. Awkward, like by rights you shouldn't be what you are. Classic case. Working-class boy betters his parents but struggles with his identity.'

'I mean about the proposal.'

'As far as I'm concerned, you *are* the proposal. Tell me, what did your father do?'

'Scotch, mainly.' Moray laughed and Reuben saw this as a good sign. 'So what about you?'

'Now, I *am* posh. Daddy was an architect, Mummy a GP. I'm just slumming for kicks.'

Reuben struggled to see Moray as anything but the down-at-heel slob he appeared to be. 'OK. Seriously though.'

'Seriously? There are issues. And I'm worried about your mental state.'

'It's a passing thing. Catastrophic few weeks.'

'Aye, well. It had better be, because—'

'Hang on,' Reuben interrupted. 'Here she is. Let me do the talking.'

Reuben caught Judith Meadows's attention as she entered the shop. Judith skirted around the hypnotized punters staring into banks of monitors. As she reached him, Reuben said, 'This is Moray Carnock. Moray, this is Judith Meadows. I guess we should talk.'

Judith shook the man's hand. It was soft and yielding, quite at odds with his rough appearance.

'Moray's a corporate security consultant.'

'Right.'

'Knows a lot of people with very specific problems.'

'How do you two know each other?'

'We met a couple of months ago in a bar, when I was working on a case. Moray had some information that might have been of use. For the right sum of money, of course. Told him where to get off.'

'And then came crawling back.'

'Yeah, well. It wasn't exactly through choice. Judith, the idea is that Moray acts as the point of contact when—'

'Look,' Moray interrupted, 'let's cut to the chase. I hate betting shops.'

As they talked, customers came and left the shop. No one appeared happy. Even those approaching the counter to cash their winnings seemed edgy and unsatisfied, as if this was just a temporary reprieve which would soon be followed by more misery.

'So, overall, what do you think of Reuben's idea, Mr Carnock?' Judith asked.

'Good and bad, depending on your perspective.' Moray turned to Reuben, his voice struggling to be heard over the background grind of defeat. 'To do what you're proposing, you're going to have to effectively disappear. Go underground. No house, car, insurance, tax, no credit cards, nothing. Anonymous hotels . . . A lab well out of view.'

Judith ran her eyes quickly over the rotund Scotsman. 'Why so cautious?'

'We're not talking about testing for colour-blindness here. If you're going after the big game you need to stay well out of the way.'

'It's important that what I do isn't illegal.'

'Aye, well.' Moray squinted at Judith and Reuben in turn. 'The sad truth is that there're going to be times when both of you will have to step over that fine line, along with the rest of us.'

'What else?' Reuben asked, his brow creased.

'CID worries me. Judith stands the obvious risk of having both sides coming after her.'

'So the real danger lies with you, Judith.'

Judith turned to Reuben, the welcoming lights of a fruit machine trying to pull her away from the conversation. 'Why don't you spit it out, Dr Maitland,' she said.

'You'll be piggy in the middle.'

'Nice image.'

'You know what I mean.'

Judith glanced around herself. 'This still doesn't feel good. Any of it.'

'Your choice . . .'

'But to quote you, Reuben, something is fucked up. GeneCrime is fucked up.'

'No one will have to be aware that we're in touch. No one at all. To all intents and purposes we no longer know each other.'

'OK.'

'If they join the dots from you to me, we're both finished.'

'Right.'

Moray Carnock monitored the door, barely listening. Reuben followed his gaze, but saw nothing untoward. A slight man in out-of-fashion denims left the shop. Moray was suddenly alert, bristling with energy. 'Call me later,' he said, nodding briskly at Judith and Reuben.

'What's up?'

Moray declined to answer. He was already pushing his way through the throng, edging towards the door.

Reuben watched him go, realizing that there was a lot he still didn't know about the hulking Scotsman, and a lot that he would probably never find out. Returning his gaze to Judith, he appreciated that, at times, this might be a good thing. 'So, are you in?'

Judith blurred through the lights of the fruit machine. On an impulse, she suddenly stepped forwards and pushed a coin into the machine's hungry mouth. Obligingly, its buttons flashed, screaming to be pressed. She hovered her finger over the largest one, marked 'Start'.

'Well, Mrs Meadows?' Reuben asked. 'Are you ready to step off the cliff?'

Judith swallowed a nervous breath. She bit into the inside of her cheek. She felt the dampness of her palm. Her hand moved. She pressed the button. The lights glimmered and the reels began to spin.

GCACGATAGCTTACGGG
AATCTA**FOUR**GTATTCC
GCTAATCGTCATAACAT

1

Two Months Later

Detective Chief Inspector Phil Kemp paused for a second, taking in the sheer carnage of the house. He had rushed over on a blue light, siren splitting the pre-dawn silence. For any emergency service the same rules applied – if a colleague was in danger, you would move heaven and earth for them. This time, however, he had been too late. Way too late.

The terraced house was deceptively long, as all terraced houses are. Phil wondered therefore why he had been surprised at the depth of the residence when he had first paced through it, checking all the rooms, opening all the doors. Maybe, he conceded, it was because his own house was a modern one, with a disappointingly functional layout. It was cubic on the outside and cubic on the inside. What you saw was exactly what you got. He pictured his bedroom, the heat from his bed slowly leaking away, light gently nudging through the curtains. Phil Kemp sighed, and walked back to the epicentre of the activity.

By now, there were at least fifteen other officers and forensics swarming along the extended narrow hallway, in and out of the rooms, up and down the stairs, like frantic insects on the trail of the deep red jam which smeared the walls and carpet. He acknowledged a number of GeneCrime members: Run Zhang, patiently scraping a dried blood sample from the cold glass of a window; Jez Hethrington-Andrews, pale and quiet, cataloguing a long row of specimen tubes; Birgit Kasper, setting up a small thermal cycler, slow and methodical; Paul Mackay, scanning a series of barcodes into a portable reader; Bernie Harrison, changing his gloves, scratching his face gratefully in-between pairs; Mina Ali, trying to take control, ordering younger forensic scientists around; Sarah Hirst, jeans and T-shirt, no make-up, her face creased, her eyes puffy, irritably signing a wad of pink and yellow forms.

Amongst the ordered bustle, the victim lay silent and unmoving on the bed, her fluids being carefully sucked up by pipettes and emptied into plastic vials. Next to her, a small travel cot sat on a chest of drawers, empty now, folded sheets showing where the baby had lain, screaming with his mother's screams, and long after she had stopped. Thankfully, a matronly WPC had taken the youngster and held him in her arms until social services had arrived to take charge. Phil Kemp felt uncomfortable around children at the best of times. In the middle of a murder scene, however, this one had shredded his nerves.

DCI Sarah Hirst finished her paperwork and walked over to Phil. She appeared uncharacteristically uncomfortable, and Phil allowed himself time to pause. This wasn't easy for any police officer.

'So what do we know so far?' Sarah asked.

Phil stared at the body as he spoke. His eyes took in the arm restraints, the cigarette burns on her cheeks, the razor cuts on her bare legs, the darkness oozing from her neck, the mutilated ear, the missing skin from her thigh, the bone poking through her split-open nose, the horror on her face. He returned to the notes he had scribbled. 'Victim appears to have deceased around midnight. CID alerted after a neighbour heard repeated screams over the course of almost an entire twenty-four-hour period. Initially thought they might "just be having an argument". Idiot. Victim's cause of death appears to be severe trauma and loss of blood . . .'

'Could you stop calling her "Victim". We all know her name.'

'Anyway, we're running with the theory that she was systematically tortured.'

'Rather than just sadistically killed?'

'Subtle difference. Her death looks almost incidental. Someone was trying to keep her alive for as long as they could.'

'Whatever for?'

'What most people are tortured for. Information. Knowledge. Access to the truth. Where's the money kept? When is so and so back? Where're the keys to the car? You know. When someone needs to know something the other is reluctant to share.'

'Christ.' Sarah risked another glance at the woman on the bed. The sight was truly shocking, and despite her training and seniority, she was unable to look for too long. All she saw was the suffering, the pain, the drawn-out leaking away of a life. She pictured the child, lying on its back, dirty, hungry, screaming and motherless. 'And the baby?'

'Unhurt. I guess, at that age, he'll never remember anything about it.'

Phil and Sarah's moment of reflection was broken by a familiar voice.

'Inspec'or Hirst?' Run Zhang asked.

'*Detective* Inspector.'

'Ri'. I got sample, and wanna take back for pre-emptive analysis.' Run held up a matchbox-sized plastic container. He looked tired and worn, his normally immaculate clothes creased, razor-straight hair rioting in all directions.

'What do you mean, pre-emptive analysis?'

'Reuben's old system. In serious crime with good probability of getting pure sample, do pre-emptive analysis for quick detection. Compare with, ah, more thorough assessment later. Save time in the long run.'

'It is, as you are well aware, almost four months since Dr Maitland left us. And if he's not with us, his systems aren't with us. And that goes for any other procedures he might have instigated along the way. Do I make myself clear?'

'Christmas.'

Sarah Hirst stared harshly at him. The name Reuben Maitland had irritated a small and angry wound like a stomach ulcer inside her. 'You mean crystal,' she said curtly.

'So what exactly have you managed to isolate, Run?' Phil Kemp asked in the calming tones which had diffused tension throughout a fraught career.

'We think we got hairs and maybe saliva.'

'Anything else?'

'Probably. But everything else take longer time.'

'OK, thanks, Run.'

Phil glanced at Sarah as Run returned to his task. She appeared bothered and unsettled, more so than he had seen her for a while. 'Are you thinking what I'm thinking?' he asked quietly.

'You tell me.'

'That if Reuben were still around, and if he'd played ball, we'd be able to sort this carnage out in a matter of days.'

'I wasn't thinking that.'

'So what were—'

'It's probably best you don't know,' Sarah said abruptly.

Phil wondered whether to ask, but decided against it. He left DCI Hirst's evasiveness hanging in the oppressive air of the house. Mention of her former colleague had evidently taken her mind somewhere she didn't want it to go. Phil swayed slightly on his feet, urging his brain to lose itself instead in the mechanics of the investigation. All around them, sloth-like forensic scientists inched across carpets, running gloved hands over the surface, unhurriedly feeling for evidence. Others opened doors, examined window-frames, pulled out drawers. The pace had slowed. Detail was more important now, the one vital hair or fibre or stain that would make all the difference. Against the backdrop of hypnotically gradual activity, an urgent shout tore down the hallway.

'Sarge. Sarge? Over here.'

Sarah and Phil were instantly animated, striding in the direction of the yell.

'You're not going to believe this,' Mina Ali said as they reached the bathroom.

Mina opened a thin plywood door. Inside was a hot-water tank, which sat below empty shelves. On the interior of the door was a series of letters. It was quickly apparent from the colour of the characters and the way they streaked downwards that the ink of choice was blood. Phil Kemp counted the letters. There were seventy-eight in total, all of which were either G, T, C or A.

'What the hell does that mean?' he asked loudly. Several of the scientists were huddled around, running through the possibilities.

'GGC. That's glycine.'

'What the fuck?'

'An amino acid.'

'Remind me?'

Mina drew in a long breath which exited again as a stream of undisguised scientific impatience. 'DNA is divided into threes. Each triplet spells out an amino acid, which collectively make polypeptides, which subsequently make proteins.'

'So how does that help us?' Phil asked, frustration clouding his excitement.

'This is genetic code, which may be indicating the sequence of something specific.'

'Like what?'

'I don't know. It's not a gene I recognize off the top of my head.'

Simon Jankowski, the most junior forensic scientist within GeneCrime, cleared his throat. 'Maybe it's not an actual gene,' he ventured. 'Perhaps they're using single-letter code. The amino acid glycine, for example, is represented by G.'

'GAG. Glutamic acid. E,' Birgit Kasper added. 'And I think AAT might be asparagine. Which, if I am remembering correctly, is N.'

'G, E, and possibly N. And the rest?'

There was an uncomfortable lull. No one wanted to profess their ignorance first. Eventually, by default, the task fell to Bernie Harrison, senior bio-statistician. 'It's not that easy,' he explained. 'I mean, a lot of people can look at a stretch of code and pull out some amino acids that they recognize. But there are four different bases – A, C, G and T – which come in sixty-four different three-letter combinations, like AAT or GAG or CCC. And, as Mina said, each triplet combination encodes an amino acid.'

'But there's only, what, twenty amino acids?'

'Exactly. So there's lots of overlap and redundancy. Three or four entirely different triplets might all give you serine, for example. I can see a lot of stop codons, and the odd isoleucine, possibly another glutamic acid or so, but we can't be certain until we get to a textbook or program. No one knows all these off by heart.'

'Well, ring someone at the lab,' Phil instructed. 'I'll text them the image. Ask them to call us back with the answer.'

Phil photographed the letters with his phone. Mina prompted Judith Meadows, who was back at the lab, to grab a textbook and expect a message. Phil keyed in Judith's mobile number and paced back and forth. Sarah Hirst stood and stared uncomprehendingly at the blood code. Bernie, Simon and Birgit also ran their eyes over the letters, exploring other possibilities, muttering about reading frame and codon usage. Jez Hethrington-Andrews focused on the thick bathroom mat. Mina Ali entered something into the keypad of her mobile. A police radio crackled away incoherently. The hot-water tank gurgled as it began to heat water for the day ahead. Perspiration ran down Run Zhang's circular face. CID shuffled restlessly, universally black footwear worrying the carpet. Phil's phone beeped.

'Christ,' Phil said, examining the display. His normally ashen skin seemed to blanch even whiter. 'Get the rest of Forensics and everyone else. You need to read this.' He passed his phone around the group. Each face changed slightly as their eyes absorbed the information. Birgit's mouth dropped open. Simon grimaced. Paul clenched his jaw. Run bit into his knuckle. Bernie swallowed hard. Jez screwed his eyes shut. Mina pursed her lips and whispered the word 'Fuck'. There was a short delay and then a shocked silence amongst the scientists and police as the implications of the message began to eat into each one of them in turn.

2

If you wanted to forget, hotels were not the place to do it. That was the problem with short-term accommodation. Time seemed to stay with you, cooped up with nowhere to go, ricocheting off the blank furniture and the featureless walls. Just when you thought you'd begun to rebuild your life, you caught sight of your reflected face, sad and drawn, and you wondered whether you were truly moving on.

But stepping back from the mirror, his breath slowly evaporating from its surface, Reuben told himself that things were getting better. Now he had something to occupy him. He walked over and sat upright on his doughy bed. He was impatient, checking his watch every couple of minutes. Soon it would be crunch time. A final glance at his watch. Six minutes until showtime. He stood up, managed a half-convincing smile in the mirror and left his room.

Across the road from the hotel, Reuben loitered in the shallow doorframe of a shop. Dusk was leaking into darkness, and streetlamps were stuttering into action. They came on like falling dominoes, travelling alongside a taxi, as if directing its solitary way through the gloom. The majority of cars had their headlights on. As these passed over Reuben's face, he stepped back into the shadows. Two days' worth of sandy stubble coarsened his skin.

He wore a baseball cap, a denim jacket and a pair of jeans. Reuben leant forwards and examined his watch in the glare of an oncoming van. It was eight-twenty-eight. Two minutes to go.

He peered across at the hotel, which was starting to show its age; it was badly in need of refurbishment. It had faded into the row of shops that surrounded it at street level, and blended almost seamlessly with the three storeys of flats above. The flakiness of its brickwork was almost like camouflage paint. He had another glance at his Dugena. Any second now his accomplice would ring, and the trap would be set. Although he was excited and scared, the way he always used to be, the balance had shifted recently. The anticipation was more intense, the fear more real. His actions were no longer protected by law. If he got it wrong, no police were going to come screeching round the corner to his rescue. This was the price he was paying. He had begun the descent into a world of scant morality.

The phone in his pocket vibrated twice and then died. Reuben pulled the baseball cap low over his eyes and stepped on to the pavement. He removed his watch and refastened it around his wrist, but over the top of his jacket. The sleeve was long enough that it partially obscured his right hand. He walked determinedly, head down, his face obscured from the CCTV cameras which dredged the streets with glassy determination. Few people were still around. Most had drained away after work. The road turned into a narrow pedestrianized section, bordered on both sides by restaurants and bars. The surface was cobbled, the lighting provided solely by the windows of eating and drinking venues. Two hundred metres ahead, where the street widened out to became a bona fide road again, Reuben could just make out the corpulent shape of Moray Carnock. Moray wore a dark suit and carried a newspaper, adopting standard City uniform. The two men approached each other, stride for stride. In between them, slightly closer to Moray, a smartly dressed man had just left a restaurant, accompanied by two larger companions. Reuben slowed. This was not in the strategy. He fingered the small implement in his pocket with uncertainty. Excitement began to be overwhelmed by fear. He chewed hard on some dying gum, his jaws resuscitating a remnant of flavour. They had rehearsed this manoeuvre a dozen times. The target would be distracted and unsuspecting. And yet no one had told them to expect bodyguards.

Reuben speeded up. The next few seconds were vital. Get it wrong and the whole thing would fall apart. Reuben's breathing was short and quick. He could see the tension in Moray's pudgy face as they converged. They had a hundred metres to rethink. He nodded at Moray. Moray scratched the back of his head. No turning back. Seventy-five metres. The bodyguards were big and wide, and stayed a step behind their client. One was black, seemingly without a neck, and the other was white, his hair in a ponytail. He realized that it was down to Moray to change the strategy.

Reuben missed a breath. Ahead, on the right-hand side of the passage, two policemen appeared from an alleyway. They were walking slowly, scanning around, taking everything in. Fuck. Reuben pulled out the SkinPunch gun and concealed it under the extended right sleeve of his jacket. The constricted alley suddenly felt claustrophobic, turning a simple sting into a risky undertaking. Moray was almost upon the man and his bodyguards. Forty metres. The coppers were ambling straight into the middle of the operation. He noted Moray's change of demeanour as he came to the same conclusion. Reuben worried that the police knew about the intended strike. He quickly dismissed this notion as paranoia. Moray stiffened and his walking became almost mechanical, aware that he was being observed from multiple angles. But it was too late to back out now. They had to do this tonight. There would never be a clear-cut opportunity again. Reuben drew mental lines, judging the speed of the four converging parties, calculating where everybody would meet. It was going to be close. Moray made the agreed abort signal, but Reuben shook his head. This was do or die.

Moray took out an *A–Z*, glanced at it, and feigned a look of frustration. Reuben had a final scan up and down. Aside from the police, the bodyguards and the omnipresent CCTV, there would be no witnesses. Twenty metres. Moray stopped the black bodyguard. Stop the target as well, Reuben hissed under his breath. The white guard and the man he was protecting came to a reluctant halt. Reuben strained to hear the conversation. Both men stared intently at Moray's *A–Z*. His colleague glanced around the alley, shuffling closer to the target. Reuben was ten metres away, the police approaching from the front. The target and his men looked further down the road, past the coppers, pointing out directions, their backs to Reuben. At the end was a extended silver Mercedes, doubtless waiting for the party. This had been the crux of the plan – knowing that the target would have to walk alone along the pedestrian alley to his transport.

Reuben heard the curt instructions, 'Straight over, past the lights.' Five metres away, and giving the target as wide a berth as possible, his jacket scraping the wall, Reuben examined his watch at eye level. As he did so, he aimed and pulled the trigger. The man scratched the back of his head irritably, just above his collar. The PCs stared hard at all of them. They were on patrol, sniffing for trouble, a hunger for action in their eyes. Reuben walked past, thrusting his right hand back in his pocket. For an instant, Reuben, Moray, the target, his bodyguards and the two coppers were all level in the passageway, almost shoulder to shoulder, and Reuben imagined one bullet could have pierced the entire septet. And then the formation changed. The target uttered something indistinct. From experience, Reuben knew the improved Skin-Punch didn't hurt. At worst, it felt like having a hair plucked. The police stopped to talk to one of the guards. Reuben headed on past the Mercedes and to a pre-arranged spot around the corner, the adrenalin still pumping fiercely.

He waited and waited, the rush subsiding, a lightness trickling into his veins, relief washing through his body. He wondered if Moray felt the same. Reuben watched the Mercedes pull away; the police were now out of sight. He bent down and untied one of his shoelaces. When his phone vibrated again, he turned and paced back to the spot. Moray had marked it, dropping a piece of pink chewing gum. Reuben approached and slowed, looking at his shoes. He bent down to tie the lace up, eyes skimming the pavement. The probe was lying next to a spent cigarette butt. It was the size of a match-head, the colour of a Swan Vesta. Reuben pocketed it and straightened, continuing on his way. Back on the main road, he flagged a taxi, and headed away from the scene. The things you could do, he said to himself, staring out of the back window. The taxi passed the two policemen. The things you could do.

3

Still fingering the small round probe, Reuben instructed the taxi driver to stop by the entrance of an unpromising industrial unit. The site, Reuben noticed as he walked through it, had the air of being imminently overwhelmed. The tarmac was being eaten by weeds, the corrugated iron consumed by rust, the concrete colonized by moss. On three sides, looming glass and steel office blocks jostled for space. On the fourth side, a train rattled slowly past on an elevated line, swaying along the uneven tracks. A series of boarded-up arches underpinned the railway. Disused warehouses with systematically broken windows littered the area. Although this small part of the city seemed no longer to be needed, a manufacturing park in an era of service industry, Reuben sensed that its time would come again. London wouldn't tolerate unused space for too long.

He entered a three-storey building, his feet fracturing small pieces of glass which had survived their initial falls from the panes above. Reuben glanced about before opening a door, which concealed a flight of basement stairs. Descending, he reached a second door, which was unlocked. Passing through, Reuben stepped into a tight, poorly lit corridor, that opened out into a large subterranean cavern. He was directly under the railway line, a dome-roofed space previously used, he guessed, for storage.

This was an archway underneath the archways. A shape came out of the shadows.

'Got it?' Moray Carnock asked.

'Uh-huh.'

'Let's have a look.'

Reuben pulled the small plastic probe out of the money pocket of his jeans and rolled it around his palm.

'Wouldn't want to do that again in a hurry,' Moray groused in his lapsed Aberdonian drawl. Reuben examined him; he had a compressed, untidy look, like a sandwich with its fillings spilling out. Through his contacts in the worlds of finance, business and detection, Moray had spent the past two months putting the word out about Reuben's services. Without him, Reuben appreciated, glancing past Moray at the surrounding equipment, there would be no laboratory. And without the laboratory, he conceded, there could be no search for the larger truths that still haunted his dreams in the early hours.

A second figure appeared from an opening on the left of the chamber. It was Judith Meadows. He detected weariness, un-happiness and distress in her face. He guessed she hadn't slept well the previous night.

'Judith,' Reuben asked, 'you OK?'

She declined to answer.

'How was work?'

Judith shuffled forwards, pulling a stray strand of hair away from her swollen eyes. 'I guess there's no way to say this other than coming straight out with it.'

'What?'

'Sandra Bantam.'

'Sandra?'

'She's dead.'

Reuben's pupils widened instantaneously in the gloom. 'You're joking.' Judith shook her head rapidly, almost violently. 'Accident?'

'Quite the opposite.'

'Fuck.' Reuben slumped. 'Fuck. When did this happen?'

'Yesterday. Half of GeneCrime spent the day going over her house.'

'She was murdered at home?'

'Worse. Her death wasn't quick.'

'Meaning?'

'She was tortured.'

'But she left to have a baby,' Reuben said, remembering, his mind drifting to the last time he had seen her. 'What about the child?'

'Found next to her. Healthy and well.'

'She was tortured?' Moray asked.

'Tied up. Beaten and assaulted. Kept alive. Mutilated . . .' Judith's eyes watered. 'And seeing her ruined body yesterday . . .' Judith began to sob. Reuben and Moray glanced quickly at each other, as if deciding who would comfort her. After a second's hesitation, Reuben wrapped an arm around Judith. He felt the taught boniness of her frame through her T-shirt, the hidden strength of her slender arms as she hugged him back. Her scent was a mix of bottled perfume and washing-machine freshness. His mind started to wander towards Sandra Bantam. He recalled her posing for a portrait, talking almost incessantly, barely keeping still, borderline hyperactive, as she always was. Until she viewed the finished painting. He retrieved the exact expression of disappointment in her face, and remembered cursing himself for his accuracy and lack of tact. Reuben tried to picture Sandra lying perfectly motionless, her exuberance drained away, her life ended in sickening pain. He steadied himself, feeling a dense and inky depression leaking into his frontal lobes.

Judith cleared her throat. She had stopped crying. Reuben looked up from the floor and let go of her, cold, numb, trying to get back to the now. Judith's arms clung a second longer, then finally let go as well. Reuben sensed a reluctance in Judith's release.

Moray broke the silence. 'Guess I'd better be off.'

'I'll ring.'

'I told the client we'd have the answer by the end of the week.'

'Maybe.' Reuben massaged his aching forehead as the shock deepened.

Moray left, locking the corridor door behind him. The silence prompted Reuben and Judith to busy themselves, needing well-rehearsed actions to paper over their respective thoughts. Reuben shook his head. When a past acquaintance dies, you suddenly have the desire to be with them, even though you drifted apart when they were alive. He walked over to a long off-white bench, salvaged from a closing hospital laboratory. The equipment which squatted on the floor and on other work surfaces, bought, leased or borrowed, were visually unimpressive machines with off-putting names – an ABI 7500 here, a PE 377 there, a Centaur 2010 in the corner. Reuben and Judith worked in silence, occasionally opening sample doors, washing plastic membranes, staring into ninety-six well plates, pipetting clear fluids. While they paused, waiting for a small microfuge to stop spinning, Judith remembered something. From her work bag she passed Reuben a copy of the *Daily Mail*. 'Look,' she said, 'Sandra made page four.'

Reuben flicked to the grim headline and scanned the accompanying text. 'What leads of enquiry have they got, exactly?' he asked.

'A few.' Judith opened the centrifuge lid and retrieved two glass slides. 'Run's pretty sure he's got good DNA. And there was—'

'Talking of which, did you manage to get those samples?'

'I took aliquots from all the suspects in the Hitch-Hiker investigation, and I borrowed DNA from the Edelstein rape, the Lamb and Flag murder, as well as the McNamara murder. They're in the freezer.'

'And the recent cases?'

'I'm working on it. But look, Reuben, we can't rush this.'

'I guess not.'

'People will become suspicious. I'm going to get fired at this rate.'

'So I'll employ you full time, instead of just evenings.'

'And you'll lose your woman on the inside of GeneCrime.' Judith attempted a grin, but her eyes remained distant. Reuben was reflective for a few moments, chewing his lower lip. He pipetted several drops of xylene on to Judith's slides, and a stream of thoughts intermingled with the fumes. The murder of Sandra Bantam. How death changes the survivors. The horror of torture. The sickness of pain. A fuzzy headache began to drift through his brain.

'What other leads have they got?' he asked.

'For Sandra? Nothing, aside from blood and saliva.'

'No motive, no suspects?'

'Nothing.'

'Huh.' Reuben nudged the slides along the bench to Judith, who slotted them on to the metallic stage of a microscope. 'I mean, what the hell could they have been after?'

Judith remained quiet, lost in memories. Reuben pipetted a small amount of toxic fluid into the SkinPunch probe, flicking through his recollections. Sandra Bantam almost seemed to enter the room and stand beside them. Together, all three silently began to process the man from the alleyway.

4

In a leafy urban park, a baby takes its first tottering steps. This follows several weeks of preparatory actions. The young infant has been crawling for three months and, more recently, has been pulling himself up against sofas and chairs wherever possible, coasting along their circumference, always maintaining contact with something solid. This is the only time the infant has actually put one foot in front of the other with no physical support. Unknown to him, the efforts of the boy mark his transition from baby to toddler.

The toddler is between a man and a woman, both of whom are crouching down, stretching their arms out, giving him a *from* and a *to*. He stumbles and falls into the arms of the woman, who laughs with joy to see her son walk. The man joins them, wrapping himself around the duo. They split up again, quickly encouraging the boy to repeat his trick, as if frightened he will forget what to do. The man points him in the direction of the woman and, with a little encouragement, he lurches forwards, taking one, two, three, four paces. The adults smile at each other over his head. In their eyes is unabashed pride.

Behind all three of them, a fleshy man watches and waits. He is hidden from their view, and has not been noticed. He ducks down in a flowerbed, concealed by two corpulent rhododendrons. He runs his thick fingers over the waxy leaves of one of the bushes, savouring its lithe flexibility.

The woman whispers to the man, who picks up the child and swings him around by the arms. The infant screams with delight. Next, he holds him by one arm and one leg, and repeats the process. The woman watches intently, disapprovingly, obviously expecting the baby to be injured in the process. After a couple of minutes, both lose interest in the game, the man becoming dizzy, the toddler ceasing his squeals. They sit down on a bench and eat sandwiches. From the way the man is dressed, it looks like he has been at work during the morning. He picks some crumbs out of the folds of his suit trousers. The baby, sitting on his mother's knee, receives the first of a series of overladen spoonfuls of blended food from a jar. A limited amount remains in his mouth, while the rest oozes out and drops on to his bib.

The man in the bushes feels a desire to get closer. He retreats from his position and skirts around a hedge until he is barely five metres away. He can almost hear their conversation from here. But that is not what he is after. Using the foliage as cover, he brings a small camera up to eye level and takes a couple of shots. His interest is in the child. He focuses in on its chubby body, its innocent face, its purity of expression. He has taken many such covert photos before. After reviewing the images on the camera screen, he smiles to himself, pleased with what he has captured. Then he takes out a compact digital camcorder and shoots some footage. He concentrates on the child's eating, the spoon being forced in and out of his mouth, and then pans around to take in the general scene. His mobile plays a tune, and he reaches for it, still filming. The couple look round, half sure they have heard something. But he is well concealed and they don't see him. They shrug and return to their lunches. The man examines the display of his phone, frowns and presses a button.

'Yes?' he asks hoarsely. 'I'm just . . . in the middle of something. You might call it an interest of mine.' He switches the camcorder off. 'Germany? Yeah, I reckon I can sort that . . . Frankfurt . . . What's his name? And where do I meet him? . . . OK . . . OK . . . Send me the details.' He ends the call and examines the camcorder. On its screen, he replays the recording he has just taken. A little bit blurred and rather too much of the adults, but it is good enough. He pulls slowly out of his hiding place, branches and twigs clawing at him to stay. He glances around, making sure no one has observed his activity, slots the camcorder into his pocket and walks away.

5

Reuben entered the pub with a burrowing unease. It was poorly lit and empty, except for one table at the back, which was crammed with a tight-knit group of drinkers. Reuben approached them, his leather shoes slapping on the wooden floor, sending a small echo ahead of him, announcing his arrival. He stopped a metre in front of the table, and took in the semi-circle of faces craning up at him.

'So,' he said, 'who wants a drink?'

There was a moment of silence, and Reuben was aware that he was being scrutinized simultaneously from multiple viewpoints. Then Sarah Hirst shook her head quickly. Run Zhang frowned at his full glass. Jez Hethrington-Andrews shrugged. Mina Ali continued to suck on her straw. Bernie Harrison stroked his beard. Judith refused to look directly at him. Reuben felt inside his pocket for some coins and gripped them hard. He hadn't expected this to be easy. He tried again.

'No one?'

In the extended silence, Reuben appreciated that four months was a long time, but not long enough for raw wounds to heal without trace. He saw that amongst the antipathy and indifference, rigid protocols were being followed. Junior members of the forensics team were gauging their reactions from the behaviour of their superiors. Reuben thought quickly about walking out, leaving them, retreating. But a memory of Sandra Bantam stopped him. They were here to remember her, a police wake in a police pub. He was going to tough it out whatever. Reuben turned and paced slowly towards the bar.

'I'll have one with you.'

Reuben stopped. He swivelled back. Phil Kemp was holding up a half-empty pint glass.

'Guinness.'

Phil half smiled, and Reuben thanked him with his eyes. He cleared his throat. 'Anyone else?'

'Small white,' Mina Ali muttered.

'Run?'

'Rum. Neat.'

Reuben stared at Sarah. 'DCI Hirst?'

Sarah stared back. 'Nothing.'

Reuben decided to quit while he was ahead. He strode over to the bar and ordered the drinks. While Phil Kemp's Guinness settled thickly and inexorably, Jez Hethrington-Andrews joined him, leaning heavily against the counter.

'Sorry about what happened,' he muttered.

'Sorry for putting you through it as well.'

'Don't worry. I had some fun with it. It's good to see you, Reuben.'

'Likewise, Jez. Likewise.'

Jez rummaged through the pockets of his dark, sculptured suit for a cigarette. 'So where've you been living?'

'Here and there.'

Judith Meadows cleared her throat behind them. 'Large white, when you're ready,' she instructed the barman. Jez and Reuben swivelled round to see her.

'Judith,' Reuben said, flashing his teeth, 'long time no see.'

'You know how things are.' Judith simulated a polite awkwardness through a quick scratch of her face and a flick of her hair. 'What are you doing these days?'

'Not a lot.'

Judith took her glass and sucked in its sweet fumes. 'Well, take care of yourself.'

Reuben passed the barman a note. 'Can't win them all, Jez,' he shrugged. 'Here, cop hold of these.'

Jez helped Reuben carry the drinks back. Phil Kemp shuffled his stool to one side, allowing Reuben room to slot himself at the table. Mina was wrapping up an anecdote about Sandra. He glanced about. Opposite him, Sarah Hirst ran her fingers through her hair. She caught his eye momentarily and looked away. Run smiled at him, a twitching raise of the eyebrows disturbing his deadpan face for a second. Mina said, 'What's your favourite Sandra story, Dr Maitland?'

Reuben was silent. He had been to a number of police wakes over the years, and they still unsettled him. The idea was simple. Get steaming drunk and remember all the good things about a colleague consigned to the ground. Not an occasion for grief or unhappiness – that was reserved for the funeral – but the celebration of a life. However, it wasn't always that easy. The news of Sandra's death was still raw to him, and he struggled for something worthwhile.

'I remember when she first started . . .' Reuben began.

'Yeah.' Mina took the ball and ran with it. 'She was so fucking twitchy I asked her if she was sitting on something. Girl couldn't stay still for a second. I thought, This one's on drugs. Wired into the mains . . .'

Reuben turned. Phil was wrapping a short, avuncular arm around his shoulder. 'So,' he said quietly, 'you bearing up?'

It was funny seeing Phil in a suit, a proper, smart black suit. It lent him a severity which was lacking in his battered and bruised work clothes. 'Not too bad.'

'I'm sorry about the tribunal. I was only following orders.'

'That's OK. It worked for the Nazi Party.'

'Talking of which, you know Sarah's running CID now?'

'I heard.'

'And that I'm overseeing your old section?'

'Yeah. They decided which one of you to appoint yet?'

'Nah. But it's close. Word is, we're going to get the nod pretty soon.'

'How are you finding Forensics?'

'Fine. Made a breakthrough with that disembowelling case at last. Matched a profile to a Korean gangster, who may or may not still be in the country. But Mark Gelson's still at large, and eerily silent.' Phil tilted his head back. 'Answer me this, though, Reuben. What is it with scientists?'

'What?'

'I mean, no offence, but where are all the normal ones?'

Reuben laughed. 'I could say the same about coppers.'

'Hey! You don't have to be crazy to work here . . .'

'But it could get you promoted.'

Phil took a slug of the thick black liquid, which Reuben imagined running down the inside of his thick black suit. 'Is that what got you to the top?'

'That and sleeping with my superiors.'

'Right . . .' Phil and Reuben both took the opportunity of a surreptitious glance in Sarah Hirst's direction, and allowed themselves a private grin. Phil stood up, unsteady on his short legs.

'Sorry, old chap, gotta shake the snake.'

Reuben watched Phil swaying towards the Gents, and then turned his attentions to his old forensics team. Visibly, little had changed over the previous four months. Simon was sporting one of his collection of loud shirts. Mina was wearing a black head-scarf and Judith was as demure as ever. Run had squeezed himself into a suit which had seen thinner times. Bernie had grown a thicker beard, and Birgit appeared, if anything, even plainer. But this was still the slightly awkward group of high-achievers it had always been, their social inarticulacy emphasized by appearance as well as actions. He sensed the alcohol beginning to join the dots, blurring their separateness, bringing them together. Sarah Hirst leant minutely forwards into his line of view.

'So what are you up to these days?'

Reuben examined her features for warmth, but saw only a cold curiosity staring back. 'This and that.'

'This and that and Predictive Phenotyping?'

'Perhaps.'

'We could have used your system.'

'You know why I took it with me.'

'Remind me.'

'Bad things were happening at GeneCrime when I left.'

Sarah's eyes rolled in the gloom. 'So you said at your exit interview.'

'People were hunting through our freezers at night. Samples were going missing. Convictions being secured on the back of questionable evidence.'

'Interesting.' Sarah smiled and Reuben anticipated trouble. 'Coming from a man who misused forensics and had someone illegally arrested.'

Reuben sighed audibly. 'OK. And here I am, paying the price. But you know what I mean. Too many ulterior motives in one building. Too many competing egos.'

'When I'm in charge, I aim to bridge the divisions and heal the rifts.'

'Sounds like you've been practising your speech.'

'Preparation, Dr Maitland, is everything.'

'But it goes deeper than that. What was going on in GeneCrime shows the fundamental flaw of science.'

'Which is?'

'Forensics is only as infallible as the people who perform it. And people are nothing if not fallible.'

'Maybe things are better these days.'

'How do you mean?'

'I mean now that our extremely fallible Senior Forensics Officer has left.'

Reuben smiled. Sarah was digging, provoking and teasing, as she always did. For a second, he realized he missed sparring with DCI Hirst.

'You know what I like about you?' he said.

'No.'

Phil Kemp returned from the toilets and squeezed himself between Reuben and Sarah. 'What did I miss?' he asked.

'Reuben was just about to say something,' Sarah answered. She angled herself slightly forwards so that she could see him.

Reuben grinned at Sarah. 'I wasn't going to say anything at all.' Despite herself, Sarah almost smiled back. 'Right, I'll get them in.' He stood up and walked to the bar. Childish and pathetic, he told himself. But, for a brief moment, it felt good.

While the drinks were poured, Reuben looked back at Sarah and Phil, scanning them quickly, the two Detective Chief Inspectors, ambitious and ill-matched, turning automatically away from each other, withdrawing and marking out their territories. One he trusted and one he didn't. One old-fashioned, the other bending new methods to meet her aims. But both of them insatiably hungry for power and influence, and on the verge of the biggest fight of their lives.

6

Reuben blinked slowly, long lazy sweeps of his eyelids, his head nodding forwards, the alcohol pulling him down, grinding him to a halt. Everyone had left, except Run, who was lying horizontal on a wooden bench. Reuben finished his drink and stood up, his bladder full, his legs unpredictable. He stabbed at Run with the point of his shoe. Run muttered under his breath in Cantonese.

'Come on. They're closing.'

Run muttered louder, his rotund form shifting on the bench, searching for comfort.

'We've got to leave.'

'I'm asleep.'

'We need to eat.'

Dr Zhang slowly sat up, rubbing his neck. 'Eat, you say?'

'Yeah.'

'Now you talking my language.'

'Run, no one talks your language.' Reuben helped his friend up by the arm. 'You know anywhere round here?'

'Not just anywhere. Best place in London.'

'That's a hell of a statement.'

'One hell of a restaurant.'

Reuben and Run left the bar and hailed a taxi. Soon they were ensconced in the dimly lit Rainbow Restaurant, with its cloudy tropical fish and laminated menus. Reuben's bloodshot eyes had barely been forced to adjust from the pub to the dark street to the interior of the Rainbow. Run caught the attention of a waiter and commenced a terse series of Cantonese exchanges.

'What was that?' Reuben asked when the waiter had left.

'I've ordered for you.'

'Should I be scared?'

'Be afraid, Dr Maitland, very afraid.'

'So, tell me, Run.' Reuben brushed away a fine tablecloth dusting of previous prawn crackers. 'Who are you lot after at the moment, besides Sandra's killer?'

'We doing, ah, some gangland stuff.'

'Anyone in particular?'

'Drug boss Mark Gelson, couple unsolved murder, Kieran Hobbs . . .'

'Kieran Hobbs?'

'We think we tie him to, ah, series attacks. But our evidence not razor-tight yet.'

'Watertight.'

'You know him?'

'Of him.' Reuben allowed himself a quick frown at the name. 'Anyway . . . tell me what's going on in GeneCrime?'

'Usual. Phil and Sarah battling for supremacy. Phil running Forensics Section like angry wasp, Sarah running CID Section with steel rod . . .'

'Iron rod . . .'

'You know how it goes. And what about you?'

'Tough.' Reuben toyed with his chopsticks. 'But getting better.'

'Yeah?'

'I don't know, everything fell apart for a bit. I lost Joshua and Lucy – my family . . .'

'There no one else?'

'Not aside from my mother. My dad died when I was nineteen, and my brother effectively disappeared from my life a few years ago.' He straightened as a waiter began to assemble an ambitious quantity of dishes between them. 'But you adapt, you survive, you piece yourself back together . . .'

'I know. When I leave my family in China . . . you feel you, ah, lose everything. Even though they all still alive, writing to me, calling me. I think is knowing you *could* be with them, but at same time knowing you can't.'

Reuben was silent for a few reflective moments, playing with his food, poking at it with ornate chopsticks. He rewound to sitting in his kitchen a few months before, facing Lucy, the storm gathering, sliding his chow mein into the bin. 'Still hurts like hell though. Comes and goes, some times better than others.'

Run leant forwards and Reuben noticed that he had abandoned his chopsticks in favour of a fork. 'You know something?' Run glanced around himself. 'I make a breakthrough with Sandra Bantam. No one knows yet.'

'Yeah? What?'

'Need to check my facts first.' Run tapped the side of his nose with the handle of his fork. 'But I think I've already got enough pure sample for matching analysis. Just need to clean it up.'

'That was quick.'

'I, ah, develop short cut. Can I call you tomorrow, when we're not pissed, get your advice?'

'Sure. Look, Run, it's great to see you. I know things are complicated, but let's stay in touch. It would be good to get together now and then, learn the gossip, find out whether Sarah and Phil actually come to blows.'

'Ri'.'

'And next time, I'll choose the restaurant.'

'You insult Rainbow, you insult me.'

Reuben gave up on his food, too drunk to appreciate it. He watched Run shovel in elaborately stacked forkfuls. He felt the buzz again. A day surrounded by CID and Forensics. The teamwork, the allegiances, the frictions, the politics. Pulling

137

together and pulling apart in the midst of multiple investigations. Knowing that they were targeting Kieran Hobbs. He realized that the last four months had been empty. He missed these people, even the ones he didn't trust. Sarah Hirst's eyes burrowed into him. He stood up, shook Run's hand, and headed back to an anonymous hotel and his fractured life.

7

Reuben rubbed his hungover face. The country was wilting in a late-summer heatwave. Sweat which had gathered on his brow slid down the bridge of his nose and interfered with his vision. There was no air and no release. The summer had started hot as well. May had been a killer. Then, true to form of the last few years, June and July had been a disappointment, with August vainly over-compensating. He took a sip of his beer, which was quickly warming, and the man returned from the toilet. Reuben had found him unexpectedly nervous. The mistrust was natural, but he hadn't anticipated that a figure such as Kieran Hobbs would be in the least bit uneasy.

Reuben felt a sudden prickle of apprehension. According to Run, Kieran Hobbs was one of GeneCrime's current priorities. A senior member of a gang with gambling and money-laundering operations in West London, he had been wanted for over two years in connection with a number of brutal attacks. And yet here he was, sitting next to him in the broad weekend daylight. Reuben scanned the bar, desperately hoping there was no surveillance, no CID camera shutters silently blinking, no grainy CCTV images recording on to tape reels, no microphones grasping their words from the surrounding cacophony.

Reuben was fascinated by Hobbs. Until recently, his contact

with criminals had been confined to the microscopic fluids and cells that they left behind at the scenes of their crimes. Seeing a whole felon in the flesh was a lot to take in. There were twitches, blinks, frowns and smiles, just like normal people. Reuben appreciated that the aftermath of a crime spoke only of decisive action and violent intent, with all the indecision, hesitancy and uncertainty lost in the freeze-frame.

Kieran had insisted, before they took a table, that Reuben accompany him to the toilet, where he had performed a search for recording devices and weapons. He talked rapidly, scanning the bar with wild mistrustful eyes. 'So,' he said, indicating that he was finally willing to get down to business, 'what can you do for me?'

'My partner Moray Carnock should have filled you in a few days ago.'

'I want to hear it from you.'

'It all depends on what you need. Moray mentioned an attack?'

'Joey Salvason. My second-in-command. Beaten to death.'

'And where is he now?'

'Hospital morgue, at a guess.'

'You have no idea who did it?'

'D'you think I'd be wasting my time talking to you if I knew who to go and fuck over?'

'All I'm saying, Mr Hobbs, is that there are two ways to go. If you suspect a specific person, I can tell you yes or no. If it could be absolutely anyone, I will show you a picture of his face. But that route is going to cost a lot more money.'

Kieran was quiet, sipping his black coffee, almost oblivious to the heat. 'There's a gang. Irish lot, led by someone called Maclyn Margulis. Been causing us problems this year. But I don't want to wade in if it's not them. They're a big outfit, and I don't need this getting out of hand. Joey had a lot of issues. You know, personal stuff. I want to be sure before we go in shooting.'

'So what you're saying is any one of a number of people could have killed Joey.'

'I guess.'

'I charge eight thousand pounds. Cash. Four now, and four when I show you a picture of the killer. Plus you'll need to pay my hotel bill while I'm working for you.'

The phrase stuck in Reuben's throat as he swallowed his warming beer. Working for you. Helping someone he had formerly hunted, someone his previous unit were actively investigating. He took another slug of beer, as if this could wash away the distaste. To aid a criminal was to be a criminal. But he was stuck and he knew it; it was an uneasy dilemma which had sweated out of him as he slept, the late-night Chinese lying heavily on his stomach. To burrow deep into GeneCrime's illicit activities required money, money that paternity and infidelity cases were only slowly beginning to bring in. Chemicals, equipment and consumables were expensive. Moray had been right from the outset. In order to find the truth, Reuben would occasionally have to cross the line. The decision was stark and inescapable and, despite its obvious logic, still eroded him. And so Reuben had to gulp down the bitter tang of betrayal, had to compare evils and had to decide what was really right and what was really wrong. But still it didn't taste good.

'This picture. Moray said it's like a photo-fit or something?'

'No. This is like a photograph.'

Reuben again studied the criminal sitting opposite him. At first glance, he was perfectly nondescript. There were no scars, tattoos or broken facial bones slowly healing without medical intervention. He dressed middle-management casual, no jewellery, smart shoes. And yet here was a man who had killed, beaten and extorted as a matter of course. In the flesh, there was something different about him, something Reuben hadn't picked out from the many surveillance photographs he had seen. It was, Reuben concluded, in his eyes. His blond eyelashes were thick and long, and remained interwoven no matter how open his eyelids. Behind, Kieran's irises were dull green, so leaden they didn't radiate any light, even when the sun breeched the gate of lashes. They were like blunt objects, poking and prodding at him, ocular baseball bats, impossible to read and still harder to stare straight into.

'I'll give you five grand, total,' Kieran stated finally. 'You can have three now—'

The late afternoon sun refused to abate. 'It's eight or nothing.'

'For a fucking photo?' The eyes slammed into him.

'For the hundred per cent certainty of your friend's killer. And for an additional sum, I'll even get you his name and address. No one in the world can offer you this service.'

'Typical copper, fucking me over.'

'Look, I need the money.'

'Bullshit. You're jerking me around, Maitland.'

'I'm serious.'

'Oh yeah? What do you want it for?'

Something snapped. 'None of your fucking business, Hobbs.' It suddenly felt wrong. Dealing with a gangster, a murderer, a monster. Going against everything right. Reuben stood up to walk away, a sickness in the pit of his stomach.

Kieran stood up as well. 'All right, all right,' he said, his hands pushed forwards, palms facing the ground. 'No harm done. Let's all calm down and start again.'

Reuben remained where he was, caught and conflicted, vainly trying to engage the eyes. He needed this job, had to have the money, had to convince Hobbs that he was no longer on the side of the law, that he was fighting the same enemy. Reuben sat slowly back in his chair, his repugnance ebbing. After a few seconds of silence, he said, 'I'm following up some cases where I don't think the force played fair, where the evidence never seemed quite right, where things were starting to get out of hand.' Reuben drained his beer, which was flat and hot, the sharpness now turned sour. 'In an ideal world, Mr Hobbs, I wouldn't be touching your case. But as you and I both know, this isn't an ideal world. Now, do you wish to buy my services or not?'

Kieran Hobbs rubbed his face rapidly and irritably. Reuben knew the sum of money wasn't an extortionate one by his standards. He wondered whether the man just didn't want to do business with ex-police. Kieran stood up. 'Wait here,' he said. He walked on to the street, to a large car with three men inside. Reuben had failed to notice that the meeting was under an altogether different sort of surveillance. Kieran returned with a rolled-up newspaper, which he slid across the table. 'It's in there,' he said. His face was flushed with the exertion, and Reuben could see through the blondness of his hair that even his scalp was pink. 'How long?'

'Seven days.' Reuben took out a small notebook. 'Now, which hospital was it?' he asked. 'And what day was he admitted? Does he have a middle name? What colour are his eyes and hair?' He scribbled the details down. 'Right. Moray will be in touch with you.' Reuben shook hands with Kieran, a wet handshake that felt repellent. As he watched the gangster go, he loitered a while, drumming his fingers on the hot aluminium table. 'The ends,' he whispered to himself, 'and the means.' Rarely, he thought, had they ever seemed so contradictory. Helping villains in order to catch villains. But that was the trouble with searching for the truth. More often than not, you had to immerse yourself in dishonesty.

8

Reuben left the café and walked languidly around the corner, carrying Kieran Hobbs's newspaper under his arm. He could feel the tight bundle of notes through the paper and against his ribcage as he entered a hotel. At Reception, he removed a small red box from his briefcase, and placed it carefully on the desk.

'Like usual?' the woman asked, a warm French accent singing through her words.

'Please.'

She turned and took the box to the safe. 'Room two hundred and seventeen,' the receptionist said as she came back. Reuben heard the numbers as notes in a scale, with the two and seven around middle C, and the one a jaunty G sharp. 'And this came for you.' She handed him a thick brown envelope with his name on it. In his small modern room, he began the ritual which always accompanied his checking in. He paced about, examining the bathroom, the chest of drawers, the bed, the wardrobe. He didn't know what he was looking for exactly, but one day Reuben hoped to find something different.

Sitting down on the bed, he took the envelope and opened it up. Reuben had been putting this moment off, but could delay no longer. Inside was a wad of photographs. He flicked through them, his fingers trembling. They were images of his son in a park. Joshua appeared to be walking for the first time. Reuben inhaled a broken breath. He was growing up. He scanned the pictures intently, curiously, smiling, frowning, with pride, guilt, anger and distress. Lucy was lurking in several shots, grinning, all teeth and eyes, an occasionally fretful look on her face. And he was there as well. Reuben suddenly felt the need to pick up the phone. 'Hello, Reception? Room two hundred and seventeen. Just wanted to make sure . . .'

A French voice cut him off. 'It's in the safe, Dr Maitland. You watched me put it there, no? And yes, before you are asking, I have double-checked.'

Reuben closed his eyes. The only thing he held precious was in the safe of a soulless London hotel. He removed his finger from the phone's receiver and punched in a rapid sequence of digits. When it was answered, he said simply, 'Two one seven.' While he waited, he began ringing the series of numbers which would slowly unite an underworld boss with a contract killer.

An hour later, there was a quiet knock at the door. Through the fish-eye aperture, Moray Carnock appeared to have gained a couple of stone and lost some height. Like the rest of the capital, he was sweating, although Moray was better at it than most. He sat heavily on the bed.

'I've only got ten minutes,' he said, pulling a wilting collar away from his clammy neck. 'Then it's Heathrow. Kieran Hobbs buying in?'

'Wants the full service.'

'We can't fuck about with big-timers like Hobbs. Are you sure you can help him?'

''Fraid so. I've found the hospital. The morgue's run by a Derek O'Shea. Here's the number. He knows me and is willing to give access to the body for two hundred. When can we go?'

'I'm in Frankfurt till tomorrow evening.'

'What's in Frankfurt?'

'Partner in an electronics firm suspected of trading in-house secrets. Might be something in it for you – they want forensics on papers and components which I'm going to intercept.'

'Store them in plastic, as cold as you can. Thanks for the photos, by the way.'

'No problem, big man. I've got some video as well. Here, have a quick scan before I go.'

Moray passed Reuben his camcorder and pressed Play. Reuben watched Joshua, Lucy and Shaun Graves playing at families. He glanced from Joshua to Shaun again and again, desperate to know. Joshua was ten months old. His features were forming with more clarity and permanence. His eye colour was changing, his hair darkening. He thought of the red box in the hotel safe. There was a simple way to find out, but he could not bring himself to do it. Yet.

'And what about Mr Loaded?' Moray asked. 'The one we did in the alley?'

Reuben remained glued to the screen. 'The woman's DNA sample was inconclusive, so we had to go back to her. But I've no idea how she's going to react to the result.'

'No?'

'The fall-out could be massive.'

'Jesus.' Moray used a sleeve of his grubby suit to interrupt the perspiration massing on his forehead. 'DNA's worse than drugs. A tiny bit can get you into a fuck lot of trouble.'

Reuben took his watch off and examined the back. 'Tell me about it,' he said softly. He walked over to the wardrobe and returned with a wad of notes. 'Here,' he offered, 'your cut. I'll give Judith hers later.'

Moray licked his lips, running the tip of his tongue over the sharp stubble of an embryonic moustache. 'Right. What are you up to?'

'Going to head to the lab in the early hours, get on with a few things.'

'Don't you ever sleep?'

'I used to sleep, Moray. In a comfortable bed with my wife, and my son next door. And then, as you know, I found out that someone else had been sleeping there as well . . .' Reuben stopped himself. Moray was not the sort of person you opened up to; he was more used to eavesdropping than dealing face to face. Already he was standing up, looking awkward.

'Anyway, time to get a taxi,' he said, retrieving his camcorder and making for the door.

'Day after tomorrow, then.'

'I don't think so.' He pocketed the money and shook his head. 'Monday's a Bank Holiday. Last one of the summer. And I've got something important to take care of.' Moray winked in conspiracy, pulled the door handle and left the room.

Reuben fingered the back of his watch through habit. Instead, he opened two Vodka miniatures and a can of Coke and poured them into a plastic beaker. He indulged in a final tortured examination of the photographs. Then he opened his briefcase and withdrew a thick file which Judith had smuggled out of work earlier in the day. It was marked 'GeneCrime, Euston: Evidence and Sample Inventory: Hitch-Hiker Killer; May 2002–'. He perused the case notes, which concerned the murder of three hitch-hikers, one male and two female, in Gloucestershire in the late eighties. Their bodies had been abandoned by the same roadside on three different days, brutalized, torn apart, their necks opened. With no witnesses and no suspect, and given the rural location, a decision had been made to test the entire male population of two neighbouring villages.

Reuben was intimately familiar with the Hitch-Hiker in-vestigation. The case had employed an early forerunner of DNA fingerprinting which was being tweaked as it went along. The Forensic Science Service had sent several of its personnel to gain hands-on experience, and as a forensics CID officer, Reuben had been seconded. Over four thousand men were bled and tested, but no matches were uncovered. The technique had failed, and enthusiasm for it faltered. Reuben returned to London after three months of fruitless investigation. However, the experience had a paradoxical effect on him. Instead of becoming dispirited, his eyes opened to the possibilities. He resumed his university education, completing a Ph.D. in molecular biology, and re-entered the forensic service eager to pioneer advanced genetic methodologies in the search for the truth. The Hitch-Hiker case had shown him that the failings of forensic detection were the same as in any detection process. What were needed were methods which overcame the obvious limitations of retrospective analysis.

And then, eleven years after the case had slipped from public consciousness, the murderer was caught. A random comparison against the original database implicated a detainee arrested for an unconnected offence. The suspect was questioned, charged and convicted. Reuben had been working on another assignment at the time of the breakthrough. He took a drink and scratched his scalp, remembering how he had never been convinced. No one performed random comparisons. Forensics simply didn't have the time.

He continued to sip and to read, absorbing the details more deeply, fascinated, his concentration snowballing over the minutes and hours, his eyes opening, his pen scribbling frantically, his brain racing through the facts, impulses rushing along networks, leaping synapses, striking up new connections, doing the wall of death around the inside of his skull, forever keeping his wife and son where they couldn't pull him apart, and desperately trying to forget that, exactly five years ago, on the last bank holiday of the summer, on a Somerset hill, he had asked Lucy to marry him.

9

Sarah Hirst faces her computer, reviewing screens of data and images. She is distracted, her concentration wavering. Light streams in through the window of her study, bouncing off the screen, causing her to squint at its contents. She can hear the traffic of escape outside, cars grinding out of the city and towards the coast, a day away from responsibility and commitment. A large part of her longs to be with them, nose to tail, edging ever closer to the restless expanse of water that smells of freedom. Killers don't take bank holidays, she tells herself. And nor do DCIs. Occasionally, she switches from pictures of Sandra Bantam's tortured body to another screen, one showing a different sort of photograph. Sarah has her arm around a tall, slender man. They are smiling, dressed casually, in a forest together. DCI Hirst sighs and flicks irritably back to Sandra's corpse.

Phil Kemp is sitting at a table in the back room of a jaded pub. In his hands he holds five playing cards. Six other people are seated around in a circle. The air is claustrophobic with smoke. A weary female in her mid-forties offers round a bottle of whiskey. All the other players except Phil take the opportunity to replenish their glasses. The chatter is rapid and tense. Coins and notes are nudged into the centre as the poker hand builds. Phil hesitates, and then drops two ten-pound notes on to the pile. Next to him, a thin man in a baseball cap lays his cards down in defeat. A tanned woman opposite matches Phil's bet and raises the stakes. Three more players fall by the wayside. When the attention returns to Phil, he is quick and decisive. Forty pounds into the pot. The woman opposite pauses, taking a nip of her drink. She stares intently at Phil and then back at her own cards. Phil holds her eye, loosening the top two buttons of his checked shirt. Then she lays her cards flat and reaches abruptly for her cigarettes. Gradually and gently, Phil turns his cards up and spreads them out. He has nothing. He reaches forwards and rakes in the pot.

Mina Ali, Simon Jankowski, Paul Mackay and Jez Hethrington-Andrews grip their steering wheels, utterly absorbed, unblinkingly enthralled. Simon is leading, followed by Mina and Jez. They career through a series of tight digital turns, narrowly missing spectators, sliding round finely rendered bends. Mina launches an overtaking move, but spins off, taking Simon with her, just as the time runs out. Jez launches his fist into the air, an unlikely winner. The quartet stand up reluctantly and make their way out of the arcade, blinking in the sunshine at the end of the pier. Despite the bank holiday sun, a determined sea breeze ruffles their hair and flaps their clothes. They lean over the rail and watch the waves below tumble towards the beach. Jez smiles in victory, before noticing an ice-cream booth ahead of them. He points to it, and the four scientists amble over, single file, each searching their pockets for change, lost in their own thoughts, coming alive in the Brighton sun.

Two male CID officers stand in front of a pale-blue door. The taller pushes the bell and clears his throat. His partner sighs and glances at his watch. The late August sun beats down on their black uniforms, warming the material, which they can feel through their white cotton shirts. The door pulls open and they introduce themselves, well-worn identity badges held out for inspection one more time in a long day of inspections. A creased photograph of Sandra Bantam is proffered by the shorter officer. The occupant, a woman in her seventies or eighties, shakes her head and shrugs, looking confused. The taller officer turns and points to a terrace several doors away, and outlines what has happened, asking if the woman has noticed anything untoward. The GeneCrime officers scribble a few notes between them. Behind, another pair of officers enter the thin driveway of a house opposite. The shorter officer thanks the woman, and they walk back to the road, grim with determination and damp with sweat, ready to try the next dwelling in the street.

Moray Carnock holds out his index finger, almost accusingly, a stubby digit with a comprehensively chewed nail. He waits patiently, biding his time. Presently, a small, colourful bird hops on to the fleshy perch. Moray bends his head slowly towards it and kisses it briefly. Then he offers it a seed, pinched between the forefinger and thumb of his other hand. The canary pecks at it, grips it in its beak and flies off with the treasure. Moray runs his eyes around the inside of the walk-in cage, and makes a kissing sound through his puckered lips. His finger is soon home to another diminutive bird, this one an iridescent blue-green. Moray tenderly strokes its back while he distracts it with a treat. The canary flaps its wings rapidly, and escapes to enjoy the snack in peace. Moray glances at the cage door, which he has locked from the inside. He pokes out his finger again, and awaits the next visitor.

Judith Meadows is lost in the mechanics of decoration. She dips her brush into a tin of matt emulsion, wipes the excess paint on the rim, and runs the bristles smoothly up and down, blending and merging, a new coat covering the old. Over her shoulder, her husband Charlie is painting the adjacent wall. They work in silence, absorbed, painting towards each other, heading into the corner which separates them. Judith watches the original colour disappear beneath her brush, and for a second feels sad that the vibrant red is disappearing under a neutral off-white, swallowed up, suppressed, pushed to the back. She dips her brush again, nearing the corner. Charlie's brush works in parallel, their hands inches apart, closing in on each other. And then Charlie stops and takes a pace back. Satisfied, he takes his brush and dips it into a plastic pot of cloudy water. Judith turns away from him, slowly and methodically starting to fill in the gap by herself.

10

DCI Sarah Hirst crossed a three-lane road with early-morning confidence. In an hour this would be a perilous endeavour. Now, however, just before seven, it was still manageable. Already, the sun was beginning to heat the tarmac, an un-British steam rising from the surface. The tube had been mercifully cool, but was gearing itself up for another onslaught. The baked air which blew along its tracks and through its tunnels was unlike any other in the country. Breathing it was the respiratory equivalent of eating candyfloss. It was thin and empty, with no nourishment or value, a hot nothingness pushing you home after the excitement had ebbed.

Sarah attempted to eat and drink as she walked. In one hand, an over-sized cup of coffee, in the other a Danish pastry. She was carrying a slim leather case, which she was forced to raise to her face every time she drank. But she had a busy day, and every second she could save meant an extra evening breath in the cool sanctuary of her flat.

Sarah took a sip of coffee, the case again obscuring her line of sight. For an instant, she pictured the different scales of attack which ravaged a dead person. After the penetration of blunt bullets or the stabbing of sharp knives lay the autopsy. Sandra Bantam's skull would be scythed open with a circular saw, her brain pulled out, her thoracic cavity sliced into with scalpels and saws, her sternum broken, ribs cracked, retractors ripping the flesh . . . truly, murder seemed tame in comparison. In Dr Bantam's case, however, the attack hadn't been an instant bullet or a quick blade. Sarah shuddered, despite the rising heat. The autopsy had confirmed that she died slowly and desperately, no single wound enough on its own to end her life.

Ahead, in an alleyway opposite the car-only entrance to Gene-Crime, a vagrant lay prone on the tarmac. Sarah bit into her pastry, appreciating that the attack on Sandra was still not over. Small parts of Dr Bantam, who had decided to leave GeneCrime a few months previously, had now returned to her former lab. They sat in cold tubes, in harsh freezers, on the bench where she used to rest her elbows. Her body had been battered and broken by assailant and pathologist alike, and now it was time for forensics to have a go. Skin and hair cells would be drowned in phenolic fluids, crushed in homogenizers, broken with sonicators, gnawed open by enzymes. The very molecules which had kept her alive would be torn out and read with unblinking lasers. On a minute level, Dr Sandra Bantam was being dissected atom by atom.

Today held a series of meetings between Forensics, Pathology and CID. As a former colleague, Sandra's death would be ruthlessly investigated. The story had made most of the papers, which tended to funnel resources into an investigation, as if the police had become media-funded, every column inch donating an extra man-hour to the inquiry. Sarah Hirst frowned, attempting another decent bite of her Danish. She was only a few metres from the tramp now. She noticed for the first time that something was wrong. The man was lying face down, and there was blood in his jet-black hair. Sarah stopped and glanced around. The street was empty. She panicked for a second. It seemed counter-intuitive to call for assistance without her police radio. Instead, she retrieved her mobile and dialled 999. Even from this distance, she could see that he was dead.

'Police,' she answered into her mobile. 'This is Detective Chief Inspector Sarah Hirst, Euston CID. I've found a man apparently dead on the pavement. Request an ambulance and some back-up.' Despite the civilian context, Sarah found it difficult to explain the situation in anything other than cop-speak. 'Yes, I'll stay on site. Roger that.' She scanned up and down the street in cold agitation, stepping away from the corpse. A road-sweeping lorry edged around the corner, its brushes kicking up dirt from the gutter, its suction hoovering the detritus of passing life. She ended the call and watched the vehicle pass, oblivious, the corpse just a few metres out of reach of its determined cleaning.

Looking at her phone, Sarah cursed. This was taking time. Her day would have to be even more rushed. She strained her ears, but there were no sirens. They say you never hear the ambulance that comes for you. A couple of cars pulled into GeneCrime, almost line astern. One contained Phil Kemp, and Sarah felt a quick flare of irritation. She considered him an inferior officer in almost all regards, and yet he seemed to be trying to overrule her at every opportunity. Sarah told herself that she had to be harder than him, colder than him, more ruthless than him if she was ultimately going to gain control of GeneCrime. She comforted herself momentarily that her opponent had weaknesses which she could exploit. An ambulance turned into the road, and she saw a squad car approaching, a junction behind. She sighed with relief. Five more minutes and her presence at the scene would be over.

The first person to address her was a paramedic, who walked calmly to the body, resisted the urge to touch it, and returned to the ambulance for a blanket. She draped the shiny black material over the corpse and said to Sarah, 'A few hours too late.'

Sarah nodded, unsure what to say.

'You found him, did you?'

'Yes.'

'Right. Over to you, boys.' The paramedic gestured as two policemen climbed out of their cars.

'OK, love,' the first began, 'it can be a bit upsetting seeing a body. Now, take a second, and tell me exactly what happened here.'

Sarah paused. Nothing had happened. She had simply found the man lying in the street.

'If you need a sit down . . .'

'I'm fine. Really.' Sarah resisted the urge to pull rank. She knew she would enjoy the cheap thrill and a large part of her wanted to say, 'I'm a fucking Detective Chief Inspector, sunshine. I've seen people mutilated in ways that your twenty-three-year-old brain couldn't even imagine. So don't fuck me around with all the fragile female nonsense.' Instead, she continued, 'Look, I'm uniform, just like you guys. I arrived here fifteen minutes ago, and this chap was lying in the road.'

There was an instant change in body language. The two PCs smiled, put away their notebooks and chatted. Sarah told them all she knew, and they radioed the information back to base. Finally, she gave them her office phone number, and left them to it, feeling somehow good about herself. There was a song she once liked by Morrissey. 'I Keep Mine Hidden'. She whistled it as she walked through the car park and into GeneCrime.

The phone call which would change Sarah Hirst's life for ever came shortly after lunch.

The morning had been hectic, fraught, laboured, divisive. Meetings between CID, Pathology, Scenes-of-Crime and Forensics had turned up more problems than had been solved. Sarah sat in her office with a sense of retreat, and double-clicked the files that had been forwarded to her. The one which made her stop showed the inside of the bathroom cupboard door at Sandra Bantam's house. As she viewed digital images of the code, magnified and sharpened, in normal light and under UV, the implications once again pricked her, and made her sweat. The message had been checked and double-checked for ambiguities and mistakes. The final task Dr Bantam's blood had performed, as her life leaked away, was to spell out the words: 'GENE. CRIMES.WILL.BE.REPAID'. Sarah wiped some dust from the screen with the back of her hand. The letters shone out at her with renewed zeal. The red letters of the code, the black letters of the translation. Since eight o'clock, ideas and theories had been whispered and shouted across GeneCrime's conference-room table. She noted the differing effect the murder had upon the building's staff – CID excited, eager, sniffing the air like bloodhounds; forensic scientists sullen, bickering, cautious that every angle was considered before venturing conclusions. The phone rang and she reached for the receiver, picking it up before the second ring.

'Hello,' she answered. 'DCI Hirst.'

There was a pause. 'PC Davies here, Euston Met. I'm sorry, ma'am, I didn't realize you were a DCI when we talked this morning.'

'No problem. Is everything OK?'

'I just wanted to follow up on the body you reported finding in the street.'

'Yes?'

There was another short silence. 'Well, it looks like he wasn't a vagrant. He had some ID on him.'

Sarah stared into her screen, annoyed that this was still encroaching on her day. She checked herself, shaking her head slowly, the phone lead rattling against her keyboard. Someone had died. This was a tragedy, not an inconvenience. But this was the side effect of chasing killers – the loss of a stranger's life had become a mundane event more likely to vex than upset. 'Right,' she muttered, not really sure what was expected of her.

'The thing is, we found something in his wallet.'

'What did you find?'

'A pass for the GeneCrime Forensics Unit.'

'What kind of pass?' Sarah asked abruptly. 'Staff or visitor?'

'Staff. We think, well, that he might be one of your colleagues.'

The letters on her computer faded in and out of focus, dancing around, revelling in their message. 'What . . .' Sarah asked, a sharp breath settling straight into the depths of her stomach, 'what is the name on the pass?'

'I'm not sure which way round this goes. It looks to be either Zhang Run or Run Zhang.'

'Run Zhang,' she repeated, the name now shocking, its abrupt syllables stabbing somewhere in her chest. 'Oh my God.'

'You knew the deceased, did you?' PC Davies asked.

'Listen carefully to what I'm about to say. Don't touch the body. Leave him where he is. Clear everybody from the room he's in. Take the name of everyone who has touched him. We'll be over. Where exactly are you?' She wrote the address on a sickeningly yellow Post-It note and slammed the phone down.

While police procedures assembled themselves into rigid pathways of thought, the rest of her mind raced around, darting in and out, delving and exploring. She stood up and rushed down the corridor to Phil Kemp's office, ideas and images streaking ahead of her, bouncing off walls and kicking through heavy double doors. This needed to be handled quickly and delicately and, knocking on Phil's door, Sarah appreciated again that these were not DCI Kemp's strengths. Phil was an old-fashioned copper, straight-laced and direct, but frequently oblivious to the subtleties of forensics. Still, they had to move fast. She flung the door open. Staff would have to be informed and, almost in the same breath, asked to examine Run's body, to pore over his naked corpse, removing small parts of him, scraping bits into tubes and bags. Just as they had done to Sandra.

Phil looked up from a thick wad of forms, eyes asking about the commotion. Sarah steadied herself and told him exactly what she knew. That she had noticed a badly beaten man lying in the street. That she had failed to examine him. That the police had identified him as Run Zhang. That his body had been dumped deliberately close to his workplace. That this was the second murder of her staff in five days. That the more she thought about it, the more it unnerved her. Someone was murdering Gene-Crime's forensic scientists.

GCACGATAGCTTACGGG
AAATCTA**FIVE**GTATTCG
GCTAATCGTCATAACAT

1

The lab was still. A trio of machines which had toiled through the night continued their programmed tasks. The forensics team of GeneCrime sat on tables and benches, subdued and quiet. As each staff member had entered, they had been told. The news spread quickly. A thick silence swallowed the shock and seemed to hold it tight around the group. No one looked at anyone, scared of seeing their own grief staring back. Birgit began to cry quietly, and Judith placed an arm around her. Paul's eyes were moist, as were Jez's. Mina clamped her hand tight over her open mouth. Simon whispered the words 'Shit shit shit' to himself. There was an empty space where Run's section of bench had been, the area demarcated with autoclave tape bearing his name. Three of his pipettes lay forlornly on their sides. Mina picked them up and slid them into a drawer.

'I bet you're wondering what the hell you've done,' Bernie said to Paul Mackay, breaking the peace. 'Four months here and two of us have kicked the bucket.'

'I guess,' Dr Mackay answered uncertainly.

'Look, if I'm next, promise you'll be gentle with me. Use something that doesn't have phenol in it. A Qiagen column, maybe. And some of those nice swabs with the soft tips.'

'Bernie?' Mina said.

'Yes?'

'Shut the hell up.'

'Just trying to lighten the atmosphere.'

'Fuck you. Run's dead. And Sandra as well. And I don't know about the rest of you, but this is freaking me out.'

'Come on, people die all the time. Do we get upset when a young girl is mutilated and we run our grubby gloves over her?'

'I won't explain to you how that's different. If you don't understand, I really don't want to work with you any more.'

Bernie glanced around the group, calculating his reaction from their body language. Mina glaring, Judith rubbing her face, Jez pale, Simon sullen, Paul scratching his scalp, Birgit's eyes filling again. 'Sorry,' he muttered. The truth was no one knew how to react. This was different. It was under their skin, a splinter driving its way through the epidermis, too slippery to be grasped. One of their number had left the lab, gone home, been mutilated and tortured, and had come back to them in a bag. Worse, until his death, he had been examining minute parts of a former colleague. Now he would be swallowed up by the GeneCrime lab, and picked apart himself. Nobody wanted to touch him. The unspoken question leaked through the group. Was Run killed because he was the scientist working most intimately on Sandra Bantam? On that basis, would assessing Run result in a similar risk? If so, this raised some even more unnerving issues. 'Look, we all understand the nature of chance, right?' Bernie asked, desperate to move on from his apology, which permeated the air like the nip of formalin.

A couple of shrugs and the odd 'Sure'.

'One of us being . . . killed, we can work it out. Jez, how many murders in London last year?'

'Two hundred, give or take,' Jez replied quietly.

'Right. And population?'

'Say eight million.'

'So, the chances one of us – Reuben's old team of ten, plus or minus – dies from an attack are . . . anybody?'

Simon, who had spent the last few seconds sullenly bruising the keys of a calculator, replied, 'One in four thousand.'

'OK, do the obvious. The risk of *two* of us dying.'

'One in sixteen million,' Judith answered.

There was a pause. In the background, a TaqMan 7500 hummed its way through a sample scan. Simon, Mina, Paul, Jez, Birgit, Judith and Bernie found reasons not to look at each other. They had all secretly been through the numbers within minutes of hearing about Run. But still, the message was clear. Hearing it out loud was confirmation. Maths never lie. The machine finished its task and lay in empathetic silence. Birgit broke the stillness.

'We don't need statistics. I am thinking that we're just being scientific about it. The only way we know how.' She dabbed at her eyes with a tissue. 'But we all can appreciate that Run and Sandra showed the same patterns. A CID guy told me that he didn't think Run was killed quickly.'

'Why don't you spell it out, Birgit?'

'I should not need to.'

'You're saying—' Mina was interrupted by the barking voice of Phil Kemp, who had entered the lab silently.

'Conference room. Now. All of you,' he instructed. He examined the group, and his demeanour softened. 'We need your considerable brains,' he explained, turning and walking back the way he had come. They filed out behind him, quizzical glances passing between them.

The conference room was long and slender and, had it possessed a second door, could almost have passed for a corridor. A highly polished table ran virtually from end to end, leaving little space to manoeuvre. Meetings in this room felt intense and claustrophobic, even when informal. It encouraged argument rather than discussion, confrontation rather than cooperation.

The members of the forensics team funnelled down one side of the room and pulled out their chairs. Opposite them sat CID, impassive, doodling, chatting. At either end of the table were DCI Sarah Hirst and DCI Phil Kemp.

Phil began. 'Right, let's talk this one through. Sarah, what have we got?'

Sarah was gripped by a momentary annoyance. Really, she should be running the meetings, giving the orders. While the irritation slowly let go of her, she brought up the relevant information on her laptop, fingers slipping over the track ball. Twenty faces monitored her intently, hungry for information, scared of what they might find. 'Right,' she started, 'since Run's body was discovered early this morning, we've only had time to run . . . to *process* crude tests. He's in the morgue downstairs.' Sarah looked up, scanning the room, her face cold and unemotional. 'I think we all have a right to be upset by recent proceedings. However, we've got to push those considerations to one side. I guess I don't have to spell it out. We need to work quickly. This will sound harsh – there will be time for grieving later.'

'That's right,' Phil added, backing her up from the far end of the table. 'We're looking into sorting a counselling service. And we're talking about twenty-four-hour protection for each one of you. But before the Met will sanction it, we need to be certain. So we have to stick together. Scientists will be accompanied by CID personnel wherever possible. We need answers, and quick. Because if we don't, well . . .' He took in the chewed fingernails, wide-open pupils, clenched jaws, and realized the implications didn't need spelling out.

'So, let's look at what we know.' Sarah opened a file on her computer. 'Run appears to have been murdered at home and then dumped in the street outside GeneCrime. There is also evidence, as many of you may have heard already, of torture. It's early days – SOCOs are at the scene, and some of you will be asked to go over there later – but a timescale in keeping with that of Sandra Bantam seems possible. We think we might get DNA from the body. And there's something else . . .' Sarah allowed the words to hang in the air, doing the dirty work for her, preparing the room for the news.

'What?' Jez Hethrington-Andrews asked.

'More code.'

'What does it say?'

Sarah plugged a USB cable into her laptop. 'Some of you might prefer not to see these pictures.'

Most of the room's occupants gazed past Sarah and at a screen behind her. On it was the projected image of a human torso, with arms, legs and head out of shot. 'A pathologist has had a very quick look. She is more or less certain that the letters were carved into him with a scalpel or modelling knife.'

'And?'

'He was alive while it was carved. The blood was wiped away later.'

Even those members of the forensics team who hadn't looked at the screen immediately now turned to take in the images. Sarah flicked through a series of colour shots, showing the body horizontal, vertical and from the side. Several of them gasped, unprepared for the atrocity of what they saw. The photos came to rest on an upright image, as if Run were standing magnified in front of the room. It was clear exactly what sort of code he was wearing.

'So what does it say?' one of the unfazed CID asked, his stare directed across the table.

Forensics were silent. Simon rushed out of the room, followed closely by Jez. Phil watched intently, noting for the second time in a week the gulf in personality between the two sides of GeneCrime. The door opened again, and Simon reappeared with a thick textbook. He sat down and started alternately to squint at the screen and scribble on a piece of paper.

167

Phil said, 'OK, while Dr Jankowski is working on that, we need a strategy. Sarah and I have talked about this and have come up with an idea. Feel free to comment.' All eyes were trained on Simon, swivelling his head between the scalpel cuts on Run's sallow body and the white opened page of his book. Phil's unruffled voice poured out regardless. 'First, we need to establish that Run and Sandra were killed by the same person. So, in a few minutes' time, half of us are going to Run's house for a thorough sweep, while the other half stay here and examine his body.' Simon was scribbling furiously, crossing out and scribbling again. 'Then we regroup, and split into two different factions, Forensics under my direction, CID under Sarah's. Forensics, with associated CID support, will begin trawling through previous GeneCrime convictions.' Dr Jankowski was moving his pencil rapidly across the page, as if performing a calculation. His face was a mix of intense concentration and puzzlement. 'CID, assimilating what DNA evidence we have by then, will work on the premise that the killer is someone unknown to us.' Phil glanced up. The twenty members of GeneCrime were unanimously focused on Simon. He followed their gaze. Simon was sitting bolt upright. He was pale; there was a sudden shocked weariness about him. 'What?' he asked.

Dr Simon Jankowski stood up and headed over to a white-board near the blinded window. His eyes were half-closed, and he almost seemed to be sleepwalking. He picked up a marker and uncapped it. Then he began to write, slowly and deliberately, from left to right in red capital letters which squeaked painfully with each movement of the pen.

'I-A-M-C-M-I-N-G-F-R-G-C'.

'What the hell is that?' Phil Kemp demanded.

Mina Ali gave a small squeal. Bernie Harrison bit into the fleshy part of his index finger. CID shuffled uncomfortably. DCI Sarah Hirst focused through the letters, almost seeing the message, her brain desperately filling in gaps and rearranging consonants.

'The genetic code is riddled with redundancy,' Simon muttered. 'There are twenty-six letters of the alphabet, but only twenty amino acids. So it's not possible to spell everything in DNA.'

'Which ones are missing?' Sarah asked.

'J, U, X, Y, Z and' – Simon rubbed his face – 'more importantly, O.'

Sarah's expression changed. 'Fuck,' she whispered.

Simon inserted a couple of squeaky letters, and CID tried it on for size, their mouths opening and closing, wrapping around the vowels and spitting out the consonants.

'What's GC?' one of them asked.

'GeneCrime.'

DCI Kemp clenched his fists and hit the table harder. '*I am coming for GeneCrime.*' His words stuck in the thin air-conditioned atmosphere and were fanned around the room. '*I am coming for GeneCrime,*' he repeated incredulously. 'No way, sunshine. *We* are coming for *you.*'

Sarah closed her laptop. Phil's outburst had lacked conviction. Sarah knew it; Phil knew it; everyone who had heard knew it. He had been unable to keep the uncertainty from his voice. Forensics sat and squirmed. CID wrote down the words. Jez re-entered the room. Phil eased himself tentatively into his chair. And the letters on the whiteboard shone out in bold red scratches of premonition.

2

In the bedroom of a fourth-storey flat in King's Cross, multiple camera flashes strobed the movements of six police personnel. On the bed, a dark cherry outline revealed the site of torture of Run Zhang. The impression was that someone had dabbed a paintbrush around his torso, leaving a white profile on the sheet framed in red.

The room betrayed the fact that its occupant was a long way from home. Its furniture was cheap and insubstantial, designed to suit a short-term purpose. The actual bed was little more than a mattress on the floor. A frail table with unsteady legs swayed under the window, which was partially obscured by a blue bedsheet. In the corner sat a mini-disc player with tiny portable speakers. The wardrobe held only a suitcase-worth of clothes, all neatly pressed and hung. No books lined the bookcase, but two thick volumes entitled *Everyday English* and *Cantonese to English and Back Again* sat heavily on the floor. However, the room did not feel empty. An intense collage of pictures decorated the walls. Photos of Run, of his family, of babies, aunties, grandmothers, uncles, cousins, sisters and brothers; of pets, classmates, tourist locations, residences and buildings; of wide-open spaces and lush countryside; of bikes and cars; of outings and events and ceremonies. Truly, Run's whole life in another country lit up the walls like miniature windows.

A member of CID was sniffing the contents of an opened can of Coke. Three of the Forensics Section examined the bed in minute detail, occasionally talking in hushed tones, snatches of their conversation darting through the room. The CID officer passed several sample bags to Phil Kemp, who had just entered.

Simon Jankowski left the photos that he had been staring at and approached his boss. 'Phil, I'm just wondering,' he said.

'What?'

'If we might know the killer already.'

Phil turned to look at him. 'I don't think we can make the link yet.'

'Do the stats.'

'This isn't statistics – this is real life. If the killer was really after GeneCrime members, why target Sandra, who had left to pursue a family life? It can't be that straightforward.'

'Either way, what are you going to do about us?'

'What do you mean?'

'Protection.'

'We're sorting it. But bear in mind, looking after a group of thirty forensics, CID and support staff twenty-four hours a day simply isn't that easy.' Phil smiled reassuringly. 'Now, let's wrap up here for the time being. Sarah's just arrived from base. Been sifting through some files. Come through when you've finished what you're doing.'

One by one, the scientists followed Phil Kemp down a short yellowing corridor, which opened into the main living room. Their white contamination suits scraped along the walls, blue shoe covers rustling with each pace. Each of them was perspiring heavily inside their outfits, which held the sweat in and away from the crime scene. Rivulets of water ran down their foreheads and soaked into the cotton masks obscuring their mouths. In the living room, they noted the overflowing ashtray on the floor, the two half-drunk cups of tea sitting on the coffee table, and the empty takeaway cartons lying on the sofa.

A police technician was hastily connecting a video projector to a laptop, focusing images on a wall which held mounted photographs of Run and various family members. In one corner of the room, DCI Sarah Hirst exchanged tense and hushed words with Phil Kemp. Despite the importance of the crime scene, neither officer wore protective clothes, a visual reminder that they rose above forensic contamination. As the room filled, they turned to face the white mass of CID and scientists. Sarah nodded at Phil, and he began to speak.

'OK. What do we think so far? The way I see it, the same person, probably a man, has carried out both murders. He has a grudge against GeneCrime. Ergo, this is either someone we have arrested previously or someone we are trying to arrest now. I know Sarah has had some thoughts.'

'There are of course two other possibilities,' Sarah said, addressing the room, and monitoring Phil from the corner of her eye. 'First, it is someone we have never encountered. A punter with a grudge against forensics in general, who knows GeneCrime is pioneering new advancements, who has a moral or ethical vendetta.'

Phil appeared unimpressed. 'And second?'

Sarah paused, taking in the discomfort of the assembled staff. She motioned for the mouth masks to be dropped. Faces came to life as their covers were pulled away. 'That it is someone inside GeneCrime. Maybe someone in this room.'

Phil, who had been slouching, straightened. 'Hang on a second . . .'

'Look, the murderer knew where Run and Sandra lived. There was no sign of forced entry. Therefore they knew their attacker. And what is the only thing that links Run and Sandra? GeneCrime.'

Scientists and CID glanced around at each other. After a sticky pause, Phil Kemp said, 'OK, this is solvable. Everybody write down on a piece of paper where you were at the time of both deaths. Give the phone number of someone who can corroborate. Pass them round to Sarah or myself. While you're doing that, Sarah will fill you in on what CID have come up with.'

'Right, let's look at the first and most probable scenario, that the attacker is someone we have dealt with in the past. While Forensics have been busy in the lab and at Run's house, CID have rifled through past cases, and have come up with a shortlist.' Sarah turned to her laptop which was perching on top of the TV. 'OK, on the screen' – she swivelled round to see if the image was projecting – 'is suspect one. Jattinder Kumar, thirty-two, whereabouts unknown, escaped from prison nine months ago.' Jattinder Kumar's grainy face appeared, vastly magnified, skin pores like black holes. Intruding into the projection, on the stubbled chin, were two framed photos of Run with his arms around a smiling, older oriental woman. 'Kumar was jailed for murdering a police officer, made a real fuss during his trial that the DNA evidence had been tampered with.' Sarah pressed the PgDn button on her laptop. 'Suspect two, Stephen Jacobs, ex-biology teacher, raped a pupil of his, recently released, attempted – as some of you may remember – to circumvent the genetic evidence by inserting salmon sperm DNA into his victim. Nice man.' She flicked on to the next image. 'Three, Lars Besser, recently released as well, jailed for murder and two serious assaults, prosecuted on genetic evidence alone. Always protested his innocence, but don't they all?' Sarah scanned the room, seeing CID nodding in agreement. 'Suspect four, Mark Gelson, never successfully charged or DNA tested, currently and previously under investigation by GeneCrime. Whereabouts unknown, probable murderer of two police informants, one of the Met's current highest priorities.'

'Why Gelson?' Birgit Kasper asked.

'We've had anonymous death-threats. One of the calls was

made from the flat of the man nailed to the wall. Anyone remember that one?'

'Can't forget it.'

'Exactly. But Gelson was, we believe, at the scene, and the call time matches CCTV footage we have of him in the area. And, more importantly, there was evidence of mutilation and torture. The victim had been sliced and diced, especially across his torso. Pathology noted internal bruising. So not a run-of-the-mill murderer.'

'Don't we have a profile for him at all?'

'He's been lucky so far. Even when we combed his house, we didn't get anything unambiguous, probably due to the large number of visitors we believe he had. And as for the crime scene, it was basically a crack house which had tens of people staggering through its doors every day.'

'This might sound like an obvious question,' a female CID officer began, wiping some perspiration away from her top lip, 'but what about the other suspects? Do we have DNA, and if we do, does it match samples from Sandra and Run?'

'Therein lies the beautiful irony. Mina – care to enlighten us?'

Mina Ali glanced from Bernie, who was technically more senior than her, to Phil Kemp, who was managing Reuben's old section. 'Sandra's DNA was being overseen by Run,' she explained. 'We're working back through his notes, but it's taking time. And we've only just begun to process Run himself. So the wheels are spinning but we're not going anywhere.'

Bernie, who looked aggrieved that he hadn't been consulted, felt the need to add, 'So a cutting-edge forensics unit suddenly finds itself relying on old-fashioned police work.'

Sarah pressed a final button, which projected all four images on to the wall. 'I guess those are our best estimates for the time being, but others might arise. Phil?'

'Any questions? Right. We need to move fast. We can get outside support – Area Commander Abner has offered us a staff of twenty – but the quickest thing is to divide and conquer. Now, I'm acutely aware that GeneCrime hasn't always been a picnic in the park, and there have been, well, divisions. What we're going to do now is something different. We're going to split into two new groups. Each group will be half CID, half Forensics. This way we can react to every eventuality. Under my auspices, Team A will be in charge of hunting down these four suspects. Our remit will be that we already know our man.'

'And Team B, headed by myself,' Sarah added, 'will work on the opposite theory – that we don't know the killer. We will sift through the forensics and crime details, as they emerge, and try to build a profile of our man.' Sarah rubbed her face, and felt a wet apprehension exuding from her skin. 'So masks back on. Let's nail this bastard.' She closed the lid of her laptop, and the picture on the wall died, leaving just the photographs of Run, smiling and content, arms wrapped around his mother.

3

Mark Gelson nursed a stolen Ford Focus slowly and gently through the slack mid-morning traffic. When you are hunting – he smiled to himself in the rear-view mirror – it is best to proceed quietly.

Every job had its conventions and regulations. For Mark Gelson, rule number one was never draw attention to yourself. Because of this, he drove a series of unremarkable cars, wore unbranded clothes and restricted his jewellery to a wedding ring. He wasn't married, and had no desire to be, but the gold band lent him a further veneer of respectability. Appearance was important, and the less conspicuous he was the more easily he could slip through the closing net of his personal and professional lives.

Although the tentacles of Mark Gelson's empire spread across half the city, he wasn't used to being this far south-east. Sometimes out here in Blackheath it hardly felt like London at all. Public transport would certainly have been quicker, but stations were bristling with CCTV. Mark Gelson's movements could have been tracked all the way from Charing Cross, a seamless montage of grey pictures, a face amongst continuously changing crowds. Cars, particularly small stolen ones, were much harder to pinpoint.

Mark pulled on to a long straight road facing a park and slotted the car into a space. From the boot he retrieved a sports bag. He cut down a side street, along a high-fenced alley and entered the loading bay for a row of shops. A grey door marked '11B' was jammed between the steel shutters of adjacent stores. Why, he wondered silently, did they all live above fucking shops? Mark rapped on the door and shouted in a disguised voice, 'Delivery. Can you sign for it?' There was a rumble on the stairs. He removed a small object from the bag and held it in his hand. Number 11B opened a fraction and a man peered through the narrowed aperture. 'Hello, Carlton,' Mark said, wedging himself in the doorway so that it couldn't close again. He pointed a gun through the gap. Carlton's body tensed within his tracksuit. He turned and walked stiffly back the way he had come.

Upstairs, under Mark Gelson's unbroken stare, Carlton sat and fidgeted. His disquiet sclerosed into fear, and he began to quiver with apprehension. Sweat seeped out of his dark skin and into his clothes, leaking through the material, making him feel sticky. Mark Gelson kept the gaping hole of the gun trained on him like a third unblinking eye.

'So, Carlton. Carlton, Carlton, Carlton.'

'Look, whatever you want—'

'Carlton. Did you really think you could?'

'You don't have to take my word for it . . .'

Mark Gelson talked quickly, at times almost without breathing. 'You really thought you could, didn't you? Some on the inside, some on the outside.' There was a violence in his words, his voice clipped and sharp. 'Inside and outside. Inside and outside.'

'I swear to you, not one word.'

'You see, everyone is leaky, Carlton. No one can keep everything they know inside them for ever. We all have our price.' Mark Gelson's brown eyes widened as he surveyed his employee. He ran an eager hand through his short, dense hair, rubbing his fingers together, feeling the sticky amalgamation of human sweat and chemical wax. 'It just takes a bent copper to name it.'

'Please, not like this. I would never . . .'

'I can't help it becoming personal. You'd feel the same, surely?'

'Whoever told you is wrong.'

'But I don't want you to suffer unnecessarily. Let me tell you what I'm going to do. I'm going to cook up a couple of rocks for you, and a couple for me. How does that sound?'

'Please don't hurt me.'

'Let's say we get this party started. Do you like parties, Carlton?'

'I'm begging you.'

'Are you turning my product down? I'd suggest you don't. Besides, how does the saying go? Never trust a skinny chef. Likewise, never trust a dealer who refuses his own drug.'

'What do you want me to do? Tell me and I'll do it.'

'You see, the thing with the rock, as you well know, is that you don't just hit the ceiling, you go through it! Tell me I'm wrong.'

'OK. Come on, let me have the pipe.'

'As I'm a polite man, you can go first. But before you do, I'm going to take some precautions. You know what a sudden high could do.' Mark Gelson took some plastic bag-ties from his pocket. He looped one around Carlton's left wrist and secured it against the arm of the chair. Then he forced his pistol into Carlton's groin and said, 'Kick me and I'll fuck you where it hurts.' He used his remaining hand to bind Carlton's ankles to the chair legs. 'Right.' He smirked, taking out a small opaque pipe, a plastic bag and a lighter. 'I'll help you hold it.' Mark tipped two white objects, which looked like injured miniature sugar cubes, into the mouth of the pipe. Under it, he sparked the lighter and kept it lit. 'Ready? Breathe.'

Carlton inhaled in desperation and fear. His eyes bulged as he sucked the smoke in, and he never took his gaze away from Mark Gelson.

'How's that? Good? Should be. That's the best product I've got. Now, as you'll notice, I've decided not to indulge. The rock may be good on the way up, but it's a fucker on the way down. So, as you start your descent, I want you to watch what I do, and listen carefully to what I say.' Mark opened the rucksack he had brought with him and began to extract its contents. There was a disposable scalpel with an orange handle, a six-inch kitchen knife, a small brown plastic bottle, a rubber belt from a car engine and a length of garden hose. 'You see, cocaine, in whatever form, brings immunity to pain. But it doesn't last long. When you crash, you hurt. We've all been there. Your thresholds drop. You become more sensitive. Your nerves are crying out. Tell me I'm wrong.'

'For fuck's sake. Let me have one more smoke . . .'

'That would defeat the object. Surely you see that? Now, I'm not unreasonable. Life is full of choices. You and other members of my staff could have colluded with the police in order to fuck me over, or you could have decided against it. So here are five objects from my house, a house I can never go back to now. I'd like you to choose which one you want.'

'I haven't done anything. Come on, some more smoke . . .'

'I mean, as I see it, there are five quick and easy ways to kill someone. Shooting. Drowning. Strangulation. Stabbing. Poisoning. Have I missed any?'

'It was Jonno Machicaran. Jonno's the cunt the cops got to first.'

'Of course, I'm counting hanging and asphyxiation broadly as strangulation.' Mark Gelson's rapid-fire delivery continued to tear through the air. 'You know, I'm grouping things in categories. Shooting could be with a gun, crossbow, fucking bow and arrow for all I care. I spend a lot of my life thinking about these matters. You have to in my position. Someone comes along who wants to take it all away from you, and you have to decide what to do about it. And you, Carlton, my friend, are a case in point. So what do you think?'

'I can't. I can't fucking think,' Carlton shouted, spit spraying his panic into the damp air.

'You want me to do the thinking for you? Because I'll stand here thinking about the business falling apart, the house I've left and the police hunting me down. I'll consider the fact that my face is on the computers of coppers all through the Met. I'll think about the forensics wankers combing my cellar, looking for the DNA of John Collins and Iqbal What's-his-name. Going through my personal stuff. My letters, my photos, my bank details. Ripping up my carpets, testing my toothbrush, taking hairs from my comb. Fucking ants gnawing away at me. You know how that feels?' Mark scratched his scalp irritably. 'Like being fucked from the inside. Having bits of you chopped up and taken to pieces. I tell you, Carlton, those cunts are the only cunts worse than cunts like you.' He stared down at him. 'So, you know which one I'll pick?'

'Not like this . . .'

'I'll choose all five of them. But I'm a libertarian.' Mark Gelson stopped pacing around. He stared intently at Carlton, the muscles of his jaw twitching. 'Do you know what that is, Carlton? Yeah? It means I believe in freedom, in people's right to choose. Now, I'll ask you again. How do you want to die?'

'It was Jonno's idea, for fuck's sake.'

'I've always liked you, Carlton. You're smart. But I've already been to see Mr Machicaran. And guess who he implicated as the next link in the chain? That's right – your good self! Now it really is time to make a decision.'

'Please. ANYTHING. Please.'

'You see, on my way here I thought you might have a problem deciding. Now, you've had plenty of opportunity to choose a preference. Time is marching on and I need information. I need to know who else fucked me over. Which coppers you dealt with and what forensic samples got taken. So it's time to speed things along. Hold out your fingers.'

Carlton bunched his fists, knuckles taut, his body shaking. Mark dragged the chair back to the wall, and punched him deep in the gut. He took a hammer out of his bag, and lined up a six-inch masonry nail. Carlton's body was limp, rasping for air. Mark Gelson pressed Carlton's left hand hard against the wall, pushed the nail quickly into his palm, and struck it smartly with the hammer. Carlton rocked upwards, swinging his head round to scream in the direction of the pain. Mark forced a tennis ball past his teeth, wedging it into his mouth. He examined the nail and hit it again, watching it burrow through skin, bone and plaster, immersing itself in the wall. Carlton spasmed and shrieked, his torture muted by the obstruction. Mark picked a Biro off the kitchen work surface and wrote the numbers one to five on successive fingers of Carlton's hand. He walked slowly back to his implements and picked up the kitchen knife. 'So what do you say? We'll let the knife decide.'

Carlton shook frantically in his chair, trying to pull his bleeding hand away from the wall.

Mark Gelson took aim, three or four metres away. Then he threw the knife. It missed Carlton's hand and dislodged some plaster a few centimetres too high. Mark picked the knife up and strolled back for another attempt.

'You know which one Jonno chose?'

Carlton wet himself, eyes wide, his wrist ligaments tearing in the struggle to be free, the nail dragging through his palm.

'Well, when he was in a similar position to yourself, he decided on drowning. With a little encouragement, of course. In fact,' Mark Gelson uttered, aiming the blade carefully, 'he lived above a shop as well.' He cast his heavy eyes around the room. 'A nicer crack-den than this though. Must have been getting more money from the cops.' He flicked his wrist and the blade somersaulted in the air, pounding handle-first into the wall, this time fractionally to the right. Mark whistled. 'Getting closer,' he said, smiling. Carlton screamed through his wedged teeth, his cheeks bellowing like a trumpet player's. 'Now I think about it, Jonno really put up a fight. I had to slice him up fairly bad before he'd give me the names of the CID he'd been dealing with.' Mark steadied himself, sighting down the blade. 'I'm aiming for your middle finger, number three,' he explained. 'Shooting. Or, if it catches your index finger, poisoning would also be good. Got some very interesting pills. Ten of those and your heart will fucking explode.' He threw again, and the knife sliced into the outside of Carlton's thumb. 'Well, well,' he said as Carlton shook, shrieked and fought, 'stabbing. Who'd have thought? My favourite!' He eyed the knife, which was embedded in the wall. A thin trickle of red leaked from the point where the blade had cut into Carlton's digit, and mingled with thicker fluid from his palm.

Every job had its conventions. Rule number two, Mark Gelson reflected, walking over and pulling the knife out of the plaster, was that the more brutal you were, the less trouble you had in the long run. He felt the heavy weight of the implement in his hand. Slowly shaking his head and smiling, Mark Gelson stooped to face Carlton. 'Now, before you give me the name of your contacts in the CID, and before you die,' he said, ripping Carlton's shirt open, 'let's see how sharp this thing is.' He ran the blade down, from nipple to navel, slicing a narrow cut into the dark skin. Carlton bawled in blind panic. 'Who was that?' Mark asked. 'I didn't get the name. You'll have to try harder with that tennis ball. Inspector who?' He gouged another rut into his victim, this time a little deeper. 'You're not going to tell me? That's fine.' He examined the blade and grinned. 'Let's play some more.'

A few hours later, Mark Gelson left the flat, satisfied. He had the next name on his list.

4

DCI Philip Kemp tried to take in the sheer physical bulk of Commander Robert Abner all at one go. Standing squarely between Sarah and himself, the Area Commander loomed over them, forcing Phil to bend his neck to observe him fully. The angularity of his black uniform, with its squared shoulders and pressed creases, lent him the air of granite, solid and immovable, an ominous outcrop reaching up to the sky.

'What, specifically,' Phil asked, 'do you want to know, sir?'

Robert Abner was an impassive and thorough man, used to getting his own way. 'Let me see what you're doing.'

Phil glanced at Sarah, who stared back. The unannounced arrival of Commander Abner had caught them both off guard.

'Well . . .' Sarah began.

'I want you to walk me through your investigation.' He turned smartly and began to stride out of Sarah's office. 'Literally.'

'OK.' Phil nodded. 'Let's start in the labs.' Phil put his arm out to guide Commander Abner in the right direction, and they set off along a carpeted corridor and down a set of bare concrete stairs.

'I need to know two things. First, what you're up to. And second, what I can do to help.'

Sarah and Phil stopped outside a heavy white door marked

'Lab 108'. Sarah cleared her throat. 'You could leave the forensics in-house, sir, but help us with external matters.'

'Such as?'

'We're tracking a few people. The Korean gang, Kieran Hobbs, a couple of others. But we need to focus closer to home.'

'I'll see what I can do.'

'So this is the first of the two large forensic labs,' Sarah said.

'Previously overseen by Dr Reuben Maitland, right?'

'I'm currently running them, sir,' Phil interjected, immediately cursing the eagerness in his voice. Robert Abner unnerved him, made him feel like a child again, desperate for the attention of his stern father. Phil silently told himself to calm down. Poker face.

The trio entered, accompanied by a faint whoosh as the negative pressure of the lab's atmosphere fought to equilibrate itself with the air outside. Inside, Bernie Harrison and Mina Ali were sharing quiet, serious words, hunched over an ultraviolet lamp. They straightened as they noticed their guests, and gave glancing acknowledgements. Behind them, Judith Meadows was solemnly swirling a boiling flask of agarose. To the left, Birgit Kasper traced a gloved finger down the screen of a VDU, following a vertical pattern of red and green bands. Two technicians filled a series of Eppendorf tubes with the same deep-blue solution. In the far corner, Jez Hethrington-Andrews tapped names and numbers from a sheet of paper into a database.

'So where are we with the pure forensics?' Commander Abner asked.

'Still playing catch-up, sir. Working back through Run's system, which appears a little unorthodox, to say the least.' Sarah puffed out her pale cheeks. 'Trying to find out exactly what he knew.'

'And exactly what did he know?'

'We think he'd extracted pure DNA from several sites on Sandra's torso, all of which were identical, ruling out the involvement of more than one person. Bernie and Mina are double-checking from the original samples that Run hadn't made any errors. Birgit' – Phil nodded in her direction – 'is proceeding with the notion that Run's new methodologies were correct, and she's busy profiling. We'll have that in . . .'

Birgit didn't turn from her monitor. 'Four hours.'

'And then we can start plugging it through the National Forensic Database. Jez is currently inputting what data we have, and setting up the search parameters.'

'Good. And Run himself?'

'Judith is beginning the preliminary sample preps. Run should be a bit quicker because we're starting from scratch, and not having to work back through someone else's . . . well, Run's . . . own system.'

Commander Abner tapped his black shoe against the white laboratory floor and frowned. 'No one say the word *ironic*. So what other lines do you have?'

'Let's check the second lab.'

Robert Abner followed Phil and Sarah through into the adjacent laboratory, where Paul Mackay was peering into the twin eyepieces of a stereoscopic microscope.

'Dr Mackay is overseeing gross samples – hairs, fibres, fingerprints and blood groups.'

Paul Mackay glanced up, his eyes struggling for a second to focus. Next to him, a technician held a row of slides on a metal tray. He removed the slide he was examining and swapped it for one in the technician's hand.

'We're fairly low on hairs and fibres. Also, no fingerprints whatsoever.'

'So despite the physical struggles, the killer was careful.'

'Appears that way,' Sarah answered, 'although we do have plenty of blood and saliva.' She shrugged sadly and glanced around the antiseptic brightness of the room, finding little comfort. Scientists and technicians inched through intricate protocols, subdued and mechanical. 'Look, why don't we head into some of the Operations Rooms.'

The three officers left the lab and headed down a long corridor populated by wood-effect office doors. Vinyl tiling gave way to a thin blue carpet, and the doors changed from wood-effect to actual wood. Phil Kemp stopped in front of one, knocked sharply and entered. Two CID officers and a couple of support staff were crowded around a large, flat-screen TV, and another pair of detectives gazed intently into a computer monitor.

'Helen,' Sarah said, 'have you got a moment? Would you care to tell Commander Abner what line of investigation you're following?'

Helen Alders, a slim, boyish CID officer in an ironed blouse and dark skirt, cleared her throat. 'Well, sir, we're tracing our four main suspects by working back through arrest records, previous addresses and known contacts. We're hammering the phone where possible, or actually going on site when we need to.' She pointed at the monitor. 'Which is easier said than done for some of the suspects.'

'Right.'

Sarah turned her attention to an officer watching high-resolution black-and-white images on the television screen. 'And Callum?'

Callum Samuels looked over from the TV screen, thick glasses reflecting the light and obscuring his eyes for a second. 'Sir, what we're examining now are CCTV records from the streets surrounding Run's and Sandra's houses, and attempting to match those with the most recent photo-identities we have for our suspects. And, more importantly, we're also looking for anyone who appears to have been at both scenes.'

'Any luck?'

'We've got over three hundred hours of footage.' The eyes disappeared again, as Detective Samuels swivelled his head from Phil to Sarah and back to the Commander. 'We've divided it up.

Two other officers are currently ploughing through their allocations.'

'How will you know if the three of you have witnessed the same punter?'

'We've developed a system, with help from IT support here. We digitize each adult male face we come across, and perform real-time match analysis.'

'Fine.' Commander Abner turned to Sarah and Phil. 'What else?'

Phil Kemp bit his bottom lip, thinking hard, eager to demonstrate that GeneCrime could run its own investigation. 'So that's Forensics and CID hard at it. We've got Pathology in the mortuary downstairs, mapping out the type of blade used, the pattern of bruises, whether the killer used latex gloves, or vinyl or rubber or whatever. We'll take the lift—'

Robert Abner held up his large right hand. 'Mortuaries give me the creeps,' he said. 'Let's walk and talk. Anything we've missed?'

Phil Kemp's short legs struggled to keep up with the long strides of the Commander, and he found himself almost jogging. 'In this office here' – he pointed to a door – 'we're collating witness statements from Sandra's and Run's locales, door-to-door reports, neighbours' testimonies.'

Commander Abner stared into the room through its small panel, breath from his nostrils steaming the glass. 'And?' he asked.

'It's taking time, sir,' Sarah answered. 'But it's fair to say nothing yet.'

'And just round the corner, in the Command Room, we've got two more CID and a couple of support staff trawling for previous evidence of torture use in the last ten years, liaising with ports and airports . . .'

Commander Abner stopped. He scowled down at Sarah Hirst and Phil Kemp. 'OK,' he sighed, straightening his tie. 'OK.' He scanned left and right. 'Exit's that way, isn't it?' he asked, nodding his head.

'Past the security desk, sir.'

'You're doing what needs to be done. I want you to keep me on top of things. I won't interfere unless you ask me.' Robert Abner craned his neck slightly down to emphasize his point. 'But end this, and quickly. I needn't spell out what it means to the two of you, and to the unit as a whole. Two staff dead in five days is no coincidence. Brace yourselves – I have a very bad feeling about this one.'

The Commander turned and strode towards the exit of the building, leaving Phil and Sarah standing silently together.

'What do you think?' Phil asked.

'Like the man says, we're doing what we can.'

'But it's taking time. Let's say Abner's right. Let's say this is just the beginning. We need something quick.'

Sarah stared down at the grainy floor tiles. 'You know,' she said, 'maybe there's another way. Something we haven't considered yet.'

5

Reuben edged down the narrow passageway that bisected a pair of smart suburban houses. As he turned a corner, his jacket scraped the rough brickwork. The light was fading. He checked his watch. Almost eight o'clock. Two thin parallel gardens stretched out behind the mirror-image houses, split by a weathered grey-brown fence. Reuben climbed on to a small outhouse and stared intently into the far garden. There were voices. The light was better here, streaming out of the patio doors and spilling on to the lawn. One of the voices was a child, the other a woman. The child stumbled around the garden, falling over, crawling, hauling itself up, moving off again. The woman vainly tried to steer the infant away from flowerbeds and other potential hazards. Reuben continued to monitor events closely, his face intent, glazed and mesmerized.

The infant screamed in the garden, and was picked up by its mother. A man appeared, wrapping an arm around them. Reuben scanned the location again, taking in a wider sweep. A row of terraces backed on to the gardens. One or two lights were on in frosted bathroom windows: the nation putting its children to bed. In another half an hour it would be dark. He felt the familiar mix of longing and excitement pulse through his body. His right leg trembled slightly, forced against a section of guttering, and he chewed his teeth restlessly. The man walked back into the house, and the mother kissed the infant's head. Reuben instantly summoned the memory of a smell. Sweet, cloying, fresh and melting. The scent of Joshua's hair. Towelling him dry after bathtime. He gazed down at the two of them. And then she caught sight of him. She started, hesitated, and gathered the toddler up, taking him inside. Reuben scrambled to the ground. He turned to run away but a voice stopped him.

'Reuben? Is that you?'

He stood, heart pounding, flushed with guilt.

'Reuben?' Lucy strode rapidly towards him. 'What the hell are you doing?'

'Nothing. I . . .'

'How did you get this address?'

'I'm sorry.'

'You've been following us?'

'No.' Reuben focused into the black surface of the floor. 'Look, it wasn't difficult to find Shaun's house. The phone directory . . .'

'But spying on us!' Lucy was swollen with anger. 'What you're doing is illegal.'

'I wasn't spying on you.'

'For Christ's sake.'

'I was watching Josh.'

'Same bloody thing.'

Reuben stared at his wife. Despite the animation of her rage, she looked tired. But the features were hard to gauge, worn smooth by too much scrutiny. When he looked at her, he didn't see the straight brown hair, the cool hazel eyes, the full lips, the slightly blunt nose, the delicate chin, the jutting cheekbones or the over-plucked eyebrows. He simply saw Lucy, the woman he had observed every day for a number of years, and then had stopped seeing. It was almost impossible for him to tell whether she was an attractive woman, because his reference point was too familiar to gain any perspective. But there was something there. Behind her, he could just make out Shaun Graves, now peering through the patio door, cradling Joshua, the one thing that truly mattered.

'But there's an exclusion order.'

'I don't see you calling the police.'

'Shaun might not be so generous.'

'I guess not.'

'And God, Reuben, you look terrible. What's happened to you?'

Reuben watched an expression of instant regret pass across Lucy's face. 'Do you need me to answer that?'

'I just meant' – Lucy's voice softened – 'what are you up to at the moment?'

'It's complicated. Very complicated.' Reuben scuffed his shoe along the ground.

'How?'

'When I was sacked, it was in a lot of people's interests. I know I fucked up, but it was almost like they wanted me gone.' Reuben appreciated that talking to Lucy came easily, a habit which he had been forced to do without. 'You remember – they even tried to promote me out of harm's way at one point.'

'So you're after your old job? Get a few people fired while you're at it?'

'I just want to know what the hell's been going on.'

'Very noble. As ever.' Lucy glanced behind her. 'Look, I think you should go.'

'Right.'

'And next time I will call them.' Lucy turned around and walked back into the garden, and then into the house.

Reuben was trembling. Not just from being discovered, but from seeing Lucy for the first time in months, and conversing with her like a normal human being. He realized that it had only taken two minutes with her to open up a multitude of suppressed feelings. He paced slowly down the narrow alleyway, cursing himself for the emotions that were erupting inside him, just through talking to Lucy and looking into her eyes.

The sharp trill of his phone cut deep into his turmoil. The call ended as soon as he said, 'Hello, Reuben Maitland.' He replaced the mobile and turned a corner. A man was standing in his way. He was tall and hooded, gripping a phone in one hand and a gun in the other.

'So, Reuben Maitland,' the man hissed, slotting his mobile away.

Reuben remained motionless, staring hard, transfixed by the face of the stranger, all thoughts of Lucy dismissed instantly.

'You have fucked with the wrong people.' The man grinned, two gold teeth winking in the gloom.

Reuben's adrenalin kicked in, hitting him like a sledgehammer. Fragments of thoughts, snatches of panic. The gun. A stranger. Cut off. Squeezed between walls. Being followed. The wrong people.

'Who?'

The smile. Pink, white, gold. Flashes of the next few minutes. Dark descending. Lying in the alleyway. Blood flowing and sticking. Forensics poking and prodding. Being *processed*. Lucy locking the back door. Joshua playing inside. Layers of brick away.

'Just people.'

Let the last thought be Joshua. The smell of his hair. The scent of his skin. The softness.

'Say goodbye to the planet.'

The aim changing. The trigger squeezing. The gunman sighting down the barrel. Reuben closed his eyes and a loud crack ricocheted through the alleyway.

6

There was a slow lingering movement. The gunman pitched towards Reuben and hit the ground. A hollow sound of skull against concrete echoed in the passage. Reuben's senses scrabbled for grip. Implications suddenly began to stick. Standing behind the fallen gunman was Shaun Graves, a baseball bat held erect in his two hands.

Reuben stared at Shaun Graves and Shaun Graves stared back.

'Fuck,' Reuben said.

Shaun was silent. He fingered the baseball bat, examining its surface as if only aware for the first time of the damage it could inflict.

Reuben dragged out the only word which felt right. 'Thanks.'

Shaun shook himself, catching up with what he had just done. 'The best way you can thank me is by leaving Lucy the fuck alone.'

'It's not that easy.'

'I think it is,' Shaun answered, peering down at the unconscious man on the ground. 'Now get the hell out of here, before this piece of shit comes to his senses, and I come to mine.'

Reuben took a last look at Shaun Graves, the man who was fucking his wife and fathering his child. The man who had just saved his life. He scraped past in the confined shade. And then he started to run. Reuben left the alleyway at full tilt and headed for his borrowed car. A large part of him wanted to turn round and return. But he swallowed his burning curiosity. He took his jacket off, appreciating that he was sweating. The consequences of the last few seconds were catching him up and overtaking him. He wiped some wetness away from the back of his neck.

His phone rang again. He examined the display, which said 'ID withheld'. Panting hard, Reuben reached Judith's car and jumped in. He drove off at speed, adrenals leaking fight, fright, flight into his blood. He watched the rear-view mirror. In the gloom he saw nothing more than the flashing of lights. Lives stopping, going and changing direction. Scenarios continued to intermingle in the headlights. His phone rang once again. He snapped it open and listened.

'Dr Maitland?'

Reuben knew the voice, but like the memory of a smell, it took a second to track down. 'Who is this?' he asked.

There was a pause. On-coming cars made him squint. He gripped the steering wheel hard, driving fast. 'It's Sarah Hirst.'

Reuben swerved into a bus stop, the engine running, the climate control freezing his perspiration, his heart thumping, his head full of too much information, his whole system about to crash. 'How did you get this number?'

'Called in a few favours. Took a lot of tracing.'

'What do you want?' he muttered.

'Just to see how you are bearing up.'

Letting go of the wheel, Reuben saw that his hands were shaking. They were oscillating like his life was oscillating: loving and hating Lucy; his existence threatened and saved in the same instant; walking in and out of trouble obliviously. 'Cut the crap.'

Sarah let out a long cold sigh. 'I've had an idea.'

'Why don't I like the sound of this?'

'Look, could we meet up?'

Reuben monitored himself in the mirror. He was pale. Shaun

Graves saving him. Warning him off, but saving him anyway. 'Why?'

'Maybe I could come to wherever it is you're working?'

'That wouldn't be possible.'

'OK, you name somewhere.'

'Look, Sarah. I'm not sure what you want from me. This isn't a good time.' The gun and the baseball bat. A stranger's blood leaking into the alleyway. 'Something weird has just—'

'You have to trust me.'

'Give me one reason why I should,' Reuben said, fighting to stay calm, unanswerable questions cramming into his head.

'OK, let me put it this way.' Sarah's magnified respiration ebbed and flowed through the speaker. 'This is important. Meet up with me, the old place on Basford Street. I have some information I need to give you.'

'Which is?'

'Something vital you need to know.'

'Come on, tell me.'

Sarah Hirst hung up, and Reuben slammed the steering wheel with the palm of his hand.

7

An hour later, and sure that he wasn't being followed, Reuben pulled up outside a dying pub. Inside, drinkers seemed to be mourning its ill health, slumped in their seats, smoking themselves breathless through deep rasping drags. He was cautious, aware that he was taking a risk being out in the open, but too wired to know what else to do.

DCI Sarah Hirst was sitting upright at a small table, holding a Coke in her long slender fingers, attracting undisguised admiration from the derelict clientele. She was wearing a dark trouser suit, and Reuben surmised that she had come straight from work. He headed for the bar and ordered a double vodka and ice. He was strung out and on edge, the need for an anaesthetic acute. As he sat down opposite Sarah, Reuben swirled his glass, watching the ice cubes climbing over each other, almost fighting to be free from the systemic poison.

Sarah stared long and hard into his eyes. The vodka warmth in his stomach mingled with a cold shot of nerves. She was too ambitious and too ruthless, he told himself, taking another sip. But there had once been a night, a night he often thought about, at a party, before he was married, when they were both drunk, when something had been said, something left hanging, something never repeated, something Reuben often wondered he might have imagined . . . Sarah's eyes bored into him, unsettling the ethanol haze. He scratched his face irritably. Today was happening too quickly, events slamming into each other and leaving him little time to think straight. 'So, come on, tell me . . .'

'There's been another murder.'

Reuben leant forwards in his seat. 'Who?'

'Bad news, I'm afraid. Someone you used to know. Run Zhang.'

'Shit.' Reuben's drinking arm stopped short of his lips. 'Run? You're joking.'

'I didn't want to tell you over the phone.'

'Fuck.' Reuben stared into the dull surface of the table. 'Fuck.' He was suddenly dizzy. 'Please no,' he muttered, steadying himself. Run Zhang. Fat, lazy and inimitable. Razor-sharp, from his hair to his clothes to his brain. He was a force of insatiable consumption, gorging himself on food and information alike. And now . . . Reuben started to feel something new, something not present in the shock which had greeted Sandra Bantam's death. He felt anger. A hardening of muscles, a clenching of sinews. Even his grey matter seemed to be tightening up, ready for violence.

'I'm sorry.'

Reuben blinked, breathing hard. 'Was he . . . was there evidence of torture?'

'I'm sorry,' Sarah repeated, 'I know you two used to be close.'

He remained quiet, scowling. He caught the eye of a drinker across the room, who quickly glanced away. Reuben had the urge to walk over and smack him. But he knew that his rage was just a reaction, a falsehood, an alibi to feel something, anything rather than the crushing pain that Run's death brought with it. He rubbed his eyes and said slowly, 'You don't know who the killer is.'

'No.' Sarah looked pale. For the first time, in the reflected light of a fruit machine, Reuben saw the hidden lines which creased with each frown. They were fine and delicate, easily covered with a layer of foundation, but appeared to have been deepening of late, burrowing their way into her skin.

'So I guess you've trawled through past convictions?'

'Phil's taking that side of the investigation.'

'How's he handling my old crew?' Reuben asked, almost absently, vivid and inebriated images from the Rainbow Restaurant swamping his consciousness.

'With all the dexterity of a fingerless man. I know you're old mates, but I think this case is finally getting to him. And to compensate, he's running round shouting orders at everyone, desperately trying to hold it all together.'

'Doesn't sound like Phil.'

'I dunno. Recently, he seems to have two settings. Cold or incandescent. Controlled or out of control.'

'I guess the murder of your staff would do that.'

'Yes, well . . .' Sarah answered coolly.

'So you're managing the team who suspect the killer isn't someone we already know?'

'In one. Yes.'

'And the forensics?'

'That's why I rang. I want to run something past you. Another alternative. A much more serious one.'

'What?'

'I hoped I wouldn't need to spell it out.'

'Perhaps you should.'

'That the killer may be someone who works at GeneCrime.' Sarah flicked her lashes at him. 'Or has worked at GeneCrime in the past.'

Reuben frowned at the implication. 'Like me?'

'Like you.'

He saw that Sarah was monitoring him, testing him, distracting him, but all the time digging. 'I won't dignify that. And what else?'

'Of course it could be someone outside GeneCrime.'

'Someone you've put away, who isn't that happy about it.'

'Or just some random punter with a grudge.'

Reuben played some more with his drink, watching the ice cubes succumbing to the odourless alcohol, being dragged down, eroding. His temperature was cooling off, and he didn't like what it left behind. 'Is that all you have?'

'More or less.'

'If you don't tell me, I can't help you.'

'OK. Two of your former employees have been torn apart. GeneCrime is under attack. These weren't coincidental attacks. Someone is actively coming for us. Look, we've kept a lot of this out of the press.' Sarah peered around the pub, and then shook her head quickly, trying to rid herself of the habit. It was difficult not to feel under surveillance even in a dingy pub. 'He's been sending us messages. Genetic messages using the triplet code. Three bases per letter.'

'Saying what?'

'Sandra's said, "Gene Crimes Will Be Repaid".'

'And Run's?' Reuben asked, eager to learn something that he didn't know already.

'"I am coming for GeneCrime".'

'Jesus. I'm beginning to see where I fit into this.'

'Whatever you think—'

'Look, Sarah. Let's cut to the chase. I see two motives for my summons here. First, you're wondering if I'm involved, and want to see my reaction. Second, you want to ask me to help, again to test my reaction, but also to see if I can make the difference, and hence further your own career.'

'Why, really, Dr Maitland,' Sarah said, instantly changing her expression, 'you do have a devious mind. Could get you into a lot of trouble.'

Reuben ignored her wide-open eyes. He pinched the bridge of his nose, watching the last frozen water liquefy. There was no alternative. Although he tried to suppress it, this was no longer a professional matter. It had just become intensely and painfully personal. 'It's OK,' he said quietly. 'I'm sold.' He swallowed the last of the drink, and thought briefly of amphetamine. He stretched the fingers of both hands wide, buried tendons twitching to the surface, hauling up taut ridges of skin, straining to be free. He ran his tongue around his gums, still numb with alcohol. 'I'll need the samples – I assume you've got unambiguous DNA?'

'From both, yeah. I'll bring it to you.'

'I've got a PO box – courier them there.' Reuben wrote down the details on a beer mat. 'Room temp will be fine.'

'OK.'

'Look, there's something you could do for me in return. I'm being followed.'

'How do you mean?'

'I don't know.' Reuben struggled to decide whether to tell Sarah about the man with the gun. He looked into her face, and saw composure in her foundation and concern in her lines. But he had never been sure. His trust in Sarah had been broken long before he left GeneCrime. 'Forget it,' he sighed.

'You sure?'

'Let's just say you owe me a favour. Deal?' Reuben held out his hand.

'A favour? Like what?'

'I don't know yet. But if I'm going to help you I want you to help me.'

Sarah sighed and shook his hand. 'Fine,' she answered quietly.

Reuben stood up. A few of the dedicated drinkers surveyed him for a couple of seconds, before returning to stare into their pints. 'And one more thing. I'm agreeing to help you on the basis that you don't tap my mobile, don't pass the number to anyone else, don't try to pinpoint my whereabouts. Our only contact is via the phone, or via my PO box. Any breach of this, and I withdraw my help. Is that clear?'

Sarah nodded, her blond hair bouncing in solemn confirmation.

Reuben turned round and left the pub. He held the image of her as he walked out towards the car. Remote, detached and sly. A career call-girl, ringing you up and offering you what you wanted, in return for her own payback. He had seen it before, Sarah chewing people up and spitting them out to make a case her own. Smiling before the act, evasive and uninterested after. Reuben shuddered in the heat, appreciating that her duplicity and ruthlessness somehow excited him. He reached the car and opened the door. Kieran Hobbs, the Hitch-Hiker investigation, the Edelstein rape, the McNamara murder . . . every other investigation would have to wait.

Someone was killing his friends. It was time to find out who.

8

Reuben left the image of Sandra Bantam that he had been
working on. Her face had been almost entirely restored. There
was a faultless serenity in her skin, her mouth had a faint
impression of mirth and her eyes were open and content. Old
habits died hard, and he still gained some solace from the
process. Soon, he would begin work on Run, painting some
dignity into his death. For the time being, though, his feelings
were too raw.

Moray Carnock closed the door behind him and skimmed a
package across the shiny lab bench like a drink along a bar.
It was plain, off-white and padded, addressed simply to Dr
Maitland at his post box number. Reuben squeezed it, feeling
plastic bubbles yield against the hard objects inside. He stretched
a pair of unpowdered nylon gloves over his hands, raising his
eyebrows at Moray, who shrugged in return. A train rumbled
overhead, vibrating Reuben's stool for several seconds. He used a
disposable scalpel to slit the envelope open, sawing gently into its
fish-belly. Two opaque tubes dropped out on to the bench,
somersaulting over each other, glad to be free. He slotted them
into a green rack. One was marked Run, the other Sandra. He
saw that they contained several tiny droplets spread around the
inside like condensation. Reuben pulsed them in a microfuge, and

the droplets duly collected in the bottom of each Eppendorf. Moray cleared his throat.

'This going to take long?'

'Twelve hours, if I don't sleep.'

'Is that twelve hours solid? Or do you get time off for being a good boy?'

'As soon as I've done the next step, I'm free for a while.' Reuben pipetted a small volume from each tube into a fresh Eppendorf.

'Only . . .'

'What?'

'I'm going to head off. See a man about a stolen dog.'

'There was one thing,' Reuben muttered, adding more clear fluid into the tubes.

'What?'

'Judith ran the tests from Xavier Trister, the nightclub owner with the bodyguards. You know – the one we tagged in the alley.'

'And what does your voodoo magic show us?'

'That Marie James is his biological daughter after all.'

Moray's eyes widened. 'Money well spent. She must be in for a share of his considerable loot.'

'I don't think she ever really cared about that. But we shall see.' Reuben glanced at his watch. It was 7 p.m., give or take, and he would work through the night. He removed the over-sized Dugena and rubbed his wrist. Judith had promised to help him finish the latter stages of the Predictive Phenotyping before her shift. Reuben took a longer look at his watch, licking his cracked lips. He flicked a thermal cycler on and began programming it. 'We said we'd have her answer today. Why don't we call round now, while this is running, and get it sorted?'

'Drop me off and you've got a deal.'

'You trust me with your car?'

'I don't trust anyone with my car. The heap of shit I'm renting at the moment though, do your worst.'

Reuben double-checked that everything was cooking, and left the lab with Moray. They picked their way through the broken building above and climbed into the rental car parked beneath a covered archway. Thirty minutes later, they neared their destination in Fulham. Reuben pulled into a side road which fed the main carriageway. They scanned the gold numbers on a blur of tired white terraces. When they reached the right house, Reuben parked London-style, half on the pavement, half intruding into the road. He passed Moray the envelope.

'Inside is everything you should need. The results are explained, there's a photo of the screen images used to make the diagnosis, a picture of the profiles, a disk housing all the data, and the sequence of three variable regions of her father's DNA.'

'And what words should I use exactly?'

'Tell her that, for court evidence, we've provided hard copies of all our analyses. The sequence of the variable regions is virtually unique for each person, and will prove beyond reasonable doubt that the DNA we used came from her father. That's if he's daft enough to dispute the findings. Inform her that, essentially, the chances of Xavier Trister not being her father are in the billions.'

'As are his assets.'

'And make sure she gives you the rest of the cash first.'

Moray pulled a stupid face. 'Do I look like an idiot?'

Reuben smiled. 'Listen,' he said, 'don't be too long. I've got something I need to talk to you about.'

'What?'

'When you've finished with Marie.'

Moray hauled his frame out of the car and sauntered up to the front door, swinging the envelope between finger and thumb. Reuben watched him enter as the door opened. He drummed the steering wheel. Paternity. The single duplicity which gnawed at his fingernails and ground at his teeth.

Of course, he had the very tools at his disposal. Reuben calculated that it would take roughly twenty-four hours to do. At any moment, he was only one day away from answering the biggest question in his life. An unequivocal resolution. Joshua: my son, or not my son. After all, he had a sample of Joshua's DNA, which he carried with him, slotting into hotel safes when necessary. It would be easy. A simple match against his own genetic material. And bingo. Paternity or no paternity.

But Reuben knew he couldn't bring himself to do it yet. He had to hear the truth from Lucy first, before he sullied Joshua by prodding and poking at his DNA. Besides, the biggest question of his existence was also the biggest hope. In the not knowing lay a lifetime of dreams, desires and expectations. If he lost these, he lost everything. And he wasn't ready to risk losing the final remnant of his optimism. For the time being, then, this was about more than simple parentage. This was about possibility. In short, he reasoned, swallowing the hypocrisy, sometimes the best solution to a problem was to ignore the science behind it. And although it ate away at him, Reuben resolved to keep his thoughts elsewhere, to lose himself in other people's problems, in their endless streams of code, in screens of red, yellow, green and blue, in the hypnotic actions of human robotics.

But the paternity of Xavier Trister had been too good to pass up. The thrill of the chase had been too great. From the second Marie James had made contact with Moray, through the instant he had fired his SkinPunch, to the final comparison of father and daughter DNA, he had been hooked, alive and excited. He realized that the hunt for other people's truths had the welcome side effect of keeping him from his own reality.

Reuben glanced through the window, watching a lorry scrape along the narrowed gap his parking had created. But there was a danger in this. He was getting sucked in. Helping Kieran Hobbs, whose eyes he had never quite seen into. He was swimming in murky water, underwater with the underworld. Reuben gripped the wheel tight. It's OK, he told himself. I'm doing this for the right reasons. One criminal, that's all. But even unsaid, the words were unconvincing. And as he continued to balance the pros and cons, an idea came to Reuben, a way to square his moral dilemma. He spent a number of minutes working through the potentials and the pitfalls, probing for weaknesses, calculating how he could carry it off. Slowly and gradually, smoothing his fingers over the polished dashboard, he came round to the unthinkable. That working for Kieran Hobbs could actually be a good thing.

But presently, even this thin sliver of hope started to drown under the seeping aftermath of delayed, shocked flashes of Run Zhang, snapshots his retinas had taken when Run was still alive, going about his business with lugubrious good humour, waddling around the laboratory, adjusting to the culture and making it his own, short-cutting to answers before most of the group had considered the question. Reuben realized that, although he was sad and shaken about Sandra Bantam's murder, he was hurting about Run. An accident would have been upsetting enough. A murder would have been terrible. But a protracted torture . . . To have a friend die in horrific pain, persecuted, slowly and methodically destroyed, his body systematically ripped apart, this began to inflict its own wounds on Reuben. The torture had left Run's dying body and entered Reuben's, digging in deeper as the hours passed, stabbing into his stomach, piercing his heart, hacking at his brain. Sarah Hirst's spare descriptions ate away at his imagination, growing and multiplying until all he could see was a blood-red horror.

Reuben tried to force his thoughts elsewhere. With the clawing notion of mortality, his mind jumped suddenly to the two minutes his life had almost ended the previous day. What troubled him most was not the fact that someone had wanted him killed, but that someone was willing to save him. Shaun

Graves, he was well aware, didn't owe him any favours. Why, he wondered again, had he intervened?

Reuben chewed a fingernail, biting in too deep, taking some skin with it. He pictured the first of a series of machines running through its allotted task, heating and cooling the killer's DNA over and over again. Then would come the labelling, the hybridization, the washing, the eluting, the expression mapping, the algorithms scurrying through the early hours. And finally, a picture on a screen. A face staring out at him. The cold features of a psychopath. The eyes which had absorbed the final moments of Sandra's and Run's lives. The lips which had curled up in satisfaction. The cheeks which had flushed with the thrill. Reuben tried to ready himself for the dawn, when he would meet the man who was killing his colleagues.

A movement outside brought him round. Moray was padding down the steps towards the car. Reuben straightened in his seat. It was going to be a long night.

'Piece of cake,' Moray said as he squeezed his inflated form into the passenger compartment.

'How did she react?'

'Like she knew already.'

'And the money?'

Moray patted his shabby jacket and grinned. Despite the heat of the summer, Reuben had never seen Moray dressed either smartly or with due regard to temperature. He seemed to have adopted a casual uniform of scruffy indifference at some point, and doggedly stuck to it. They pulled off the pavement and began to thread their way to Moray's flat. Reuben didn't know where Moray lived, but followed his instructions. He had the impression that he would never discover the exact address or location. As they became mired in traffic trying to funnel itself through a junction, he started to tell Moray about the events of the previous day. Something else was bugging him.

'OK, so a man I've never seen points a gun at my head. But how could someone have tracked me down in the first place? I thought I was invisible. No bank accounts, no registered address, no car, no nothing. Anonymous hotels, everything paid in cash. This was the whole point. Underground and immune. Not even the force knows where I am. Or at least I didn't think so.'

Moray rubbed his double chin with weary indifference. 'No one is invisible,' he growled. 'You got a mobile: you got a way of being pinpointed. Talk to the right people and they could track your progress down this very street even when you're not using the phone. Besides, you were probably followed, maybe for several days. Which is not the exclusive domain of the cops.'

'I guess. But who's coming for me? I don't remember having any enemies before.'

'It seems like you have now. And it seems like it's time for extra precautions.'

'Such as?'

'Siege mentality.' Moray shifted in his seat to face Reuben, his chubby knees scraping against the shiny plastic dashboard. 'I had this guy once. The last surviving member of a family who manufactured a well-known fizzy drink. Had sole access to the recipe. An American super-fucking-conglomerate had been trying to take over the company for two years. Think they had some sort of master plan for shutting him down and taking his rather large slice of the UK market. You know, aggressive bastards. This guy was being followed and harassed, which is when he contacted me. Completely freaked out. Didn't feel safe in his house, his car, anywhere. So we set him up with living quarters in the factory. Beefed up the security. Had a quiet word with the local constabulary. Sorted everything out for him.'

'What happened?'

'He didn't emerge for over four months. The Yanks were unable to track him without committing commercial trespass, at which point they could be arrested. They lost interest eventually and he got on with his life.'

'You're saying I should do the same?'

'The point is this. Out here' – Moray swept his arm in an arc which encompassed the windscreen and side windows – 'you're easy meat. You won't know you're being followed until it's too late. And, while we're on the subject, hanging around the house of your ex-wife's boyfriend is fucking suicidal behaviour.'

Reuben was silent for a second. A car tried to lever its way in from the right. He steered slightly towards it, forcing the driver to stop sharply. With the horn piercing his ears he muttered, 'It's all I have left. To look. To snoop. It's all I'm allowed. They have a fucking exclusion order. I can't even touch him, hold him, kiss him. He's growing every day. Do you know how much an eleven-month-old grows every day?'

Moray shrugged, uninterested.

'One millimetre. If I don't see him for a week he's grown over half a centimetre. It eats me up. He's growing and dividing and learning and smiling and all without me. When I last held him he was half as big. It's like I'm stuck. For me, Joshua will always be that baby I fed and loved.'

Moray glossed over Reuben's outpouring. 'I'm just saying stop staying in hotels. Lie low. Only come out when it's safe. And in the meantime, I'll have a nose around, see what I can dig up. Someone always knows something.' Moray pointed through the screen at a bus stop. 'You can drop me there. I'll walk the rest.'

Reuben pulled over, lost in his thoughts. Moray walked across the road and disappeared into a shopping centre. Reuben pointed the car back towards the laboratory that was about to become his home. He worked through the processes which would unite him with the face of the GeneCrime killer. He called Judith, who promised to help out from around 6 a.m. He pictured Lucy, readying Joshua for bed, playing games in the bath, smiling with his smiles, squealing with his squeals. He saw Shaun Graves, running his fingers over the bloody baseball bat. He cursed himself for once again opening up to Moray. He focused on the tarmac in front of him and the concrete all around him. Mostly, though, Reuben found himself wondering what the face would look like. And, as he reached the industrial estate, whether the killer was someone he already knew.

9

Blur, tweak, adjust. Calculations and comparisons. Remap and reassess. Almost two thousand genes scanned, corrected and quantified. Colours drifting back and forth across spectra. Fluid features flowing and hardening. Vast directories of data plundered and assimilated. A 3D face coming to pixel life. Eyebrows sprouting, hair by hair. Ears germinating and budding. Teeth multiplying behind reddening lips. Irises coming into focus. Cheeks narrowing and widening, as if sucking air in and out. Eyelashes proliferating, growing longer, lightening and darkening. Nose narrowing and widening, beginning to push out of the screen. Jaws squaring and jowling, pulling the cheeks back and forth. The forehead stretching and receding, frontal lobes curling and uncurling.

Reuben glanced at Judith. She was mesmerized, the screen projecting its developing image across her pale features. The hard-drive of the computer flickered like a hummingbird, the algorithms smoothing and editing. The face started to become human, features sticking, adjustments increasingly subtle. Colours stabilized. The eyes, the hair, the chin. Reuben stared into the image, taking in the traits of the killer. In seconds, the picture would be complete.

The only sound above the whizzing computer was Judith's

breathing. The face crystallized. It went past photo-fit and entered the realms of Pheno-Fit. The image was photographic, holographic even. A face with texture, depth and definition, which could almost be touched. The PC stood silent, happy with the work which illuminated its VDU. In the bottom left corner, the Psycho-Fit appeared, summarized in red by three key characteristics. Obsessive behaviour. Individualism. Fierce intelligence. The physical and behavioural intermingled. Reuben was unable to take it in. Here was the man who was killing GeneCrime. Judith broke the silence.

'Fuck,' she whispered. 'You know what this means?'

'I have no idea,' Reuben muttered. He stared and stared, absorbing the cold eyes of the face. 'No idea at all.' Reuben tapped his forehead against the screen, provoking an angry burst of static. 'Except that things are much more fucked up than even I had imagined.'

GCACGATAGCTTACGGG
AATCTAG**SIX**GGTTTCCG
GCTAATCGTCATAACAT

1

Jimmy Dunst closed his pub till and scanned the floor. There, just in his line of view, was a baseball bat. He peered over at the man in the corner and changed his mind. He walked to a private ground-floor room at the rear of the pub, an unsettling sharpness of odours from the toilets mingling with his growing nervousness. Jimmy Dunst locked the door, paced over to the phone and pulled a betting slip out of his pocket. In the corner was a number, which he dialled hurriedly, punching the buttons with badly chewed fingers. As he listened to the ring tone, he watched the door. Even though he had locked himself in, Jimmy was careful to speak quietly.

'Is that Detective Chief Inspector Kemp?' he said as his call was answered. 'This is Jimmy Dunst, landlord of the Lamb and Flag, Streatham. You asked me to ring. He's here. Yes. I recognized him straightaway. No, I don't think so. Long black coat, brown shoes.' The barman shuffled uneasily on his feet. 'OK. I'll look out for you.'

The barman replaced the receiver and thought for a second. Twenty years of pub work had taught him not to rely on the police arriving at the right second. He reached behind a sofa which was lined up facing an oversized TV. Pulling out a First World War bayonet, Jimmy unsheathed it and examined the short, brutal blade. He saw his stubbled mouth reflected in its polished form, and noted the confidence the weapon inspired. The fucker had chosen the wrong pub to come back to. He would just have time before the police arrived. A life for a life. That was justice. And now he had the chance to do what he had wanted to do for almost a decade. The barman carefully tucked the small weapon into the belt at the back of his jeans, unlocked the door and returned to the lounge. The man was still sitting at the table, running his eyes around the room, coldly absorbing all of its features.

'Another, is it?' Jimmy said.

The man turned his eyes on him. The stare was harsh and intimidating. 'What?' he asked.

'Another drink?' Jimmy repeated.

The man ignored him, and continued to scan the nicotine walls, the smudged windows and the sullied carpet. Jimmy Dunst pulled him a pint, seeing the atrocity which had happened in this pub nine years ago. This, he said to himself, as the glass filled with dark liquid, was the moment. He topped the pint off, checked the bayonet behind his back and headed towards the man. His breathing was rapid and shallow, his stomach as fluid as the drink. Through the window, there was no sign of the police. The room was empty, too early even for hardened regulars. The man didn't look up as he put the glass down. Jimmy reached round for the knife and pulled it out in one movement.

'So you thought you'd come back?' he breathed, stabbing the blade forward, holding it millimetres from the man's face.

The man didn't react.

'Let you out, did they?'

The man remained silent, focusing into the carpet.

'I've seen some bottle in my time, but this . . .'

He still didn't look up.

'I'm talking to you,' Jimmy screamed, pushing the knife so that its tip touched the man's crooked nose. 'The police will be here soon.' The blade made a small indent. 'But not soon enough.'

'Put the knife down,' the man answered quietly.

'You don't give the fucking orders here. In fact you don't fucking come back here and expect to live.' Jimmy lowered the blade, tracing along the silhouette of the man's face, until it plunged off his chin and dug into his neck. A small red line appeared, where it had bitten into the skin.

'Put the knife down,' the man repeated, staring straight ahead.

'In this very fucking room. You animal.'

'I won't ask you again.'

Jimmy stifled a laugh and then felt a sudden surge of anger. He retracted the blade a fraction and stabbed it into the man's neck. Except that as he did so, the wrought-iron table lifted instantaneously, crashing into his elbows and forcing the knife up and away. A second later and a vice-like grip had torn the bayonet from his hands. He felt his hair rip as his face smashed into an adjacent table. As his lungs fought to breathe, he inhaled the stale powder of an overflowing ashtray, and felt a thin film of decaying beer under his cheek. Jimmy fought to see the man, but he was behind him, pinning him down. The grip was as heavy and solid as the table. Seconds passed. Jimmy strained his ears. He heard the rumble and whoosh of traffic. He willed a car to stop, the police to rush out, DCI Kemp to take the man down. Then his hair began to tear in a different direction, pulling his face up to its normal elevation, his chin pushed into the table, his eyes running across its surface. Jimmy's bowels fought to push their cold liquid out of him, and his legs shook uncontrollably. Then the man spoke.

'Lick it up,' he said.

A stain of beer had half dried into the varnished wood and mingled with ash and dust. Jimmy felt sick. He yearned to scream. But instead, self-preservation kicked in. Through his half-closed teeth his tongue snaked out as far as it would go. The surface was cold and sticky. He licked back and forth, tasting the bitterness.

'More,' the man whispered.

Jimmy poked his tongue as far as he could. He urged the police to kick through the door, told himself he was simply playing for time, refused to believe he was utterly terrified, tried not to see the events of that fateful night. Then the man pushed down on his head, forcing his jaw further into the table, making his teeth cut into his tongue. Jimmy tried to retract it, to no avail. He watched the man, still crushing his head, swivel round to face him.

'I asked you to drop the knife,' he said quietly. 'And I also hoped you wouldn't call the police.' He lifted the bayonet up for him to inspect, but Jimmy was transfixed by the face in front of him. The cold black pupils seemed to be sucking in his discomfort, the mouth distorted by a mix of anticipation and violence.

The man holding the knife felt himself swell. His mouth flooded with saliva and he pulled in deep, wet breaths. A rush of energy made him tingle, all the way down to the tip of his glans. It was in these moments that he was alive, truly alive, in the way that animals in the kill are alive. He saw the purity of pain, the cock-tensing pleasure of watching another being experience the power of his rage. His torso stiffened, his stomach flattened and his toes curled. He recognized in himself a leonine power and a desire for flesh. He understood that he was his father's son. In these instants of mania, of bloodlust, this fact only served to make him stronger. He licked the bayonet, slowly running his tongue along its under-surface, and pictured steel penetrating meat, again and again. The metallic essence lingered in the back of his throat. He reached the point, and pressed it into his lip. When he was this excited, he was immune to hurt. He pushed until it breached the skin, a warm trickle of red running down his face. The man monitored the effect this had on his captive, and experienced a fresh rush of excitement. He pictured the times he had been in the barman's place, almost wanting to be wounded himself, just to feel the smart of fresh agony as his father laid into him. He began to visualize the possibilities, his eyes watering, daydreaming about what he might do. He pictured deep, sawing cuts, sneaking glimpses of bones and intestines, repeated lacerations, the ebbing away of one existence as another grew in strength. And then, spiking through his sweet stupor came the sour prick of a siren. His eyes blinked rapidly, flicking through options. He scanned the room, tensing his solid frame, ready. He looked down at his prisoner. And, having lingered as long as he safely could, he brought the knife down hard.

For Jimmy Dunst, there was a second of nothingness. His brain frantically tried to calculate what was wrong. He stood outside himself, surveying his body, finding what the problem was, knowing only that pain was on its way. A numbness, which leaked into an ache, which grew colder and sharper, and pierced his consciousness, until the agony was all he could feel. There was the squeal of hard-braking tyres. With his peripheral vision he saw DCI Kemp burst in through the door, but something was in his line of sight. Phil shouted at him, but Jimmy was unable to answer. The words started in his throat but got no further. He began to scream.

'Where the fuck is he?' Phil yelled, scanning the bar wildly. He saw three potential exits that led into the back yard or directly into the street. He turned to his deputy. 'Call an ambulance. The rest of you, round the back. I'll watch the front. He can't be far. Christ. Someone help him.'

Jimmy continued to scream, but it was strangled. He started to see the problem, and it scared the shit out of him. Phil Kemp put a hand on his shoulder. 'You're sure it was him?' he asked, surveying the bayonet and knowing already that it was.

The barman shrieked and cried as fresh agonies spasmed through his tongue.

'You're sure it was him?' Phil asked again. He listened to the scurry of boots across the wooden floor, the slamming of doors, the muffled shouts. Phil knew that if they were going to catch him, they would have done so by now.

Jimmy gripped the table, watching his blood leak across the surface he had just cleaned. Phil hovered, putting his fingers close to the handle of the bayonet, and then taking them away again. 'Fuck,' he repeated. 'Fuck. In this pub of all places.' As the barman continued to scream, Phil closed his eyes tight and rubbed his face. 'In this fucking pub,' he repeated, 'in this fucking pub.' A shocked WPC approached and glanced cautiously at DCI Kemp.

'He seems to have got away, sir,' she said.

Phil glared at her, knowing they had missed him by seconds. 'Bag the handle,' he ordered, 'and then pull the fucker out.'

The WPC peered dubiously at the bayonet impaling the barman's tongue, which was firmly wedged into the table. 'Are you sure?' she asked.

Phil shot the WPC and the barman murderous looks. 'Just do it,' he said.

Jimmy Dunst closed his eyes and swallowed a mouthful of blood. He sensed the blade move sideways as the WPC took hold of it. He screwed up his eyes, ready. This was going to hurt.

2

'So, are you going to ring Sarah Hirst, or shall I?' Reuben asked, tension straining his voice.

Judith Meadows held up her hand.

'I mean, the sooner we get the information to GeneCrime . . .'

'Wait. Patience. We need to be certain first.' Judith always needed to be certain. Sometimes when the obvious was staring at her, too many years of scientific rigour refused to believe it. Judith's instinct was often overwhelmed by her training. The attitude that something wasn't definite until all other avenues have been investigated was characteristic of the Forensic Service. There was even a term for it: disproving hypotheses. Judith spent a frustratingly large amount of her time disproving hypotheses. It was, she felt, a crushingly pessimistic way to live, but it had taken root, and now ensnared all of her thought processes. 'Look, let's double-check before we do anything hasty.' She stepped back a pace and ran her eyes repeatedly across the projected face.

'And?' Reuben asked irritably. He hadn't slept for twenty-four hours. And now this.

'Stop talking. I'm just making a hundred per cent sure.'

'Come on. You know it and I know it.'

'A few more seconds, that's all.' Judith continued to peer at the Pheno-Fit of the killer. Although she knew the answer, and had done from the second the Predictive Phenotyping crystallized, there was another potential conclusion, one she was sure Reuben hadn't spotted. 'OK,' she said, 'I reckon we can be certain.'

Reuben slumped on a lab stool. This was a head-fuck. His fatigued brain circled and circled around the truth, never quite landing on it. He wanted Judith to leave so that he could sleep. He would worry about the consequences later. She had other ideas, however.

'I just don't understand,' she muttered, half to herself.

Reuben watched her go through the mental gymnastics, wondering if he would detect a change in her body language. Surely one of the strongest possibilities would occur to her, and frighten her. Judith pulled a strand of hair away from her mouth. She walked back and forth, occasionally stopping and tapping her right foot rapidly. After a couple of minutes, she said, 'I see five options.'

'Which are?'

'One. You contaminated the samples with your own genetic material.'

'Unlikely.'

'Two. Your Predictive Phenotyping is bollocks.'

Reuben shrugged. 'Three?'

'You have accidentally been sent the wrong samples.'

'No way of knowing. But it's doubtful.'

'Four. You are a cold-hearted murderer with a grudge against forensic scientists, bumping your ex-colleagues off one by one . . . In which case I should leave.' Judith squinted at Reuben, who felt a flood of affection. In this moment he wanted to lunge forwards and wrap his arms around her. Instead, he dragged his eyes away.

'And five?' he asked.

'It's not you.'

Reuben swivelled to examine the picture once again. It was there, down to the hair colour, the nose length, the chin cleft, the eyebrows . . . the lot. On the screen was an almost identical image of his face. The eyes were a little dark, the jaw on the jowled side and the earlobes too padded, but it was like staring into a virtual mirror. In fact, when Reuben had first looked at the visage, he wondered why it didn't move when he did. He was also disconcerted by the fact that the face appeared fresher than his own. Clearly, he had quickly reasoned, his phenotype had lived harder than his genotype had designed. But all of this was inconsequential compared to the real issue. His own technology predicted that he was the killer.

Judith's words struggled through the cacophony of his thoughts and finally made themselves heard. 'What do you mean?' he asked.

'It's not you on the screen.'

Reuben examined Judith's face for clues. 'So who else is it?'

'Someone who shares your DNA.'

Aaron. The single word crashed into Reuben's consciousness.

'I remember you telling me once that you have a brother. Whom you're not close to any more. Well, how alike are you?'

'Physically?'

'Yes.'

Reuben stared into the dull brickwork. He hadn't seen Aaron for nearly three years. 'Reasonably similar.'

'How similar?'

'He had the brains and I had the looks . . .'

'But could this be a picture of him?'

He glanced up, scanning the features hard, trying to see them differently. As he did, key fragments of his adolescence played themselves within his optic centres. He saw his brother happy, angry, indifferent, protective, destructive and unfathomable. Born only fifteen minutes before him but always a world apart. 'No,' he lied, 'Aaron and I are different.' Judith appeared slightly put out, and Reuben realized that she had been proud of her explanation. 'I'm sorry, Sherlock, I don't think it's him.'

'So where does that leave us?'

'Fuck knows.' Reuben was on the verge of exhaustion. He rubbed his face, the killer's face.

Judith swapped her shapeless lab coat for a tight cardigan which hugged her slender figure. For the first time, Reuben saw vulnerability in her. 'I'd better be making tracks.'

'Right.'

'Here, before I forget.' Judith passed him a small plastic tube. 'The dried-down sample.'

As Reuben took the Eppendorf, both sets of fingers lingered momentarily, skin brushing skin, a brief warmth in the contact, before he moved his hand.

'Judith . . .' Reuben looked into her eyes.

'Uh-uh?'

'You still believe in me?'

Judith stood facing him, pupils huge, not moving. He held back, longing for her, caught for a second, the warmth still in his fingers, yet knowing she was married, wondering whether his motive was simply loneliness. She stepped closer, her arms by her side, her eyes wide. 'Yes.'

'You sure?'

Slowly, she raised her arm and placed it on Reuben's shoulder. 'I always have been,' she said, still staring into him with the faintest of smiles. Reuben tingled. She moved her other hand. He paused, fighting it. Then he leant forwards and kissed her.

Instantly, they were in each other's mouths. Wet desperate kisses. Pulling at clothes. Grabbing at flesh. Lifting her on to the cold lab bench. Riding her skirt up. Opening her blouse, frantic and needy. Swiping away the clutter. Tubes and racks and tips cascading on to the floor. Sensing her yearning. Her abandoned, almost rough, touches. Widening her legs. Kissing her neck. Moving her knickers. Pushing into her. Hearing her sighs. Images of Lucy. Judith's eyes screwed shut. Her palms down on the lab bench. Pushing against him. Flashes of his wife. Judith getting louder. Sighs becoming moans. Neck arched, cheeks red, mouth open, fingers grabbing the edge of the bench. Reuben starting. The itch, the ache, the burning, the tightening. Eyes wide. Trying to escape Lucy. Pushing and pushing, teeth clenched, muscles spasming, time stopping . . . Breathing. Quiet. Holding her. Beginning to sense her discomfort. Stepping slowly back and hitching up his jeans. Silence. Deep, laboratory silence. Barely looking at each other. The hum of a train. Judith standing up and readjusting her skirt and cardigan.

'Are you OK?' Reuben began.

'I'd better go,' she answered, flushed and awkward.

'I just . . .'

Judith pecked him on the cheek. 'I know.' With an edgy smile, she made for the door.

'Judith . . .'

'I've really got to go,' she repeated. Judith left the lab and picked her way hurriedly out of the building.

Reuben stayed where he was, trying not to think about what had just happened. He blinked slowly, in a dream-like state. It had been almost automatic, two needy humans slaking their thirsts, rapid and unthinking. A few moments of pleasure after years of business. And then nothing. Judith leaving before he'd even got his breath back.

After a couple of quiet minutes, he walked back to the computer. However depressing, loneliness was at least simple. In a corner of the lab lay a mattress and a sleeping bag. Next to it, propped on a packing crate, the half-finished face of an oriental male. Reuben hesitated. Despite his exhaustion, a nervous energy tingled within him. He had two options, and he drummed his fingers as he worked through them. First, he could discard the evidence of the Predictive Phenotyping, and pretend the technique had failed. This would not solve the problem, however. Sarah Hirst would ask him to repeat it. Reuben scratched the back of his hand with three days' worth of stubble, and sighed Judith's name. The second option was tantamount to suicide. But, as he thought about it, the only alternative. He opened his email and typed a message.

sarah, attached the results of pp. ring me when youve
thought what this means

He deliberated over the words for a couple of seconds, then added,

think about the reason I have sent this to you

Reuben inserted the words 'dirty science' into the Subject box. He attached the Pheno-Fit picture, grimaced and pressed Send. He was tense and edgy, pacing slowly towards his make-shift bed alone. Tell the truth, he muttered to himself. Always tell the truth. No matter what the consequences. As he tossed and turned, urging his body to ignore the adrenalin pricking at his heart, his brother began to appear increasingly. Coming home in squad cars in the early hours as a teenager, his mother's exasperation, his father's drunken indifference, the solvents, the cannabis, the ecstasy, passing Reuben small wraps of amphetamine under the kitchen table, refusing to meet Reuben's eye at their father's funeral. The phrase which had marked him like a tattoo: Too clever for his own good. Reuben screwed his eyes and forced his breathing to slow. Too clever for his own good.

3

The new information arrived in Phil Kemp's office through the wires of his phone and into his red, spongy ear, courtesy of *Sun* reporter Colin Megson. What was significant was that it hadn't come via the usual routes. Even amongst the media frenzy for knowledge, any knowledge, the police usually got there first. Phil often wondered if there would be more newshounds than detectives soon. It was an increasingly close-run thing. And today was a case in point. The media knew before the police.

Megson played hard to get. Phil, who had taken the call languishing with his feet on the desk, straightened bit by bit until he was sitting bolt upright with his shoes pushing hard into the carpet. 'Cut to the chase,' he growled, on the verge of losing his temper.

The hack continued to play the situation for all it was worth. 'As I say, Chief Inspector, all in good time. But first, you have to help me. A few details of the other two. That's all.'

'Look, Megson, don't mess with me. I'm a bad enemy to have.'

'Easy, plod. I'm only trying to get my back scratched.'

'Besides, I'm going to know very soon.'

'Are you? You think someone's going to make the link? What, in twenty-four hours? A couple of days? Fine. But in the meantime, you have a psycho on the loose. Your funeral.' Megson chuckled, a dry laugh aimed to irritate as well as insinuate. 'Could be, anyway.'

DCI Kemp's voice tore through the reporter's cackle. 'You don't start talking to me now, and I mean fucking NOW, I'm going to send a couple of officers over . . .'

'Which will all take time. Now, a few details. You show me yours—'

'For fuck's sake!' Phil slammed his hand on his desk. 'I'm running a fucking murder investigation here, and I could do it a hell of a lot better without pricks like you.' He paused, letting his anger stabilize, picturing Colin Megson doodling on a piece of paper, waiting, knowing he had him by the balls. 'Look,' he began, softening, 'one titbit, and then you tell me, and no fucking about. Right?'

'I'm all ears.'

Phil sighed. 'He's leaving us clues, like he wants to be tracked down.'

'What kind?'

'Genetic clues – not in the normal sense – but code, which when translated spells out words.'

'Like it. The Boffin Butcher.'

'I'm not sure—'

'And what words might they be?'

'Taunts, threats. I'm coming to get you, sort of thing.'

'"You" being?'

'You, impersonal. Now, show me yours.'

'And where are these clues? On the bodies? At the scene?'

'Megson. Don't fuck me about. Tell me what you know.'

Colin Megson muttered something inaudible. 'OK,' he said. 'But I think you're holding out on me. Right. I got called to nose around. You know, the usual. Random murder – state of modern Britain – that sort of thing. Quarter-page editorial. Anyway, I asked one of the pigs – sorry, Inspector – *filth* at the scene, and they were clueless. Middle-aged man, middle class, attacked in his own middle terrace. They didn't have an occupation for him, so I dig around, and guess what?'

'What?'

'Forensic scientist. Lloyd Granger.'

'Granger? Doesn't ring any. Where did he work?'

'Small unit in South London. Recently privatized, specializing in, I think, something unpleasant which goes by the name of buccal swabs.'

Phil Kemp wrote the details hurriedly, a blue Biro pushing deep into his notepad. 'Go on.'

'There is more,' Megson exuded, 'if you're willing to play a bit more ball. Just give me a couple extra niceties to flesh the story out.'

'Colin?'

'Yes?'

'How offended would you be if I just put the phone down?' Phil replaced the receiver. 'I guess I'll never know,' he said quietly to himself. Picking up the phone again, he began to track the details of Lloyd Granger's recent demise, all the time thinking, wondering, puzzling, trying to decide what the death of another forensic scientist could mean, knowing that Granger wasn't one of his staff, hoping and praying that the killer had finally turned his attention away from GeneCrime.

The Metropolitan switchboards treated him to a variety of crackly silences and electronic approximations of classical works. As he moved closer and closer to the information he needed, the time spent on hold increased. Phil tapped the desk with his thumb. He had spoken to the duty sergeant at the South London station, the constable who had attended the scene of Lloyd Granger's death, the assistant to the pathologist who was due to examine the body later, a member of the SOCO team, a DCI overseeing serious crime in the area, as well as a number of middle-ranking officers who were putting a murder team together. Currently, he was waiting for an operator to connect him with a unit commander, to request special GeneCrime access. He hummed along to a keyboard mutilation of Handel's Water Music. The door opened, and he craned his neck, the lead wrapping around his forearm. It was Sarah Hirst.

'Holding,' he said by way of explanation. 'Sit down.'

Sarah lifted a pile of papers off the room's only spare chair. She was carrying a slim brown folder, which she placed carefully on her lap. 'We've got some progress.'

'Yeah? Me too. We've been able to rule out one of the suspects.'

'Who?'

'Jattinder Kumar.'

'How come?'

'Turns out that he died in an RTA a few months ago.'

'And you're sure?'

'As we can be.'

'And what about the rest? Your other three suspects?'

'Stephen Jacobs, ex-biology teacher and serial attacker . . . No. I'll keep holding, thank you . . . skipped his bail-house in May. Hasn't been seen since.'

Sarah fought the impulse to smile. 'And I understand you managed to lose Lars Besser.' Every time Phil fucked up, she edged closer to the overall command of GeneCrime.

Phil's eyes narrowed. 'Who told you?'

'It's common knowledge.'

'Fuckers.' Phil rubbed the right side of his face.

'Well?' Sarah asked, no longer holding back a grin. 'Did you lose him?'

'We wouldn't have, except a barman decided to make a hero of himself. Ended up with a fashionably pierced tongue.'

'You're sure it was him?'

'He hasn't been able to tell us much, as you might imagine. But he seems reasonably certain.' Phil Kemp shook his head, trying to suppress his anger, seeing the bayonet, feeling the after-presence in the smoky pub, averting his eyes from Sarah's self-satisfaction. 'And Mark Gelson' – he grimaced, changing the subject – 'some reported sightings. Plus, we think he's killed again. A former dealer of his – Carlton Morrison – found dead, badly cut up, evidence of torture.'

'Any genetic code?'

'Not that we've found yet. But the multiple lacerations apparently bear a lot of resemblance to those found on Run's torso. We're doing tests which will confirm either way. So we're a bit . . . He *is* definitely on duty today? I need to speak with him ASAP. OK . . . further forward. We can rule one of our four potentials out, two of them appear still active and one is missing in action.'

'But that's assuming it's someone we know.'

'Well, yes.' Phil nodded. 'And you're looking after the other explanation. So what have you got?'

'Something that will interest you a lot.' She began to unzip her slim leather folder. There was a loud knock at the door and two of DCI Kemp's CID team walked in. Sarah nodded at the officers and continued, 'I've got the results of the—'

Phil cut her off dead. 'Sarah, you might as well hear this at the same time. I've just learnt some fresh information, boys. A third murder. This time a low-ranking forensics officer called Lloyd Granger from south of the river. We don't know if it's connected yet, but I'm making some calls to seal the scene for us.' He waggled the phone to show he was on the case.

'Any torture, guv?' one of the stocky officers asked.

'Too early.'

'Anything else that might link it to Sandra or Run?'

'I'm still getting the prelims.'

'What branch of forensics was he?'

'Just routine batch-testing by the sounds.'

'And no affiliation with GeneCrime at all?'

'No. But you should get a team together, be ready to head over there as soon as we've got clearance. And ask around. See if anyone has ever heard of a Lloyd Granger. Sorry, Sarah, you were about to say . . .'

Sarah glared at the CID officers. It continued to rankle with her that she was treated as a lesser being on Phil's territory, her information of secondary importance, even though this news was the biggest news yet. 'Look, we either run this thing together or we don't.' Her face was flushed with quick-tempered anger. 'I'm warning you, DCI Kemp, don't try and make this case your own. And don't ever make the mistake of treating me as an inferior.'

The CID officers stared pointedly at the floor. Phil took a moment to answer. 'OK,' he said quietly. 'Now, what's your news?'

'Maybe later.'

'No, come on. I've shown you mine. Let's see yours.'

The three men stared expectantly at her. Sarah told herself to calm down. Lose your temper and you lose the argument. She held the zip fob between her fingers, unsure. This had to be dealt with carefully. 'I'll talk to you later. Privately.'

Phil Kemp's pale, jowly face came alive. 'This is a fucking murder investigation,' he barked. 'We don't have time for delicacies. People are dying. Now, if you've got something to say, for Christ's sake spit it out.'

Sarah hesitated for a second longer. Her opposite number, snapping terrier that he was, was right. She remembered the mantra from her training days. All information is good information. She opened her wallet file and carefully pulled out a piece of photographic paper. 'The results,' she said, 'of Predictive Phenotyping on DNA samples taken from Run and Sandra.' Phil took the paper from her. On it was a Pheno-Fit. He passed it in silence to the two CID men, one of whom whistled. Phil replaced the receiver of the phone and rocked back in his chair, fingers interlinked beneath his chin. No one said anything. Sarah retrieved the Pheno-Fit and slid it back into her case. She watched a scuffle of emotions enliven Phil's features. He was seeing the possibilities, fighting his loyalties, suppressing his subjectivity, peering through the myopia of friendship, linking everything together in a painful trudge towards a conclusion.

'I know this is upsetting,' she said, breaking the silence, 'but we have to consider him. I don't know why he would do this, or what his motives are. We can't ignore it, though. No matter whether you two are old friends or not.'

'Surely the very fact that Reuben sent us this goes a long way to proving his innocence.'

'Perhaps,' Sarah uttered. 'And yet . . .'

'But why else would he . . .'

'I don't know. Forget everything else and look at the facts. Let's be impartial about this. Run and Sandra knew their attacker. No sign of forced entry. The killer uses genetic codes. Reuben is sacked for misusing his powers.'

'Didn't he also take that phenotypic profiling thing with him?' one of the CID asked.

'Predictive Phenotyping,' Sarah corrected.

'Either way, ma'am, it stops us using it against him. You know, to check if he's the killer.'

'And Surveillance have recently seen him hanging out with the gangster Kieran Hobbs,' the other CID officer ventured.

'Really?'

'But Lloyd Granger? What's he got to do with it?' Phil asked.

Sarah picked at the skin surrounding a fingernail. 'I don't know. It may even be coincidental.'

'Guv, have we got a whereabouts for Dr Maitland?'

'Sarah? You've obviously been in touch with him.'

'No idea. Genuinely. Everything has been done through email or phone calls.'

'So he's in hiding?'

'Yes, but not necessarily because . . .'

Phil Kemp stood up. He was slightly unsteady. Sarah saw that he was rife with uncertainty. 'Get everyone together,' he in-structed the CID men. 'Meeting room in five minutes.' He tightened his tie and ran a hand through his hair. There was a sadness in his manner which told Sarah that he was considering the unthinkable. 'I'm afraid it looks like we've just got a new suspect,' he mumbled, heading towards the door.

4

As Judith watched Reuben pace the laboratory confines, she saw in him the first eruptions of the obsessive behaviour which had always simmered under the surface of his skin. It had been there in the twenty-four-hour stretches of work, the refusal to eat or sleep until all the evidence was gathered, the drive to quantify, to determine, to conclude, to know the truth. She wondered what he reminded her of. A trapped animal was close, but not right. He was in a restricted area of his own volition, able to escape whenever he wanted. No, she thought, pushing her arms into the familiar stiffness of her lab coat, this was a mental rather than physical restraint. And as with all matters of the brain, the results were etched on his face. He was haggard and unshaven, his eyes bloodshot. Clearly, the results of the Predictive Phenotyping had been festering away, refusing to leave the strip-lit room, ricocheting around the uneven walls, forcing Reuben to confront scenarios which eroded and disturbed.

Reuben finally noticed her, and stopped momentarily, a pale form against the dark brickwork, almost an inverse silhouette. He half smiled, aware that he had been observed, before rubbing his head self-consciously and walking over to her. 'So,' he said, in a manner that suggested he had no idea what to say.

'So, indeed,' Judith replied. They stood in silence. Despite what had happened in the same room fewer than twenty-four hours previously, Judith sensed a vast gulf between them. 'I can't do this,' she said.

'What?'

'Yesterday.'

'I thought you . . .'

'No. Just be silent and listen.' Judith paused, and Reuben noted the hesitation in her quiet beauty. 'Charlie and I have been having a few difficulties. Not really getting on. But that doesn't excuse . . .' Her eyes were wet, and she was trying not to cry. 'Look, I'm married, for Christ's sake. What I did yesterday was wrong. Very wrong. And I don't feel good about myself today.'

'It's OK.'

'No, it's not OK.'

'So what do we do?'

'We carry on. Work colleagues. Business as usual.' Judith dragged her moist eyes up from the floor. 'Listen, it's not about you, Reuben.'

'No?'

'This is about my marriage. Which I still happen to believe in.'

'It's fine. Honestly.' Reuben appreciated that the situation was less than ideal. In desperation and under enormous stress, they had crossed a line they shouldn't have. Even then, it had struck Reuben that he was unable to shut Lucy out of his mind. He was, he could see, still not ready. 'Sure you can face being in the lab?'

Judith sighed. 'It won't be easy. But yes. We're grown-ups. We'll manage.'

Reuben watched her, noting the cold distance in her voice, wondering how authentic it was. He was aware that he would soon be pushing her friendship and loyalty to its very edges, propelling her in a direction she didn't want to go. 'And what about today?'

'Not good,' she answered sullenly, blowing her nose on a tissue.

'We have to keep the work coming in, Jude. Otherwise all this' – Reuben swept his hand around the laboratory – 'has to go back to the shop. The sad reality is that without Kieran Hobbs's cash, we'll grind to a halt.'

'But surely there's a safer way?'

Reuben pulled his jacket off a chair and hunted around the room for the equipment he would need. 'If we don't do the bad things, we can't do the good things,' he answered. 'Now, you're clear about what we have to do?'

'Clear, yes. Convinced, no.'

'No?'

'It still seems too risky.'

Reuben shrugged. He was asking a lot, but tried not to let it show. 'You've known that all along, Judith.'

'There's a difference between knowing and doing. I'm sorry, Reuben, but sometimes this piggy-in-the-middle arrangement scares the hell out of me. Like I'm being torn in two.'

'Nature of the beast, I'm afraid.'

'But it's OK for you. I, on the other hand, still work for the police. One mistake and I'm out in Loserville. No offence.' Judith took three yellow tubes from a packet and closed their lids, being careful not to touch the inside of the caps with her gloved fingers. She placed them in a cigarette box, removed her gloves and lab coat, and handed the box to him. Reuben saw in her actions that she had made a decision. He prayed that nothing would go wrong.

'Just promise me we'll be sorted by lunch. My shift starts at two.'

'Promise,' Reuben said, slotting the box into his shirt pocket. 'And I also guarantee you'll come to no harm.'

Judith appeared less than convinced.

In the taxi, Judith began to rehearse her lines. They talked through the details. Reuben played with a slim roll of double-sided tape, thinking, working out the best way. He told her about the murder of Joey Salvason, the unproven charges against Maclyn Margulis, Kieran Hobbs's suspicions, the henchmen, the danger, escape plans if it all went wrong. Judith scrutinized Reuben out of the corner of her eye. He was animated and alive. This, she told herself, was what he lived for. She examined her fingers, knowing that in a few short minutes, in an atmosphere of menace, she would be holding hands with Reuben. Images of yesterday hunted her down again. Judith ran her palm over the surface of her jeans, pushing the moisture into the material, her wedding ring dragging along the surface.

As she monitored the passing streets, Judith wondered what the day would hold when her shift started, and felt the tension building already. She pictured her husband sitting in an office, his hair grey, his clothes grey, his words grey. Judith prayed to God that he never found out about Reuben. Catholic families weren't big on divorce. Looking up, she saw that they had arrived in Covent Garden. Fieldwork was what Reuben had called this. Judith appreciated that this was a benign term. They left the taxi and walked towards the bar. Reuben reached for her hand, hesitated a second and then squeezed it. She felt a tingle in her stomach, which she fought to suppress. His palm was wet, and this worried her. For an instant, she caught their reflection in a window, lovers walking together through the early lunchtime streets. As they approached the door, he turned to her and said, 'Let's do this.'

Judith swallowed hard. They were making their way to a table, threading through chairs, still tightly joined at the hand. As they had rehearsed, on the verge of sitting down, Reuben exclaimed and waved at two men sitting further back. They headed over, smiling brightly, surprise beaming out of their faces. 'Kieran, you old dog!' Reuben said. 'How the hell are you?'

Kieran Hobbs opened his gated eyelashes and stood up, smiling in return. 'David.' He grinned. 'Long time.'

'This is Annalie,' Reuben gestured, pulling Judith forwards.

'Kieran,' she effused, wrapping her arms around him and kissing him on both cheeks, 'David is telling me a lot about you.'

'So what are you up to these days?' Reuben asked.

'You know, a bit of this . . .' Kieran swivelled round, an awkward introduction looming. 'Sorry, this is Maclyn, a business associate of mine.'

Reuben stuck out his hand, and Maclyn Margulis reluctantly did the same. He was tanned and good-looking, with a square jaw and Roman nose. His hair was crow-black, his eyes swimming-pool blue. Over Maclyn's shoulder, Reuben noticed the presence of three well-built men, loitering at the back of the restaurant and paying close attention to proceedings. One of them stood up and began to approach. He was leaning forwards, walking slowly, threading through diners. Reuben edged nearer to Judith. Maclyn Margulis moved his head slightly and raised his hand. The minder stopped dead, turned reluctantly and made his way back to his associates. Reuben smiled obliviously at Maclyn Margulis. Broad daylight, in an upmarket restaurant, surrounded by his bouncers. This was one careful motherfucker. 'Hello, David,' Maclyn said in a tone which suggested goodbye. 'And Annalie.'

Judith bent down and kissed him stiffly on both cheeks, placing her hands on his shoulders.

'How's your mum these days, David?' Kieran asked Reuben.

'Oh, you know, soldiering on,' he answered.

Maclyn Margulis fidgeted in his chair. His men stared with a threatening mixture of contempt and hostility. On the other side of the restaurant Reuben noticed for the first time a couple of Kieran's gang. And, somewhere unseen, he wondered whether Metropolitan CID would also be paying close attention.

'Listen.' Kieran smiled. 'Let's catch up soon. I'm kind of in the middle of a business meeting here.'

Reuben tried to look disappointed. 'Oh right. I suppose we

ought to leave these gentlemen.' He wrapped his arm around Judith and gave her a peck on the cheek. 'Come on, honey, let's get something to eat.'

'You know, I've changed my mind. Shall we drink instead?'

He shrugged apologetically at Maclyn and Kieran. In his peripheral vision, both sets of minders continued to watch. 'Sure. I know a good pub. I'll give you a bell sometime, Kier.' They picked their way out of the restaurant and walked back towards the taxi, which was waiting around the corner. Thirty metres before it, Reuben caught a reflection in a shop window, his arm around Judith's waist. He let go of her, almost guiltily. And then he said, 'Walk past the cab.'

'Why?' Judith asked.

'We need a corner pub, and fast.'

Behind, one of Maclyn Margulis's minders was tracking their progress. Reuben checked again.

'Over there,' Judith nodded.

A Covent Garden pub decorated with flowers and drunks occupied the junction between two roads. Reuben and Judith entered, squinting in the dark. As he guided Judith through the lounge, he listened for the door opening again after them. Hearing nothing, he led Judith out of the rear door, which opened on to the adjacent street. Reuben waved briskly at a black cab, which squealed to a halt. They pulled away and he risked a glance back.

'Reuben, what the hell's going on?'

'Trouble,' he answered. Through the rear window, the minder had reappeared. He was writing down the registration number of the taxi.

'Shit,' Judith said, taking a small pair of tweezers out of her pocket and examining her right hand. Small dabs of double-sized tape were stuck to the ends of each finger. On them were a number of thick black hairs. Reuben passed her the cigarette packet, and she levered the hairs into the tubes inside. They were silent as the cab headed away, swallowed by the frantic gallop of traffic through the city. After a few minutes, Reuben told the driver to pull over. They climbed out and stopped a fresh taxi. Later, he asked, 'Do you think he twigged?'

'No. My fingers only brushed his collar for an instant.' Judith glanced at her boss's face, wondering what he had felt the previous day, and whether he had been happy to call it a mistake.

Reuben watched the digital meter tick in twenty-pence increments as they slid back and forth along the vinyl seats, the driver short-cutting through tangled streets no wider than alleyways. 'Look,' he said, 'should I drop you at work? Or thereabouts?'

Judith turned from the window and checked her watch. She had been lost in her own journey. 'I guess so,' she replied. 'Won't hurt to be a bit early, catch up with the state of play. Whatever that is. You never know, there might even have been a break-through.'

'Anything's possible.'

Reuben redirected the driver, who cursed under his breath before pulling a U turn. They spent the rest of the journey in silence. As she left the taxi, a couple of streets away from GeneCrime, Judith handed the cigarette box over to Reuben, saying, 'That's enough excitement for one day.'

Reuben grimaced. 'Goodbye,' he muttered as the driver pulled away, with the distinct feeling that the excitement was only just beginning.

5

DCI Phil Kemp stood close behind Jez Hethrington-Andrews, who was scrolling through a long list of computer records. Despite the efficiency of the air-conditioning, Jez still sensed a dank wetness emanating from his boss. His proximity was uncomfortable, breaching the safe gap that Jez liked to put between himself and other workers. Names and details flashed on the screen, and Jez opened folders and perused their contents. An awkward silence hung in the recirculated air, disturbed only by Phil's breathing and the double-clicking of Jez's mouse.

'So,' Phil said, waiting impatiently for the information he had requested, 'when's your brother out?'

'Not for another year,' Jez replied, staring deep into the screen and rubbing his dry eyes. The skin beneath was red and inflamed, deep bags which had been scratched almost raw over the last few harrowing days.

DCI Kemp cleared his throat. 'You do realize that could present us with a problem. Interpreting the rules strictly.'

'How, sir?'

'Immediate family with on-going criminal activity. There are guidelines about that sort of thing. I know Dr Maitland took you on, fully aware of your brother's record, but, technically, he shouldn't have done. And while your brother's incarcerated, the

242

situation has been, let's say, stable. But when he's back on the street there could be a conflict of interest, wouldn't you say?'

Jez partially turned in his seat, trying to read his boss's expression. 'I'm not sure . . .'

'Come on. A forensics information officer. A repeat offender. Suppose he does something more serious than B and E this time. At the very least your position of responsibility could compromise an investigation.'

'A bit unlikely, if you don't mind me saying, sir.' Jez dug a finger deep into the bag under one of his eyes, pushing it upwards until it seemed to press on to his eyeball. For a second, he lost himself in the dull ache of discomfort. 'I mean, I'm nowhere near the front line. And the chances of Davie committing a murder or rape or . . .'

Phil shrugged. 'Happens.'

'Look, he's not daft. He just got caught up in drugs. Davie is not exactly a career criminal.' Jez finally found the folder he had been seeking and pointed to it. 'That the one?'

'Yeah.'

'Besides, the last time I visited him he looked a lot better.' Jez shivered with the memory of the place, a cold recollection gripping his stomach. 'He says Belmarsh has sorted him out, made him determined never to go back.'

Phil snorted. 'That's what they all say. The universal junkie mantra. I'll never go back. I'm not who I used to be.' He leant over Jez's shoulder, his baggy white shirt brushing against the top of Jez's head. 'Can you bring all the picture files up at once?'

'If I display them as thumbnails.'

'But you and I both know the statistics on reoffending, and on returning to a former drug habit. Put the two together and it's dynamite. Tell me I'm being unfair?'

Jez ground his teeth hard and remained silent.

'There, that's the one,' Phil indicated, pointing at a small image. 'Just lighten it a fraction. And show me full screen.'

'OK?'

'Perfect.' Phil squinted for a moment to make sure. 'Yep, that's the one. No, I'm afraid we'll have to review your employment when your brother is released. Not my rules, I'm sure you understand. And for what it's worth, I feel bad about it. But there was a recent directive about this, and as part of my duty I have to take it seriously. Right. Let's have a colour print of that.'

Jez pressed the print icon, the movement of his mouse swift and irate. He stared into the screen, chewing his molars, pursing his lips, his heart beating faster than normal. Phil snatched the printed image from the printer and ran his eyes over it. 'So, my old friend Reuben' – he frowned – 'what the hell has happened to you?'

6

'Lloyd Granger,' Reuben whispered quietly to himself. 'What have I done?' The call came from Judith, who had gradually been brought up to speed with developments at the start of her shift. Reuben buried his face beneath his hands. He let out a long melancholic moan, which ground through the empty lab. 'You poor bastard.' Reuben inhaled deeply and blew the hot moist breath through his fingers. He moaned again, reclining from sitting on the bench to stretching out on it. Against his side he felt the warmth of a slab-like ABI 377 sequencer. On its screen, which nuzzled into his jeans, the DNA of Maclyn Margulis was being assembled base by base into technicolor barcodes, which unlicensed software would later decipher.

Since the restaurant, Reuben had spent three hours processing Maclyn Margulis. The menace of the bodyguard had lived with him as he DNA-extracted four black hairs and performed parallel sequencing reactions. While the machine carried blindly on, however, Judith's two pieces of news had stopped him dead. She had simply said, 'I've got some bad news and some badder news.'

'Give me the bad news,' he had answered.

'Another death. Have you ever heard of a Lloyd Granger?'

Reuben had tried to sound non-committal. 'I don't think so.'

'Low-level forensics at a privatized screening lab somewhere in

245

SE6. Possible evidence of torture.' Judith's voice was weary with shock. It said, Another one of us is dead and the trauma is too much to take in right now. 'Phil and Sarah aren't sure what to make of it. We're heading out there in the next few minutes.'

'Are you ringing from work?' Reuben had asked quietly.

'Yes. Why?'

'Keep the conversation short. And next time use your mobile.'

'Why?'

'Long story. Anyway, let me have a guess at the badder news.'

'Go on. But you're not going to—'

'A new suspect?'

Judith exhaled a long, depressed breath. 'Yes.'

'My good self?'

'Did someone warn you?'

'No need,' Reuben sighed. 'It doesn't take rocket science to know we're not dealing with rocket scientists.'

'But you know what this means?'

'I've got a few ideas.'

'You're going to have to be careful.'

'And so are you. Don't take this the wrong way, Jude, but don't say any more. Ring me on your mobile when you know what's going on. But for now, periscope down.'

Reuben had flipped his phone shut. Second by second he had reached the point where lying down on his lab bench seemed the only sensible course of action. And now a neon fatigue was burning into his closed eyelids. The hum of mechanized action was buzzing in his ears. A sickening certainty was beginning to ball itself tight in his stomach. The death of Lloyd Granger changed everything. Reuben realized with lethargic sorrow that he was the only person in the world who knew this. GeneCrime and CID had missed the whole point.

Reuben exhaled his creeping grief and yawned. Another torture. Long hours of helpless pain, of slipping in and out of consciousness, of watching your skin tear open, of seeing the knife enter slowly and deliberately, of feeling the cold metal burn through your flesh, of utter vulnerability, of wanting only to die. Reuben slept fitfully for a couple of hours, a depressed semi-consciousness haunted by pain and suffering. When he awoke, the face of Moray Carnock was peering down at him. Moray was munching a sandwich and swigging from a can of Pepsi. Up close, small dark hairs sprouted from the pores of his nose.

'Comfy?' he asked in his thick Aberdonian drawl.

Reuben propped himself up on his elbows. 'Like a bed of nails,' he said.

'You see, that's what happens with all this scientific mumbo-jumbo.' He took a colossal bite of his late lunch. 'Your perceptions get buggered about.'

'It's been a life-long problem.'

'So I take it you nailed Maclyn Margulis,' Moray guessed, sweeping his can of pop in the direction of the sequencer.

'Yeah. We'll know in a few hours whether Kieran Hobbs's hunch is right.' Reuben shook himself round, shrugging off the horror of Lloyd Granger's death, knowing that it would come right back and find him soon enough. But for now he wanted to be sharp. He needed to pick Moray's brain. 'It's just a bit weird.'

'How so?'

'We did the Predictive Phenotyping on DNA samples taken from Hobbs's second-in-command Joey Salvason. Only Hobbs didn't recognize the Pheno-Fit we gave him. But he was still convinced that Maclyn Margulis was behind the killing.'

'So?'

'So it doesn't add up. The Pheno-Fit suggests that Kieran Hobbs is wrong, and that his man was killed by person or persons unknown. Normally I'd recommend we use the suspect's ID to trawl through DNA and photographic databases, and nail him. But Hobbs wants this confirmatory test doing instead. It seems counter-intuitive. I mean, what do you really know about Kieran Hobbs?'

Moray drained his drink, his thick throat bobbing as he glugged the final remnants. 'I only know what you know. Big crime boss, really nasty, a lot of clout in this end of town, loyal to his men. But as for a hidden agenda, who knows? You said that CID were interested.'

'Run told me they were stepping things up. But I guess they've got other priorities at the moment.'

'And, of course, there could be major issues between Kieran and Maclyn Margulis.'

'Which is what scares me.'

'That, my friend, is the danger of providing the service you're providing. Suggesting that someone is a killer can be taken a little personally.'

'I've had an idea on that subject.'

'What?'

'About how to settle a few scores. Forensics aren't ready to nail Kieran Hobbs yet. But I could help.'

'Why don't I like the sound of this?'

'Look, I'm in a unique position. CID can't get close to him, but I can. When Hobbs has paid up, well, let's just say that all bets are off.'

Moray looked extremely unimpressed. 'Don't do anything daft.'

'I'm doing this for me, Moray. My career has been about catching criminals. That's who I am, and that's what I do.'

'These aren't the sort of people to fuck with. You're in deep enough as it is.'

'Talking of which.'

'What?'

'Have a guess who the new number-one suspect in the murder of forensic scientists is?'

Moray arched his bushy eyebrows. 'And how did they make that genius leap?'

'Don't ask. But there's something else, something much worse.'

'Go on.'

Reuben swivelled round and hopped on to the floor. He paced the confines of the lab for a few seconds. Moray watched him intently. Reuben appeared to be psyching himself up. 'There's been a third death. A mediocre private forensics officer called Lloyd Granger.'

'You're kidding.'

'I wish I was.'

'Fuck.'

'This changes things. Before, with Run and Sandra, it was GeneCrime.'

'And now?'

Reuben turned to face Moray, burning into him. 'Now it's me.'

'Meaning?'

'Lloyd had no connection with GeneCrime. DCIs Kemp and Hirst don't know this, but Lloyd and I were friends. We met at a conference a few years back. He was . . .' Reuben's eyes watered and he turned away from Moray, forcing himself not to break down in front of him, sensing the ache in his mouth which he hadn't felt for just over four months. He clenched his teeth and drove his fingernails into his palms, realizing too much isolation and too little sleep was fucking with his composure. 'We had some shared interests. He painted as well.' Reuben turned back to Moray, his face emotionless. 'We used to get together occasionally at weekends. Or he'd come round to my place. You know, every few weeks. We'd stay up all night just painting, trying to get the perfect lips, or nose, or whatever . . .' Despite his best efforts, Reuben's eyes were filmed with the evidence of sad nostalgia. 'He only ever met one or two of the GeneCrime crew, and that was through me. So this changes the whole scenario. The killer isn't after GeneCrime at all.'

'No?'

'He's after me.'

Moray was quiet, allowing the words to settle. He appeared

249

unusually serious. Now that Reuben was still, he found he couldn't help but pace the same confined area, peering down at his shoes, scratching his brow. A piece of his sandwich had lodged between two teeth, and he worked at it with his tongue while he thought. A train juddered by overhead. 'OK, so you've got motive. They have strong forensic evidence against you. That's good enough for most courts. How about alibis?'

'You're acting like you think I'm guilty.'

'We have to think like they think. Where were you at the time of death of Sandra, Run and Lloyd?'

'Ah, you'll like this. Either in here by myself, or else . . .'

'Yes?'

'With you.'

'You're fucked.' Moray stopped and muttered, 'Shady slobs like myself aren't good alibi material. And, for reasons of professional survival, I would be extremely disinclined to help you out.'

'Thanks.'

'So, with strong motive, clear forensic evidence and no alibi . . .'

'What?'

'I'd stay the hell underground for now.' Moray drummed his fingers on the back of a lab stool. His greasy face scrutinized Reuben for a reaction. Reuben looked away. With trembling fingers he opened the sequencer and removed its heavy glass plates. As he prised the plates apart and scraped an almost invisible layer of acrylamide off their surface, Moray slid an envelope across the bench and left the lab. Reuben folded his stiff arms around himself. He squeezed tight, as if he could crush the fear which was beginning to cling to his insides. Someone was coming for him. Someone who had killed time and time again. Someone who wanted him torn apart.

7

The varied streets which encircled GeneCrime were just as he pictured them almost every day. GeneCrime's environs were alternately grubby, exclusive, commercial, residential, tired and new. When he left it had been May, and the first awakenings of summer. Now it was just September, and the sun was pounding down with fierce defiance. Reuben chose the exposed side of the road, sucking in the heat and light like an emerging butterfly. As he walked, he felt his shoulders push back, his arms stretch, his lips curl upwards, his body come to life. He had nearly forgotten how good summer could feel.

Reuben pulled a baseball cap from his rear pocket and slid a pair of sunglasses up the slippery bridge of his nose. GeneCrime was only a street away. He crossed the road and headed up an alleyway which housed a small restaurant. Inside, covered tables were each flanked by a pair of wooden chairs. On one of the chairs, at one of the tables, was sitting DCI Sarah Hirst. But he had to be careful. He scanned the alleyway, looking for plain-clothes, searching for watchful workmen, sensing a trap. Twenty metres from the door, Reuben spied a member of GeneCrime and stopped. He glanced quickly behind him, checking for an escape route, but didn't find one. The man headed directly towards him. Reuben hoped against hope that this was coincidence. The man appeared to notice him, and then not to. Reuben guessed that he hadn't been recognized behind his cap and glasses. Running his eyes up and down the road he made a judgement call. 'Jez,' he hissed.

The man turned his head and kept walking.

'Jez!' Reuben cried, a little louder, removing his sunglasses. 'It's me.'

Jez Hethrington-Andrews glanced nervously around, looked again, and came to a reluctant halt. 'Reuben,' he said quietly. 'Didn't see you.'

'Must have been the disguise.'

'Call that a disguise?' he mocked as Reuben pulled his cap a little lower.

'What were you expecting? Chin putty?'

'At the very least.' Jez stared past Reuben and scrutinized passers-by. 'Look . . . I don't know. I shouldn't be here. What are you doing so close to . . .'

'Meeting someone.'

'Right. Right.'

Reuben saw that Jez was uncomfortable. His usual playful state had been gnawed away. Reuben imagined that events at GeneCrime were picking apart even the more relaxed scientists. He seemed desperate to be somewhere else, and Reuben suddenly understood his conflict. 'Are you lot coming for me?' he asked.

'Yes,' Jez replied without emotion.

'When?'

'Soon.'

'Jez, whom can I trust?'

'No one.'

'Sarah?'

'No.'

'Phil?'

'No. No one.'

'No one at all?'

252

'Especially not Sarah or Phil. There's a lot of stuff going on which . . . I don't know, things have got fucked up. I can't talk to you about it. I wish I could. But I can't. I'm sorry. Very sorry. Look, it's best you aren't seen with me. I mean it. I have to go. Got to go somewhere.'

'But, Jez . . .'

'Reuben, let me just say this.' Jez was impassioned, his eyes wide, as if they had glimpsed a horror he could only half describe. 'Go and hide. Hide well. Stay there and don't come out. It's all you can do. You don't realize . . . You have no idea how much danger you're in. No idea at all.' Jez began walking. 'Go,' he implored. 'Hide. There are things . . .' He turned his head and carried on.

Reuben stood blinking in the sunlight. On one side was the restaurant where he was due to meet Sarah; on the other, Jez Hethrington-Andrews, scurrying away with something in his face that spoke bluntly to Reuben's adrenal glands. Jez's words echoed in the street. Trust no one. Especially not Sarah or Phil. He pictured Sarah handing his Pheno-Fit over to Phil Kemp, smiling, the fine lines of her eyes fanning out in satisfaction. Reuben stood still. He could see the restaurant door. At the end of the street it would only take a couple of minutes to hail a cab. The sunny side or the shady side. Stick or twist. Play it safe or gamble. Fuck it, he whispered under his breath. Reuben made a decision. He turned and walked.

8

Sarah was seated at a table in the basement of the restaurant. Reuben picked his way slowly and cautiously towards her, weighing up the other diners. He appreciated that his actions verged on the reckless, and acknowledged that his curiosity was a perpetual danger to him. For a second, he pictured Moray lecturing him between mouthfuls of food.

Sarah was unexpectedly pale, and he sensed that she was spending too much time inside, planted in front of her computer, facts and figures radiating from her monitor and bleaching her skin. Her sky-blue blouse was rolled up at the sleeves to reveal slender, hairless wrists. Reuben pulled out the chair opposite and sat down. Before he had time to speak, a waiter shuffled over and lit the candle which lay between them. Reuben glanced around the dingy subterranean room. Couples nuzzled together at small tables, leaning forwards, holding hands, wisps of candle smoke dancing in their words.

'Nice restaurant,' he said.

'Intimate,' Sarah replied.

Reuben ordered a drink, and muttered, 'I very nearly didn't come in.'

'So why did you?'

'I wanted to talk to you, face to face.'

'Well, here we are. Face to face.'

Reuben looked across at Sarah, who smiled back at him. It was a smile of utter control, and Reuben sensed that this was not going to be straightforward.

'Maybe you shouldn't have come,' she said.

'No?'

'No.' Sarah took a long, slow sip of her red wine. 'After all, you do know we're hunting you down?'

'So I hear.'

'See, the way I figure it, you're either very brave or very foolish.'

'Maybe I'm just a sucker for a free meal.'

'And Phil's finally starting to believe it is actually you.'

'Is he?'

'I'm working on him.'

'And what do *you* think?' Reuben asked, holding her gaze.

'That you're the killer.'

'What makes you so sure?'

'This and that. Come on, Reuben, you can tell me the truth. Unburden yourself.' Sarah's eyes sparkled with mischief. 'Get it out in the open.'

'If you're so certain, why not just arrest me?'

'What's to say I won't?'

'Because a deal's a deal. I agreed to help you, and you promised a favour in return. And now it's time to keep your word.'

'But you don't trust me, Reuben, do you? Never have.'

Reuben remained quiet, letting the silence answer for him.

'So what's the favour?'

'I'll come to that. But first I need to know what you know.'

'Confidential. Surely you understand that.'

'Otherwise I can't be any help.'

'Your best help would lie in not murdering anyone else.'

'Sometimes I get the impression you're just playing with me.'

'What makes you think I'm not?'

Reuben shook his head, holding it like he was being attacked. Talking to Sarah was always a head-fuck. She could get inside without even trying. But, just as in the pub, there was also something else in her eyes. Suppressed, disguised, but still leaking through. Reuben decided to play Sarah at her own game.

'I wonder what a police psychologist would make of you choosing to meet me in a romantic restaurant?'

'That I had a warped sense of humour.'

'Or else . . .'

'What?'

'You know what I'm saying.'

Reuben stared hard into her face. It was there. The faintest hint of a blush struggling through. With a summer tan, he wouldn't have spotted it. But Sarah was pale, and Reuben had keen eyes.

'I don't think I do.'

Reuben chewed an ice cube. He had just learnt something valuable. 'Two can play at this.'

'At what?'

'Hot and cold. Push and prod. Nice and nasty. Call it what you will.'

'Look, what is it you want to know?' she asked impatiently.

'Tell me what you've got,' he said.

'Just some murders. Forensics team tortured one by one. A scientist with a grudge against his former colleagues. And guess what? All the DNA evidence points to him being the killer.'

Reuben reached across and clenched Sarah's hand. 'I mean it. Stop fucking me about. Be straight for once.' A pair of couples glanced surreptitiously over. For an instant, Reuben saw what they saw. Two lovers arguing in a restaurant, trying to salvage their relationship. He let go of Sarah and took a cool slug of his vodka.

Sarah stroked her long fingers reflectively. Her brow furrowed and her smile disappeared. A genuine look of empathy settled into her features, as if aware that she'd pushed Reuben too far. 'What I'm going to say is entirely confidential and must never resurface. OK?' Reuben nodded. 'Right,' she sighed, 'you're the top priority on our list, but there are others. Three others. All have relevant form, of one sort or another.'

'Who?'

'No names. We've just tied one to twenty-four-hour surveillance. The other two are on the loose, but we've got CCTV putting them in the city on or about the days of the murders. We don't have DNA from one, but we do from the other. The switch to Lloyd Granger threw us for a bit, but we think we've made a breakthrough.'

'How?'

'Can't say – it's too preliminary. But I think you know already.' Sarah swirled the wine in her glass and took a sip. 'So we've divided into two teams, trawling through past convictions, CCTV footage, multiple profiles. Forensics pulling double shifts, trying to keep up. CID knocking on doors, checking last known locations, sifting for witnesses. Myself and Phil cross-checking the data, coming up with ideas, planning tactics. We've got the whole of GeneCrime sweating their arses off, trying to do the one thing we've never done before.'

'Which is?'

'Solve a case in real time. Catch a murderer as he murders.' Sarah stood up. 'Give me a second,' she said.

Reuben watched her stride towards the toilets. Sarah Hirst was not invulnerable. He ordered a second vodka and savoured its cold nothingness. 'Look,' he uttered as she sat down again, 'I want you to do something for me.'

'Don't push it,' Sarah answered. 'You're not exactly in a strong bargaining position.' It was clear that she had used her time in the Ladies to stitch her composure back together. Her foundation was suddenly thicker, her cheeks rouged. She had slammed the door, afraid how much of her was leaking out.

'Number-one suspects rarely get to dictate the course of an investigation.'

'I might be able to help.'

'You already have. You identified yourself as the killer.'

'I mean, really help.'

'How?'

'I want to get involved in the investigation. Let me examine the bodies.'

'You're joking, right?'

'This is the favour I want. Come on, Sarah. You don't trust me any more than I trust you. But these murders are stacking up. The pressure's on. Senior brass must be jumping all over you. And at least you'll know where the main suspect is for a few hours.'

Sarah stared coolly into Reuben's face, calculating. He watched her eyes narrow as she considered the options. A thin smile worried her freshly painted lips. Her eyes widened again, pupils opening up like flowers. 'Sure,' she said. 'I think that might work.' Her smile thickened. 'For both of us.'

9

Mina Ali shivers slightly as she leaves the GeneCrime car park. It is cold in the building, regardless of the outside temperature, and cold in the subterranean car park, now the sun has set. As she makes her way to the bus stop, she pictures her ageing Polo sulking alone in a garage somewhere, having been assaulted all day by a succession of indifferent mechanics. She shakes her head, hoping it will be fixed in time for her morning shift.

Her feet ache from a day spent standing at the bench, and the walk at the other end is easily half a mile. She checks her watch and swears. It is almost 1 a.m. Mina waits hopefully at the stop. As she rifles her purse for spare change she realizes that her fingers and wrist ache nearly as badly as her feet. It has been a long double shift, pipetting huge numbers of samples from Sandra and Run's crime scenes. Worse, the first batch of specimens from Lloyd Granger has meant that all forensic officers are working flat out.

A night-bus approaches, and Mina gratefully climbs aboard. The journey south takes twenty minutes, the traffic thin at this time of day. When she leaves the bus, all she can think about is an extended soak in a hot bath. Mina cuts across the school playing fields which lead towards her flat. It is so dark and she knows the way so well that she barely bothers to open her eyes.

She hears the background hum of early-hours London, a light breeze wafting the noise of a car alarm towards her. Above the restlessness of the city, she suddenly realizes that she is not alone. She senses acutely that someone else is in the park with her. Mina strides quickly towards the road, looking around. She is unable to see anyone in the blackness. But she is sure that another person is close. A terrible notion comes to her. *She is next.* She begins to sprint blindly. The road is fifty metres ahead. In her ears are the sounds of hurried progress, to the left and behind her.

She reaches the street and turns right, away from the direction of the noise, but also away from her flat. She glances back towards the playing fields but cannot see anyone. Mina keeps running, a single thought pushing her forwards. In the gloom she sees images of Sandra, Run and Lloyd. A hundred metres further on, she clearly hears rapid footsteps. She spins around. Fifteen car lengths behind a man is coming towards her. He is at full pelt, leaning forwards, vulpine hunger in his momentum. She runs again, scanning her environs, fighting her panic. She is surrounded by dense rows of terraces, intersecting and cutting each other up. Mina slows, checking the street names. There are three options ahead. Left, right and straight on. Behind, the dark figure is moving swiftly on the other side of the road, forty metres back and gaining. She can hear him panting, almost feel the slap of his shoes against the pavement. She knows the police won't get here quickly enough. A sudden icy premonition squeezes her lungs. She needs another strategy. Something quicker than the police. She pleads with her brain for help.

Glancing at a sign, she chooses left, and renews her sprint. The street is increasingly derelict. Boarded-up windows become the norm. The road dog-legs to the right. She pulls her phone out as soon as she rounds the bend and can't be seen. When her call is answered, she simply says, 'Dunkirk, Tiverton Avenue. Repeat, Dunkirk.' Mina slides the mobile back in her jacket pocket.

Ahead, the houses stop. Thirty metres beyond, the road ends as well. A high brick wall tattooed with fading graffiti. Mina slows. She begins to back away, turning to face him. His footsteps echo towards her. His shadow. And finally his form.

He is wary, making sure she is trapped. She cannot see his face. She is panicking. The light is poor. Smashed streetlights, spaced well apart. She retreats as far as she can. She feels the wall behind her. It is sharp and uneven. He seems to gain confidence. His face is obscured by a SOCO mask. She sees that beneath his jacket he is wearing SOCO gear. He walks towards her. She is trapped. He has latex gloves on. She steels herself, fighting the urge to scream. Her eyes are wide, her breathing hard, her chest tight. He is ten paces away. She stares at him, trying to gauge his size, his build, his general appearance. Belatedly she appreciates that the light is too dim, and that he has come prepared for this. His SOCO mask pulls in and out with his breathing. She realizes she has to play for time.

He has a good look around himself, and then steps forwards. He is pulling something out of his bag. Mina sees that it is a white cloth. Even from three metres she recognizes the smell. It is an odour she experiences most days. But now, in the cool air of outside, the sweet waft of chloroform scares her. She sees her fate. She utters the single questioning word, 'Reuben?' The man stops, frozen. And then he begins to lunge forwards. Suddenly the narrow street is bathed in light. A rattling cavalry. The clatter of a dozen diesel engines. Black cabs stream towards them. He stares at her. Even through the concealment of his clothing she detects anger and surprise. He turns and runs directly at the taxis. Two of them are forced to swerve. He vaults over a fence, disappearing into the dark. Mina notes that despite his bulk, he is athletic. She takes her phone out and dials the police. While she speaks, all she can think is, I almost had him. I almost trapped him. Drivers emerge from their cabs. Some have weapons. They approach each other, bemused. Mina's father climbs out of one of the taxis. 'What the hell are you doing here?' he asks gruffly. And then, 'Are you OK?' Mina simply nods. The adrenalin is leaving behind a sting in its tail. She is trembling. Through the windows of a couple of cabs she sees passengers, inquisitive faces steaming the glass.

'And I suppose it was you who called in the Dunkirk?' he says, wrapping an arm around her.

'There was a man . . . he was . . .'

'It's OK, my daughter,' he soothes, squeezing her gently.

Mina stares out into the darkness, vainly searching for traces of him. Breathing through the night air come the sound of approaching sirens. 'Thanks, Dad. I'm all right, honestly.'

Asad Ali signals to the huddle of drivers who have leapt out of their cabs expecting to find one of their own number in trouble. They climb back in, and begin a noisy retreat from the dead end. Drivers and passengers stare at her as they leave.

'Right,' Mina's father begins, 'I'm taking you home.'

Mina shakes her head. 'No. I can't. I have to stay. They'll need to know where to look for the man who chased me. They'll take care of me.' She stays in her father's embrace, shivering, willing the police to arrive. By the sound of the sirens, they are still tangled up in the side streets, looking for the dead-end road.

'I'm sure they'll catch him,' Mina's father says.

'No. He'll be long gone,' she answers. Mina has an almost overwhelming desire to cry, but fights it. She hasn't cried in front of her father for a number of years, and wishes to keep it that way. A few minutes later, the first squad car finally pulls into Tiverton Avenue.

10

Phil Kemp held up a newspaper and displayed it in an arc of 180 degrees around the room. It was a quality daily, and had been folded to show a page-five story which filled half the sheet. The headline announced, 'Scientist Linked to Forensics Murders'. Phil wrestled it closed and picked up a tabloid edition. He was silent, his rage evident in the stiffness of his movements. He similarly displayed the paper. The front page screamed, 'Boffin Killer On The Loose'. Phil allowed the room to sense his anger. It was a technique learnt from years of interrogation. The implied threat, the simmering violence. He spoke quietly, and every word was listened to intently. 'I want to know who has been dealing with the press.' He glared at the room's occupants, who largely avoided eye contact. 'When I get back to my office I will turn my computer on. If I don't get an email today from the guilty FUCK who has leaked the details I will tear this division apart until I do.' He allowed his voice to raise a notch, key words spat out, echoing around the room. 'Do I make myself clear?' There was a silent affirmation. 'I will NOT tolerate this sort of activity. Journalists are SCUM. Once they start to twist the story they FUCK an investigation over. We're OUT in the open, now. In the public FUCKING domain.' He glowered in the same slow arc he had shown the papers around. One or two people cleared their throats. The air-conditioning eased off. Phil looked down at the back of his hands. Veins knotted their surface like tree roots. His knuckles, as he clenched his fingers, were angry and white. 'Right,' he grunted, 'we have other business. You'll notice Mina isn't here. For those of you who haven't heard, Mina almost became victim number four last night.' DCI Kemp raised his head towards a young CID officer. 'Keith?'

'That's correct,' Keith said, standing up self-consciously. 'Dr Ali was followed home in the early hours of this morning, after working late. She had apparently refused CID assistance point blank, for reasons we don't quite understand yet. If it hadn't been for some quick thinking, well, it's more than likely that . . .' Phil Kemp motioned to hurry him along. The officer turned to a piece of paper he had been holding. 'Well, we now have a description of our man.' He paused, his fingers shaking slightly, aware of the utter concentration focused upon him. 'He was above average height, well built and athletic. Dressed in dark clothing.'

There was another pause, longer this time.

'And?' Helen Alders, the blond, snub-nosed detective, asked.

'That's it.'

'That's the best she could do? I mean she's a senior forensic officer for Christ's sake. Blunkett's fucking dog could have come up with more detail.'

'In her defence, it was dark, she was about to be hacked to pieces, and she's more used to dealing with people who have entirely lost the ability to chase her through the streets.' Phil raised his eyebrows briskly in the direction of the detective. 'Tell them the other bit, Keith.'

'Here's the thing. The description is limited because the man was wearing an anti-contamination face mask. According to Mina, he was also wearing SOCO gear beneath his overcoat, and nylon gloves. He even had shoe covers.'

There was a restless silence. Scientists, CID and support staff allowed their thoughts to meander. Each one of them saw their own set of images, drew their own set of conclusions. Phil inhaled a long breath as a prelude to speaking. 'I'm afraid we have to confront something uncomfortable here. Now I know how uneasy we all felt after we examined the Pheno-Fit of Reuben Maitland a couple of days ago. And I understand that. In fact, I've probably had more doubts than anyone. But, gathering everything together, and being entirely objective . . . I mean, the sad fact is, we cannot ignore what is in front of our eyes. Motive. Evidence. Description. This kills me, but we have to be transparent and honest. If this was someone else, someone whom none of us knew, would we be so reticent?'

Bernie Harrison rose slowly to his feet. He knew Forensics were with him, and took confidence from the quiet which greeted Phil Kemp's words. 'Intuition,' he stated firmly. 'What we need here is intuition.'

'Meaning?'

'In science, logic can only take you so far.' He wiped his forehead with the back of a hand. 'Perspiration is fine, but without inspiration, you will never make any real breakthroughs.'

'For fuck's sake,' muttered a burly CID officer facing Bernie.

Phil Kemp scowled at him. 'Bernie, what are you trying to say?'

'The point is this. My intuition tells me that Reuben is not killing people. For a start, we have no independent forensics. Now, Dr Maitland may have his own reasons for sending us a Pheno-Fit of himself, he might be playing mind games, throwing us off the scent of something, but he certainly isn't butchering us. We need our own data.'

'Wherein lies the problem. If the very scientists processing the killer's samples are being murdered, the supply chain is going to be impaired. Besides, I don't see your point. We already have forensics from Run and Sandra which Reuben processed—'

'Implicating himself. But as I say, you are then relying on the evidence of a sacked member of staff, evidence which, logically, points away from him being the culprit. And what about Lloyd

Granger? He had no connection with GeneCrime. How do you explain Reuben's involvement in that one?'

Phil Kemp sighed out loud. 'Because we have news on Lloyd. We think we've made a breakthrough.' Phil fiddled with a document projector for a couple of seconds, switching it on and attempting to focus it on the whiteboard. 'Although we don't have in-house forensics yet, clearly, those should start filtering through in the next twenty-four hours or so, when Mina comes back to work. But what we did find – Helen Alders, well done – was a name and address in the deceased's address book.' Phil squinted at the screen, and then back at his audience, lingering a few seconds on Bernie. 'Ergo, we have made a link. Up until this point, Lloyd Granger's death might have signalled a change in direction. But, Bernie, you will notice that although Lloyd's murder was not connected directly with GeneCrime, it *was* connected with one of its former staff. As you can see, Reuben's name, along with his wife and son's, their previous address and their telephone number all appear prominently under "R". Not under "M" for Maitland. Lloyd and Reuben knew each other well. It is time, I'm afraid, for us all to face the unpleasant probability that Reuben Maitland is involved in the killings.'

Bernie sat down. He examined his colleagues' faces for support but found little. CID, as he looked at them, were leaning forwards in their chairs, murmuring, comparing notes. He envied their togetherness. By contrast, the intelligentsia of Forensics were sullen, isolated from other staff as much as they were from each other. Phil Kemp, whose job was Head of Forensics, seemed to be slowly reverting to form, old-school detective sniffing a trail, hungry in the chase. The support staff of programmers, statisticians and database-miners remained neutral, almost un-interested. There was, he acknowledged sadly, a shortage of coherency. And the murder of forensics officers, rather than uniting its personnel, was pulling them apart, rubbing disparate careers up against each other, opening old wounds.

'Judith,' Phil said, 'I believe you've talked most recently to Path.'

Bernie ran his eyes over to Judith, who appeared somehow both composed and worried. 'Pathology says that Mr Granger's injuries are entirely in keeping with those found on Run and Sandra. A small, sharp blade; multiple lacerations. Maximum pain while keeping the victim alive.'

'Anything else? Do we have a message?'

'We've just got the translation. But we don't know what to make of it.'

'And what is it?'

'It's two words, simply that.'

'Which are?' Phil asked impatiently.

'Hitch and hiker. Hitch-hiker.'

Phil sat down heavily. Glances were exchanged around the room. A couple of senior CID raised eyebrows at each other.

'What?' Dr Paul Mackay asked. 'What is it?'

Phil Kemp's phone rang and he left the room. No one said anything.

11

'Before I kill you I want to make you understand.'

Jimmy Dunst, barman of the Lamb and Flag pub, stared wildly through the gloom. A hand was clamped over his mouth and a loud ripping sound pierced the stillness of the bedroom. Seconds later, the hand withdrew, and a wide section of tape was wound under his head and across his closed lips. The swiftness and strength of the movement brought an instant reminder, cutting through the blurriness of broken sleep. Jimmy Dunst's tongue started to throb in memory of his last encounter with this man. This was no burglar, here to demand the code for the safe, intent on removing the night's takings. No, this was far worse.

The small reading light by the bed was switched on, and the barman's nightmare was confirmed. Leaning over him, the man said, 'You know what I think?'

Jimmy shook his head, utterly petrified.

'That the truth is everything. So you should have the truth before you die.'

The barman struggled, grunting and panting. A large hand was pushing down on his chest, pinning him to the mattress.

'You threatened my life with a bayonet. And you called the police. You recall?'

A rising panic made Jimmy tremble involuntarily.

'This is the main reason I have come back for you.' The man sat down heavily on the bed, and eased his grip slightly. 'You know, my mother was killed by a policeman.'

'Mmm.'

'And do you know who that policeman was? No?'

Jimmy shook his head vigorously.

'He was my father. He was a very brutal man. Sadistic and merciless. Went a long way in the police. But, of course, I never knew he was the killer.' He talked slowly and softly, almost to himself. 'He lied to me about my mother's demise. Right up until the last few seconds before he himself died. He said that she had deserved to go, that she was, how do you say, bipolar, schizophrenic. She was crazy, prone to terrible tantrums and mood swings, where she would provoke my father, mock him, threaten him even. You understand?'

Jimmy tried to plead, but the tape around his mouth and the still-fresh stitches in his tongue reduced his efforts to a grunt.

'And later I realized I should have known. The times he had beaten me, just for being like my mother – unpredictable, he would say. Erratic. Never knowing what I was thinking. Impossible to read.' He examined the barman intensely. 'Do you think I'm difficult to read? No? I hope not. I hope I'm making myself very clear. Good. Now I have to ask you a couple of questions, and I realize I have hampered your efforts to speak. So what I'm going to do, ever so carefully, is slit a hole in your gag with my knife.'

Jimmy's eyes widened, and he began to fight the crushing pressure on his chest.

'I'd advise you not to struggle. One slip and the blade will be in your neck. Just like the bayonet you tried to thrust into me a few days ago. So hold very still.' He positioned a small, sharp knife over the tape and carved a hole in it, carefully and slowly, pushing the blade through and into the barman's mouth before retracting it. 'There,' he said, 'let me hear you say I'm sorry.'

'I'm sorry,' Jimmy said quietly.

'For threatening you with a knife and then calling the police.'

Jimmy repeated the words as clearly as he could.

'Good. Now let's talk about that other event. What would it have been? Nine or ten years ago?'

'Yes.'

'And that's what encouraged you to try and attack me a few days back, wasn't it?'

'Yes.'

'Tell me what you saw with your own eyes. Not what the police found, or what the trial alleged, but exactly what your recollections are.'

'It's a long time ago.'

'I'm not going anywhere. So, take me through it from the beginning.'

Over the next two hours, Jimmy described what he had seen, and the man dissected his answers, repeatedly pushing him, separating fact from supposition, truth from allegation. Jimmy came to see that he had a chance, if only he could engage him long enough. It was 4.55 a.m. The cleaner arrived at seven, the deliveries shortly after. If no one answered, they would become suspicious. Maybe even suspicious enough to call the police. He gained a degree of confidence. Although the man was difficult to read, Jimmy could see he had become increasingly friendly, warm almost, as the questioning had progressed.

'And the dead man, I'm sure you still remember him vividly, was he lying on his back or his side?'

'His side, I think. Though the doctor could've moved him.'

'Moved him how?'

'Rolled him over.'

'You told me there was blood around his head?'

'Yeah. Like an outline, or a shadow or something, a big round pool . . .' Jimmy Dunst stopped. Something had changed. The face in front of him was suddenly different. The eyes were fixed, the eyelids retracted, the pupils huge. His cheeks were ruddy, his lips drained of blood. Jimmy stared at him. It was almost as if he had taken a drug. His jaw twitched, muscles spasming in his cheek as he chewed his teeth. Still the eyes were large and distant, seeing something Jimmy couldn't. He decided to continue his story, eking out the time, hoping that this would bring him round. 'And it was leaking into the carpet. I remember that because I tried to scrub it out with . . .' He halted again. The man was staring straight at him, eyes boring into his face. Without warning the knife plunged into Jimmy's arm, just above the elbow. The barman screamed, blowing air in and out through the hole in his gag, thrashing around in the bed. A second attack, the small knife puncturing his thigh. And then the razor-like blade slid up his leg, slicing through flesh, towards the groin.

'What is the number of the safe?' the man demanded, with-drawing the knife.

'Fuck, fuck, fuck,' Jimmy shrieked.

Pushing him hard into the bed, he slit a shallow gash in Jimmy's bloated torso, just above the line of his boxer shorts. 'The fucking number.'

'Eleven, forty, eleven, sixteen.'

Jimmy Dunst had no time to wonder what had changed. He saw only that the man was on fire, maniacal, intensely and defeatingly strong. There was a power in him that seemed to defy normal human musculature. Another wound opened up and Jimmy screamed. He had the sudden impression that the questioning had merely been filling time until this moment.

'How many tills fit in the safe?'

Jimmy had already learnt to answer first time. Despite the burning pain of his wounds, he gasped, 'Three.'

The man stopped for a second, examining his victim as a cat examines a rodent trapped by the tail. Jimmy saw the pleasure, the thrill of the chase, the expectation in his eyes. There was hunger and need, and for the first time, he realized with absolute certainty that he was going to die. With sickening premonition, he saw that he would be forced into the pub safe, whether it required broken bones or not, and that his crumpled body wouldn't be found for days. As he studied the knife, Jimmy felt a warmness trickling through his legs, which began to sting as it mixed with blood and entered a wound. He wondered at the man's mental state, imagining quick flashes of what he had been told. The sadistic father, the schizophrenic mother, the murder, the lies. And as the knife was slowly and deliberately lowered towards his nose, Jimmy Dunst suddenly and finally understood the truth of that night ten years previously. And the truth scared him almost as much as the impending torture.

GCACGATAGCTTACGGG
AATCTA**SEVEN**ATTCGC
GCTAATCGTCATAACAT

1

Reuben gazed into the monitor. It was a stare of slow, dawning comprehension, of the solving of a puzzle, of seeing the inherent beauty in an enigma. 'Gotcha,' he whispered at the multiple peaks of colour on a vastly elongated graph, 'you sly mother-fucker.' He flicked to a Pheno-Fit and let out a low, satisfied sigh. 'So nurture wins this one.' Reuben continued to focus into the screen and pressed a button on his phone.

'Moray,' he said, 'you doing anything you can't drop? Can you come over? Where are you? See you in a couple of hours.'

With his free right hand, he scrolled through a screen littered with clustered digits, some red and some blue. As he did so, he dialled another number with his left.

'Kieran. It's Reuben,' he began. 'I think I've got some news you might be interested in. Not on the phone. I'm going to send Moray Carnock over to you. Can you give me a location? Right. Three hours. And he'll need to be paid in full.' Reuben breathed in and frowned, mustering a quick calculation. 'All together, six K. Yep. He'll see you there. Bye.'

He shook his head slowly, and swung his legs off the stool. Stretching, Reuben pulled in a deep breath and held it. 'Sly, sly, sly,' he grunted, letting the air out, the long period of dry concentration ebbing away. Working for gangsters like Kieran

Hobbs was ugly and demeaning, a parasitic necessity, but occasionally, like today, taught him something he could never have learnt in the police force.

He rubbed his eyes and moved on, taking a piece of paper from his pocket. For a few seconds he held his head to the side, weighing up the options. Almost reluctantly, he entered a number from the paper into his mobile. When it was answered, he stood up erect.

'Hello. I'm trying to track down someone by the name of Aaron . . . Yes . . . Did he? How long ago? Did he leave a forwarding address? A telephone number? Anything? . . . Well, has he been back to collect his post? . . . Oh, right.' He was quiet for a few seconds. 'Yes, that sounds like him. Fair enough.'

Reuben walked over to the canvas he had been working on and ran his eyes across its surface. So far there were two irises, the faint impression of an Asian nose, and a slightly down-turned mouth. A solitary strand of black hair jutted straight upwards. Run Zhang was proving difficult. He chewed his lip and dialled another number from the piece of paper. 'Oh, hi. I'm trying to trace Aaron. This is one of the numbers given to me by . . . No, I'm his brother . . . And when was that? Look, I'm only his brother . . . Are you there? The reception is terrible . . . Hello? . . . Sorry, I didn't think you could hear me. But do you know where he is now? . . . Hello? Hello?' Reuben pulled the phone away from his ear and examined the screen. The words 'Connection Lost' were imprinted blackly on its surface. 'You can say that again,' he whispered. He stabbed his blunt pencil deep into the canvas, forcing it between the roughly woven fibres, piercing it, opening a hole where a dark iris had sat.

A reflective couple of moments later, Reuben grabbed his coat and keys with sudden urgency and headed out of the lab, through the industrial estate, along the long soulless road which served it, and towards relative civilization. He walked quickly, with grim resolution, a baseball cap pulled down tight over his face. Twenty minutes later, he entered a tube station, which deposited him, through its subterranean magic, in another area of the city. Reuben burst through the entrance of a glass-fronted building, ignored the receptionist and ran up the stairs to the third floor. He paced down a long corridor of closed offices, before settling on one and swinging open the door.

'Don't call Security,' he said, stepping in.

Lucy Maitland looked up from her desk. 'Reuben! Why the hell are you—'

'I want some answers.'

'I thought I made it clear the other day that if I complained you'd be in serious breach.'

'What more damage could they do to me? I don't have a lot left to lose.'

'They'd lock you up. And from what I've read in the newspaper . . .'

'So why didn't you?'

Lucy was quiet for a few seconds. Reuben noticed that her hair was different, as rigid and shiny as polished wood.

'Look, something's been bothering me, going round and round in my head. I had to see you. Away from him.' Reuben sat down on a chair facing his wife, breathing hard. 'I don't understand why Shaun saved my life.'

'He didn't mean to.'

'No?'

'No.'

'Well, what then?'

'He was coming to attack you.'

'Attack me?'

'He was cutting round the front to make sure he got you. Since you assaulted him, he's been taking self-defence classes. Fanatically. In fact, I think he's getting a bit carried away.'

'But what happened to the man?'

'At a guess, he woke up with a massive headache, none the wiser, and sloped off home.'

For the first time, Reuben noticed a secretary in an adjoining annexe. She peered over her glasses at him, holding his stare. 'He was really coming to get me?'

'You have him arrested and beaten, then you punch him yourself, and finally you start spying on us. What else is he going to do?'

'So why . . .'

'Much as he doesn't exactly appreciate your actions, he didn't want to see you killed. Maybe he realized it would upset me too much. Maybe he's just a better person than you—'

'It would have upset you?'

'Not the way you think.'

'I miss us,' he muttered, almost to himself, his impetus subsiding. He knew he shouldn't have said it. 'I mean, I miss us as a family. You, me and Josh.'

Lucy sighed and interlocked her fingers beneath her chin. She stared into Reuben's face for a long second. After a pause, she glanced away and said, 'Things are different now.'

'Look, three people I know . . . I miss being with someone.'

'Anyone?'

'You know what I'm saying.'

Lucy peered past him and out into the corridor. 'This isn't helpful.'

'So what is helpful? Betraying me?'

'Reuben . . .'

'I need to know.' Something in Reuben's composure snapped, his hurt breaking through and tumbling out. He leant forwards in his seat. Having sex with Judith had brought the issue of fidelity sharply back into focus. 'Why did you betray me?' he demanded. 'Why? Why couldn't you have just loved me? Why couldn't you have been happy with me?

278

Why couldn't you have meant it when you said you loved me?'

'Reuben . . . you were never there. You were always wrapped up in crime scenes, or doing interviews . . .'

'But why did you have to fuck someone else?' Reuben stood up. 'In our fucking bed?' He took a pace towards her. 'Why did you feel you had to do that? Why couldn't you have talked to me?'

'I tried . . .'

'And what about Joshua?' Reuben banged the glass desk with his fist. 'Why the hell did you risk the happiness of our child?' He was shouting. 'If he is my fucking child.' He sensed another presence. A pin-stripe in the doorway.

'You OK, Lucy?'

Lucy glanced away from Reuben and shook her head.

'Lucy, I need to know. I'm asking you. Please. Is he mine?' The secretary was craning her neck to see. The pin-stripe inched forwards into the room 'Lucy? You want me to call Security?' he asked.

'I'm her fucking husband,' Reuben spat.

'And I'm her boss.'

'Is he mine, Lucy?'

'I'm surprised you haven't done some sort of bloody test.'

'I can't bring myself to do it. Not until you've said the words. I need to hear it from your mouth first. Please, tell me the truth.'

Lucy stared icily into the middle distance, assiduously averting her gaze. The secretary picked up her phone and dialled a quick number. The pin-stripe walked over and stood behind Lucy.

'I'm asking you a question.'

Still she refused to speak.

'I think you'd better leave.'

Reuben suddenly felt exposed, his feelings sprayed out as clumsy words that assailed the ears of strangers. He realized

Security were charging up the stairs to meet him. Reuben turned and walked out. He took the stairs up to the fourth floor, and then descended in the lift. Reuben strode out of Lucy's building, not looking back, cursing himself for letting all the pressure erupt, and longing for the sanctuary of his laboratory.

2

Back in the lab, Reuben turned despondently to his computer and brought up the original Pheno-Fit. Then he pulled Judith's small make-up mirror out of one of the drawers. His throat was tight and his heartbeat rapid and empty. He wanted to sprint headlong into the lab wall. Instead, he stood in front of the screen and held the mirror at face height in his right hand. He ran his frowning eyes from the reflected image to the projected image and back again. He made himself collect and compare, focus and blur, retain and ignore. He remembered being called Aaron, his brother Reuben. He saw photographs of the twins, arms stiffly around shoulders, each recoiling from the intimacy. He pictured them both in matching school uniforms, football shirts, funeral suits. He recalled the initial confusion on people's brows, hesitating, avoiding names where possible. He saw the later years: different haircuts, different clothes, no longer being mistaken. He darted his eyes back and forth, returning to the present. He hadn't seen his brother for three years, but knew his face would have changed just as his own had. He scrutinized the mouth, lips, ears and eyes. As he considered what to do next, the door opened, and Moray Carnock's considerable bulk entered the room. Reuben put the mirror back in the drawer, and slid it shut.

'How's that new mascara working out, big man?' Moray asked.

Reuben raised his eyebrows and attempted to lift his mood. 'Didn't realize you cared.'

'Ach. The long hours, the close contact, the intimate phone calls. How could I not?' Moray wedged half his backside on a stool. 'Besides, I go for the dangerous outlaw type.'

'Great. I like them plump and butch.'

'That's big-boned. And anyway, it's my metabolism.' Moray patted his belly with satisfaction. 'Which tells me, incidentally, to eat a colossal amount of pies.' Moray loosened his tie, which was already on the verge of slipping through its knot. 'So enough of this pillow talk. What's the news?'

'You'll enjoy this one,' Reuben began.

'First time for everything.'

'Maclyn Margulis. He's either enviably clever or just breath-takingly vain. You recall Kieran Hobbs was less than impressed that our Pheno-Fit failed to identify the killer of his right-hand man, Joey Salvason. And that he then suggested we test Maclyn Margulis, his best guess at the culprit?'

Moray pulled a sausage roll out of his pocket and tenderly unwrapped it. Reuben had observed him extract a wide variety of foodstuffs from his jacket over the months. It was a portable pantry of convenience. 'I remember you moaning about it, yes.'

'Well, I guess Kieran has taught me a valuable lesson. Some-times technology over-complicates things. Sometimes the message is simple, easy and obvious.'

'How so?'

'When I examined Maclyn Margulis's hair follicles, their sequence matched the DNA samples we took from Joey Salvason. You've seen Maclyn Margulis, from a distance?'

'Wouldn't like to get too close. But, yes.'

'Here, look at the Pheno-Fit.' Reuben closed his own image and opened another up. 'What do you see?'

'A fairly unpleasant ginger-haired man with a big nose and buck teeth.'

'So what do you conclude, Holmes?'

'Your Pheno-Fit isn't worth shit.'

'Or, the jet-black, tanned, straight-nosed, perfectly dentured Maclyn Margulis owes less to his genes than to his hairdresser, plastic surgeon and dentist. Have another look.' Reuben typed a few commands into the computer, and the hair darkened, the eyebrows blackened, the skin lost its pallor, the nose shrank, the teeth levelled. 'Nurture outwitting nature.'

'And you think this is deliberate?'

'I guess he's just a rich gangster who took the decision at some point in his past to drastically improve his looks.' Reuben stretched again. 'It was a moment of revelation – the hairs Judith took were black, but their DNA said red.'

'And I guess you want me to explain all this to Kieran Hobbs?'

'Aha. But be careful. The more I think about it the less I like coming between men like Kieran and Maclyn.'

Moray tapped his nose with the sausage roll. 'Careful is what I do best.'

Reuben examined the minute crumbs which had been transferred to Moray's skin. Behind him, the handle turned, and the door eased open. Judith entered, carrying a briefcase. She approached the two men warily. Her clothes and face were tired and drawn. One word struck Reuben as he looked at her. *Simmering.* She nodded quickly at Moray, before turning to her former boss, who anticipated bad news. 'What?' he asked.

'It's finally happened. You're out there, Reuben. On the streets. In the papers. On the news. In people's conversations.' She fiddled with the handle of her briefcase. 'You're going through the city like a retrovirus.'

'How, exactly?'

'You've become a headline.'

'Which is?'

'Forensic scientist killing forensic scientists.'

'Fuck. So who leaked the details?'

'No idea. Phil Kemp was livid. Look, Reuben, we knew from the start that I would be taking risks, and that was my decision. It seemed to be worth it. But now the risk has gone through the roof.'

'Why?'

'I'm hanging around with the number-one suspect in a serial-murder case, while spending the rest of the time trying to track him down. Talk about fucked up.'

'But if you abandon me now—' Reuben stopped himself just short. 'I'm sorry. You're in an impossible situation. I'm being selfish.' He raised his eyebrows, his eyes widening. 'See it from my side, though. I'm being pushed into a corner by someone. My only hope is to find out who. Without you on the inside of GeneCrime, I don't stand a chance.' He pointed at Judith. 'You are my forensics team.' And then at Moray. 'You are my police force. And you think *you're* scared.' Reuben ferreted for support, but there was something in Judith's face – doubt, maybe – that he had not witnessed before. 'They will hunt me down. They're coming for me. The evidence is strong enough.' He glanced around the confines of the laboratory. 'I'm going to be locked away for ever. If you trust me one hundred per cent, then please, please, help me.'

'One hundred is a large number.'

'Et tu, Judith?'

Judith merely shrugged.

'So you'll help me?'

She stared deep into her former boss's eyes. Reuben held the stare for a few seconds. It was a disturbingly different look than the one of desire and need which had passed between them only two days ago.

He turned to Moray. 'And you?'

'As long as you keep paying me, I don't care who you kill.'

Judith opened her case slowly and deliberately, pulling out several scraps of newspaper. 'You might as well see what they're saying about you.' Reuben scanned the articles, passing them along the line to Moray as he finished with each one in turn. To see your own name printed for public consumption . . . he suddenly understood how it must feel to have your DNA sequenced and published.

Moray let out a deep rumbling laugh which shook his belly. '"Police have issued a DNA policy – Do Not Approach – for boffin-slayer Reuben Maitland . . ." Who writes this crap?'

'Colin Megson of the *Sun* was first to break the story,' Judith answered.

Moray turned to a broadsheet.

'DCI Sarah Hirst of Euston CID confirmed that her team were eager to speak with Dr Maitland, who was sacked from an elite North London forensics unit in May. The unit, GeneCrime, which is pioneering advances in detection technologies, is barely known about outside the upper echelons of the Metropolitan police force. However, GeneCrime has maintained a policy of publishing its breakthroughs in scientific journals. Dr Maitland, 38, was previously a regular contributor to media analysis of crime, and at the forefront of UK forensics, before his dismissal on grounds of alleged misuse of powers . . .

'Alleged? Blatant misuse, more like,' Moray muttered.

Reuben didn't look up. He was absorbed in an article from the *Daily Express*. Judith had passed it to him silently, questioningly. It was haunted by the word 'Exclusive', white on black, an ominous box hovering over the headline. 'Fuck,' Reuben whispered to himself. He searched the item with a desperate hope, but it soon faded. Someone had been digging deep. The facts were virtually all accurate. Police records had been mined, even the arresting officers had been interviewed. Reuben felt an arctic cold in his bones, a metallic clamp squeezing his brain. His own truths had been pursued with the fervour he applied to others. Events that had been absorbed, stored away, glossed over and denied were exposed. Deeds which were known only to one other person. At least until now. He let the paper slip from his fingers, watching it feather downwards, sliding along the floor as it landed, rearing up and finally settling. Reuben held the lab bench with both hands, arms straight, his head bowed. Moray picked the article up, glanced at Judith and then read it. He whistled.

'This true?' he asked.

Out of the corner of his eye, Reuben saw that Judith was watching him intently.

'Some of it,' he muttered.

Moray whistled again. '"Hunted Scientist is Convicted Drug Dealer".' Anything else we need to know?'

'It's more complicated than that.'

'How?'

Reuben stared into a brown bottle of phenol on the shelf in front of him. 'I'm not sure I want to talk about it.'

'And the sentence?'

'It was only three months, not six as suggested. But other than that, yes. Brixton. One of the country's finest.'

Judith, who had been quiet, cleared her throat. 'You know the rules. No previous. If a reporter can find out . . . What's been going on, Reuben? There's no way on earth you could have had a police career with a record, not to mention jail time. Surely it isn't true?'

Reuben turned to look at her. There was a disquieting mix of emotion in her face. Her eyes reflected betrayal, her mouth curiosity, her nose disgust. He wanted to tell her the truth, to be straight with her, anything, as long as she didn't stare at him that way. He felt compelled to open himself up to her. 'As the article implies, my actual name is not Maitland. I changed it. Only slightly. Background checks are crude, as you know. My dad succumbed to cirrhosis when I was nineteen, and my mum reverted to her maiden name, mainly to be free from his memory. There wasn't a lot of contradictory evidence.'

'But cocaine – what were you doing?'

'Long story. Wrong place at the wrong time, helping the wrong brother. Look, I don't see how any of this changes anything . . .'

'Don't you?' Judith was busy closing her case. 'Don't you see this has all been about the truth? Always the truth. That's why your team worshipped you. You were a purist.' Her eyes were moist; she turned to leave the lab. 'And yet . . . this goes beyond hypocrisy. This makes me worry about a lot of things. Jesus, when I think about the power, the trust, the loyalty you've had. And all along, a liar, an ex-con.' She pulled the door open. Her face was flushed, her words strained. 'Who the hell are you, Reuben?'

'Judith . . .'

'Have you any idea what I've put on the line for you? Jeopardizing my career. Undermining my colleagues. Going behind their backs. Working for you on the inside.' Judith glanced at Moray. There were tears in her eyes. 'Not to mention anything else.'

'I know it seems . . .'

'And what was it you called me? Piggy in the middle?'

'But . . .'

'Well, this little piggy's going to market.'

'Judith . . .'

'And she isn't coming back.'

The door slammed. Reuben bit hard into his lip. He screwed up his face, rubbing his forehead with his knuckles. He turned to Moray, who shrugged, heading for the exit as well. 'Get some sleep,' he said, swallowing the last of his sausage roll. 'You're going to need it.'

3

Mark Gelson crouched behind a brimming yellow skip, which sat pregnant in front of a renovated house in Dulwich. Disused doors had been wedged along the skip's length, its bulging contents in imminent danger of overwhelming them. From his position beneath the slight overhang, Mark Gelson could monitor the road, the short drive and the front door of the house. More importantly, given that the skip was backed close to a neighbouring brick wall, he couldn't be seen.

Originally, he had planned simply to sit in his car and wait, but this was far better. To be out in the fresh air, the falling sun still warming the tarmac, this was the life. He looked up, above the house, past its shiny new guttering, and saw that the sky was slowly filling with clouds, drifting in and parking, like old American cars. A light wind toyed with an empty cement bag dangling out of the skip. Mark Gelson zipped his jacket up and checked his watch. It was almost seven-thirty. He rubbed his hands together impatiently, wondering why the fuck CID seemed to work so many hours for so little pay.

To pass the time, and sure that he couldn't be observed, Mark Gelson opened the sports bag at his feet and risked a glance inside. He was met by the knowing wink of a blade. In the gloom he also noted a gag, a pistol, a length of wire, some handcuffs and a bottle of pills. In each he pictured procedures and protocols, fun and games. Ever ambitious with his arsenal, he stood up and surveyed the skip. Its swollen innards spoke of repair and replacement, of DIY and modernization. Period skirting boards, window-frames and fire-surrounds had been ripped out, to be substituted, no doubt, for less ornate, more functional entities. It saddened him momentarily that items discarded after a hundred years of domestic service would now be of no more use to anyone. Mark Gelson scoured the contents until he found something he could utilize, an object he could rescue from futility. Amongst bricks, tiles and pieces of wood, he spied the ideal implement. He extracted a thick shard of glass from under a light fitting. Beside it he found a strip of cloth coated in paint. He wound the material around the blunt end of the glass to make a handle and slotted it into his bag.

Crouching down once more, Mark Gelson's knees grated, femur and tibia grinding unhappily together. The pace of his life was eating into his bones. His thirty seven years had been lived in a frenzy that would have exhausted lesser men. He had taken more drugs, been more places, seen more desperation and earned more money than an entire town of ordinary people. It had been an existence of extremes, of brutality, of desperation. At the current moment, his skeletal complaints told him that he was more extreme, brutal and desperate than ever before. And, listening to the lament of his body, Mark Gelson vowed to himself that his rampage would soon be over. He would disappear as easily as he had broken cover, with the marrow-deep satisfaction that only true retribution could bring.

A car slowed, coming from the right, and Mark Gelson zipped up his sports bag. His bones instantly felt strong and alive again, gripped as they were by tightening muscles and eager tendons. He adjusted his position, and watched a silver Vectra pull on to the drive. It was a pool car, an unmarked squad car, obvious from a mile off. He congratulated himself that the last interrogation had brought the truth. Here was the next link in the chain. This time a CID officer. A change of tack. But this was where things started to get more interesting. With the information a copper could provide, there was no one he couldn't get to. Mark Gelson checked his watch again. It was just after eight. He had no plans until the following morning. It was going to be a long night, particularly for the CID officer now climbing wearily out of his car. Mark watched him walk to his front door, carrying a wad of files and notes. Again, he marvelled at the dedication of a copper to his case. He allowed the officer to unlock his door and close it behind him. Mark Gelson counted a slow hundred. He wanted the CID man to dump his homework, loosen his tie, kick off his shoes, and then stride impatiently to the door without checking the spyhole. A little agitation would throw him off his guard. Ninety-five. He stood up. Ninety-six. He stretched a little. Ninety-seven. He stepped up to the front door. Ninety-eight. He clenched and unclenched his fists a few times. Ninety-nine. He pulled out his gun. One hundred. He rang the bell.

4

Reuben and Moray left the car nearly a kilometre from Gene-Crime. Both were silent, Reuben swinging a slim attaché case, Moray a closed umbrella. A fine summer drizzle wet their foreheads, the humid air swallowing their thoughts. The pavement reflected what light there was like a greasy mirror. The streets were known to Reuben in almost microscopic detail. As he turned a corner he saw the spot where he had encountered Jez Hethrington-Andrews. Reuben glanced at the restaurant he met Sarah Hirst in, half expecting her to be there. But it was closed, as were all the other shops, offices and cafés. Ramraid-proof shutters lined the street so that it almost felt like walking down a steel tube. Reuben checked his watch. At this time, even London slept. Moray fastened an extra button on his coat and let out a grunt. 'Better do it,' he said. He raised his over-sized umbrella and opened it wide. Reuben hopped on to the pavement and walked under the umbrella's shadow. Moray held it inches above their heads.

'Thank God it's raining,' Reuben said. 'I'm getting sick of baseball caps.'

'I cannot stand umbrellas.'

'You think they make you look effeminate?'

'Aye.'

Reuben glanced at Moray's untidy bulk. 'Listen, a pink fucking parasol wouldn't make you look effeminate.'

'I'll try and take that as a compliment.' Moray wiped the moisture from his face. It was the sort of drizzle that pervades, soaking through clothing, leaking through umbrellas. 'Now, you're sure about all this? I mean, talk about the lion's den.'

'I'm not sure about anything.' Ahead Reuben spotted the faceless rear wall of GeneCrime. There were no windows or doors. It merely served as a partition, closing off a dead end. People passed all day long, oblivious. Reuben and Moray turned sharply into a narrow side street fifty metres before it, too tight for traffic, but brightly lit. Above and around their progress was monitored by a swarm of security cameras. 'Something Sarah Hirst said rang true.'

'So you're friends now, all of a sudden?' Moray asked, pulling the umbrella tighter over their heads.

'Not by a long stretch. But a deal's a deal. She owes me a favour, and I expect her to keep her word, just like I kept mine and sent her the Predictive Phenotyping results. She could have had me arrested when I met her in the restaurant, but she didn't. Who knows, maybe she is playing fair.'

'Maybe. Or maybe this is a trap.'

'Which is where you come in.'

'Right,' Moray whispered, 'like I get all the glamorous jobs. OK, you stay here. Keep the brolly down low. There's an alcove twenty yards ahead which can't be seen on camera. I will be a while. If I'm not back in an hour, go home, making sure you're not followed.' Moray pulled a small radio receiver from his pocket, along with a digital heat-sensing camera. Reuben watched him walk slowly down the alley, adjusting the camera and listening to the receiver. In his environment of stealth, Moray had transformed into a professional, the kind you would trust your life with.

Reuben tried one final time to weigh up whether he was doing the right thing. He saw the way Sarah had toyed with him in the restaurant, the rising enthusiasm in her face, the unexpected ease with which she agreed to this favour. He recalled the warning in Jez's eyes, confiding in him, telling him to trust no one. He contemplated how Judith Meadows was losing weight, jumpers baggy, cardigans not hugging so tight. He pictured the newspaper headlines. He imagined the rumours spreading through the capital's forensic teams. He envisaged the CID meetings, Phil Kemp banging the desk, spitting through the air. He saw printers spewing his photo out, his image being distributed, becoming the man in the manhunt. He ran through views of his lab, first as a sanctuary and second as a prison. He lived the soaring moment he had conceived of Predictive Phenotyping, and the crushing moment it had trapped him. He concluded that he had little choice. Bite back. Play them at their game. Be smart. Stay ahead. Use the skills they had instilled in him. Think like they thought; act like they acted. Understand them from the inside and overcome them from the outside. Gamekeeper turned poacher. And now he was about to enter GeneCrime, the epicentre of the organization which was hunting him down.

A figure appeared and passed by. There was silence. Reuben shivered. Minutes later, another figure entered the alley, a drunk who staggered past, barely noticing him. He realized that there was a strong possibility of a trap. Reuben imagined what he would do if he had to go back again. Three months had been horrible. But Reuben knew it would be even harder this time. He would go in labelled with the tag of copper. It didn't matter that he was civilian force. How many fellow prisoners had been locked up on forensic evidence? he wondered. And how many of them had he personally sent there? He shivered again. This time would be murder. Reuben clenched his fists involuntarily. Then he recognized the rotund form of Moray. Reuben inspected his watch. Moray had been forty minutes. 'It's clear,' he said, ducking under the umbrella.

'You sure?' Reuben asked.

'It's clear,' Moray repeated. 'No police communication within half a mile, no one in the morgue except DCI Sarah Hirst.' He waggled the infra-red camera. 'Well, no one who's alive. And no one hanging around the streets in parked cars. Shall we?'

They began walking. On the right, around a shallow corner, was a set of tall, metal gates, opening into a cobbled courtyard. The capital was full of such anonymous incursions, hiding who knew what. The gates pushed open, and Reuben and Moray approached a door. Reuben moved his hand towards the metal keypad, but Moray grabbed his wrist.

'Fingers,' he said.

'Sorry, force of habit. The combination is—'

'Don't tell me,' Moray interrupted. He squinted at the pad from a couple of oblique angles. 'It's two seven nine four.'

'Two nine four seven,' Reuben corrected.

'Close enough.' Moray entered the numbers.

'How did you do that?' Reuben asked.

'Companies rarely wipe their keypads. Hence the correct keys of the combination tend to be greasy. And the number two appeared greasiest of all. I'd have cracked it in a couple of minutes.'

Reuben shook his head. 'Rule number one of being shady. Never deliberately break into police stations.'

'So?' Moray held the door open. 'Shall we?'

Reuben sensed the cold pinch of formalin reach his nose from within. A figure was moving behind the frosted window. A tired clock on the corridor wall pointed to 3.15 a.m. Reuben drew in a deeper breath. 'What could possibly go wrong?' he answered, pushing through and entering the morgue.

5

Mina Ali is sitting up in bed, hugging her knees, another pounding sweaty nightmare having woken her. She looks at the blood-red digital numbers: 3:15 a.m. The house creaks and groans like a heavy piece of furniture. Through the nearest wall to her single bed comes the sound of her father snoring. She finds some comfort in the deep vibration, and convinces herself that moving back in with her parents is a good thing, for the time being at least. Mina peers across the room in the half-darkness. The wallpaper and curtains have been changed since she moved out. They have depersonalized her room, she realizes belatedly. Mina touches her forehead, which is sticky. She runs her fingers down the length of her nose, feeling the grease which has exuded from her nightmare. A single LED bar switches the time to 3:16. She returns to hugging her knees and closes her eyes, trying to think of something to pull her brain away from its nocturnal chases.

Bernie Harrison is inside and on top of his wife. He has the faint impression that she is slumbering, but it doesn't concern him. He has been unable to sleep, and knows that he has coerced his wife into sex. She is offering him comfort in the form of penetration. He speeds his stroke. She is quiet. He opens his eyes in the darkness. Whenever he closes them he sees things which terrify him. His wife begins to breathe more deeply, and for a second he worries that she really is dozing. But she grabs his hands tight, the sign that she is close. He forces his eyes open, picturing one of the female CID support staff naked, bending over, offering herself. Bernie begins to come. It is over almost instantly, a weak orgasm, forced, conjured up, a physical solution to a mental problem. His wife whispers that she loves him. He withdraws slowly, reluctantly, and lies on his back. The luminous hands of his watch tell him that it is quarter past three. He sighs. His wife starts to snore. Bernie closes his eyes and attempts to join her.

Paul Mackay reaches his hands skyward. Above, smoke is made solid by lights and drilled through with lasers. The man dancing behind begins to rub his crotch against him. A rush of ecstasy coincides with the stranger's contact. Paul's muscles are rigid, the contact between them so hard they almost rebound. The throbbing, banging noise is melting into a second rhythm, equally sublime. The DJ, hunched over in concentration, is jumping from one speeding train of a record to another. The bass vibrates Paul's chest with delicious warmth. He feels good. The stranger wraps his arms around him from behind. Paul is still extending upwards, through the lights, towards the invisible roof of the nightclub, and out and beyond, up and away from his problems. The stranger's wrists are gleaming and almost hairless. Paul notices the time on the man's watch. He dances with renewed mania, feeling aroused, excited and free. The club is open for another three hours. Until then, the world outside doesn't exist.

Birgit Kasper is talking on the phone. She flicks at a cigarette. There are several butts in the plastic cup she is using as an ashtray. The cigarette never gets the chance to accumulate a growth of ash, as she taps at it almost constantly. Birgit is speaking in Swedish. She is wearing a pair of unisex pyjamas and some slippers which are decorated with small woollen sheep. From time to time she rubs the skin beneath her eyes with forefinger and thumb, the phone held in the crook of her neck. She has been crying. As she listens, she takes a deep drag, a needy red cone glowing at the tip of the cigarette. Occasionally she peppers her speech with terse words of English. The microwave in her studio flat shows the time. Birgit notices it, and speaks rapidly. She ends the conversation with the word 'Ciao', slumps back in her chair and opens a fresh packet of Marlboro Lights.

Simon Jankowski is tapping a stream of letters into his computer. He is reading them from a piece of paper, and never once looks at the keyboard. Two of his fingers hover over the characters A and C, and two more touch the surface of G and T. He is in the living room of his bed-sit. The dining table is littered with scraps of paper, photographs and evidence forms. A Pheno-Fit of Reuben Maitland is taped on his wall. He is chewing a Biro, and his concentration is absolute. Simon Alt-Tabs to another screen of sequence data, and then to a public database of gene accession numbers. The small speakers of his laptop are playing a CD by the Stone Roses, which reminds him of his student days in Manchester. In the bottom right of his screen are four tiny digits. Out of the corner of his eye he notices that they say 03:15. He stops typing and stretches, only aware how tired he is now he knows how late it is. Simon saves his work, stands up and stretches again. He looks in the direction of his bed, pauses for a second, and then sits down and continues his work, typing, collating, comparing and validating with reluctant discipline.

Judith Meadows is sitting on the edge of her bed, silently crying. Her husband lies next to her, fast asleep. She glances down at him, before returning to stare out of the window. An orange streetlight opposite shines sadly through the night, its head bent over, as if examining its feet. Judith blows her nose on a tissue. Tears continue to pour out of her eyes and slip down her face, dropping off her chin and on to her bare legs. She is startled by a noise. A cat appears on the ledge, meowing to come in. Judith shrugs at it with a half-smile which quickly fades. She points her eyes at a pair of freshly fitted locks bolting the window closed. Turning round, she wonders if the cat has disturbed her husband. He mumbles something incoherent and resumes his slumber. Judith stands up and walks into the newly decorated room next door. She pulls back the cold sheets of the spare bed and climbs in.

Phil Kemp is asleep at his desk in the GeneCrime building. His left cheek is lying on a small stack of newspapers, and two empty horizontal bottles of Shiraz loll on the table. Forms, papers and evidence are strewn everywhere. His arms are spreadeagled, as if he is about to gather up all the information in front of him. A penholder on the desk has a small analogue clock at its centre, short stubby hands climbing over each other, and both pointing to the number three. His computer monitor shows the home page of an on-line poker club. Phil lifts his head and turns to face the other wall. His left cheek bears smudged black letters of print from the newspaper. He grunts and slides back into his shallow slumber.

Jez Hethrington-Andrews is sitting and staring into his TV. He is chain-smoking joints, swallowing strong lager, staring and staring. His eyes are glassy, his thoughts a long way from the film which is showing. There is a noise. He turns his head slowly to look at the front door of his flat. It is a gesture of resignation and acceptance. Jez hears another noise, louder this time, and away from the door. He remains where he is, drawing heavily on the joint, his fingers shaking so that the burning end flickers in the glow of the television. Swigging from his can, Jez mutters to himself. 'This is so fucked up,' he says. 'This is so fucked up.' He picks up the remote and presses a button. The film gives way to Teletext. One of the headlines is 'Scientist Killer Still on Loose'. So fucked up. Jez takes another drag and continues to talk to himself. 'So fucked up,' he repeats. 'So very fucked up.'

6

'So, Dr Reuben Maitland returns to the scene of his crimes.' Sarah Hirst's eyes are wide, already accustomed to the bright light. She is wearing a lab coat with pinched sleeves and an enclosed collar.

'Hello, Sarah,' Reuben replies. 'This is a friend of mine, here to make sure nothing happens to me. Any trouble and we're gone.'

Sarah nods an unenthusiastic hello in the direction of Moray. 'This has meant pulling a lot of strings,' she intones. 'We don't have long – an hour max – and we'll have to get everything back as it was.' As ever, Reuben is drawn to her air of detachment, which mimics the perpetual separateness he feels. Separate from friends, family, Joshua, from society. In Sarah's isolation he sees his own remoteness staring back. 'Now, some rules. You mustn't take any gross samples like skin punches. Nothing noticeable. The bodies stay on their trays. We don't have time to transfer them to the autopsy table. You must work quietly – there are a couple of CID on night shifts in the building above, and imagine how pleased they'd be to see you. And your friend can't touch anything. OK?'

'Wouldn't dream of it,' Moray answers flatly.

'Right, I guess we ought to get this party started.' Sarah walks over to what appears to be an elongated stack of filing cabinets.

Reuben follows her. He is nervous, worried about his reaction when he sees the corpses, concerned that this could still be an ambush. 'I have to warn you,' Sarah Hirst adds, 'that they are a mess.'

Reuben grunts. He places his case on the floor and opens it. From within he extracts a pair of surgical gloves, some elongated forceps, a rack of tubes, several self-sealing plastic bags, a roll of Sellotape and a packet of cotton-wool earbuds. Reuben has seen many bodies before, but knows this is different. He has feelings for these people. He tells himself all he has to do is examine them as if he has never met them. Reuben tries to do this, to make them strangers. But it doesn't quite work. Sarah withdraws a shiny steel drawer, and Reuben gasps quietly.

Lying naked on the table is the body of Sandra Bantam. Even though her wounds have been cleaned, her torso is stricken with slashes, bite marks and cigarette burns. The sick pallor of her skin contrasts with the reddy-brown lacerations. Her face, slightly bloated, shows local swelling and bruising, oozing cuts apparent on her lips and nose. One of her earlobes is missing, a bite-sized chunk where an earring might have hung. There are finger-bruises on her upper arms and neck. Reuben's eyes wander over the rawness of her knees, the bushiness of her pubis, the serenity of her navel, the darkness of her nipples, the contusions on her forehead, the unkemptness of her hair. He breathes hard, sweat running down his back. Sarah is watching him. He knows now that she wanted to see his reaction. She is still making her mind up. Extracting a cotton bud and a vial of blue dye, he realizes that this is a good thing.

Reuben wipes small dabs of the solution around the bite marks, and examines for DNA staining. He can see that this has been done already, but needs routine to steady himself. The smell of Sandra is nauseating, and he tries not to swallow it. He remembers the perfume she used to wear. Reuben crouches down and runs his gaze across the surface of Sandra's skin. He hears the near silence, penetrated only by the hallway clock. Moray has turned away and is fiddling with his camera, finding less gruesome things to occupy his attention. Reuben notices that Sarah is continuing to monitor his body language. 'Plenty of DNA,' he mutters to her.

'Run was leading Sandra's processing. He got DNA early on.'

'Bite marks. The big forensic no-no. I suppose you've done dental?'

'Of course.'

'And?'

'Slightly ambiguous, so we haven't made a big deal of it.' Sarah grins in a way that spells trouble. 'But the bite marks were similar to your own.'

'How do you work that out?'

'You left a gumshield in your locker, presumably from your spell in the infamously poor Forensics Rugby Club. We made an internal cast and matched it to the marks. Path were a bit fifty-fifty about it.'

Reuben turns away from Sandra's skin. 'I guess I shouldn't think about that too much.'

'I guess not,' Sarah says.

'So, apart from the suspect dentition, do you know exactly where they took DNA from?'

'Not *exactly*. But follow the blue staining.'

Reuben frowns. 'I mean, did they swab internally?'

Sarah leafs through a wad of notes and forms. 'Vaginal, anal, buccal.'

'That's my boy. Run was as thorough as . . .' Reuben stops, glancing over at the metal drawers. He shivers with sick anticipation. Run's body is next.

'Look, Dr Maitland, what do you think you're going to find that we haven't already?'

'I don't know,' he answers. 'But let's get the next one out as well.'

Sarah tracks her finger along a row of metal doors, squeaking over the surface until she stops at a name. Reuben watches her. He glances at Moray who appears pale. Sarah pulls the drawer, sliding Run Zhang out into the harsh whiteness. Reuben readies himself. He knows this one will be difficult. Pretend this is a stranger, he tells himself again. Pretend you are not about to throw up. Pretend the death of Run hasn't gnawed away at you for sleepless night after sleepless night. Reuben steps slowly forwards. The first thing he sees is the lettering, carved with short, fine angular slices. He clenches his jaw, forces himself to be objective. He skims his reluctant eyes along the length of the body, from feet to head, noticing the smoothness of the skin, the relative hairlessness, the trauma and leaking of internal wounds. Burns, cuts and abrasions are scattered over the loose surface. In places, the skin gapes open like small mouths, with red flesh lips and white fat teeth. In their throats is a burgundy blackness which seems ready to ooze out into the light. All around are slow budding bruises which occurred just before the time of death, fighting their way through the adiposity to flower at the surface. Reuben's wet eyes are dragged back to the site of the most intense damage. Across the flabby chest, multiple cuts lie in intersecting patterns, slicing into Run as his life ebbed away. Reuben checks Sandra's face momentarily.

'Tell me, were Sandra and Run's eyes closed at the time of death? Or were the lids dropped by pathology?'

'They were closed at death. I attended the scenes.'

'Aha,' Reuben says.

Moray turns from his camera. Sarah steps forwards. 'What?' she asks.

'We might be on to something.' Reuben pulls Run's eyelids back, feeling the coldness through his nylon gloves. A sudden detective urge moves him away from the feeling that he is about to retch. 'I read about this once.' The pupils are large, hard to see against their enveloping irises. He takes a fresh bud and dips it in the solution, before wiping it gently over Run's eyeballs. The cotton wool drags across the surface, and Reuben shudders with it. He retracts Sandra's eyelids and performs the same sick procedure with a separate stick. Bending over them in turn, he says, 'Bingo.'

'Reuben . . .'

'You saw the lack of blueness in the whites of their eyes?'

'Kind of.'

'So no one has tested under the lids. Until now.'

'And?'

'And maybe that's important.'

Sarah walks round to stand opposite him, Run's head between them, gazing up, the whites of his opened eyes slowly turning blue. 'How? Could just be the same DNA – your DNA – which is all over the body.'

'Could be,' Reuben answers. 'But think about this. Eyes are like amber. They trap the moment. A fly stuck in the resin of a tree becomes fossilized, there for eternity.'

'I'm still not really following you.'

'Get used to it,' Moray Carnock grumbles.

'The eyes witness the murder, wide open in shock. Then sometimes they close. And when they close they seal in any sample, contaminant or whatever, safely away from harm.' Reuben dabs a cotton-wool bud onto Run's iris, and then into a plastic tube of clear liquid. 'Very few forensic scientists ever check the eyes, especially if there's abundant sample elsewhere.' He performs the same careful process on Sandra. 'But I think we may have just found our fly.'

7

When they reached the car, which was parked several streets away from GeneCrime, Moray said, 'So Sarah believes you?'

'Not at all. She just owed me. And the main reason she let me cash it in was to see how I reacted to the bodies. Classic procedure.'

'Aye, well. Best keep our distance.'

'As long as we can. But face it, Moray, someone is fucking me over.'

'Who?'

'No idea. Except that they're smart and they know about forensics.' The central locking made the noise of a belt being pulled quickly through the inside of the doors. 'Think about it,' Reuben urged, climbing in. 'Three scientists die, each of them smeared in my DNA. Someone even goes to the trouble of attempting to plant bite marks. You think that's easy?'

'Not something I've ever considered.' Moray started the car and pulled off. The intermittent wipers dissected rivulets of water and tossed them away. 'Where would they get your DNA?'

'Wouldn't be hard. It's possible to take a minute quantity and amplify it up, if you know what you're doing.'

'And your gumshield?'

305

'As Sarah said, I obviously left it in my old sports locker. I'm not sure how she found out about it.'

'But we're looking at someone from GeneCrime? Someone on the inside. Someone with access to things the average criminal could never get hold of.'

Warm air from the fan blew the moisture from Reuben's eyes and he blinked with slow, dry lids. 'Indeed.'

'You scared, big man?' Moray asked.

'Would you be?'

'I'd be bricking myself.'

Reuben was quiet. 'Yes,' he said eventually. 'When I'm on my own. I sit there and just listen. You know, like when you're in a house alone at night. But knowing someone is coming for you, that they want to hurt you . . . Yes, it's eating me up.'

'So what now?'

Reuben lifted his head and looked at Moray. 'Sandra was murdered ten days ago. Run five days. Lloyd three days, give or take. Just as Run was about to come up with answers on Sandra, he is killed. Just as Mina was processing Run, she is chased, and has a near miss.'

'So what about Lloyd Granger?'

'Lloyd represents a change in tack.'

'Any names spring to mind?'

Reuben stared sadly out of the window. The light was improving, dawn about to make its pale presence felt. The wipers dragged across the screen as the mist-like rain began to ease. 'One or two. But the eyeball samples might give us a clue.'

'So what are you going to do?'

'Take the DNA from Run's and Sandra's eyes and phenotypically profile it.'

'And what will that show us?'

'All being well, the face of the killer.'

'Won't your samples be contaminated with Run's and Sandra's own DNA, though?'

'It's OK. When Sarah wasn't looking I took buccal swabs from both bodies, so that I can isolate the killer's DNA away from the background.'

'You can do that?'

'You never know. Where are you going?'

Moray accelerated off a stretch of dual carriageway, and flung the car round a roundabout. 'I think we're being followed,' he said, wrestling with the steering wheel, a frown pinching his brow. The surface was greasy, and Reuben pictured a fine film of moisture separating rubber from tarmac. He checked the side mirror. A hundred metres behind, a white Fiesta was making rapid progress.

'You see who it is?'

'Male. Caucasian. That's about all.'

'Fuck.'

'Indeed.'

'What are we going to do?'

'Your call.'

Reuben stared hard into the mirror again. The Fiesta was gaining. 'He's quick,' he said.

'Quicker than this big thing.'

Moray changed down a gear and floored it, the engine whining. The speedo climbed slowly clockwise and he gripped the wheel with greater force.

'He's going to catch us.'

'The cops are out. No other option,' Moray grunted.

'Than what?'

'Than this.' Moray screeched the car around another traffic island. 'Basic level-one training for security consultants.' He yanked the handbrake up and spun the vehicle down a side street. Almost instantly, he pulled the handbrake again and pointed back the way he had come. Reuben grabbed hold of his belt, thrown back and forth across the passenger seat. The stench of burning rubber seeped into his nostrils. Adrenalin encouraged blood to flow out of his gut and into his muscles, leaving his stomach feeling tight and sick. Moray revved the engine. 'You ready?'

'You'll kill us, for fuck's sake.'

Moray drove the accelerator deep into the nylon carpet. He teased the clutch. The large rental car howled. The smell of burning intensified. The white car blurred by. Moray jumped off the clutch and the car sprung out of the alley, wheels slewing round the corner, digging for grip. He found second and Reuben pitched back in his seat. Third and the rev counter dipped momentarily out of the red, before quickly returning again. Within seconds they were up behind the Fiesta. 'Got you, you motherfucker.' Moray grimaced. They were approaching the industrial estate. The car in front slowed. Moray nudged up to its bumper. He thrashed the engine. The clutch screamed, held just below biting point. Ahead, the road split into two carriageways.

'Easy,' Reuben warned.

Moray accelerated forwards and thumped into the car. Its driver sped up, and Moray followed. He tried to ram it another time. Reuben saw the broken indicator and brake lights. The Fiesta, smaller and quicker off the mark, avoided the second contact. The junction loomed. Moray floored the hire car again. Reuben checked his seatbelt, and glanced at his friend. Moray had changed. He was now dangerous. A series of images appeared to Reuben as they broke eighty miles an hour. Moray chasing and being chased, attacking and being attacked, hunting and being hunted.

They were gaining. The rental car was eating up the tarmac at higher speeds. Reuben braked involuntarily, forcing his right shoe into the footwell. They were seconds from impact. The junction started to fork. Cross-hatched white lines marked a no-man's land between the two turns. The Fiesta swerved to the left. Moray followed. And then, yards from the concrete divider, he swung the vehicle right. They watched the Fiesta peel off and away, confined to a raised overpass. Moray was breathing heavily. The hair at the back of his neck was wet. He didn't slow. Reuben saw that the needle was nudging eighty-five.

'Moray,' he barked.

Moray shook his head and followed the direction of Reuben's gaze. He took his foot off the accelerator. The car coasted, its engine starved of petrol, slowing down over quarter of a mile. After a few silent moments, he said, 'Where do you want to be dropped?'

'I know we're close to home, but take me to an all-night chemist's. I need some things.'

'How will you get back?'

'Cab or tube. Don't worry, it's still early. Don't think the Met will be combing the streets for me at six a.m.'

Moray yawned, the excitement subsiding. 'Be careful,' he replied. 'We don't want to fuck things up now.'

'Surviving your driving – that was the big thing. Everything else is easy.'

Reuben felt a shaky fatigue tugging at his limbs. The road was almost dry. They passed a small number of taxis and buses, and the occasional car. He made a mental list of what he needed from the chemist's. Toothpaste. Soap. Wet wipes. Vaseline for the sequencing plates. Tweezers for sample preparation. Paracetamol for his head. Cough medicine for a few hours' sleep. He saw a frantic day of Predictive Phenotyping. And at the end of it, the image of a murderer. Moray slowed and stopped. Reuben climbed out and walked towards an all-night chemist, trance-like, lost in the mechanics of detection.

8

Dave Hillier, Assistant Security Officer, stretched, arching his back, pushing his swollen belly outwards and dropping his head over the back of the chair. When he looked down again, he saw that a dusting of orange biscuit crumbs had begun to edge into the creases of his jumper, which was folded like an extra layer of fat. Dave brushed them away, where they lingered on his trouser legs, before finally being despatched to the vinyl floor. As he stood, the rollers of his seat crunched over the powdered debris.

Dave ambled to his locker in the corner of the control room. It was bluish-grey and rusted around its lock. From inside he retrieved a wounded copy of *Razzle*, which he thumbed hungrily on the way back to his seat. The cover proclaimed a 'Readers' Wives Special'. Dave extracted another biscuit and pored over the pages. From time to time, he glanced upwards, squinting at the vast bank of monitors which surrounded him like an electric panorama. The screens were pale, the summer dawn beginning to emerge, a lull between illicit late-night activities and the morning scramble to work.

Dave spent a long time examining two photographs. They depicted different women, one on her back, one on all fours. They weren't particularly attractive, and there was an almost deliberate artlessness to the shots. But he began to become aroused again. Dave moved the fingers of his right hand inside his trouser pocket. He knew these women might not be pretty, or airbrushed, or flattered by camera angles, but they were out there. Dave scanned the monitors momentarily, allowing his eyes to follow a shapely female form as it hopped from one monitor to another. Maybe one of these women would walk across his screens today. Maybe hundreds of the females who paraded in front of the CCTV cameras had also paraded in front of bedroom cameras. This was the thought that kept him going through the sterile night shifts, and the cacophonous day shifts. That the women who walked through the televisual windows of his life were naked, were needy, were secretly exhibitionist.

A noise arrested him mid-stroke. Dave noted that it was nearly six o'clock. The next shift was about to begin. As slowly and naturally as he could, the guard moved his right hand on to the desk, and ran his fingers over the tracker ball. Dave gripped the small metallic joystick with his left, zooming and scanning, swooping into people's lives, banking around office blocks, following fast-moving cars. Another day of uninterrupted surveillance was about to resume. The door opened and his replacement entered.

Dave nodded. 'Jim.'

'Dave,' his replacement replied.

Dave was reluctant to hand over control. Particularly, he was disinclined to stand up until he knew he was safe. He pulled his jumper down slightly.

'Anything good been going on?'

'Fight outside a chip shop about three. Attempted mugging, some whoring – you know. Nothing unusual.'

'Cops get the mugger?'

'Nah. Way too slow. I called it in as soon as it happened, but they said they would be ten minutes. So I follows him across but lost him on eighteen, which has stopped panning.'

'Stopped panning? Here, give us a go.'

Dave stood up, happy now that his erection had subsided. The new guard sat down and stared intently at Monitor 18, attacking the joystick and rollerball with thick stubby fingers. 'The fucker's broken. What you been doing to it? You see some skirt?'

Dave chuckled. 'Cheeky cunt,' he said. 'Here, you want me to leave the mag?'

Jim examined the cover and frowned. '*Razzle*? You sick fuck. Your missus in again?'

'Chance'd be a fine thing,' Dave answered, a genuine look of regret seeping into his features. 'Anyway, you want a brew before I go?'

Jim nodded. 'But make it —' He was interrupted by an insistent buzzing from one of the screens. 'Fuck's that?' he asked.

Dave stopped. 'Pattern recognition. Euston branch installed some experimental system, spots people out of a crowd. We used it about four months ago to pick some bloke up.'

'And then what?'

'There was a bit of flack about whether we should have used it. Shit hit the proverbial.'

'How come no fucker told me?'

'It was a one-off. And then last week, out of the blue, some weedy fuck with a double-barrelled name came over from Euston CID and gave it a new face to search for.' Dave took the joystick from the tattooed hand of his colleague. 'Here, budge over,' he said. The guard frowned, zooming the camera, his tongue moving in unison with his fingers, as if it was working their strings. 'And that' – he scrutinized the close-up of a face bobbing slightly as it walked along a pavement – 'is the one they're after.' Dave picked up a phone, watching his captive as if he could escape the square screen at any moment. 'Druids Lane CCTV. We've got a target walking east along Junction Road, just passing a zebra crossing, approaching Somerset Ave. Wanted by the Euston branch. Special request.' The face disappeared, and Dave followed new buzzing on an adjacent screen. 'Yep. Heading left on to Somerset. They called it in as a Priority One. I dunno. It's here, hang on.' Dave indicated for Jim to pass him a log book from the far side of the semi-circular desk. He tapped his fingers rapidly, and then flicked quickly through the book as he received it. 'We've got a Reuben Mait . . . Reuben Mait-*land*. Dr Maitland, it says here.' Dave scanned the bank of monitors. 'I'd guess towards the Mayfield Centre. But he's still on Somerset.'

'Looks a right shifty mother.' The man on the screen glanced warily about him, as if aware that his progress was suddenly being scrutinized.

'Yeah, I've just got contact.' A squad car made feline progress, pouncing from screen to screen, honing in. It took corners wide, overtook on the wrong side, tearing towards the man. 'Looks like blue jeans, light tracksuit top, trainers. Can't miss him – he's the only fucker on the pavement.' A second car appeared from the other direction, its blue lights flashing, silently screeching around roundabouts. 'I'll stay with it,' Dave spoke into the receiver. 'Looks like about thirty or forty seconds.' The man was walking hurriedly, leaning forwards, making progress. The two vehicles dashed along straight roads, hurtling towards each other like speeding trains. Between them, the man continued to examine the road as he marched on.

'Shit.' Jim was the first to spot the problem.

'What?'

'There's a fucking underground,' he said, 'fifty yards.'

'We've seen an underground,' Dave repeated into the phone. 'Charing Cross. Tell your boys to step on it.'

The guards watched the man pat his pockets. They saw him pull a ticket out. They scanned the screens, willing the cars closer. They were seconds away. A police motorcycle had also joined in, but it was too remote. The man reached the station. They saw him register the flashing lights heading towards him. He stepped smartly inside. 'He's gone in, he's gone in,' Dave shouted. The car slowed, hesitated and then stopped. There was a short pause. They could see the coppers talking into their radios. The message was gradual. Dave felt his words crawling through the wires, fighting through switchboards, crackling into radiowaves, spitting out of speakers.

'Come on!' Jim shouted, forming tattooed fists and slamming the desk with them.

'He's gone in the fucking station!' Dave screamed.

The policemen opened their doors and ran inside. Dave and Jim exchanged glances, and Dave replaced the receiver. 'What do you think?' he said.

'He's got a ticket, he'll be long gone.' They monitored the screen forlornly. A couple of early-morning tourists asked for directions, their rucksacks almost pulling them over. A newspaper seller shouted inaudibly. A businesswoman scanned a piece of paper as she entered the tube station. The two coppers reappeared from the same exit, returning to their car, speaking into their radios. The motorcycle pulled up, joined by the second car.

'Right, about that cuppa,' Dave muttered, checking his watch and noticing, now the excitement was over, that he wasn't currently being paid. 'Then I'm off.'

Jim nodded. 'Milk and two,' he said. 'And if they ask me about this . . .'

'They might. Just tell them exactly what happened.'

'But you said last time—'

'Hang on,' Dave interrupted. 'Hang the fuck on.'

Screen 42 showed a grainy image of washed-out colour, as lifeless as the side street it monitored. A helmeted constable was emerging from a different underground exit. His head was cocked to one side, and he appeared to be talking into a shoulder radio. He was holding the captive firm by the elbow. Jim and Dave whooped, watching as the other officers ran around the corner. The man didn't struggle. He walked with sad acceptance. Within seconds he was besieged. He was pushed to the floor, his arms bent behind his back. One copper whispered in his ear. Another pressed firmly between the man's shoulder blades with his knee, cuffing his hands. A WPC searched him, patting up his legs, around his torso and along his manacled arms. They lifted him up and bundled him towards a car. His head banged as they forced him, battering-ram style, into the rear seats.

'Gotcha, Dr Maitland,' Dave said triumphantly. 'Whoever you are.'

GCACGATAGCTTACGGG
GATCTA**EIGHT**GGTTTC
GCTAATCGTCATAACAT

1

Davie Hethrington-Andrews wound his index finger around the helical phone flex, coiling and uncoiling it, watching his fingertip turn white as the lead tightened, and redden again in between. He pictured the blood being alternately trapped and then released. He was hunched forwards. The corridor was quiet. Aside from the large man standing over him, he was alone.

Davie knew what he could and couldn't say. He had been told the rules. They had especially warned him away from hints and insinuations. This was to be just one more weekly call, a son enquiring about the health and well-being of his mother. The large man leant against a straight arm, palm pushing into the wall, slightly too close. Davie could smell the sourness of his armpit, and see the conviction of his tattoos. He cleared his throat as the call was answered.

'Hello,' he said flatly. 'Is my mother there?'

A few seconds later, he said, 'Mum? It's Davie. Are you OK?'

He wound the flex tighter, constricting the circulation of his finger and feeling the dull ache of oxygen starvation. 'Yes, you know. The usual,' he answered. And then, 'Well what can you expect? It was never going to be a bed of roses.'

While he listened patiently to the reply, his cellmate Griff walked by, studiously avoiding eye contact. Davie smiled, breathing in more of the acrid odour of recent exercise, a smell which conveyed protection. People were afraid of him now. Not directly, but because of the baggage he carried. It was an uneasy privilege, however. Often Davie feared the men protecting him more than anyone.

'You know I can't talk about that,' he answered. Davie saw out of the corner of his eye that the man was glaring intently down at him.

'Mum? Are you all right? I just worried that they were . . .'

'Really?'

'No, don't cry. Everything will be OK in the end. Seriously. He's made guarantees. He needs us. Look, Mum, soon it will all be back to normal. I promise. And we'll be able to forget . . . we'll be a family again. All of us. And I'll stay out of trouble.'

His mother talked rapidly, almost hysterically, and Davie tried to calm her.

'Trust me, Mum. Just hang in there. We'll be all right. We'll be all right.'

'No, no. Really. I can see light.'

The smell of the man assigned to babysit him grew less intense. Davie scratched a long fingernail into the faded green plaster.

'You know I can't talk about that.'

Davie hesitated. His personal bodyguard appeared to be losing interest. He was edging away, lighting a cigarette, passing the time of day with another inmate. Davie decided this was his only chance.

'I spoke to Jez,' he said, urgently and quietly, cupping the end of the receiver with both hands, holding the mouthpiece like a flame about to go out, 'and he seemed . . . I don't know, I'm just worried about him. Have you been able to?'

He monitored his babysitter warily, but found him still distracted.

'Look, this may be the only chance I get to say this, Mum. Listen carefully. You know what this is all about? You know why they're watching you? You know why they monitor what I say to you, and why you can't come and visit? It's all about Jez. He has the one thing that they—'

Davie was falling forwards, the floor looming, his head hitting, teeth jarring together, his nose on fire. He scrambled up. The babysitter stood over him, cigarette in his mouth, muscles twitching, gripping the phone like a blunt instrument. He waved his index finger back and forth a couple of times, mouthing the word 'No'. Davie felt his nose, which wasn't bleeding. He spat out a small chip of tooth. The babysitter turned and walked back to the communal lounge. Davie ran his fingers over his face and blinked with watery shock. There was an unpleasant numbness in his top lip. He eyed the phone, swore to himself, and then followed.

2

'So, Dr Maitland. You understand that we're not officially charging you yet, but we are going to hold you here while the charge sheets are drawn up? You are free to contact legal representation, and everything you say will be taken down . . . yadda yadda yadda. You know how it all works.'

The prisoner said nothing. He searched their expressions, making up his mind, calculating the best options.

'WPC Marsh and myself, Detective Gommershall, will question you first, before we hand you over to your old team at Euston CID. Is that clear?'

He remained impassive. He had been here before, and knew that silence bought a lot of thinking time.

'Right, Reuben. What say we get started? We just need the basics. So, how about your current address.'

The detainee shuffled in his seat, feeling the cold complaint of future bruises. The arrest had been rough, and his torso was stiffening up. He examined the questioning officers and figured them for also-rans. He needed a reaction, had to know what they knew before he committed himself.

'I'll ask you again,' Detective Gommershall said. 'What is your current address?'

'Look,' the WPC soothed, 'there's nothing to gain now. We're not taking a statement. We just want to confirm your details, seeing as you were apprehended on our patch. Where are you living, Reuben?'

The edge of the desk was dappled with a wood-grain effect. Against the grain were the sawing scratches of a hundred pairs of bored handcuffs. 'Dunno,' he answered quietly.

'Right. OK,' the detective replied. 'Fine.' There was irritation in the brevity of his words. 'How about your date of birth?'

'Dunno.'

'Your place of birth?'

'Dunno.'

'Occupation?'

'Dunno.'

'Do you know today's date?'

'Dunno.'

'We're only trying to help you, Dr Maitland,' the WPC said, leaning forwards. 'As I say, all we need to do—'

'Stop fucking us about,' Detective Gommershall interrupted. He ran both sets of fingers up his brow and through his fine dark hair. It had been a long night shift. All they wanted were the detainee's basics, and they could hand him over and escape to their beds. 'You're wasting my time, WPC Marsh's time, and your time. We'll charge you anyway. Now, for the last fucking time, give me your current address.'

'Dunno.'

'You don't know very much, do you?'

'I don't know anything until I've spoken to a brief.'

'We just need you to confirm your name and address, and then we'll organize legal for you. Now, what's your name?'

'Dunno.'

The automatic answer echoed in the small subterranean room, was sucked in by the tape recorder, magnetized on to its dual rotating reels, and rang in the detective's ears. He jumped to his feet and shouted, 'Look, you little prick, I don't care who you are, or who you once were, fuck me about any more and I'll turn that machine off and I'll make you say anything I want you to say. This is a serious fucking charge, so stop fucking with us. Give me your address or you're going to lose some fucking teeth.' Detective Gommershall glanced sideways at his colleague, who avoided eye contact, and sat slowly back in his seat, battling his anger. He stared down at his knuckles, which were so white that the bones appeared to be breaking through the skin. When he looked back up, the prisoner's expression had changed. He asked him, with noticeable control in his voice, 'Where do you live?'

The detainee coughed, a muffled clearing of his throat. He had elicited the reaction he'd been looking for. However, he appreciated that the situation was worse than he had imagined. He had to think quickly. 'I'll tell you where I live,' he answered. 'But first I have to tell you a few other things. And then I want to talk to a brief.'

'Like what, Dr Maitland?' the WPC asked.

He hesitated. Ahead of him lay a series of unpleasant questions and situations. He had to be careful. He had seen enough to know that there was no benefit or protection in subterfuge, and that the truth was just as dangerous. He was almost caught, but there might be a way out. 'First, my name isn't Maitland. It's Mitland. Without the first A.'

'*Mit*-land?'

'Yep. And my Christian name is not Reuben.'

'No?'

'What is it?'

'It's Aaron.'

'Aaron Mitland. *Mit*-land?' Detective Gommershall's eyes bugged again. 'I thought I told you—'

There was a sharp rap on the door. WPC Marsh walked over and opened it. A short, terse exchange rattled the corridor outside. A female officer entered. She was pretty, in a fragile sort of way. The prisoner noted that her irises were dark-edged saucers of pearlescent blue, drawing light into her face, swallowing it up. He saw doubt in her brow, unease in her features, a hesitation he had watched a million times before. While he scrutinized her face she stared deeper into him. It was like the meeting of partial amnesiacs. A second officer entered the room. He was squat, broad and businesslike. He joined the female officer, running bloodshot whites over him. There was something disconcerting about the stare, like his eyes were exuding rather than extracting information.

'What do you think, Sarah?' the officer asked, maintaining his stare.

'Bit of a poser, Phil.'

'Come on, Reuben,' Phil Kemp encouraged, 'it's over.'

The prisoner smiled. 'Like I told the other two officers, I'm not Reuben. I'm Aaron Mitland. Reuben's brother. You did know he had a brother?' He watched the nascent disappointment in the faces of the two new CID, and appreciated that they did indeed know this.

'How can we check this out?' DCI Sarah Hirst asked no one in particular.

'No point DNA-testing him.'

'Exactly. If they're identical, they're identical.' Sarah turned to the detainee. 'You *are* identical, are you not?'

The prisoner shrugged. While he feigned comfortable indifference, his mind darted and raced, concocted stories and alibis, grasped for ways out. He needed to know exactly what evidence they had.

'Look, Aaron – if you are Aaron – why play along till now?'

'I didn't exactly get the chance for discussion.' As he answered, he considered the implications, shivered at what they might find out. 'They jump me in a tube station, bundle me straight here and then start the questions. Thought I ought to see what my brother was accused of first.'

'You mean you didn't know?'

'No.'

'And you never saw any of this on the news?'

'I live in a squat.' He clenched his fists under the table, picturing them in cuffs, seeing them sawing into the surface, adding to the multitude of ruts. 'We're not big on TV.'

'But you must have spoken with GeneCrime?'

Aaron Mitland blew cool air out of the side of his mouth. 'You'll have to work harder than that if you want to catch me out.'

'Hang on,' Sarah said, holding up her hand with traffic-cop abruptness. 'How was the arrest made?'

WPC Marsh, who had been watching proceedings slouched against a far wall, stood upright. 'Called in via CCTV. We got word of some sort of pattern-recognition ID . . .'

Phil Kemp and Sarah Hirst exchanged glances. Aaron Mitland watched their faces intently. The WPC rested her hands on her hips, unsure whether to relax again. Detective Gommershall brooded in his seat, refusing to make eye contact with anyone. Aaron waited for the attention to return to him. He pictured his brother, excelling, obsessing, a string pulled slightly too tight. Watching the reactions of people who clearly knew Reuben and who had worked beside him, for an instant he longed to swap places with them, to experience Reuben not as a brother, but as a neutral, as a normal person with no baggage, no shared history of conflict and strife, and no guilt. But then he pulled back. He retreated within the four magnolia walls, the thin blue carpet, the bare, strip-lit ceiling. Familiar ground. Another cell; another bunch of coppers.

'Let's say you're not Reuben,' Phil began, 'where is your squat? Could you give us an address?'

Fuck no. The worst thing. 'I want my brief. Now.'

'And what do you do for a living?'

'This and that.' Aaron cast his eyes around the cell. 'Mainly this.' He tried to untangle the growing knot in his stomach, acutely aware of how much danger he was in. It was only a matter of time before they obtained his arrest record, started picking through the details, ran his name and appearance through their Unsolved databases, started to generate a few hits, got more interested in him, began to piece his activities together. He had to get out, away, disappear for a while. And that meant convincing them that he wasn't his brother. But this was a fine line to tread. There was a big snag looming. He anticipated the next discussion, which duly permeated the cell with grim inevitability.

'Think about it, Sarah,' Phil whispered, loudly enough that Aaron could hear it, 'we've become obsessed with Reuben. But if this is his monozygous brother, he has identical DNA to him.'

'And hence identical DNA to the murderer.'

'Don't forget the Pheno-Fit. And the pattern recognition. Maybe we already have our man.'

DCIs Kemp and Hirst turned as one to face him, almost as though they'd choreographed the movement. Its effect was unnerving, like meeting two lanes of the truth head on, hurtling round a blind bend. Aaron saw in an instant that these were not people to fuck with. They were different. Something set them apart from the run-of-the-mill coppers who asked direct questions to solve direct crimes.

'Where were you on the following dates?' Phil Kemp asked, scribbling some numbers down on a notepad.

'Or maybe you can prove to me you're NOT Reuben,' Sarah said.

'Call Fingerprints,' Phil instructed WPC Marsh.

'I'll instruct a team to swab his squat,' Sarah added.

'Come on, Reuben, the game's up.'

'I'm not—'

'We know who you are.'

'Reuben. Aaron. What's the difference?'

'It's your DNA on the victims.'

'Where is your brother?'

'When was the last time you saw him?'

'Did you help him?'

'You were doing this together.'

'Covering for each other.'

'Classic alibi strategy.'

'Always in two places at once.'

'Let's get the CCTV from this morning, find out exactly where you're staying.'

'We'll work back from your arrest, hunt down your residence.'

'See what people know.'

Aaron Mitland glanced up at them. They could smell blood. They thought they were on to something. If they could trace his movements back to the squat, he was fucked. His brother was fucked anyway. They were both in trouble. The questions kept coming. He tried to focus through them. He had to think, and think fast.

3

Maclyn Margulis stretched his legs in the front seat of his BMW X5, running his fingers lightly around the leather steering wheel. Today, he had insisted on driving. There was a time to be guided, and a time to guide. He glanced at his associate in the rear-view mirror, using the excuse to examine his own profile, his jet-black hair, his chiselled jaw.

'Mart,' he said, 'you're sure about the address?'

'Yeah.'

'How sure?'

'Pretty sure.'

'As a percentage?'

'What do you mean?'

Maclyn Margulis swivelled slightly in his upholstered luxury, raising his eyebrows at the other man, who was hunched in the passenger seat beside him. 'Out of a hundred.'

'Ninety. Give or take.'

'And who exactly did the info come from?'

'Bluey Jones. He followed the target's associate, some fat Scotsman, who had a meeting with Kieran Hobbs.'

'Is Bluey still working for Hobbs?'

'Seems that way.'

'Can you trust him?'

'Pretty much.'

'As a percentage?'

'Same again.'

'I just don't get what Hobbs has to gain from this,' Maclyn Margulis said, partially to himself. 'Why's he putting this our way?'

'Maybe the geezer's outlived his usefulness.'

'Maybe. Or perhaps Reuben Maitland knows something that he shouldn't.' Maclyn turned to the other man, who was broad and mustachioed, a bony hardness in his face, a muscular readiness about his torso. His scalp was so clean shaven that it almost shone. 'Anyway, that sound OK for you?'

'What's the background?' the man asked, emotionless.

'Look, we need a hit. That's it. The details aren't important.'

'The details are all that's important. The last man you sent, there was a rumour . . .'

'One of my own. A good boy, bit on the sadistic side, but a good boy. Marcus Archer.'

'I heard he got whacked.'

Maclyn Margulis sighed. 'Not whacked in the way you're thinking. Whacked over the head. In an alleyway, by the cunt he was sent to sort out. Turns out he must have had prior knowledge, or protection or something. Probably knocked some sense into him.'

'So as I say, the details.'

Maclyn Margulis hesitated. Focusing past the bulky passenger, he took in the sheer exoticism of London's newest skyscraper behind. It had already been christened the Gherkin. To Maclyn it was a huge bullet, thrusting its slug into the gunsmoke clouds. It was not his policy to share information with anybody. But this had to be sorted. 'Right,' he relented. 'Reuben Maitland is ex-police, a forensics officer. Here's his force picture.'

'So what's your interest?'

Maclyn Margulis breathed deep. This kind of curiosity was

usually fatal. 'You know Kieran Hobbs's gang over in West London?'

'Bits and pieces.'

'Hobbs's second-in-command, Joey Salvason, got mixed up in something we were doing. Nasty piece of work, overstepped the bounds. Wouldn't back down so I had to sort him out. Gave him a severe beating, which turned out to be a little bit too severe, if you catch my drift.' He smiled at the man, but elicited no reaction. 'So we lie low for a bit. We're a big operation, but we don't want to take Kieran Hobbs on. No point. Then I hear some fucking forensic scientist is sniffing around Joey Salvason's body, on a mission for Hobbs. This is going to stir things up big time. So I send Marcus Archer to track him down and silence him. Only Marcus, as we've mentioned, goes and gets himself knocked unconscious. Next thing I know, Kieran Hobbs has arranged a meeting, out in the open so no one's going to get hurt, lunchtime restaurant, Covent Garden, that sort of thing. Tells me he now knows for certain that I killed Joey Salvason.'

'Yeah?'

'Yeah. So, during the meal, this ponce comes over with a flowery bit, long-lost friend of Kieran's. Afterwards, I send a minder after them to check them out, but they jump in a cab. I think no more about it. I deny hurting his boy, we leave the meal, then nothing. Not till yesterday' – Maclyn Margulis closed his eyes for a moment – 'when Hobbs comes round to my place, mob-handed. He's got a picture in his hand. It looks like me, except ginger-haired, buck-toothed, big chin, you know, a right lemon.' Maclyn ran a hand through his shiny black hair. He took a quick glance in the rear-view mirror at his employee in the back seat. 'Cut a long story short, he accuses me of being the killer. Tells me he's now got cast-iron forensic evidence. Says DNA taken from Joey Salvason proves it. Reckons the tests were done by the ponce in the restaurant, who, it just turns out, is not his long-lost friend, but – you guessed it – the ex-copper Reuben

Maitland. Of course I deny it. They're standing there, shooters out, we're fucking helpless. And then Hobbs walks forwards, pushes his pistol into the chest of Tony, my right-hand man, and pops him. In front of me and everything. Says an eye for one, and now we're square, turns round and leaves. And there's Tony, squirming on the ground, fucking bleeding to death.' Maclyn Margulis stared bitterly into the man with his incongruously blue eyes. 'You think you can finish the job?'

The man didn't bother to look at him. 'So why has Hobbs now given you Reuben Maitland's whereabouts?'

'Why do I give a fuck? The only issue I'm interested in is whether you can you do the job.'

'Never failed yet,' the man replied, running a hand over his shaven scalp, and then through his moustache, as if savouring the contrast.

'Well, you do come highly recommended. And, if I might say so, highly expensive.'

'You get what you pay for. You want ex-special forces, you pay the going rate.'

'Now when're you going to do it?'

'Soon.'

'Make sure it is. Don't leave this long. I want it taken care of by the end of the week.'

The man tucked the envelope into his jacket. He opened the door and climbed out, walking away without looking back. Maclyn Margulis monitored his progress. 'Job done,' he said to Martin, craning his head round. He watched the man heading towards the Gherkin, being swallowed up by suited City workers. 'Actually, Martin,' he frowned, 'why don't you drive?'

The heavy black X5 pulled away, trailing a dual stream of exhaust gases, which dissolved in the warm air. A few seconds later, an unmarked Ford Mondeo parked a hundred metres behind indicated and followed, maintaining a discreet distance, its CID officers monitoring the BMW's progress intently.

4

Judith Meadows jerked a bedroom drawer open and quickly counted five pairs of knickers. She pulled out a lower drawer and extracted five pairs of socks. Then she stuffed everything into a black leather bag. On top of this, she planted two pairs of jeans and a couple of light jumpers. She moved rapidly over to the wardrobe and flicked through coat hangers like vinyl albums. There was no time to choose outfits. It was simply a case of selecting a range of garments which would roughly match. As she rummaged, Judith glanced nervously out of the window. She was pale and unsteady, and her eyes were ringed with the evidence of missed sleep. Judith pressed a button on her mobile, and gripped it in the tense crook of her neck.

'Hi,' she said when it was answered. 'It's me.'

On the other end, Reuben began to say, 'You sound—'

'I'm fine,' Judith declared. 'Just fine.' She pulled a blouse off a hanger and it rocked emptily back and forth. 'Look, Reuben, I'll cut straight to the point. I've been thinking about the situation I'm in, and I've made a decision.'

'Sounds like the end of a relationship.'

'In a way it is.'

'Yeah?'

'Yeah. I want out of this.' Judith nudged the curtain back

slightly and peered out into the street. 'Despite what I said the other day, it's not that I don't trust you . . . it's just that everything's terrible, horrible . . .'

'What's happened?'

'I came to my senses, realized I can't go on living this way. Whatever may have happened at GeneCrime in the past is irrelevant now. People are dying.' She threw the blouse on to the bed and ran her fingers over the densely packed array of dresses and tops hanging in her wardrobe. 'And someone is coming for me. They're going to torture me and kill me. I need protection, and yet I'm protecting the main suspect. It has to stop. I have to take sides. Surely you understand? I could lose my job, everything . . .'

Reuben was quiet for a second. 'I understand,' he said.

'Look, I know you didn't do those things, but that's not the point. You always taught me about loyalty.' She tugged a pale-blue polo-neck from its skeletal coat hanger and pushed it roughly into her bag. 'Now my loyalty has to be with the team. We have to stay alive and we have to stick together. I can't undermine the people who are trying to catch the murderer.'

'Like I say, Jude, I understand.'

'And there's something else you should know.'

'What?'

'I guess you won't have heard yet, but they've . . . *we've* . . . arrested your brother.'

'Aaron? Christ. When was this?'

'Early today. Apparently a case of mistaken identity.' Judith paced into the bathroom and began to throw a range of products into a toiletries bag. 'They thought it was you, Picasso.'

Despite himself, Reuben snorted. 'I bet he loved that.'

'It was weird seeing him. He was like an edgy version of yourself. I kept having to remind myself that it wasn't you.'

'So . . . Shit! I bet they're going to try and pin it on him.'

'Oh yes. After all, we've got DNA, samples . . .'

'Where's he being held?'

'Why? You can't exactly go and visit him.'

'I'd just like to know.'

'He's down at Ludgate Road. And between you and me, I get the distinct impression they're going to use him to get to you.'

'How?'

'I'm not sure. But think about it. They're holding your brother while really all they want is you.'

Judith pushed her palm down flat on a can of deodorant and a hairbrush, willing them into the narrow confines of her toiletries bag. The brush left a small battalion of dents in her hand. She forced the zip bluntly around the bag's periphery, poking stray items out of the way of the zip's progress. Carrying it with her, she returned to the main bedroom and dropped it heavily into the case.

'What are you doing?' Reuben asked her after a couple of seconds' pause.

'Packing,' she replied.

'To go where?'

'I have to get away. I'm not safe. CID are meant to be looking after us, but they're by no means infallible.' Judith's face struggled to regain its usual serenity, and she exhaled heavily. 'And things aren't working out with Charlie. I'm drowning in guilt, and I'm worried he's starting to suspect something.'

'I'm sorry.'

'Are you?'

'Of course.'

'I mean sorry that it happened, or . . .'

'Or what?'

'Sorry for what has subsequently happened?' Judith stopped, her soft breathing filling the silence.

'I don't understand what you're asking.'

'Yes you do, Reuben.'

'Look, Jude . . .' Reuben saw it for the first time. In this moment, on a phone, in desperate times, he realized that, close as they had come, they were not destined to be together. He pictured Judith's long years of loyalty. The willingness to help him, to take risks for him. It had always been there, simmering. He knew, because he had felt it too. But still, Reuben realized that this was not to be. It was the wrong time, the wrong place, the wrong set of circumstances. 'I'm just not ready.'

'It's OK,' she whispered. 'It's nothing. Things are a little crazy, that's all. I'm trying not to come apart at the seams.'

'Jude, I don't regret what went on between us at all. I wish . . .'

'Ignore me. I'm really all over the place.'

'I don't know what to say.'

'So say nothing.'

Reuben listened to the falling waves of her breathing, closing his eyes, understanding how fucked up things had become. With him, with Judith, with everything. 'Where are you going to stay?'

'Friends. People who don't know anything about this. People who will look after me.' Her voice had gained a cold briskness, as if she merely wanted to fast-forward through the discomfiture.

On the other end of the line, Reuben hung his head and stared at his feet. 'But don't you think you should stay—'

'And be the next on the list? No chance. Look, I shouldn't tell you this, and this is the last piece of insider information that I'm going to give you, but Jez is missing. Hasn't been seen for a couple of days, and isn't answering at home.'

'I'll give his mobile a try.'

'So that's why I'm not saying where I'm going or who I'm staying with. Someone knows where we all live. Mina was followed home. Run and Sandra were attacked at their houses, and Lloyd . . . I know I'm next. Reuben, he's coming for me.'

'So what about the other suspects in the case? What's happened to them?'

Judith rammed two pairs of shoes into the side of her bag and tried it for weight. 'I said no more info.'

'OK. Last piece.'

'We haven't got a whereabouts for the other two strongest potentials, Lars Besser and Mark Gelson. We've got CCTV, and we know they're in London, but that's all. It's been difficult to tie them to the crime scenes, and not much has emerged from house-to-house in Lloyd Granger's street. But there is some good news.'

'What?'

'The forensics on Lloyd are due imminently. Literally hours until we get the profile.'

'Which will probably be mine again.'

'Not this time. Sarah suggested eyeball sweeps—'

'Wonder where she got that idea?'

'And Mina reckons she has something promising. Then we can start to trawl the databases and look for previous. We've also been able to exclude one more of our initial four – Stephen Jacobs – who turned out to be very cooperative, largely because he'd been seen hanging around schools, and was desperate not to go down again. So that just leaves Besser and Gelson, both of whom are on the loose. And, of course, Maitland.'

'I thought I was a done deal. Why are they persisting with Besser and Gelson?'

'I get the impression that, at heart, Phil Kemp still isn't a hundred per cent convinced it's you.'

'Nice to know.'

'It's about as good as you're going to get.' Judith took a final glance out of the window. 'And that, Reuben, is as much as I can tell you.' She hoisted the bag over her shoulder and took the phone into her hand. 'So I guess this is it,' she said, almost formally.

'I guess it is.'

Judith walked briskly down the stairs, the extra weight magnifying the thump of her shoes on the carpet. 'Look after yourself, Reuben,' she said. 'Because no one else is going to.'

Judith pressed the Off button on her phone and left the house. She ran to her car and engaged the central locking, checking the doors were safe before she started the engine. As she drove, she monitored the rear-view mirror and cursed herself. Although she was shaky and uncertain, a lead-weight of regret clung to her and refused to leave. Judith decided it was best for everyone concerned if she disappeared for the time being.

5

Reuben placed his phone on the lab bench beside him. Jez's mobile had rung straight through to Messages. Staring intently down, he saw for the first time a fine layer of dust on the surface of the worktop, and noticed a couple of hairs languishing next to a brightly coloured plastic rack. Spraying 70% ethanol on to a paper towel, he scrubbed the bench slowly and methodically, a surgeon washing his hands before an operation. Even when it was clean, he continued to scour, lulled by the motion, soothed by the mechanics of preparation. The tissue dried, its alcohol evaporating in fine films, and began to squeak in complaint.

Reuben stopped cleaning and began to search around, on the shelves, in the small fridge under the bench, in an upright freezer at his side, once again picking out the ingredients he needed for the cookery of molecular biology. He entered a trance-like state, calculating volumes, estimating temperatures, working out concentrations, labelling tubes, scribbling notes, programming cycles, assembling plates, pipetting liquids, extracting nucleic acids, equilibrating arrays, scanning read-areas, gauging quantities, loading reactions, monitoring electrophoreses and initiating algorithms.

He thought about his brother, repeated the words he had said to Judith, listened in his head to her short, rushed sentences, mulled over Jez's disappearance, attempted to guess what the eyeball samples were going to show him, chewed a sandwich, etched the uninjured face of Lloyd Granger into a fresh square of canvas, called Moray, who was stuck in Finland, of all places, paced around, monitored the door, scratched his stubble, slept, screwed up the canvas image and threw it in the bin, considered Kieran Hobbs and Maclyn Margulis, thought of the warm rush of pure amphetamine, tried to shut out images of his alcoholic father, wondered again who had attempted to kill him in the alleyway, leafed sadly through photos of Joshua, stifled notions of Lucy and Shaun Graves raising his son, repressed the notion that Joshua would become someone else's boy, someone armed with a baseball bat, and fought the tightening in his throat and the cold ache in his ribs.

Seconds, minutes and hours were measured out in micro-litres, millilitres and litres. Every press of the pipette inched him towards a feature; every action of each procedure brought him closer to the face. He battled an itchy, greasy, burning tiredness. Reuben entered a stretch of thoughtless action, the mechanics taking over, scientific autopilot pulling him through. He shut down the peripherals, the distractions, the worries and cleared his head. There came a point where thinking was actually detrimental. Lost in the purity of his procedures, Reuben moved into the final stages of Predictive Phenotyping. He had re-suspended, extracted, amplified, labelled, hybridized and washed. The array was complete, with signals which would turn into numbers, which would be compared with data-sets, which would be dragged through algorithms, which would appear as shades and tones and sizes and locations and characteristics. Reuben transferred the RNA chip data from the fluorescent reader to his laptop.

Coming alive again, he ran his middle finger, with its chewed nail and slender carpals, over the tracker ball. He selected the Run button, drew a nervous breath, and pressed it. The hard-drive buzzed with eagerness, galloping through the calculations and comparisons. Blurry digits scrolled upwards, flashing green and red as they went. Reuben glanced at his watch. It was 11 a.m. Somewhere he had lost another day. Time slipping through his fingers as he sought other people's truths. The face was thirty minutes away. Already, a framework was appearing, crude lines mapping out the 3D surface it would colour and stretch into a photographic image. Reuben's mobile rang, vibrating along the bench towards him. The ID was masked. He hesitated, appreciating that calls from Finland wouldn't necessarily be recognized by his phone. 'Hello,' he said flatly, rubbing his eyes.

'Reuben Maitland?' the voice asked.

Reuben straightened. 'Who is this?'

'I think you know already.'

He stood up involuntarily, his guts filled with ice. 'Tell me.'

'First things first. I think you should know that I have someone with me.'

'Who?'

'Jeremy Hethrington-Andrews. Your old colleague, I believe?'

'Jez? Let me speak to him.'

The phone was handed over, crackling, becoming quiet and then going live again. 'Help me, Reuben,' Jez said suddenly, his words bursting out of the earpiece. 'He's serious. I'm next. He's going to—'

Jez's thin, terrified plea was replaced by a firmer, broader utterance. 'That's enough.'

The line went dead momentarily, before Reuben could hear the scraping and scuffling sounds of the receiver being passed back.

'Look, who are you?' Reuben asked, almost desperately. 'At least tell me your name.'

'Let me get straight to the point. You have been very elusive, Dr Maitland, and now I wish to meet you.' The voice was calm, in control, almost hypnotic. Reuben appreciated that the last utterances Sandra, Run and Lloyd had heard were the soothing tones of a man who took comfort from the distress of others. 'As an incentive, I will be executing Jeremy in one hour if you don't turn up. We're at Flat one hundred and thirteen B, Alcester Towers, Penny Drive, Walthamstow. As the number suggests, we're on the eleventh floor. It won't be too difficult to spot whether you have come alone or not. And if you do have company, Jeremy will be exploring the pavement with a great deal of momentum.' Reuben scribbled the address frantically, unplugging his laptop, folding it up, grabbing his wallet and keys. 'You have fifty-nine minutes,' the man stated. 'And then we can finally get down to business.'

Reuben scanned the laboratory wildly, then ran for the door, carrying his computer. He dashed along the underground passageway which linked into the wrecked factory above, and out, over the broken glass, into the light. He sprinted through the elongated industrial estate, which was fed by a long, straight road with no pavement. He glanced left and right before deciding on the latter. About six hundred metres further was a busy intersection. As he ran he checked his watch, swivelling the diving bezel around to fifty minutes. There was just time. He pictured Jez, pupils wide, knowing that death could be within the hour.

Racing towards the junction, Reuben felt the warm laptop nuzzling into his armpit. He saw cars slowing and stopping, but no taxis. Surely he would be able to flag one down? There was no time to be standing around. Just as he reached his destination, he heard the familiar clatter of a black cab behind him. Please let the light be on, he gasped through burning lungs. He swivelled round, stuck out his arm and saw a flash of yellow. The taxi sped by, and entered the junction. Reuben swore, running his eyes desperately up and down the three intersecting roads. No other taxis were in sight. Then he saw that the cab was turning around. Reuben realized that there had been nowhere to stop. It beeped at him and pulled over. He climbed in the back and said breathlessly, 'Walthamstow. Quick. Fifty quid if you can make it in half an hour.'

The driver pulled off and Reuben opened the laptop on his knee. It was still buzzing, and the face had changed. Colours were deepening, the relief map gaining contours, sprouting hairs and cutting teeth. He typed in a couple of commands and then took out his phone. He dialled DCI Sarah Hirst's number, saying 'Come on, come on' with each ring.

'Dr Maitland?' Sarah said. 'Why are you—'

'No time,' he interrupted. 'We're into the endgame. The killer called me. He's holding Jez, and is about to execute him. I've got' – Reuben examined his Dugena – 'forty-four minutes to get to Walthamstow. He wants a face to face.'

'Why you?'

'I guess this is where we've been heading.'

'Are you armed?'

'No. I want to be met somewhere within a mile of Penny Drive, Walthamstow. A firearm, something small like an S and W. Then I'll go on alone.'

'It's going to take a bit of organizing.'

The taxi swung through corners, its hard suspension rocking over the bumps, throwing Reuben around in his seat. He clung on to the computer. 'Organize it or Jez dies.'

'Look, give me the address. We'll get a team out there.'

'There's no time. And he's promised to teach Jez how to fly if he sees anyone but me.'

'Where are you now?'

He peered through the window. 'Hurtling through the back streets of Bermondsey.'

'And do you think you're going to get there?'

'Should just about do it.' Reuben braced himself in the corner of the seat. 'So you'll ring me with an address for the handover?'

'I'm typing the route in. Can you see any street names?'

He careered through a T-junction. 'Jamaica Road.'

'Jamaica. Jamaica. OK. Let me see. Bermondsey. Come on, come on. Right, got it. I can see where you're heading, give or take. We'll set something up, meet you en route. How long now?'

'Forty-one minutes.'

'Shit.' Reuben heard echoing footsteps and appreciated that Sarah was running down a corridor in GeneCrime. He was with her as she crashed through a door and clopped down a flight of stairs to the Incident Room. 'Reuben,' she breathed, 'no heroics. You're not a copper. You don't shoot people.'

'I don't intend to,' he answered.

'I've got to go. Phil – we've got a situation. Reuben's in a cab, on his way to the killer. Yep, he's on the line. Bermondsey. You want a word? Phil says good luck. Right. Reuben, remember what I said. See you on the other side. Bye.'

Reuben mouthed the word 'Bye' and slipped the phone back into his pocket. He stared into the screen, captivated, nerves firing, stomach churning, heart galloping, sweat forming, fingers clenching. The image was becoming real. Features which before were simply budding were now flowering. The program had moved from constructing to tweaking. It was, he realized, just playing, trying things on for size, like painting on the final layer of make-up before a night out. This was the man he was about to meet. And as he stared into the face before him, Reuben knew for the first time that this was the killer. Because the face was familiar. He had seen it, and within the last few days. This time there was no resemblance to himself or to his brother. The features were coarser, darker, more menacing even on the screen. He gazed into the eyes, then took in the peripheral characteristics: the thick lips, the heavy brow, the padded earlobes, the dense hair. But still the identity was elusive.

Reuben shook his head, fast-winding through recent events, flashing up everyone he had encountered: people he had walked past in the street; images he had seen in Judith's case notes; members of Kieran Hobbs's gang he had observed in the café;

344

Maclyn Margulis and his accomplices in the restaurant; the bodyguards of Xavier Trister; everyone his retinas had scanned since the death of Sandra Bantam. He gritted his teeth and tapped his forehead. The taxi swung through a mini-roundabout. Reuben checked his watch. Thirty-four minutes. He looked for street signs. Still the face wouldn't come. It was an itch at the back of his brain that refused to be scratched. He noted that the roads appeared familiar. Reuben glanced at the taxi driver's eyes in the rear-view mirror. He felt a sick premonition. He recognized the bumps of the street they were on. He examined the screen of his laptop again. He heard the central locking kick in. He rewound to the junction. The taxi. The driver. The man. The face. The face. The cab slowed. They were at the junction again. They pulled over. The driver looked round. Reuben saw two similar images, one on his laptop, one behind the driver's screen. One of them was neutral; the other was smiling. Through the payment hole poked the dead eye of a gun. Reuben folded his laptop shut. He was looking at the killer.

'You direct from here,' the man said.

'Where's Jez?' Reuben asked.

'Jez has gone. Now you'll have to show me the way. I know we're close. And no fucking about if you want to live.'

Reuben swallowed hard. 'Third left. Then follow it round towards the arches.'

The taxi lurched forwards and headed into the industrial estate.

'You recognize me?' the man asked.

'I recognize you. But it's been a while since I saw you properly.'

'It certainly has,' he answered.

'On the right,' Reuben instructed. He ground his teeth together to stop the sickness climbing his throat. He saw Sarah Hirst heading desperately towards Walthamstow, half of London's CID in pursuit. He saw Moray Carnock bugging a hotel room in Helsinki. But mostly, he pictured the cuts, the burns and the protracted tortures of Sandra, Run and Lloyd. As they picked their way through the broken building and down into the basement, the sharp, honest nose of the gun digging into his back, Reuben realized he was utterly alone in a city of eight million. He entered the lab and blinked along with the neon lights. He could scream for days and not be heard.

GCACGATAGCTTACGGG
AAATCCT**NINE**GTATTCC
GCTAATCGTCATAACAT

1

External chaos had a perversely calming influence on Phil Kemp's state of mind. In the midst of panic, he alone walked clearly through, considering the information, separating the extraneous noise from the main signal. Although frequently absent of late, his calmness had helped him in his steady rise to the position of Detective Chief Inspector. During the early days, caught up in flammable situations or messy crime scenes, he had been able to exert an authority absent in many of his peers, purely through the ability to remain unruffled. And now, as Sarah Hirst barked orders and scribbled frenzied notes, he forced his brain to regain its customary composure and focus on the single important issue.

Sarah had arranged for an Armed Response Unit to meet Reuben Maitland's taxi, for the illicit handing over of a small revolver, for roads to be sealed, and for helicopter back-up. But, Phil realized grimly, this was potentially a lose-lose situation. He picked up Sarah's CID mobile and scrolled through Options until he reached Records, and then Calls Received. Phil wrote the number down. He knew that there was little point informing his colleagues of his actions. No one would listen. Experience had told him that in the heat of battle, people only heard the firing of guns.

Sarah approached him and retrieved her phone.

'Well, here we are,' Phil said. 'The endgame.'

'Indeed.'

'Look, Sarah, what matters is we catch the bastard. That's all.'

'And don't tell me' – Sarah glared – 'you want to be the one to take him down.'

Phil was unusually contemplative, weighing up his answer. 'No, I'm not saying that.'

'So what, then?'

'Just . . . let's get this right,' he replied. 'You go get him, and I'll cover the base.'

'You sure?'

Phil nodded. 'I'm sure.'

Sarah's eyes thanked him. She turned and left the room, CID officers swirling behind her. Phil watched her hurried departure. The real glory was in the chase, in capturing the killer. Running the Incident Room was unrewarding and remote. But whatever he had to do. For once, he was content to let Sarah take the praise. As he tapped the telephone number into a computer, he reflected that it had been an intense struggle from the moment Sandra Bantam had been murdered. GeneCrime had suffered. The death of its personnel would taint GeneCrime's name for ever, given that the unit was now public knowledge, written about on front pages, speculated about in filler pieces.

But there had been another problem. The murders had opened up deep schisms in the ranks, scientists versus CID; gouges had been carved out between the two which might never be healed. Even Sarah and himself had been sucked in, failing to agree, fighting like children, vying for promotion. He wondered what the future held for his Division, and failed to see anything positive. A small flare of regret singed his calm. Phil had dedicated his professional life to running the advanced forensics unit, and it was possible this would be taken away from him after the killer was caught. There would be an investigation into his actions during the manhunt. Questions would be asked about morale, cooperation, the sharing of knowledge and a whole host of other policing issues. Sarah, he realized sadly, was on the verge of victory. As he scrolled through screens of data, Phil picked up his phone and dialled an on-screen number. He reflected that as his self-control had leaked away in the course of the investigation, he had gradually been losing the game.

'DCI Phil Kemp, Euston CID, GeneCrime Unit,' he said as the call was answered. He chewed his thumbnail, eyes wide, brow creased, and then read out the telephone digits. After a few more seconds, he gave his own phone number. He wrote a few lines of text on an A4 piece of paper, then folded it up, slotting it into his shirt pocket.

Phil replaced the receiver and sat absolutely still for a whole minute. His mind raced through a series of rapid calculations. Serenity within chaos. He considered the options, shaking his head slowly, pulling a headset on and listening to the gunfire communications shooting back and forth between officers heading for the scene.

Somewhere in the mix he detected Sarah's voice, giving orders, cajoling, seeking advice and running through scenarios. Phil could hear sirens intertwined in each statement, changing pitch and tone as various CID in different squad cars entered and left the dialogue. He jotted down locations and street names as he heard them, and tapped them into his computer, keeping a close eye on progress, watching the vehicles chase each other, being joined by new cars and vans, all inextricably converging on Walthamstow.

Phil's mobile rang and he listened intently, pulling one of his headphones away from his ear. He took the piece of paper from his breast pocket and scrawled some more numbers and figures on it. Again, he was motionless for a short period of time, temporarily cut off from the rapid events around him. Then Phil turned to a junior member of CID and said, 'Can you take over for a minute?'

The officer nodded, and Phil noted the panic in his eyes.

'You'll be fine. Good experience. Just keep a record of everything that strikes you as important, and give locations and ETAs.' He waggled his phone. 'And call me if things get out of hand.'

Phil left the Incident Room and headed for the floor below. He put his jacket on and walked down a long vinyl-floored corridor, past a succession of laboratories and offices, and towards the toilets. Inside a cubicle, he unfolded the piece of paper again and stared at it, pushing himself towards a final decision.

2

'Nice lab.'

'Thanks.'

'Very discreet, difficult to track down.'

'That's the idea.'

'Some of your colleagues were extremely unwilling to give me your address. Even after a lot of encouragement.'

'They wouldn't have known.'

'Unfortunate. You abandon your marital house, leave no forwarding address, quit your job, disappear into thin air. But now I can see why I didn't run into you earlier.'

'The torture was to get to me?'

'Not just that. As you will see.'

Reuben felt oddly calm, but knew it wouldn't last. 'So you've found me. Now what?'

'It's funny. You plan something for so long, rehearse your words, and when it happens . . . Let's say I have a strategy. You will be different from the others. More pain, but also more gain. I'll explain as we go along. Now, where's the phenol?'

Reuben moved his eyes towards a large brown bottle on a shelf above the lab bench.

'No gimmicky kits for you. Just go with what has worked for twenty years.' He frowned. 'Interrogation and truth, that's what you're taught. The truth at any cost. Is it not? All right, let's begin your very own interrogation.' He reached for the bottle and played with its cap. 'You know who I am?'

Reuben stared hard into his face, taking in the very features Predictive Phenotyping had forecast. The black eyes, the heavy eyebrows, the full lips, the barbed teeth. 'Yes, I recognize you.'

'And I am?'

'Lars Besser.'

'Very good. And why do you recognize me?'

'I've come across you before. A pub murder in the nineties.'

'Excellent. What you might also recall is the fact that you led the team which convicted me?'

'Yep.'

Something seemed to snap in the serene features of Lars Besser: there was a redness in his cheeks, a tightening of his serrated mouth; his bristling lashes dragged in the light, revealing the fiercest of eyes beneath. 'You see, extracting information is easy. Just like extracting DNA. All you need are the correct tools. Am I right?'

Reuben shrugged.

Lars Besser uncapped the phenol. 'I said, am I right?'

'Yes,' Reuben acknowledged quickly. And then he asked the question that had been haunting him for the last ten minutes. 'You've killed Jez?'

Lars smiled, a thin serpentine smile, lips snaking coldly upwards. 'Oh yes,' he answered.

'Where?'

'At his house. Only a few minutes from here.'

Reuben felt a tightening in his abdomen and a hardening of his muscles. His adrenals were working overtime, leaking their endocrine panic into his blood, pushing Reuben to maximum alert. In his heightened state he knew that pain was imminent and for a second he sensed his own transience. He had lived, burnt bright, and was now close to being snuffed out. But still his curiosity flickered. 'So you didn't torture him? You couldn't have had time . . .'

'No, I didn't torture him – there was no need. I finally had all I wanted from Jeremy. You see, Jeremy has been most helpful to me, in ways you couldn't imagine.'

Reuben looked at his watch. The hour wasn't yet up. In the fictionalized chase across London, there would still have been hope for Jez. Reuben appreciated the reason for the deception. 'It was you in the white Fiesta, following us a couple of days ago? You tailed us from the lab when we went to meet Sarah. And from that you gained the vicinity but not the address. So you flushed me out into the open and picked me off. Forced me to break cover to help a friend. Then in a stolen taxi you let me dial CID and throw them in the wrong direction before bringing me to the lab.'

'More or less.'

'So this has something to do with the laboratory? Otherwise, why not take me elsewhere?'

'You know, it's fascinating to watch your brain in action. I mean, I've heard you on the radio and read your articles – mostly derivative, narrow and poorly focused – but I can see now there's an intellect in there somewhere, struggling to get out.' Lars Besser took a step forwards, bold, in command, ramming home Reuben's powerlessness. 'Maybe it's time to return to the interrogation.' Keeping his pistol at waist height, resting against his hip, Lars passed Reuben a pair of handcuffs. 'Try these on, hands to the front.'

Reuben picked them off the bench and slotted one manacle to his left wrist, while joining the second to his right. He kept his eyes on Lars. Behind the stare a thousand thoughts and impulses tore silently through his cerebral cortex, forging connections and striking up alliances.

'Place your hands on the bench, palm down,' Lars instructed.

Reuben did as he was told, slow and automatic in his

movements, letting his brain fight for its survival. He watched Lars take a pipettor, plant it into a box of tips, then pull it out. It became increasingly obvious to Reuben that Lars knew what he was doing. Lars then dipped the instrument into the phenol, and withdrew a millilitre. Reuben had to think fast. Lars was about to interrogate and kill him. Reuben would die, surrounded by the very equipment and samples upon which he had based his investigation.

'Keep your hands very still. If you move them, I will shoot you. It's up to you, Dr Maitland – a bullet through the hand, or a drop of phenol.' Lars grabbed a marker pen and drew around Reuben's fingers, leaving a black outline on the surface of the bench and against Reuben's skin. He brought the pipette tip so that it hovered over Reuben's right hand. The drop of phenol exuded slightly, held back by its viscosity. Reuben clenched his teeth. Phenol was nasty because it had to be. When you wanted to extract DNA from muscle, or skin, or hair, you needed a chemical which would devour human cells and burst them open. Which was the very problem. You had to be careful with the stuff, otherwise it would eat you up. 'Now, this might sting a little.' Lars Besser smiled. 'But I want it to serve as a taster, a hint at what's to come. And not just with the phenol. Why, we could drink a little TRI Reagent, gargle some chloroform' – he cast his eyes around the laboratory – 'maybe snort some ethidium bromide. And that's before we even begin with the acrylamide or mercapto-ethanol.'

'What do you want?' Reuben asked, his eyes wide, the pipette slowly lowering towards his flesh.

'What do any of us want? Peace. Love. Understanding.' Lars Besser moved his thumb over the plunger. 'But mainly understanding.' He pushed down. The thick, clear fluid with its antiseptic smell oozed out of the blue tip. It bounced for a second in elastic hesitation, and then fell on to Reuben's skin.

Reuben fought the urge to snatch his hand away, to run for the sink and wash it off. Phenol was bad, but a bullet would be worse. For a moment, all he felt was a coldness, as if the fluid had simply been water. But then the burning started. He watched his skin rise, blistering white. The phenol seeped through and into his bloodstream below. Seemingly every muscle in his body clenched tight. His hand spasmed. Flesh was being eaten by the burning teeth of the fluid. He saw an image of sulphuric acid consuming metal. His head was silently screaming. Reuben concentrated on his fingers, holding them still, impossibly still. When he looked up, he was truly afraid for the first time. Lars Besser was alight, his face sucking in the distress, his senses exalting in Reuben's pain. He seemed to have swelled, to have gained power from his victim's helplessness. Truly, he was unpredictable, impossible to gauge from one moment to the next. Since the taxi, Lars Besser had been threatening, persuasive, withdrawn, reasonable, ebullient and sadistic. Reuben realized he would have difficulty second-guessing him. He tried to keep his thoughts away, urging them to ignore the siren of hurt. But it was no good. They were dragged back into the agony and consumed.

'You see what's happening?' Lars asked gleefully. 'You see how this all works as a metaphor? We're stripping away layers, getting to the real meat and bones. Extracting information and understanding like we extract and read DNA. You do see the beauty of it?'

Reuben clenched his jaw. The pain was throbbing with migrainous intensity. It was like being burnt with a cigar, but having the cigar pushed through the epidermis, someone still dragging on it, until the flesh below started to snub it out.

'What's nice as well is that all you've really achieved in your frantic attempts to track me down is to incriminate yourself. The more you've struggled to find me, the closer you've come to establishing yourself as the killer.'

Reuben grunted.

'I guess I've got your attention now. That was one single drop of phenol. You have a large bottleful here. Imagine what that will feel like!' Reuben pictured the mutilated bodies of Sandra Bantam, Run Zhang and Lloyd Granger. For the first time he saw that these injuries had been inflicted with alacrity and zeal. It was there in Lars Besser's jerky, excited movements. He was a schoolboy, attaching fishing line around a sparrow's neck and letting it fly off to its bone-snapping death. 'But as you know, phenol is much more effective when it's been properly equilibrated.'

Reuben watched Lars Besser pour the litre of phenol out of its brown bottle into a tall, thin measuring cylinder. He was careful, entranced by the evil liquid. Then he pipetted a smaller volume of isoamyl alcohol into the phenol, where it formed an unstable top layer, clearer than the brown-tinged liquid below it. Droplets of the ethanol fell slowly through the viscous phenol, lava-lamp fashion. Partially mesmerized, Lars whispered, 'When the phenol is fully equilibrated, we will begin. And when I've watched you die sitting at your bench – and I imagine from the literature that this could take quite a while – an anonymous tip-off will give the police the address of this lab. With your DNA at every crime scene, and Pheno-Fit pictures up all over the capital, the case will quickly become what newspapers really want: a single all-encapsulating headline. "Bitter scientist goes on rampage and then kills himself". End of story.' Lars pushed the pipette tip into the blister on Reuben's hand, popping it and encouraging a thin, watery fluid to leak out. 'And then I just have one more person to deal with.'

'Who?'

Lars merely tapped the side of his nose and winked.

Reuben mustered some defiance, watching drops of alcohol plunging through, each one taking days of his life with them. 'But what the fuck do you want from me?'

'Let's talk about the point at which our paths crossed before, Dr Maitland. Let's pick through the evidence, see what conclusions we can draw.' He ran his fingers along a fierce bushy eyebrow, stroking it, suddenly reflective. 'So, it's the mid-nineties. A wet-arse student gets beaten to death in a fight which spills out behind a pub in South London. Police arrive at the scene almost immediately, and no one is observed running away. All males in the pub are questioned and later DNA-tested. Ring any bells?'

'A few.'

'So what about me? I'm drinking alone in the bar, thinking a few things through. You see, Dr Maitland, I've had what you might call a disturbed life. An atypical upbringing. And as I sat there, I was considering my mother and my father. Everything that went on. The wordless beatings. The turmoil. The funeral. The lies. Wanting to go back to Gothenburg and destroy my father's grave. Astonished that I had managed to escape to England, my mother's country. You know, flicking through the last few years, resolving what to do next. And then? A fight breaks out. I sit still and watch. I get DNA-tested along with everyone else, questioned and released. And guess what? A few weeks after, my DNA is discovered on the clothing of the victim! I'm arrested and charged, and with two previous convictions for serious assault, well, clearly I'm the man.' Lars smiled ferociously, bringing his face close to Reuben's. The mania was resurfacing. 'The only problem is that I didn't do it. And the team who fitted me up? Led by none other than Reuben Maitland.'

Reuben remained quiet. Droplets continued to fall, measuring out the minutes he had left to live. Recollections were gnawing away at him. This wasn't simply revenge. There was something else. The memories were sparking an unease, a feeling that simple truths were no longer simple. Focusing past Lars's gun, he pictured the scene at the Lamb and Flag, as it had appeared a decade previously.

3

Reuben Maitland enters the bar. He is nervous and the CID who look up at him are almost all more senior. They aren't actively hostile, but there is precious little bonhomie as they examine a small patch of carpet. He can see it in their shrugs and raised eyebrows. They are asking, Where's the proper Lead Forensics Officer? Reuben scans the room. In the corner, as in the Lounge, which he can see through the Bar, a group of twenty to thirty drinkers are being questioned one by one. A stocky barman is talking with a WPC. Two round tables have been commandeered, and an officer sits at each, asking for personal details, taking notes, checking identification.

For a moment, Reuben remains where he is. A large part of him wants to run away. I do not belong here, a voice whispers. And then another says, This is your first time in charge, don't fuck it up. Do a good job and they might make this permanent. With the sudden fear of being paralysed by responsibility, he begins to do what he has repeatedly witnessed his boss do at the scene of a murder.

'So what have we got?' he asks, borrowing the phrase straight from his supervisor.

A tall, thick-set officer straightens and says, 'Body of a young male, believed to be one Gabriel Trask, is outside. All those here at the time of death are being questioned. We're examining the place the deceased was actually sitting just before he went into the back yard.'

'Right. Look, I want this area, and the area around the body, sealed off. No officers within three paces. All right?'

'You're the boss.'

'And keep the punters here. I want to take DNA from all of them.'

'All of them?'

'Yes.'

'Are you sure?'

'Entirely. There's a forensics technician on her way over.'

'But we've already got witness statements—'

'Look, this is my investigation. We will be doing DNA, whether you like it or not. OK?'

The tall officer appears momentarily petulant, and Reuben wonders whether he is trying too hard to sound in charge. As long as the tremor stays out of his voice he will be all right.

'Fine,' the officer answers.

Reuben walks through the pub, out past the damp smell of the toilets and into the back yard. Lying on his back on the cement floor is the body of a scruffy young man. His waxen features are lit by a harsh security light on the wall opposite. Blood has leaked under his lank hair, and forms a halo around his head, which appears black in the artificial lighting. A police pathologist is kneeling next to him, the corrugated concrete surface forcing him to shift his weight from time to time. Reuben introduces himself.

'Reuben Maitland, acting Lead Forensics Officer,' he says, holding out his hand.

The pathologist, a bearded man in his late fifties, cranes up at him and shows Reuben his bloody gloves.

Reuben withdraws his hand and asks, 'So what was the cause?'

'At a guess, a few heavy punches, followed by an unfortunate contact between cranium and concrete.'

'So he fell back pole-axed, and cracked his head?'

'As I say, that's a guess.'

Kneeling beside the pathologist is a junior officer, Philip Kemp, who has been promoted at the same time as Reuben. He is now a Detective, and Reuben can tell from the body language of the pathologist that he is on his way to becoming a respected copper. Philip Kemp stands up and shakes his hand.

'So they've put you in charge for one, have they?'

'Boss is on another case.'

'Better not fuck it up then.' He smiles, and Reuben appreciates he has made a friend at the scene.

'Look,' Reuben says, 'what exactly happened?'

'We got a call from Jimmy Dunst, he's the landlord. Said there was a big fight happening. Some of it spilt into the back here, which is where Gabriel Trask' – he thumbs at the prostrate figure – 'ran out of luck. We don't have any direct witnesses, but it's likely the culprit either climbed over the wall there, or else ran back into the bar. We got here pretty sharpish, while most people were still in the thick of things.'

'Have to be a fucking mountaineer to get over that wall.'

'If you're desperate you'll climb anything.'

'So the killer is probably still in the bar.'

'I guess so.' Phil Kemp shrugs. He looks quickly at Reuben. 'Tell you the truth, this is my first big investigation as well.'

'So we're bluffing it together. Well, there's only one way to find out.'

'Yeah?'

'I'm going to DNA-test everyone at the scene.'

'What about the people already here? It's not exactly clean.'

'Between you and me, I think it's time we did this more.' Reuben glances at the corpse. 'Even just for assaults which go too far.'

'Look, don't get me wrong, but wouldn't it be easier to question them all, take statements, do identity parades?'

'I dunno. This could be different.'

'How so?'

'You've got a pub full of people, most of whom are probably drunk, and half of whom have been fighting each other. The deceased was killed outside, away from obvious scrutiny. My feeling is that it'll be difficult to get reliable witness statements, ones which won't get pissed on in court.'

Phil Kemp stands, several inches shorter, gazing up at him. He chews his lower lip and examines his fingers for a second. And then he says, 'You think this gets easier? You know, for the bigger boys inside?'

Reuben frowns. 'I hope to fuck it does,' he answers.

Phil grins, walking past Reuben and into the pub. A few moments later Reuben hears the sound of laughter, and imagines he detects Phil's chuckle amongst it. Reuben follows him in and sits down at an empty table, observing the mechanics of the investigation, and willing the forensics technician to turn up. Several of the established coppers glance over. It is, he concludes sadly, a battle to introduce new methods to old policemen, and even to new ones. But, as he scans the line of drinkers patiently waiting to be interviewed, he guesses that this is nothing compared to the battle that lies ahead.

4

The only thing keeping him alive, Reuben appreciated, was the difference in viscosity between two liquids. He wondered about the surface tension dispute holding the fluids apart, phenolic riot police intermittently breached by protesting drops of alcohol bursting through their cordon.

Reuben had contemplated his mortality on numerous occasions during his professional life. It had been hard not to. Confronting death and its ugly aftermath made you think about your own. Certainly, he had never imagined dying at his laboratory bench. Reuben looked around. Laboratories were where people ended up *after* being killed. They shouldn't constitute the actual scene. They were too ordered for the chaos of dying – the futile thrashing, the desperate gasp for oxygen.

'Did you send a man to shoot me?' he asked Lars Besser.

'Your ignorance continues to astound me. I had no idea where you were. If you hadn't disappeared so effectively, I wouldn't have had to torture your colleagues to get to you. Think about that for a second. Your sudden anonymity cost several people their lives. Besides, I intend to savour the pleasure of your death all to myself. So someone else wants your blood?'

'Looks like it.'

Lars grinned. 'Well, finders keepers.' He turned his eyes to the measuring cylinder. 'Not long now till we get the show started. It's best we cut right to the heart of the issue in your last few minutes.' Lars Besser turned his pistol over in his hands. 'First, I want to tell you another story, in many ways a more important one. How I made the link between a couple of seemingly un-related events. How I realized what was really going on. A year before I was released from prison, a new inmate arrived, broad-casting the fact that he had been fitted up for the unsolved murder of three hitch-hikers in Gloucestershire in the late eighties. You are familiar with this case, Dr Maitland?'

'I worked on it.'

'And the forensics unit who fitted him up? GeneCrime.'

'Look, Lars, that conviction had nothing to do with me. I was working on something else—'

'Shut the fuck up,' Lars screamed. 'I'm the one who's talking.'

The ferocity of Lars Besser's reaction encouraged Reuben to remain quiet.

Lars squeezed one of his fists tight. And then, without warning, he slammed the butt of the gun down on Reuben's hand. A burning ferocity travelled instantly from the site of contact. The whole of Reuben's nervous system screamed. His stomach convulsed. The hand curled up like a wounded animal. A buzzing agony broke out through the bones; knuckles which had only recently mended screeched in pain. The skin, already opened up by the phenol, was pulsing blood over the bench. Lars trained the pistol on Reuben's injured hand.

'Move it again and you get the other end.' The force of his voice shook the lab. Reuben squeezed his jaws together. The pain was intensifying, swamping him. He had no notion of anything other than his broken hand. As he tried to unfurl his fingers there was an agonizing disagreement between carpals, tendons and metacarpals. He bit into the flesh of his cheek. Lars was virtually willing him to move his palms from the bench. He pushed them hard into the surface and screwed his eyes shut.

He was dying, and he knew it. Not now, but the process was taking hold. The systematic torture, the chemical assault, the sickening minutes as the poison leaked through his skin and circulation, burning cells and stripping nerves. Reuben pictured himself begging and pleading, Lars Besser staring down, eyes moist with pleasure, writing a new code with Reuben's seeping blood. He saw the day fade, the cloudy London sky, the city preparing for bedtime, people going about their rituals as if the world would last for ever. He saw that as he stopped everyone else continued. Joshua sleeping fitfully in his cot; Judith staring out of an anonymous window; Moray on surveillance in Finland; Lucy and Shaun Graves making love with the window open; his mother sitting in her still front room; Sarah Hirst returning to base, perplexed and agitated; the Forensics team talking in hushed tones about Jez; his brother pacing a small police cell. He imagined the pain in his hand spreading throughout his whole body.

Reuben realized that he actually wanted to die.

'Of course, everyone is innocent in prison. Everyone has been fitted up. But this one case began to get me interested. You know why?'

Reuben winced, the crushed bones throbbing more acutely. He shook his head, partly at the question, and partly to dispel the notion that he actively wanted a quick death.

'I believed him. You could see it in his face. He was no saint. In fact he had probably done a lot worse than fool around with a few hitch-hikers in his time. But I was the only one who made the link.'

'Which was?'

'That the same forensic fuckers who had framed me were framing others. Putting people away based on false evidence.'

'But there are safeguards . . .'

'Right. Safeguards. Controls. *Mechanisms*.' He screamed the word. 'There's one thing you're forgetting.'

'What?'

'That in the search for a killer only one person really knows the truth. And I was that person.'

'You?'

'The guy was stitched up. Clearly. Because, in the late eighties, when I was working near Gloucester, I inconvenienced three young people thumbing for lifts. Showed them the authority someone could have. Made them see how human flesh is there to be enjoyed, in whatever way possible. That as one person dies so another comes alive. That as my father killed my mother he became more powerful, more forceful.' Lars examined the phenol. It was very nearly ready. He was almost quivering with excitement.

Reuben studied the face of the Hitch-Hiker Killer. He could see that Lars Besser was a rare breed. Sadistic, intelligent and psychotic. There was a bipolarity about him: rational and furious, measured and delirious, controlling and unpredictable. A complexity which rendered normal detection useless, overwhelmed by a superior acumen, outplayed by an unanticipated malice.

'Of course I saw the beauty of it. In prison, everyone is scared to fucking death of forensics: the unblinking eye, following them everywhere they go, sticking its nose into everything they do. They fear it more than the police. It's more deadly than an Armed Response Unit.' Lars ground his teeth together, chewing at his words. 'No one doubts forensics. Juries just love the fucking stuff. You see, in the good old days, you beat a confession out of someone. Now, in a force which is ever scrutinized, who has power over everything? Who can convict whoever the fuck they want to convict? Who are infallible? Scientists. Instead of the truncheon, the pipette. The new short cut to locking up whoever you want locked up.' Lars lowered the volume of his words. 'How could you know how it feels to spend a decade in prison for something you didn't do? Knowing that one bent scientist had put you there, and was doing the same to others. Wondering whether he'll try and do it again when you get out.'

Reuben remained quiet.

'So I thought I'd beat you with your own stick. Take forensics and fuck you up. Destroy you from the inside. Make you see that you don't have absolute power. Claim back some of the years you had taken from me and everyone else you were busy framing.'

Scrabbling, clawing, grasping, Reuben's brain fought for an answer. There had to be a way out. See Lars's story, he told himself. See it from his side. See his injustice and use it, divert it.

Only a few drops of alcohol remained. Lars was wrapping up his argument, eager that Reuben died with full knowledge of his crimes. Reuben half listened, half snatched at piscine thoughts darting back and forth in his watery consciousness.

'So I began to plan, reading texts on genetics and molecular biology. Got to know the field. Convinced the warders I was a reformed character, going to study for a degree when I left prison. Of course, none of those halfwits realized that molecular biology is the same thing as forensic science. Identical principles, just a different name. Biology? What could be dangerous in that? So I spent all day every day absorbing and learning, until I knew just about everything. GeneCrime was taking liberties, and now it was payback. I even read some of your sorry excuses for papers. And then a breakthrough. I noted that one of your co-authors was a man with an unusual surname, one which matched with a fellow prisoner in Belmarsh. I couldn't believe my luck! Jeremy Hethrington-Andrews was easy to get to. A promise to have his brother Davie killed in prison. Holding his dear mother captive in her flat in Walthamstow. And he agreed to help me. Just to switch a few samples, that was all. Take some of Reuben Maitland's DNA from his GeneCrime exclusion profile and exchange it for crime-scene DNA. All this chaos just through the deliberate mislabelling of a few tubes. And then, with a man on the inside of the Forensics team, I was virtually immune to detection, as you have seen. Unstoppable. Untraceable. Until Jez began to – how should we put it? – crack under the strain. Poor Jez. Didn't really know what he had let himself in for. Entirely unaware of the scale of what I had planned. But he was smart enough to know that if he opened his mouth, he would instantly lose his brother and his mother. And by the time I had your rough whereabouts, Jez had outlived his usefulness.'

Reuben watched the last drop of alcohol wobble and hesitate on its less viscous bed. This was the end. Think. Think. Think. He wondered whether to antagonize Lars. He needed to be shot. Death by phenol was not an option. If you were going to die anyway, speed was the thing.

'And so . . .' Lars Besser turned to the measuring cylinder. The final drop was small, just visible. It was teetering. Lars gave the cylinder a nudge. The amyl alcohol rode the wave of phenol sloshing thickly from right to left and back again. And then, a diver with lead boots, it immersed itself and plunged through the phenol. Both men watched it, hypnotized, a silent reverse bubble. 'We are equilibrated. We are at a steady state. We are ready.' Lars picked up the long cylinder with one hand, the other still pointing the gun at Reuben. He took in a slow, deep breath, his eyes momentarily closed. When he opened them again, he said, 'Let's do this thing.'

Reuben scanned the laboratory frantically. Fridges, freezers, machines, chemicals, brightly coloured plastics and bare walls stared back at him. The cold antiseptic glare of science. The hush was interrupted by the passing of a train above. In the far corner, Lloyd Granger's unfinished portrait jolted slightly with the tremor. Lars moved the cylinder of phenol. Reuben closed his eyes. Lars Besser felt the weight of the container, gauging how best to launch it. Reuben clenched tight. He said a silent good-bye. His teeth gnashed together. Lars pulled his arm back.

Reuben held a cold empty breath. His right leg shook uncontrollably. Another train juddered by, vibrating the bench. And then there was a voice in the room.

'Stand exactly still,' it said from the shadows. 'Don't move a fucking muscle.'

5

Reuben and Lars turned as one. Reuben saw that Lars's gun was lying impotent on the bench. He tried to track the voice down, knowing this could only be bad news. Moray was away, and the police were returning from a mad hunt in the wrong direction. Someone else finding the laboratory could only spell trouble. He pictured the man sent to kill him in the alleyway. Slowly, the figure emerged from the shadows, pistol first, then hand, then arm, shoulder and face. And as he looked into Phil Kemp's eyes, Reuben felt a deep joy rising from his stomach and filling his body. Here, in the form of a stocky, straight-laced Detective Chief Inspector, was the cavalry. Phil approached cautiously.

'Put the cylinder down and slide your gun out of reach,' he ordered, motioning with his own weapon.

Lars Besser balanced the phenol on the bench and stared at him. There was hatred in his face. 'Kemp, isn't it?' he said.

'I won't ask you again. Should you fail to slide your gun out of reach I will have no option other than to shoot you.'

Reuben stepped gradually away from Lars, skirting round to be behind Phil. He was impressed with DCI Kemp's composure. This was a side of him he had never witnessed before: the calm control of a live situation. Phil held his arm straight, sighting down the barrel of the police-issue pistol. Reuben felt protected, as if his father had intervened in a school fight and was now confronting the bully.

'I'm counting to five. Then I will have no choice other than to discharge my firearm.' Reuben even found himself moved by Phil's use of language. This was the sort of clichéd cop-speak that he generally detested. However, he could see now that its simplicity and power cut right to the chase.

'Phil Kemp. Mediocrity personified.'

'One.'

Lars scowled. 'And to think I was coming to shoot you next.'

'Two.'

'Big hero thinks he's going to save the day.'

'Three.'

'You see, I'm really still in charge here. Just a question of whether I want to die or not.'

'Four.'

'Live or die.' Lars glanced down at his gun. 'Live or die.'

'Five.'

Lars moved his hands to grab his gun. Phil squeezed the trigger, the echoing crack of a shot stopping Lars dead. Reuben glanced past Lars at the hole in the wall.

Phil shouted, 'Drop it, you motherfucker.'

Lars stared at his gun. Phil aimed at Lars's head. Reuben watched Lars. He seemed to be deciding if he had time to grab the gun and aim. Phil squeezed the trigger again. He screamed, 'This time it's your head.'

Lars looked at him. He smiled, and then slowly, almost imperceptibly, began to push his arms into the air, nudging his pistol on to the floor.

'Kick it over to Reuben,' Phil ordered, still focusing his weapon on Lars's head.

Lars obliged, but without a hint of defeat. Reuben sensed that they were still not safe. Lars had the air of a pit bull allowing a lead around its neck, knowing that it could break free whenever it chose.

Reuben bent down to pick up the gun, noting the warmth of the handle. He slid the handcuff keys off the bench and removed his manacles. Phil cast his eyes over Reuben.

'You OK?' he asked. 'Your hand looks—'

'I'm fine.' Reuben felt a second wave of almost overpowering affection towards DCI Kemp. He appreciated that their jobs had gradually come between them. At GeneCrime, Phil was another under-pressure team leader, needing to do what he felt right, constantly battling to make sense of a unit which was divided and incoherent. And he and Phil had fractured along the same lines as the rest of the outfit. 'But how did you get here?'

'I tapped your mobile. Wanted to double-check you were definitely heading out east.' Phil was sweating slightly, still holding the gun. 'Used a contact in the Intelligence Service to have your progress scanned, got some GPS, located you here. All strictly illegal, of course.'

'Of course,' Reuben agreed, smiling. 'You know, Phil, in the past—'

'Forget it,' Phil said. 'Like you say, the past. Only thing that matters now is where we go from here. Now that we have finally caught the killer.' He passed his gun to Reuben. 'Here,' he instructed, 'guard him with this.'

Reuben watched Phil extract a pair of surgical gloves from a cardboard box and manoeuvre his fingers into them. 'Let's seal this scene,' he said. 'And that' – Phil gestured at the measuring cylinder full of phenol – 'was the intended murder weapon?'

'You saw that?' Reuben asked. 'How long were you—'

'Just long enough to make sure I heard what I needed to hear.'

'Typical fucking copper,' Lars spat.

'Reuben, pass me the phenol, carefully.'

Reuben took a step closer to Lars Besser, and then inched the measuring cylinder along the bench towards Phil. It felt good, as if he was disarming Lars. For a second, the relief which had been surging through him mixed with a sense of rage, and he considered pulling the trigger. But no, it was vital that Lars was arrested, charged and isolated from society. That was how justice should work. Revenge never truly repaid any debt. With his gloved hands, Phil Kemp took the phenol and examined it.

'Nasty,' he tutted.

'Very nasty,' Reuben answered.

Phil appeared mesmerized by the noxious liquid. Pacing towards Lars Besser, he said, 'Looks like the final nail in your coffin, Mr Besser.'

'If you say so.'

'Anything you want to share before I officially charge you?'

Lars sneered at him. 'Big fucking hero,' he answered.

And then Phil launched the phenol into his face.

Lars screamed, staggering backwards, clutching his eyes. He bent over, silent for a second, before shrieking again. The sound made Reuben shudder, cutting through him, rebounding off the walls. Lars sucked air in and out of his lungs with a ferocity that seemed to pull the oxygen from the room. He fell on to his side, and Reuben watched his face being eaten away beneath his fingers. His flesh blistered white and started to peel in sickening strips. Lars screeched and screeched, and Reuben realized that his death would take minutes rather than the hours he had estimated. Besser turned on to his back, spasming, legs and arms flailing, emitting a noise Reuben hoped to never hear again. His limbs smashed into the floor, the heavy legs of the lab bench and the base of a lab stool. Reuben swivelled round to look at Phil. Still holding the empty cylinder, Phil was entranced by the scene. 'Fucking hell,' he whispered under his breath.

Lars's breathing became fluidic, a mixing of gases and liquids in a condenser. He was clawing at his face, tearing through blisters, opening up deep bloody wounds, as if he was trying to dig the affected flesh out. Reuben turned away; the howls grew louder. At last, Lars seemed to be trying to say something. It took Reuben a few seconds to pin it down. 'Shoot me. Shoot me,' he was squealing. Again Reuben looked at Phil, whose features didn't change. The dearth of expression and sympathy seemed to be saying, 'Got what he deserved.' Lars's cries were becoming pitiful sobs. Reuben realized he was observing a sadist understand his own reward. His undoubted power was ebbing and melting. Phil took a pace nearer and crouched down. Lars's body was just twitching, no longer thrashing, and his face looked like it had been skinned. His laboured breathing seemed now to be composed only of inhalations, sudden, abrupt and rasping, convulsing his whole torso every few seconds.

'Give me his gun,' Phil said without turning round.

'You going to shoot him?'

'Something like that.'

Reuben passed the weapon, and Phil studied it, occasionally running his eyes over Lars. He appeared to be considering what to do.

'Should I call for support?' Reuben asked.

Still crouching, and with his back to Reuben, Phil answered, 'We've got the situation covered. This cunt isn't going anywhere. I'm just making sure.'

'But CID . . .'

'I said I'm just making sure. This fucker has caused me enough trouble. It was time he suffered the way he made others suffer. You know how this game works, Reuben. He would have pleaded innocent, clogged the courts up, maybe got twenty-five years in a cushy cell. Where's the justice? The proper human justice? Surely you can see that. Come on, think of Sandra. Think of Run. Think of Lloyd.'

'And Jez.'

'Jez? Fucking animal!' Phil lifted the butt of Lars's gun and held it above his head for a few seconds. He ground his teeth.

'Phil,' Reuben said.

'It's OK.' Phil lowered the pistol. 'Modern policing and all that. Sometimes you forget.' He rubbed his face and sighed.

'Is he finally dead?' Reuben asked quietly.

'I think so. Jesus, that stuff is evil. I mean, I would never have . . .'

'You did. And it's over now.' Reuben straightened, slowly clenching and unclenching his damaged hand, which was beginning to cooperate a little. 'What a God-awful way to go.' He felt suddenly sick. Despite all the aftermaths, all the cold, mutilated bodies he had witnessed in his career, nothing could have prepared him for what he had just seen.

'What did he want from you anyway?'

'Details of an old case.'

Phil swivelled, squatting close to Lars's head. 'Which one?'

'The Lamb and Flag murder in the mid-nineties. You remember?'

'And that's all that drove him to these lengths?'

'He said he was framed. Said our evidence was false.'

'In what way false?'

'That he couldn't have been the killer.'

'That's right.' Phil arched his eyebrows at Reuben and allowed himself a small laugh. 'Fine upstanding chap like him.'

'Hell no.'

'Anyway . . .' Phil pushed the gun into Lars's palm, seeing how it fitted. 'The investigation is closed. Has been for years. And now' – he grinned up – 'I have caught the Forensics Killer.'

Reuben smiled back as the tension finally left his body. 'I guess so.'

Phil pressed Lars's still-warm index finger on to the trigger of the gun. He moved Lars's arm around, looking along its line.

'What are you doing?'

'As I said, I have caught the Forensics Killer.' He aimed the gun at Reuben.

'What?'

376

'You see the state of play, don't you? This is the conclusion, the answer to the case. The truth is in front of you, behind you, around you. In fact, you are the truth. The thing you've been hunting all these years is you.'

'Phil, stop fucking around.'

'And the truth is this. Forensics Killer Reuben Maitland murders Lars Besser, key suspect in the investigation, by pouring phenol over him. But as Besser dies, he manages to shoot Dr Maitland. The forensics and fingerprints are watertight. Case closed.' Phil squeezed Lars Besser's slippery finger on the trigger. 'Unless I've missed anything?'

Reuben held his mouth, betrayed, in shock, staring at Phil with a mix of fear and incredulity.

'But, Phil . . .'

'Bye bye, Reuben,' Phil said.

'I don't understand . . .'

'Been a pleasure knowing you, Dr Maitland. Goodbye. *Mate*.'

Staring past the gun, Reuben noticed a movement, a twitch of the feet. Phil hadn't seen it. And another. 'Phil . . .' he said. But it was too late. Lars Besser reared up and lunged. He grabbed for flesh. He was roaring, a wounded grizzly, hands pawing the air. Phil tried to scramble away, but slipped, the gun falling to ground. Lars launched himself, eyes huge and monstrous, their lids melted. Reuben leapt forwards instinctively and clutched hold of Phil, who was on his back. Lars wrapped his arms around Phil's legs and squeezed. Phil was screaming, 'Get him off me, get him off me.' Reuben pulled Phil by the shoulders. Lars inched his grip up Phil's legs. His frozen stare was fixed on Phil's neck. 'Shoot him, for fuck's sake.' Reuben couldn't see Phil's gun. 'Shoot him.' Lars's pistol was trapped under Phil's body. Lars was on top of Phil, his immense strength pulling him up so that he was wrapped around his chest. One arm reached for Phil's neck.

Reuben let go of Phil and stood up. He shook his head. What

the fuck was he doing? 'Help me,' Phil shrieked, almost over-come. Reuben scanned the lab, conflict raging through his body. He dived for the lab bench and picked up a bottle. It was simply marked 'Nitric'. Lars was roaring and snarling and bellowing. Reuben uncapped the bottle. He stopped. A terrible thought came to him. Of course he could save Phil. But he could also save Lars instead. Both had tried to kill him. Which one did he want to live? Phil's shrieks for help jolted through Reuben's vacillation. His hands shook as he held the bottle above their heads.

Reuben stood over them, hesitating as Phil's cries became more desperate, more frantic. 'Kill him. Kill the fucker.' If he did nothing Phil would be dead inside a minute, a victim of Lars's immense power. But if he eliminated Lars, Phil was still a threat. Maybe he could overpower him, find one of the guns, call for back-up? But letting Phil live would create more problems than it solved. Reuben saw Phil's face start to change colour, his limbs thrashing uselessly. Still he waited. He couldn't think straight. It was kill or be killed. All he had to do was tip the nitric acid one way or the other, but he couldn't.

Reuben closed his eyes and grimaced. He would have to end the life of a human being. Phil was whimpering; Lars was gaining in strength. Reuben swayed on his feet. Phil or Lars. Lars or Phil. Both of them wanted him dead, and now it was his turn. Phil was turning purple, his eyes pushing out of their sockets. Lars was forcing his fingers further into Phil's neck, forearms bulging, muscles clamping tighter. Lars or Phil. Either would solve a lot of problems. An abhorrent decision crystallized. He adjusted the angle of his wrist. And then he poured the clear fluid out of its bottle.

6

There was a scream of pure undiluted horror. A burning smell, flesh and hair, filled the room. Reuben watched, sickened and fascinated. A whiff of vapour hung around the bottle mouth like smoke from a gun. Another howl pierced the lab and almost seemed to make the glassware shake, cutting through Reuben and scratching at his nerves.

Phil Kemp stared up at him, bug-eyed and dying. Lars Besser swivelled his distorted face upwards as well. Four eyes, four terrible eyes, digging into him. Reuben knew he would never forget those looks. He doused Lars Besser a second time; only a few drops remained. Lars finally stopped, his damaged eyes staying open. A burrowing blackness appeared in his flesh, steam escaping from the wound. The phenol had melted the outer layer of skin. The nitric acid was devouring flesh and bones. Lars twitched, grabbing the back of his hair. Phil writhed away from him, managing to shake him off. Lars rolled on to his front. The back of his head was red and white, skin giving way to bone, and then to membrane.

Phil climbed slowly to his feet, gasping for air. 'Fuck, fuck, fuck,' he said. He walked over and kicked Lars hard in the kidneys. Lars's breathing was becoming shallow. The fight was seeping away as the acid entered his brain.

Reuben picked Lars's gun up from the floor, wiping it clean with a tissue. Phil paced about in small circles, muttering to himself, unsteady on his feet. He skirted around Lars's body, seemingly oblivious to everything else. He kicked Lars again. This time there was no grunt of objection.

Reuben belatedly realized that he was in the very act of murdering someone. Even though he had hesitated before administering the acid, he knew that a small part of him, a region of his brain he battled to suppress, saw the justice in it. But he guessed that when the adrenalin subsided, the guilt would start to kick in. Not just because of the pain he had inflicted, but because it was now clear that Lars Besser, despite his sadism, had been motivated by injustice. There was a similarity in their plights which unnerved him as he watched Phil examine the body, lifting one of Lars's arms up and letting it fall limply back to the floor. Reuben was more wary, and stayed well away from the prone figure. Phil lifted Lars's other arm and glanced over at Reuben. For the first time he noticed the gun.

'I guess things are a bit fucked up,' Phil muttered.

Reuben shrugged blankly, not knowing what to say.

Phil cradled his head with wide-spaced fingers, rocking it slowly back and forth. 'Fuck. Fuck. Fuck. This is the sickest thing . . . I thought he was going to kill me.'

Reuben released the pistol's safety catch and extracted his mobile from his jeans. He dialled a number with his thumb. 'Come here alone and unarmed,' he said when the call was answered. 'I've got what we might call a situation.' He gave the address and brief directions. 'I'm holding DCI Phil Kemp at gunpoint, and can't be responsible for my actions. If you want to see him alive, you'd better get here now.' Reuben flipped his phone shut. He took a stiff, white lab coat and draped it over Lars Besser's body.

'So, DCI Kemp.' He frowned. 'This is where things get interesting.'

GCACGATAGCTTACGGG
TATCTTA**TEN**GGTATTCG
GCTAATCGTCATAACAT

1

Reuben listened to his stomach complain. It had seen too much adrenalin and not enough food. He hadn't eaten for as long as he could recall. He leant his empty body against the fridge. He was trembling slightly, the vibration of the compressor at one with his own oscillations. Behind Phil Kemp he saw that he had failed to give Lloyd Granger any posthumous dignity. Things had become so fucked up that they spilt on to the canvas. Lloyd would have to wait.

Phil remained silent, his face gradually greying. There was a noise at the door, and Reuben walked swiftly behind Phil, pointing the gun at his head and covering the entrance.

'So,' he said, as DCI Sarah Hirst stepped into the lab.

'So,' she answered. He watched her absorb the scene of chaos in the lab, coolly detached, drawing her own story from the pictures. The figure lying on the floor, the spilt liquids, the burning skin, Phil standing with a gun at his head. Sarah straightened her hair, adjusted her collar and smoothed her skirt, as if distancing herself from the mess around her. She walked slowly forwards. 'This is the situation you mentioned.'

'Show me you're not armed,' Reuben instructed.

Sarah Hirst unbuttoned her jacket. Reuben took in the sculptured look of her white blouse as she turned around.

'Want to tell me what's going on?' Sarah asked, facing him.

'Sarah, for Christ's sake,' Phil implored.

'One more word, DCI Kemp, and it will be your last.' Reuben pushed the bevelled mouth of the gun hard into Phil's hair.

'Well?'

'Lars Besser was the Forensics Killer.'

'What I'm really asking you, Dr Maitland, is why you're holding a senior CID officer at gunpoint.'

'It's complicated.'

'You'll have to do better than that. And you don't have a lot of time. I told Mina Ali where I was going. If I'm not out by two, she's going to raise the alarm. And you know what that means.'

Reuben sighed. True to form, Sarah had broken her word. If time was limited, he needed help. 'I'm going to make a call,' he said. 'And then we can start getting down to business.' He picked up his phone and dialled a number. 'Judith,' he began, 'I'm in the lab. I think you should come here. Things have changed. A lot of things. But it's safe. And I need your technical help. How long till you get here? Right. See you then.'

Reuben put his mobile down and glanced at Sarah, who was now standing in front of Lloyd Granger's unfinished portrait. 'Of course,' she said, running her eyes over the canvas, 'you know why you paint?'

'Enlighten me.'

'Because deep inside you can't bear the truth.'

Reuben grunted. 'I'd say it was an outlet. Something maybe you could benefit from. So where do you get your kicks, DCI Hirst?'

'From being in control.'

'Inspect your surroundings. Do you think you're in control now?'

Sarah Hirst swung round instantly as the door opened. Reuben stepped back and trained his pistol on the entrance, careful to keep the gun behind Phil's head. Out of the shadows emerged the large figure of Moray Carnock.

'What's up?' he asked, his face clouding as he glanced around the room.

'Long story. What happened to Helsinki?'

'Outstayed my welcome and had to leave in a hurry.'

'Well, make yourself useful. Take the gun and keep it trained on DCI Kemp.'

Reuben paced over to Sarah, pulling her by the elbow, guiding her away from the picture. 'We're going to run some tests,' he said, sucking in her perfume. 'Find out what's been going on. Now, I've taken a risk asking you here. But I need all this to be legal and open. I need to know that I can trust you.'

'Why start now, Dr Maitland?'

'Because I haven't any other option.'

'Your man's the one holding the gun.'

'Do I have your cooperation or not?'

Sarah shrugged. 'We shall see.'

'Never mind. Moray, keep a watch on DCI Hirst as well.'

Sarah flushed with anger, shaking herself free from Reuben's grip. 'That's enough, Dr Maitland. You're going to tell me what you know. You're going to convince me that when this is all over I shouldn't have you taken to pieces.'

Reuben glanced quickly in Phil's direction. He was monitoring Sarah with quiet desperation. Reuben saw that there was still hope in his eyes. Behind, Moray was leaning against a bench, holding the revolver and rummaging in his pockets for something to eat. Noticing the hunger in Reuben's stare, he passed him a banana and a can of drink. Reuben faced Sarah and muttered, 'OK, here goes nothing. Did you ever hear about the Lamb and Flag murder? A student called Gabriel Trask?'

Sarah frowned. 'Yeah. I remember.'

'Lars Besser, lying there on the floor, was the man we sent down. Old-school DNA fingerprinting was struggling. It wasn't until maybe three months after the murder that we made the breakthrough, discovering Besser's DNA on the student's clothing.' Reuben swigged a mouthful of apple juice, savouring the sweet-acid coolness.

'What's your point?'

'It's the only thing that links DCI Kemp to Lars. Phil was on the case and when Besser laid eyes on him today, he said he was going to shoot him next. I'm going to find out why. Judith Meadows is on her way over to assist. For reasons I'd rather not explain at the moment, I've got archived samples from that investigation.'

Reuben walked over to a vertical freezer and opened it. Inside were four shelves, each stacked with around ten rectangular plastic boxes that looked like ice-cream tubs. He pulled individual containers out, examined their labels, and piled them on the floor. After a couple of minutes, he found one marked 'Lamb and Flag 1995'. He passed it to Sarah, replacing the other boxes in the freezer. Sarah removed the lid and stared for several seconds at the contents. Inside were thirty white tubes, bullet-shaped and numbered consecutively. In one small plastic bag were six or seven smaller tubes, red in colour. In another, several slips of paper, and five more Eppendorfs. 'I won't ask why you have GeneCrime specimens in your freezers,' she said, examining a damp Contamination Notice. 'But what good is this going to do you?'

'I'm going to run the original samples through Predictive Phenotyping, so we can meet everyone who was in the pub that day.'

'Really?' Sarah asked coolly. 'You haven't got long before the cavalry arrives.' She glanced at Phil. 'And he's going to be one angry wasp released from its jar.'

'I take the hint.' Reuben ate quickly, flicked a chip-reader on, picked up a rack of tips and began to work as swiftly as he had ever worked. He wrestled with the issue of why Phil had wanted

Lars and himself dead. What was he so scared of? Phil had to be shielding someone, and it had to be a person Reuben knew. Otherwise why go to such lengths? Phil had arrived at the pub after Gabriel Trask died, so his role could only have been in diverting the investigation away from someone who was eager to avoid detection. He pictured the people he had come across recently. The fair-haired Kieran Hobbs, with his gated eyelashes; the cosmetically enhanced gangster Maclyn Margulis; the night-club entrepreneur Xavier Trister. He saw Phil's henchmen at GeneCrime, Metropolitan officers who would lay their lives down for their boss. He considered the man sent to kill him behind Shaun Graves's house. He once again put himself in the Lamb and Flag ten years previously, recalling the junior Phil Kemp whispering with senior CID, the pathologist, other officers, the stale smoky air, the closed circle. Four or five policemen, two of whom had risen high through the ranks since then. He ran through the dirty-science cases he had processed in the last few months: the industrial espionage; the victim identities; the infidelity cases. He searched for links between events he had previously considered to be separate. This was, he belatedly appreciated, the secret of science: forging connections between discrete strands of evidence.

While he thought, he flicked open tubes with his left hand, dispensed liquids, pulsed samples in a microfuge, bit into an apple, which clashed with the apple juice, washed filters, amplified signals, hybridized probes, programmed machines, and opened up his laptop, which still held the frozen face of Lars Besser, undamaged and immaculate. Judith Meadows finally entered the lab, cautious and suspicious. He watched her take in the disarray, her face changing as she saw Phil Kemp, Sarah Hirst, the dead man on the floor, Moray Carnock aiming the gun. There was a slight hesitation and awkwardness. Judith propped herself against a freezer, toying with the two rings on her third finger. Reuben walked over and hugged her. It was a brief embrace, stiff and mechanical, before Judith broke free, asked what Reuben was doing and what stage he was at, and opened a box of gloves. Silently, she began to involve herself in the procedures.

'Clock's ticking, Reuben,' Sarah said, glancing at her watch and disrupting the hum of activity.

'I'm taking all the short cuts I can,' he replied. 'I'll use the Predictive Phenotyping on low resolution, which should be accurate enough. Also, we won't run the usual controls or calibration steps. And, as a final strategy, I'm going to give precedence to samples that we overlooked before. Should be an order of magnitude quicker than normal.'

Sarah's mobile rang, a polyphonic imitation of a classical song. She ignored it. The phone rang again, and she examined the display with irritation. The third time it sounded, she looked pleadingly at Moray, and then at Reuben. He nodded. 'Moray, listen in. And, Sarah, don't say anything that would jeopardize your life, or that of DCI Kemp.'

Sarah pressed a button. Moray cocked an ear in her direction, listening intently. Phil transferred his weight from foot to foot, hopefully watching his opposite number. Sarah said a lot of yeses, nos and maybes. Nothing incriminating. When she ended the call, she announced, 'They've picked up Jez's body from his flat. People are asking questions. Mina has opened her big mouth. And,' she added, keeping the best for last, 'they're on their way over.'

2

The words entered Reuben's embattled consciousness. Gene-Crime personnel were on their way to the laboratory, doubtless aided by any number of Metropolitan officers, bloodhounds in the chase, sniffing the capture of the Forensics Killer. He saw the room as they would see it. A corpse, a senior officer held at gunpoint, a shady security consultant, and the chief suspect of the case *in situ*. There were many ways to interpret such a scene, few of which gave him hope. He quickened his efforts.

'How long have we got?'

'As long as it takes them to find us.'

Phil raised his chin. There was victory in his eyes.

'The first image will be through in minutes.'

'Reuben, why not just surrender now? We can sort everything out after.'

Reuben stared hard at Sarah. She had adopted her negotiator voice, soft tones designed to bend his will. 'Because we're going to sit here and I'm going to show you what really happened. Before everything gets swarmed over and poked at. Before police procedures complicate matters. Before you try and take me into custody.'

While Judith pipetted a long row of small nylon filters like a static conveyor belt, Reuben opened his program and entered a quick list of commands. 'Right,' he muttered at the screen, 'let's start with a couple of the punters who were in the bar at the time of the death. See if anyone recognizes them.'

Over the next few seconds, two crudely digitized faces appeared. They improved and sharpened, but remained grainy cousins of finished Pheno-Fits. Reuben swivelled the laptop round so that it could be viewed by everyone in the room. Most importantly, he wanted Phil to see the images. Reuben scrutinized his reaction, which was impassive. 'Anyone come across either of this motley pair before? Maybe in another investigation? Hanging around with Phil at social events?'

No one said anything, and so Reuben began on the next two pictures. In the background, the processor of his laptop ground through the data which Judith was sending it via the imager. As soon as he had closed one image he was able to open another up. 'How about these?' he asked. Again, there was no response. 'Or this chap? His girlfriend?'

'How many do we have to go through?' Sarah enquired, tapping her mobile impatiently against her chin.

'A few more, and then we'll start on the Exclusions and Victim Samples.'

Reuben exhibited three further pairs of mug shots to Sarah, Moray, Phil and Judith. One was recognizable as Lars Besser, the rest were anonymous. Phil didn't blink. He was watching the screen, emotionless, a weary indifference haunting his features. But when Reuben stared hard into Phil's face, he saw that, amongst the unconcern, his pupils were like saucers. They were sucking in all the details. Something was spooking him.

'Anything on your mind, Phil?'

'The only words I'm saying to you are "You're fucking nicked, Maitland." Just as soon as my CID boys and girls get here.'

Reuben ignored the taunt, losing himself in the images. 'I still don't understand . . . who the hell were you protecting?'

Phil stared back, expressionless. On the collar of his blue shirt,

Reuben could just make out an advancing front of sweat, soaking into the material from his neck.

'Who attended the incident? Who ran the investigation, Phil? It's time for a trip down memory lane. My first crime scene as Lead Forensics Officer,' Reuben said. 'Let's take a look at the Exclusions, the officers initially present. You call them out.' He brought up a succession of picture files.

The first two officers were identified by Sarah, who had become increasingly interested in the pictures. 'That's Nick Temple on the left, and Bob Smetter on the right.'

Reuben opened another duo of grey JPEGs, and waited impatiently as they came to life, pixel by pixel.

'Helen Parker, I think, on the right. But I don't recognize the other. Anyone?'

No one could put a name to the WPC on the left.

'Last two,' Reuben said.

'James Truman,' Sarah said. 'Now a commander. Real big boy in the Essex force. And the other one's Cumali Kyriacou.'

'Hmm,' Reuben shrugged. 'So what have we got? Couple of big people going big places. Lots of influence to a young officer. A copper could go far with that sort of clout behind him. Don't you think?'

'Fuck off,' Phil answered.

'Reuben, you're running out of minutes.'

'I'm thinking. I'm thinking.' Reuben glanced down at the final few samples, taken from Gabriel Trask, the dead student. Judith was frantically typing them. This was quick and approximate science, but the only sort they had time for.

'Give it up, Reuben,' Phil said. 'Look, Sarah, this man's a murderer, for Christ's sake. Even if you don't believe he killed Run and Sandra and everyone, look what he's done to Lars Besser.'

Again, Moray encouraged his silence. 'Shut the fuck up,' he growled.

'The clock is ticking, Dr Maitland. In a very short time, CID will be here. And you've yet to convince anyone . . .' Sarah's mobile came to life and she answered it with short, clipped words. 'They're just reaching the industrial estate,' she said to Reuben.

'Fuck,' Reuben answered. He screwed up his eyes. This was his only chance. After this, Phil would seize control of the situation. No one was going to accept Reuben's explanation for the events. Maybe they would believe that Lars had killed Jez, Sandra and Run, maybe the forensics could prove it, but it still left Reuben in a lot of trouble. He had helped to murder Lars, was holding two officers at gunpoint, had misled the police. And now he was struggling. The last few days were taking their toll. His breathing was fast and shallow. There was no other option than to thrash his way to the end. 'Judith,' he gasped, 'let's have a look at the Victim Samples. Are they done?'

'More or less. But they're going to be a bit rough around the edges.'

Reuben entered a few lightning commands into the laptop. Seconds later, a specimen labelled 'Coat' was processed. The depiction of a man lit up the screen. It was a low-resolution version of Lars Besser. 'Next,' Reuben commanded. The sample came from a tube marked 'Buccal'. The image was of a young man, slightly gaunt, with dark hair. 'Gabriel Trask, I think.'

From above come the rumble of a train, quickly followed by a concatenation of loud footsteps. There was also a sustained burst of gunfire. Reuben and Moray exchanged glances.

'They're shooting,' Moray exclaimed. 'Fuck.'

'Who at?'

'No idea. But they're shooting at someone. And whoever it is, they're in the building.'

'Come on,' Phil whispered.

'OK, Dr Maitland, you're going to have to let DCI Kemp go. Otherwise they're going to take you down. They won't stop and ask politely. Tell us what you know before the whole scene gets swallowed up.'

'I'm not sure.' He rocked back and forth, eyes closed. Who the fuck was Phil protecting? The next image began to appear, from a specimen called 'Facial'. Moray, Sarah, Judith and Reuben all stared intently at the laptop. The face appeared, coming alive, bit by bit.

'Lars fucking Besser again,' Moray grumbled.

Reuben took in the disappointment all around him. He appreciated that they wanted to believe his hunch, hoped that there was an explanation for all the deaths, a meaning to the terrible last two weeks of their lives. The police were shouting. He heard a dog bark. They would find the door, the stairs and then the corridor. Reuben opened up the final file, named 'Fingernails', distracted from the screen by the sound of fresh gunshots above them. He was watching the expressions of the others, delaying the moment he'd have to confirm that it was all over. He watched Moray's pudgy chin drop slightly, Sarah's magnificent eyes open, Judith's brow crease, Phil's cheeks redden. 'What?' he asked. The door was kicked open. Three uniformed GeneCrime CID burst in. Moray dropped his pistol. They were followed quickly by a dog-handler with an angry German Shepherd. 'Stand still,' one of them ordered. Another approached the body lying on the floor. 'Do we need medics?' he asked.

'Too late,' Sarah replied.

'And is DCI Kemp OK?'

'I'm fine,' Phil answered, relief washing through him. 'Now arrest Dr Maitland and this fat fucking Jock.'

The broadest of the officers stepped forwards, extracting his handcuffs.

3

DCI Sarah Hirst was the first to move. She grabbed for Phil Kemp's pistol and trained it on the head of the CID officer approaching Reuben Maitland.

'Stop,' she shouted.

The officer spun round, handcuffs gripped between forefinger and thumb. 'Ma'am?'

'No one is doing anything until I say. I am taking control of this crime scene. You want to walk over and wedge the door, Constable Parish?'

Constable Parish did as he was told. Sarah waved the gun at the other men.

'We have a state of affairs here, that I want preserved for the next ten minutes. After that, I will put the weapon down, and we can proceed normally. But during this time, no other officer will enter the room. OK?'

Two of the CID glanced at each other. Having a superior officer wave a gun at them was unfamiliar territory. They nodded slowly, unsurely.

'You and you' – she pointed them out with the barrel – 'will stand by the entrance. You may explain to those trying to get in that DCI Hirst is securing the scene for Forensics, and that nobody, regardless of rank, is to trespass. Clear?' Sarah checked the pistol's safety catch. 'And you are not to converse with DCI Kemp. If he attempts to pull rank on you, please remember that I am the one carrying the firearm.'

Sarah returned her attention to her opposite number, satisfied that CID were playing along. 'The problem we have now, as I see it, DCI Kemp, is a simple one.'

'Which is?'

'Dead men don't scratch.'

Phil implored the officer closer to him, 'Geoff, this is a direct order. Get Armed Response in here.'

Geoff looked at both of his superior officers in turn: at Phil's desperation, and at Sarah's gun.

'Come on. Do it, for Christ's sake.'

He remained still.

'Phil?' Sarah repeated. 'Dead men don't scratch. Do you disagree?'

Reuben was suddenly alive to the possibilities. Sarah was sharp, and just ahead of him this time. While she raced down the main road, he had been exploring the back streets. How the Lamb and Flag incident was not as it seemed. Why a student had been beaten to death. Who had administered the fatal blows. Why the initial genetic screen had failed. Whose samples had automatically been excluded from the investigation. The identity of the person Phil had been protecting all this time.

'It's beautiful,' Judith murmured, catching up. 'Perfect.'

'And then you realize that one of the punters has previous.'

'And Lars Besser pays the price,' Sarah added.

'Geoff, sort it, for fuck's sake.'

'I knew he was protecting someone.' Reuben stared into Phil's face. He was pale, his image on the screen contrastingly ruddy. 'I just didn't realize it was himself.'

Moray screwed up a chocolate wrapper and slotted it in his pocket. 'Is this a private party,' he grumbled, 'or can anyone join in?'

'You see, Moray,' Reuben said, 'the reports stated that Phil had arrived just after the death, that he had been witnessed entering the pub. But what happened, Phil? You go out for a pint that evening, get caught up in the fight, let that famous temper of yours go too far, floor this poor lad, see he's in trouble? You climb over the wall and make sure you are witnessed entering the pub, ostensibly for the first time? So Sarah's right. Dead men don't scratch. There can't be any other reason that your DNA was under his fingernails. Other than there being physical contact between you while he was still alive.'

'Geoff . . .'

'And then he makes sure he contaminates the body with his DNA . . .'

'I remember seeing him,' Reuben recalled, 'crouching down with the pathologist, probably there before him . . .'

'Then Phil has tied all the loose ends. By contaminating the scene he is automatically excluded.'

Phil Kemp lifted his head and examined his surroundings. He took in the laboratory, its walls detention-cell white, harsh and unforgiving. He saw three of GeneCrime's officers staring back in a way that alarmed him. He noted Sarah Hirst enjoying the feel of his gun, aiming it at him like she wanted to fire, quietly controlling the situation. He heard the commotion outside the room, restless CID wanting to break down the door, senior Metropolitan brass barking orders. He observed his own face on a computer screen, pixelated and impassive, like the newspaper photo of a suspect, and immersed himself in the central question. If I was in charge of this investigation, what would I think when I came through the door? When I took in the scene? Who would I believe? What was the real evidence and what was superfluous? Would I believe Sarah Hirst, Reuben Maitland, Moray Carnock and Judith Meadows, or would I believe me? Would I listen to their story and dismiss it? Would I pick through the forensic evidence and pull it apart? And, finally, would I look into my eyes and ignore what was there? 'It wasn't like that,' he whispered.

Reuben glanced up from the keyboard he was hammering. 'Enlighten us.'

Phil's face whitened even further, colour retreating into pores, hiding behind the black stubble which permanently threatened to break through his skin. 'The student. Things happened. It got messy,' he mumbled.

'So you got caught up in it?' Reuben said.

'I didn't say that.'

'You fought, you punched him, he hit his head . . .'

'Ma'am, they want the door open. They say they're coming in regardless.'

'Stall them. Another two minutes.'

The door started to give. Phil stopped talking. Three pounding blows echoed in quick succession. Orange brick dust clouded out around its hinges. The CID officer closest to it took a sharp step backwards. Phil Kemp eyed the entrance uneasily. The laboratory door smashed open. A blur of black uniforms swarmed into the room, with shouts and commands echoing into the high, arched ceiling. Out of the corner of his eye Reuben detected the presence of Area Commander Robert Abner. Sarah was talking to him. In the background, he noticed that the remaining members of his old team had entered, dressed in white, loitering around, waiting to begin. Bernie Harrison looked over and half smiled. Mina Ali gave a brief thumbs-up and turned away. Paul Mackay avoided his eye. Birgit Kasper raised her eyebrows. Simon Jankowski flushed, and attempted to busy himself. Reuben realized that this was as close as the reunion was going to get. He longed to walk over and hug all five of them, but knew that the lines had been drawn. Out of habit, his eyes scanned for Run Zhang and Jez Hethrington-Andrews, but saw only scientists he didn't recognize, staff drafted in to replace the dead. Commander Abner and DCI Sarah Hirst approached.

'Dr Maitland.' The Commander frowned. 'I think we need to have some words.' He placed a massive hand on Reuben's shoulder. 'Back at GeneCrime.'

4

It was like looking into an unreliable mirror, or examining an old photograph of yourself. The appearance was almost what you expected. Almost. And yet there were differences, subtle changes that the years had wrought, faint alterations which caught you slightly by surprise, even now.

'How are things?' he asked.

'Great,' his brother answered.

'Three years.'

'Three years.'

Reuben stared into Aaron's pale-green eyes. It didn't matter how identical you were, discrepancies still shone through. Aaron's eyes were as impenetrable as ever. The one person Reuben had always struggled to read shared his DNA. They had nature and nurture and still Aaron was an enigma. Of course, there was communication, but only on the mundane things. They understood music together, and art, and politics. But on the wider issues, on *feelings*, they were as far apart as any other brothers.

'They released you?' Reuben said.

'For now. And you? They told me you had backed yourself into a serious dilemma.'

'Something like that.'

'Which is why they arrested me in the first place.' Aaron shrugged, impatience twitching his shoulders. 'Who'd have thought? You getting me into trouble.'

'You still owe me big time.'

'Look, bro', that thing with the coke in my car . . . I never meant for you to be the one . . .'

Reuben knew that Aaron was unable to apologize. He'd had over fifteen years and still hadn't managed it. Reuben had taken his brother's punishment. At the time, part of him had wanted to know his brother's life, to live his darkness, to understand him. But Reuben appreciated he would never understand Aaron. 'That's one thing I will never forgive you for,' he sighed.

Aaron shuffled his feet, eager to move the conversation on. He thumbed in the direction of an interview room. 'Did they take you to pieces?'

'Interrogations are easy when you tell the truth. You should try it some day.'

'Best not. I remember Dad only ever giving me one piece of advice in his life. "If the cops tell you they know the whole story, they're lying. The police never know the whole story."'

'Great advice. And Mum gave me a piece recently. "Keep in touch with your brother."'

'Yeah. Me too.'

'So what now?'

'I go back to mine, you go back to yours.'

'But what is yours?'

Aaron Mitland glanced apprehensively up and down the corridor. 'Lying low for a while. Disappearing from these insidious motherfuckers.'

'You in trouble?'

'No more than usual.'

Reuben sensed his discomfort. Aaron was agitated, desperate to be somewhere else. 'Look, Aaron, I want you to take this.' He pulled out a scrap of paper and scribbled a number on it. 'My mobile. You don't have to call me. That's fine. But take the number.'

Aaron screwed his eyes up and kept his hands where they were, firmly planted in his pockets. 'No, ta,' he answered.

'We live in the same city, for Christ's sake,' Reuben implored. 'You might need me one day.'

'I said, No, ta.'

Reuben balled the piece of paper and clenched his fingers tight around it. He had learnt enough about his brother to know that he would do only what he wanted to do, and nothing else. As Reuben stared into the face opposite, he felt the closing of a door, the end of part of him, the loss of a limb. Aaron was already turning, walking away, sauntering out of his life. Reuben's other half, practically identical, and yet poles apart in every way that actually mattered, was leaving his life for ever. He felt abandoned, let down in the most acutely painful way. He watched him go, transfixed. This was the central theme of Reuben's life, he thought. He lost everyone he held precious. Lucy, Joshua, Run, Jez, his father, and now Aaron. For a second, Reuben saw himself more isolated than ever before, with a vacuum surrounding him that failed to support substantial relationships or meaningful interactions. His brother reached an oversized pair of swing doors and turned.

'Hey, Rubinio,' he shouted.

'What?' Reuben asked flatly.

Aaron tapped the side of his head with his index finger and winked. 'O seven seven six five six one nine one three two eight. Right?'

Reuben tried to hold back a smile, but failed.

'OK if I reverse the charges?'

Reuben grinned again, and then Aaron was gone, swallowed by the doors, which squealed open and shut a few times, laughing like hyenas. Reuben felt himself straighten. He sucked in a couple of deep breaths, which seemed to inflate him. He had been at

GeneCrime for a day and a half. The creeping paranoia of the building which had infused him again was now evaporating into the dry air. He knew he was free to leave, but he was reluctant to go. This would be his last time, and to step outside into the sunshine would be to close the heavy security door on a large proportion of his life. Then Sarah Hirst strode through the entrance, almost swinging the doors off their hinges.

'Come on,' she said, 'let's walk and talk. We'll head out through the car park.' Reuben turned and matched her pace, which slowed as they progressed along the whitened corridors and past the offices and laboratories that Reuben had once occupied, the toilets where Reuben had consumed the drug which had kept him sane at work and paranoid at home, and, finally, near the cells in which he had been held and questioned.

Sarah explained what she knew. How they had found an early version of Predictive Phenotyping on Phil Kemp's computer, one which pre-dated Reuben's dismissal from GeneCrime. How, although they were still picking through its files, they realized that he had been trying to use it to put away villains the software identified as potential dangers to society. How the four-strong team from the Met had dug and dug into Phil until they began to unearth a rich seam of inconsistencies and contradictions. How Phil had argued and struggled, kicked and screamed, denied and accused. How he had been played tapes of his conversations with Gary Megson of the *Sun*, leaking stories to the press. How he had been shown key forensics files, with evidence of manipulation. How two of his CID team, threatened with dishonourable dismissal, had begun to implicate their boss in a series of un-orthodox practices. How documents and witness statements and computer files and emails and directives and testimonies had quickly begun to stitch themselves into a smothering blanket of truth. How Phil had suddenly stopped talking. How he had stared into the distance. How the flushed innocence had leaked away, replaced by a leaden guilt. How he had started to tremble.

And how, after thirty-six hours of questioning, thirty-six hours of being subjected to the same interrogations he had inflicted upon others, he had begun quietly and tearfully to capitulate. How he had finally admitted to the Lamb and Flag murder. How, with a second forensic sweep looming, he had panicked, and made sure that Lars Besser's DNA was discovered on the body. How he had contaminated the scene with his own DNA to ensure his subsequent elimination from forensic analyses. How he had then begun to manipulate convictions to further his career. How he had done all in his power to try and assume overall command of GeneCrime.

Sarah and Reuben turned the final corner. There, waiting by the exit, was Area Commander Robert Abner. Reuben glanced at Sarah, who glanced back. Robert Abner was a tall, looming presence. Despite his age, which Reuben estimated to be early fifties, the Commander was as physically daunting as he had ever been.

Robert Abner scratched the cropped hair at the base of his neck, letting them approach. 'One more thing, Dr Maitland, before you leave this building for good.'

'Sir?'

'Above your lab, on the industrial estate, there was a bald-headed man with a moustache, and an ex-service revolver. Found himself on the wrong end of an Armed Response Unit. We've been monitoring him for a while. We think a gangster called Maclyn Margulis hired him to kill you. Any ideas why that might be?'

'None,' Reuben lied.

'We've an inkling that Kieran Hobbs was involved as well. May have helped the hitman get close to you. Now why would he do that?'

Reuben checked himself. The final piece. Kieran Hobbs had double-crossed him. He screwed up his eyes. Just as he was planning to provide CID with enough genetic evidence finally to put Kieran away. 'As I told you before . . .'

Commander Abner frowned, displacing a lifetime of wrinkles. 'Dr Maitland, you might think we owe you an apology.' Reuben noticed that his cheeks were contrastingly smooth; shiny skin stretched taut across protruding bones. 'But you'd be wrong. I see what's been happening here, and I see some culpability, and a lot of rule-bending.' He pulled the sleeves of his jacket straight. 'What I will do for you, however, is what Sarah suggested to me. I won't ask why you have police files, police samples and police manpower doing your work for you. But that's all. And I want your lab closed down. Do you understand me?'

Reuben nodded silently.

'Right, Sarah,' Robert Abner continued. 'From this moment on, I'm relieving you of your input into this investigation.'

'Sir?' Sarah asked, her brow creasing.

'You're too involved. We need impartiality. All the subsequent forensics will be handled by the Service, and not by GeneCrime. But show them the computer files, explain where the samples have come from, bring them up to speed, find out how far back we need to look. We need to wrap this up as soon as we can.'

'OK,' Sarah replied sullenly, her influence dripping away.

'Besides, there are other cases.' A twinkle of promise appeared in the Commander's eyes. 'Mark Gelson is still out there, and we think he's killed again – another CID officer, found this morning. And a wealthy London club owner has gone missing, his daughter murdered.'

'That wouldn't be Xavier Trister, would it?' Reuben interrupted.

'Do you know him?'

Reuben recalled firing the SkinPunch weapon at him in the alleyway. He caught the eye of the Commander, and wished he hadn't. 'Just heard the name, that's all.'

Commander Robert Abner hesitated, rotating his head again to scowl full-on at Reuben. 'I'll be visiting your lab, Dr Maitland. And if I see that you're still fucking about with forensics, I will have you prosecuted. Am I clear?'

Reuben nodded slowly. 'Christmas,' he answered.

The Commander raised his eyebrows. 'I hope you're not being flippant.'

'It's just what someone here used to say.'

'Watch your step, Dr Maitland. And watch it well.'

Robert Abner strode angrily past them and around the corner, his shoes slapping the floor tiles. Reuben found himself standing directly in front of Sarah. He was uncomfortable, unsure of himself, silently running his eyes back and forth between her face and her feet, assessing her strengths and weaknesses, her perfections and flaws. Sarah was beaming, and he felt the warmth. He guessed that if you managed to break through the exterior, you really broke through in style. He basked in her sudden attention a while, savouring it, weighing it up, deciding how genuine it was. Seeing the case from her perspective, Reuben acknowledged that she had had more than ample grounds for suspicion.

Sarah smiled and said, 'Sorry.'

'For what?'

'For not believing in you.'

'And now?'

'As we interrogated you and Phil it quickly became apparent who was playing straight. There was nothing to do but take sides.'

'So you're on my side?'

'Don't push it, Dr Maitland.' The tone was chill, but there was playfulness in her eyes. And possibilities. Reuben cast his mind back to the party they had both attended, before Reuben was married, when Sarah had said something which had played on his mind for years.

'Do you remember that party?'

'I never remember parties.'

'When you said that—'

Sarah put her finger to her lips to shush him.

'I've always wondered about those words.'

'Then you won't mind wondering a bit longer.'

Reuben ran his fingers through his fair hair. The ice was melting. Fish were swimming. Nature was coming to the boil.

'Well, you're still in one piece, but the lab's got to go. You going to get a proper job?' she asked, changing the subject.

'What? Become legit again?' Reuben made a mental decision to ask Sarah out for a date. He would take his time, but he would do it. He felt some strength returning, adrenalin pumping through his heart. 'Besides' – he smiled – 'I'm having too much fun. I'll be in touch.' And with the sweet regret that walking away from beauty inspires, Reuben strode out of GeneCrime, through the car park, into the sunshine, swallowing lungfuls of warm, balmy air, coming alive, the tiredness ebbing, the humid fatigue burning off in the heat.

Waiting for him, shuffling fitfully in the sun, focusing through cameras and scribbling in notebooks, were half a dozen restless journalists. They came alive as Reuben approached, shouting questions, trying to slow him, shoving microphones in his face, strobing his face with flashes.

'Any comment, Dr Maitland?'

'How do you feel at being exonerated?'

'A message for the families of the dead?'

'Is it true that you will be pressing charges of your own?'

Reuben pushed through. Behind the reporters, slouched against a wall, was Moray Carnock. Moray started to walk around the corner. By the time Reuben caught up with him, he almost felt like a normal human being, and barely like a scientist at all. He wrapped an arm around his corpulent partner. 'Thanks for everything,' he said.

'No, thank you,' Moray answered.

'So which one do you fancy?'

'Which what?'

'Which baddie. Xavier Trister or Mark Gelson?'

'Haven't you had enough of this?'

'I'm just getting started. Besides, they're struggling. But they can't reach the places we can.'

'Keep paying me, I'll see what I can do.'

'We'll have to build a new lab.'

'No, you'll have to build a new lab.'

'Whatever.'

Reuben let go of Moray and closed his eyes. He shut out the image of Phil Kemp, his betrayal of everything and everyone he had ever held dear, his life in ruins, his career over; and of Lars Besser, distorted and destroyed; and the dead forensic scientists lying flat on metal trays; and Aaron released back into his underground world; and Judith Meadows with her loveless marriage and quiet dignity; and Sarah Hirst with her thawing exterior; and Kieran Hobbs and Maclyn Margulis and their hidden agendas; and Joshua Maitland growing and developing and learning to call a new man Daddy; and the DNA of his son which he kept in a hotel safe, too shit-scared to perform genotyping on, petrified that the single, last thing he cared about in the whole world might not be his anyway, that the one person he had ever truly loved could be made up of the genes of someone else.

'Fuck it,' he said, opening his lids and scanning for a taxi, 'let's get them both.'

Reuben's mind made a sudden leap as he walked on. He took out his phone and dialled a number. 'Lucy,' he said, 'I want you to do me a small favour. Clear it with Shaun if you must. I won't ask again, and, yes, you have to do this. You have no other option.'

5

The taxi dropped Moray in the middle of a crowded street, and he shuffled out towards an underground entrance. As he looked back, he waved, clenching his fist, as if in victory. Reuben instructed the driver and they moved away. There was no victory for Reuben. At least not yet.

Twenty nervous minutes later, Reuben entered a brightly coloured building and was immediately challenged by a matronly woman with greying hair tied ferociously above her scalp.

'Can I help you?' she demanded briskly.

'I'm Reuben Maitland,' Reuben replied.

'Ah, yes. Just wait here a minute.'

Reuben looked around for a chair but couldn't see one. The odours seeped into him, sneaking in images and memories along for the ride. He had been here many times, but never had the smells been so intense. In fact, they almost overpowered him as he leant against a lurid yellow wall, waiting, wondering and worrying. In front of him was a row of coat-hooks at waist height, with bags and coats hanging down. He scanned the names, but didn't see the one he was looking for. And then he guessed that he had been moved into a different room.

A younger female approached, frowning and unsure of herself. 'Mr Maitland?' she asked.

Reuben nodded.

'Come with me. He's actually asleep at the moment, but he's due for some food soon.'

She walked back the way she had come, opening doors with shoulder-level handles and plastic protectors on their corners. They went upstairs and Reuben followed, step for step, nervous and excited, wanting to break into a sprint. A final door was breached and they entered a darkened room. In it, fifteen to twenty small forms lay still on white blankets, on their fronts or their backs, their arms cradling teddies or dolls, their mouths open or sucking vigorously on dummies.

'He's there,' she pointed, 'at the back on the left.'

Reuben paused, unsure.

'It's OK,' the woman whispered, 'you can pick your way through.'

He peered at the toddler lying serenely in the corner, and tiptoed forwards. When he arrived, Reuben was almost over-come. Up close, the months away had left their marks. In his open mouth, Reuben counted eight teeth, four in the lower jaw and four in the upper. The hair was slightly lighter, the cheeks chubbier, the chin more pointed. Reuben bent down and pushed his face close, until he could hear his breathing. Joshua twitched and moved his head to the side. Reuben examined his ears and nose, and his eyebrows, and his neck. But not this time, he told himself, as a geneticist. Instead, he scrutinized his son with the desperate love of a father.

Reuben appreciated that he was being monitored by the nursery nurse, but ignored the attention. This was more import-ant than anything in the world. He reached slowly out and touched Joshua's hot hand, watching it flinch slightly. He stroked his hair and kissed his cheek. His son began to wake, and instantly started to cry. Reuben smiled in wonder. He grabbed a nearby dummy and slotted it in Joshua's mouth.

'I don't blame you,' Reuben whispered. 'You don't really

know me.' He stroked his hair. 'But you will, my son. You will.'

He picked Joshua up, sensing the heaviness in his plump legs and arms, guessing that he now weighed double what he had when he last held him. Joshua wriggled and squirmed, wanting to be free to crawl and explore. As Reuben hugged him close, smelling his hair and his skin, he resolved to seek visiting rights from Lucy. Joshua, here in his arms, was all that really mattered. He was still the father, his name on the birth certificate, his bloody fingers cutting the umbilical cord. After all, genetics was, as his brother and the forensics murders had painfully illustrated, only part of any story. Love was the ultimate truth. Biology, in comparison, was almost irrelevant. And gazing into Joshua's wide-open eyes, he decided he would love him no matter what.

Reuben kissed his son tenderly, and blew a quiet raspberry on his cheek. Joshua stopped wriggling. Reuben blew a second, and his son giggled. A third and he was squealing, eyes screwed shut in delight. The nursery assistant glowered over. Reuben turned his back, away from her, away from the other staff, and away from the world, the answer finally in his hands.

ACKNOWLEDGEMENTS

John Macken would like to thank the National Endowment for Science, Technology and the Arts (NESTA) for funding through the DreamTime Award; the peoples of Siberia and India for listening patiently to his lecture series; his agent for really earning his money; his Thursday Nighters for their sustained disinterest; and his wife and children for putting up with the dual nightmare of living with a scientist and writer.